PERTINENDI

by Morgan McLendon

Black Rose Writing
www.blackrosewriting.com

© 2013 by Morgan McLendon

All rights reserved. No part of this book may be reproduced, stored in a retrieval system or transmitted in any form or by any means without the prior written permission of the publishers, except by a reviewer who may quote brief passages in a review to be printed in a newspaper, magazine or journal.

The final approval for this literary material is granted by the author.

First printing

All characters appearing in this work are fictitious. Any resemblance to real persons, living or dead, is purely coincidental.

ISBN: 978-1-61296-194-1
PUBLISHED BY BLACK ROSE WRITING
www.blackrosewriting.com

Printed in the United States of America

Pertinendi is printed in Times New Roman

For anyone who has ever been so lost in their own depression. You are not alone.

May hope and love guide you home.

PERTINENDI

Dear Everyone,

    I can't pretend anymore. I'll be the first to say I'm not who you think I am. I'm not sure when exactly I changed, but something is severely wrong...inside me. There's this thing... You'd call it a monster if you really knew. But it's all wrong. It's all wrong inside. I'm all wrong. But now I'm making it right.

    This is the <u>only</u> way...

    Because...

Pertinendi

PART 1

WHERE THE HELL AM I?

A jagged breath scrapes against my skin. Over and over and over. Faster and faster. The sound raspy and short. It stops, just as I close my lips to gulp down a smothering bubble of steaming air. It's so hot where I am.

I look around.

But where am I?

It's dark, yet I can make out the molten rock enclosing my trembling body; pockets of sulfurous lava ooze through the cracks then seep into the ground, as scarlet flames whip the darkness and tame it into a dim light. A curious set of steel bars puncture through the rocks where there is a wide opening, like a window, at the front of this prison cell I seemed to be caged inside.

Slowly, with great effort, I push myself off the blistering ground —a horrible spectacle of bones and ash painted in vibrant blood colors. But for my own selfish comfort, I tell myself it's all fake, the bones and the ash, and that the blood is actually just paint. *Yes, just paint. That's all.*

Despite myself, I kick away the bones and sweep the ash into the corner, dousing a flame in the process. It dies out with a snake-like *hisssss*.

I curl into a ball in my now clean spot and take a moment to reflect. I can't remember anything. How I got here, who I am. My mind is as dark as my surroundings. And as for my memory... It's even darker.

I crawl to the opening in this cell, panic coursing through my veins as I grasp hold of the bars and try pulling against their metallic strength. They don't budge.

"Help!" I holler. "Help me, please!"

Nothing.

I bang my wrists upon the bars, hoping to make a sound or a dent.

Nothing.

My lips begin to tremor, olive eyes sting with foretell of tears.

Nothing.

I cannot cry.

I sit back on my bottom; defeat along with sweat shroud my body. I press my back against the bars and upturn my gaze to the ceiling, but there is no end to the roof. It's like the midnight sky that keeps going and going, starless.

"How'd I get here? Somebody…just…*please*, help me. *Please*," I sob, my fingers reaching for something around my neck—a somehow comforting and natural movement to calm my nerves. Five silver blocks collect in my palm, all attached to a black chain around my neck. And letters. Letters are inscribed on each dented and chewed block. The charms spell out: JOVIE. I tilt my head to the side, eyes shrinking to slits.

"Jovie," I whisper. A faint twitch curls the side of my lips as recognition dashes through my mind. Jovie. *That's my name…*

Something suddenly yanks out the plugs of my memory…

A sound…

A voice…

Thick and hoarse like a chain smoker's…

"You won't get any sort of help with *those* manners. Saying 'please'," the voice sneers. "You're in Hell, baby doll. No one says *por favor* here."

I scramble to the bars once again, panting, "Who's there?"

The rocks below suddenly quake beneath me. I spread out on all fours to balance myself. When the ground steadies, I look up, my black locks parting before my face like a curtain, revealing to me…a monster…

Beyond my own cage is another right across, and inside a peculiar thing stands with its head cocked to the side. A woman. Her skin is ghoulishly green, stretching in patches over her skeletal figure that is covered in a ragged, blood-spattered gown. Blackened veins weed along her cheeks, blending into her inky lips. Her hair touches the ground with black strands that mirror Hell's darkness or perhaps mirrors my own black hair.

She sits down swiftly, her movements a blur. "What is your name?" Her grating voice echoes. It carries in an eerie breath of wind that slaps my cheek with the foul stench of death.

"J-Jovie," I stammer. "Jovie…" I trail off. A glimmer snatches my attention. A rock bound to my pointer finger. Sapphire gleams on the tip of a silver ring, and in my memory it shines… "Blue," I say more to myself. "My name's Jovie Blue!" *How could I almost forget my own name?* I shake my head at the silliness of it all. "Please, ma'am, where am I? How'd I get here?"

The woman's hair sways from side to side as she shakes her faceless head. "I told you, *chica*, it is not wise to be polite. You're in Hell. How did you get here, you ask? Well, I do not know. You tell me." She pauses for a moment, sniffs the air, then slaps her hand down on something in her cell. My stomach churns at the following sight… She's devouring a spider!

After coughing once and licking her lips and fingers viciously, she clears her throat to say, "Jovie, mmmm, I like that name. Jovie Blue."

"W-what's yours?" I ask, imitating the woman and sitting cross-legged near the bars.

"Oh, Monica is what you can call me. It is short for *Demonica*."

"Okay," I gulp. "So, Monica, how long have you been here?"

"Well, I would guess a couple hundred years, but time is tricky here, Jovie Blue. What seems like only minutes could be a week, and what truly is a year to you could actually be only a second. However, my dear, you arrived this evening. Welcome to Hell. Welcome to your own Personal Eternal Nightmare. Welcome to…" She heaves a sigh. "Whatever you want to call it. I call it Hell. So. Do you know why you end here? I mean, how you got here? Can you remember anything at all?"

I look to the ground, away from her cloud of a face, and pain myself trying to recall who I am or was. But all that remains is a simple name, Jovie Blue. "I can't remember," I cry tearlessly.

"Aww, one simply cannot cry here, my darling. Your tears dry up before they hit the fire."

"But I don't understand why I'm here!" I wail. "I shouldn't be here. I can't be in Hell. I can't be dead!"

"Oh but you are, you are," Monica sings in a hushed whisper that fails to soothe my dead heart. She cocks her head to the side at my panic-stricken face, then staggers to her knees, keeping her face down. "You know," she says, voice muffled by her hair, "there are ways to remember who you were before all this." She looks up at me, and I see, for the first time, her eyes. They glow red, like a stoplight—a warning not to go any further.

I wonder, for a moment, if mine look the same. "How?" I inquire with a hint of suspicion.

She shoves her arms between the two bars in her cell, as if she's reaching for me. Then, as her limbs hover in the light of a flickering flame, the garish color of her flesh melting to a sallow yellow, she rakes her nails up her arms, digging, clawing, and bleeding herself dry. "Cry," she answers in a voice that quivers with agony. "Make yourself cry."

"I thought you said it's impossible to cry here," I say, confused. "You said tears dry up too fast."

"Not if you catch them before they taste the flames. This place can't make you cry, Jovie, only you can. When you do cry, catch the tear, for a tear is just a memory of the heart bleeding out. It's probably the last human thing you can do. Cry and cry. All else is monstrosity, trust me." Hysterical cackles erupt from the back of her throat as she laps at the blood dripping from her arms.

My eyebrows arch high on my forehead at this, but I soon find myself thinking of ways to make myself cry. When a flame ignites near my hand, an idea sparks. Hesitantly, I let my fingers hover over the fiery orange heat. I inch closer, only to back off when I feel the awful singe.

I want to remember, I tell myself firmly.

I slam my hand down on the smoldering fire, the burn a dreadful sensation that releases a high shriek from my lungs. My cry echoes and echoes throughout the dark hallway of cells, awakening other souls who growl and snarl, their chains clanking together as they stir. I recoil to the swept and tidy patch in my prison, tears swelling in my eyes. I quickly catch one tear in my good palm, then another as it slides down my lip. When the pain subsides, I peer down into the puddle of saltwater, awaiting a memory to appear…

The tear, once a puddle, suddenly parts into tiny shards of glass-like liquid in my hand. Then, as if a magnetic force is pulling them back together, the shattered tear vibrates, and is instantly put back together like a puzzle. It shapes itself into a small square, mirror-like in its reflection of the blackness above. I lean over the precious tear and see a monster looking back at me…

Jolts of shock electrocute through my soul, ensnaring my body and thrusting my mind down into the memory… To make me see, perhaps, what my soul refuses to remember…

Hell melts away as I fall into the tearful memory—a very moist space in time that flushes out the acidic odors of Hell and all of its horrors. I land in a huff inside a real mirror. The glass hangs on a wall in a room I don't recognize anymore, because objects, life, the world—it's all blurry through the mirror. But one thing is clear, one thing is distinct…so vivid that it sends a shudder down my spine…

It's me.

Alive.

I see the Jovie I was. We exist again in this memory. And I am her and she is me. We are one again. Only, I am the monster inside the mirror and she is the body standing before the glass.

The Jovie I used to be has skin white as magnolia pedals and beetle-black hair wielding the shimmer of moonlight in every strand. Her luminous eyes of emerald have faded with the tears I can tell have already been shed. But more tears well in her…*our* eyes. We stare at each other, noting the gray crescents under our eyes and the puffiness in our pink lips.

I am that doleful girl again. I ease into her pain just as I felt it when I was her—alive. The pain we feel weighs down to the floor, though nothing but our feet are there. I can't see her thoughts. They are hidden behind a mask of silence that is breaking in tears, wrinkling with sobs. But I feel them. I feel her thoughts, and they feel *bad*. They feel worse than anything I've ever felt, an insurmountable glut of hopelessness that just won't go away!

And the mirror won't tell us who we are anymore. The mirror simply reflects a monster, not a soul. We are nothing. Jovie is nothing. I…am…nothing.

And no one cares.

And we feel sick that people really do care, but…it's really that *we* don't care.

I am the problem.
I am sick.
And I'm tired.
So tired.

But the worst emotion lurking deep inside our still-beating heart is a feeling of instability, as if our body is constantly wandering through life, because we don't belong anywhere. And we can't make ourselves fit. Our feet are planted on the floor but we don't want to be where we stand, where we live, or even who we are. Because revulsion saturates us…

We hate… I hate…*her*. Us. *Me*.

This hate fills us to the brim. And the Jovie I used to be is wheezing now. So much hate rattles her body, our body. This rage, we are its puppet, and it draws back our arm, closing our hand to a fist, and thrusts it forward towards the monster's face—my face. The mirror cracks; some shards fall into the sink. We look down at our bloodied knuckles; the pain and the sight of blood a numbing bliss flittering throughout our body.

But when our eyes meet again, I see a beast standing before the looking-glass instead of a human. It's a dead girl, with a corpse's skin and hollow eyes—the one going to Hell.

We are both a monster. She is now what she always saw in the mirror—me.

But before I can warn her, the living Jovie slips out of my skin—the green skin with black veins and dried blood—and walks away

Pertinendi

from the mirror which is where I am trapped...

Jovie leaves me to do something... The only thing she can think of to do... The only thing to make us feel as if we're doing something right for once... To put an end to the nothing we already are...

I know what she's going to do, yet all I can do is stand inside the mirror, because I am the monster and this is where I belong. I belong in the mirror, in this confining square that presses against my shoulders and the top of my head. I am what I used to always see when I was alive—a monster.

I don't know how Jovie is doing it, but I know the final outcome. She will be me. She will take her own life. And I, the monster, am okay with that...because I feel her pain...and...I don't want to feel it anymore.

My hands tremble as I reach through the broken glass and grab a handful of mirror shards. Looking down at them, I close my eyes; I breathe out a slow breath of vitality, of air still within me in unison with the last breath being sighed from the dying Jovie...

◉

"Do you remember now?"

My head is thrown back out of the memory, the momentum of it all knocking me flat on my back. I stare up at the nothingness above, Hell's lightless forever. I wipe my face dry of sweat, trying to recover from what I'd witnessed.

"Just..." I catch my breath. "Just the end. It was awful. Self-inflicted."

"Aww, poor baby's a Suicide." She clicks her tongue three times, seemingly disappointed by this.

"Is-is that why I'm here?" I whisper the ultimate inquiry. "Is it because I *killed* myself that I'm in Hell?" I look at my hellish surroundings, heartfelt sobs erupting in my chest again.

"Oh no. Oh no, no, no, no, *no*, my dear. No Suicide is here because they died on their own account. They are here for much different reasons. But they will never know that, for they just wallow in the sorrow that got them here. They never do try to *remember*."

"Remember what?"

"Why they killed themselves in the first place," Monica answers, leaning into the bars of her cell. "*Escucha*, Jovie—listen. I have been here for very long time. I have listened to many Suicide cries and they all say the same thing. They feel as if something is *missing*. It was missing from their human life and now it's missing in their afterlife. Now, I cannot tell you what it is that went missing from their lives, but it is something that keeps them here in Hell."

A minute passes or perhaps a year does—I don't know—but silence sets in as well. The only noise is the faint clanking of chains echoing from down the endless corridor of prison cells.

"You hear those chains, don't you?"

I nod my head.

"Those chains—" Monica points down the hallway. "—those chains are bound to those souls because they want them to be. They are guilty about something. Something just won't let them go. And the chains won't unlock until they figure out what."

I look down at my wrists, the reopened scars present and still stinging. "I don't have chains," I note.

"Me neither. I ate them." And with that, howling laughter slices the air, the shrill sound reverberating from Monica's lungs like an upchuck reflex to emotion. I'm not even sure if it counts as a laugh, for there is no trace of happiness in her face.

"Well," I say as I study my hands, "what d'you think happened to my chains?"

"Oh, they've been missing since you got here." She plops onto her bony back, spidery hands folding at her stomach. "You know what I think? I think maybe you don't want to feel guilty. You're happy you're dead. I know I am." Unexpectedly, Monica, lost in a zombie-like trance, rises to her feet, turns her back to my prison, and glides to the corner of her cell. She rests her head against the sighing wall, her body curling with vulnerability of what I remember to be human. "I deserve to be." Emotion, if it is even possible coming from her, drips from the glow in her eye. She never catches the tear though, just lets it fall to its demise.

Does she not wanna remember something? I wonder.

After that episode, I leave Monica be for a while. I crawl to the back of my chamber and collect myself in my arms. My hair pillows the ground for me as I lay in Hell, staring at the bones swept aside to the corner. I let close my lids, let the darkness of my soul settle in on itself, and allow what feels like nighttime blanket me with a moment's peace...

But there is no peace here.

As I try to sleep, I hear the awful cries of lost souls. Their confusion. Their *rage*.

And somewhere inside the darkness, I hear my own...

Why don't I feel guilty? I killed myself. I'm in Hell. Why do I feel like this is where I belong? Was I that awful of a human, even aware of it then, that I expected this?

◉

Along the brims of nowhere and sleeplessness, something overflows and quakes.

I sit upright at the alarming ruckus. The ground is convulsing erratically again. I scramble to my hands and knees, dodging hissing rocks crumbling down from the walls. But this quake is more violent than the first. The ground slams me against the wall; dripping lava just barely misses my face.

"Ooof!" I puff, when I'm thrown against the bars. I hang on, squeezing my eyes shut.

Down the hallway in other cells, I hear moaning and nonsensical wailing.

Why is everyone so much more afraid than before?

Even Hell itself seems to be shivering in terror.

But then I hear the ringing noise, like white noise, distant at first, gradually maximizing into an excruciating screech. Nails on a chalkboard would sound like Mozart compared to this awful racket.

I'm forced to let go of the bars and slap my hands over my ears. I yell, "What's happening?!" over the commotion, hoping Monica can hear me despite it.

"SSSSHHHH!" she hisses, as the ground settles with an exasperated groan.

I shut up immediately. And it's not Monica's hiss bringing me to a dead silence—it's the herd of shadowy beasts flying by our cells in a stormy blur. They snarl and hiss, making that awful screeching sound that penetrates so deep that even my sanity cringes.

The monsters look like black smoke at first. But the ones lagging behind, stopping in front of certain cells, I can make out much more vividly…

Veiled in gossamer, pepper-black and bone-tight suits they are, with smoky ends cascading into the darkness. Faceless and legless, these volatile phantoms police the prisons of Hell.

I peak through the spaces between the bars, quietly lowering my body down to the ground. I watch as the demonic creature hovering near the cell diagonally from my own scrapes its long, curved, tusk-like nail against the bars. The soul locked inside the cell is nowhere to be seen. I suspect he or she is hiding—I would too, from a horrid thing like that. And I do, when the featureless head of the monster turns slowly in my direction. Eerily, it breezes over to my cell, casting a dark shadow upon my Hell…

I gasp in horror under my breath, cowering to the back of my cell where bones prick at my bare feet and fire singes the wilted clothes dangling from my body. I press my back against the steaming wall, my chest rising and falling with every deep, silent breath I inhale…

The monster's blackened claws strangle the bars of my cell. And, as it watches me, a noise, something between a growl and an intrigued purr, escapes its invisible lips. Its skeletal head tilts to the side curiously. Then, as if there are no impenetrable boundaries between us, the supernatural being glides right through the bars…entering my chamber…

I kick against the ground, pressing myself into the wall, hoping to just sink into it and disappear. But I don't. I stand there still, as still as I possibly can, for something behind my ear tickles and itches; I want *so* badly to scratch at it! But the monster is at arm's length, its face closing in as I'm leaning away and turning my head to the side. Hell is clammed up in darkness as I squeeze my eyes shut…

Sharp, incomprehensible gibberish whispers from the beast. It's rhythmic, like an incantation. The droning spell stiffens my body, freezing me against my will and luring my gaze to its monstrous features…

I stare at its hazy face, the up-close view dizzying.

And it's only when I blink, that, behind my lids, I see its face, floating there like a stain on my vision. I blink three more times, the image of its black and gray face sharpening in my view. The monster is indescribably maleficent, smirking at me with bloody fangs. It has thick eyebrows contorting in a devilish glare, and bulging, wrinkled eyes popping from their sockets, swimming in the air at my face, *staring*.

My mouth sags, eyes widen at the pure malice raising its claw to my cheek. Just when I think it's going to take a slice out of me, the smoke monster gingerly reaches behind my ear where that persistent little itch keeps tormenting me…

For a moment, I feel the touch of the beast on my skin. My lips part as a strange sensation of weightlessness tingles throughout my body, diluting my skin into the same transparent blur of the monster's. My feet sink into the ground, the feel of the rocks jelly-like and permeable. I even slide into the wall an inch just before…

There's a distinct *crunch* and a faint *hissss*.

The claw pulls away from my ear, taking along with it a speared cockroach and the light, ethereal feelings I felt.

My lips curl in disgust as the monster slits its own face where its lips should be, then shoves its claw down its throat with the cockroach. When the claw comes up again, the cockroach is gone.

The Hell-monster's flapping lips mesh back together as it grunts a cloud of smoke.

I blink, noticing that the monster is looking down at me again, angrier this time, less interested in food. The claws of the shadow reach into the darkness above, then come back down swiftly, in a blur, slicing at my cheek. I yelp and scramble away, holding pressure on the rows of deep, crimson scratches the monster left behind.

A violent shiver fingers my spine as I look over my shoulder to watch the entity fly back through the bars of my cell and disappear down the lightless corridor.

After a while, when all of the cloaked monsters go away, I drag myself to the bars and whisper to Monica, "What were those things?" My voice is frighteningly loud, echoing against the darkness. It's so quiet now, as if everyone is either dead again or asleep.

"Demons," she answers, her voice weary. "They work for the

Devil."

"Oh," I say, leaning my head against the bars. "So it's like this for all eternity? Just sitting in this cell?"

Monica exerts an impatient grumble.

"I mean, I guess I always imagined Hell being a…a…" I stroke the blood drizzling down my cheek, trying to think of the most fitting adjective. "I don't know the word."

"Bloodbath," Monica guesses.

"Yeah, exactly."

A deep, throaty chuckle echoes from the back of Monica's cell. "You just wait till morning, Jovie Blue. You just wait."

Even after Monica has turned away from me for the night, her chilling giggle still haunts my mind as I try to sleep.

You just wait till morning.

Her voice swirls around inside my head, the scratchy words mixing with the dark hues of Hell, creating a kaleidoscope nightmare. I fall into this nightmare, and, when I wake, live it…

◉

I lay on my back inside an artificially-lit and sterile room. I try to sit up but am strapped to a rectangular board.

I move my arms.

Stuck.

I try to move my head, but a belt pins my forehead down.

My heart *thump thump thumps* inside my chest, pumping fear throughout my barren veins.

My eyes scan the room. The tiles on the floor are hospital-white, while the gravelly walls are jam-packed with skeletons—the skulls face me, their jaws set in a scream…

Beside where I lay is a table supporting a tray of shiny silver tools; all of them sharp and gleaming lethally under the harsh light. The board I lay upon is firm but something clammy and supple fabricates it.

"MMMMMMMMMM!" I scream when I realize what the board is cushioned with. But I can't scream; something is taped over my lips, sealing them shut. *"MMMM!"* I struggle against the straps. I

don't want to be here! I don't want to be lying on a bed made of human flesh!

As I thrash against the straps, my frantic stare upturns. I see, beyond the piercing light, the same never-ending tunnel of darkness above me. This tunnel is present in my cell too. But the more I stare up at it, the brighter a dull red light at the end glows…

My mind suddenly plummets to the bottom to meet it…

I see my soul inside my cell, possessed with rage, screaming and beating on everything like a caged animal. I let loose the most gut-wrenching scream, as I tear at my hair and fall to my knees. I'm so scared. *I want out, I want out, I want out!*

My mind warps into reverse; I fall back up through the tunnel of darkness and land back in the flesh-veiled torture table.

Dazed, I look around at the dark shadows surrounding me. I feel so dizzy watching, without blinking, a demon inject me with a violet serum. I wince when the needle enters my skin and, *"MMMMMMMMM!"* sears my throat when agony manifests at the injection sight.

What did it inject me with?

It burns. It burns so terribly. Like volcanic lava.

With one of the surgical knives, another demon slits the opening where my lips should be, proceeding to remove the tape over my mouth.

"OUCH!" I cry. "Stop it! Stop! Please!" God the spot where the needle poked through *burns* and it's spreading like a wildfire!

The demons whisper amongst themselves in that fast, unfathomable gibberish. Then one eagerly slices at my left wrist with its claw.

I scream—a scream so high that it echoes down the dark tunnel leading to my cell. I get lost in this scream, as warm blood dribbles over the hacked membrane. For a moment, looking into the darkness above and seeing the caged Jovie looking up at the tortured Jovie, something elusive and hazy flashes in my head.

Images.

Familiar things.

"I think we should stop seeing each other," a voice says to me, then the figure walks away.

I see an empty hallway and I stand in it, alone and afraid. I'm lost. I'm so lost, clutching my books to my chest and walking along, Converse shoes tapping the ground with each step.

I see faces wagging their heads at me, disappointed in me.

I just want to disappear.

I just want to run away.

I see mirror shards falling, or are they razors?

I see pills, so many of them falling too.

And then I feel like I'm falling…

Through an empty darkness…

I can't see. I can't see. But I feel—I feel the falling sickness…

God help me.

A boulder slams against my stomach when I crash-land. I roll over onto my back and, with a strain, open my eyes to find myself staring up at the tunnel of darkness I know in my cell. But, this time, I see a lingering white light at the end; it's harsh, bright, and in my memory it burns as it winks one last time then fades out.

I'm back in my cell. And being back here… It is inexpressible how much better it is to be here than where I was…

The torture.

I look down at myself, somehow put back together after it all.

"So, how was it?" a groggy voice calls from Monica's cell.

I limp to the bars, only to lifelessly mutter through bruising lips, "There aren't words to describe it."

Monica laughs, but it's not a mocking laugh. It's an understanding kind. "I guessed your visit to Tormentum Tower would be in the morning or in the afternoon."

"Tormentum Tower?" I echo.

"Yes, we all have one. It's right up there." Monica points to the roofless part of her cell. "But when we go there depends on who we were as humans. As for me, afternoons were the worst, and I go to Tormentum Tower then. You, however, went this morning. So…as a human, morning's must have been…pretty rough."

I turn away from her probing red eyes. "I guess so." I pause. "So you're next, huh?"

"Yes, my turn will be soon. The flames whisper it is almost noon." Monica shuffles around in her cell, settling cross-legged near the bars. She folds her slender arthritic fingers in her lap, looking at me expectantly. "Can I ask you something, Jovie girl?"

I perk my head up, cautiously meeting her gaze. "Sure."

"Did you...*remember* anything while you were, *you know*, suffering up there?" Her eyes flit to the top of my cell.

I inhale a deep breath and wait a long moment before I answer. For some reason, remembering my human life was more painful than the ripping and slicing of my soul. "Yes," I say, my voice thick. "I did remember some things. They weren't as vivid as the tear memory, but —but I remembered flashes."

"Mmhmm," Monica hums. "I'm just curious, because it happens to me, too. I've never met anyone else who remembers their human life." She looks down at her fidgeting hands and says tentatively, "Being tortured is one thing, but being forced to recall awful things from life, now that's just cruel." She meets my stare, offering a weak smile as if she knows how badly the memories burned me. I nod back at her, then the shadows of her cell consume her as she crawls away.

By now I understand why Monica looks the creepy way she looks and acts the crazy way she acts. Being tortured like that every day for who knows how many years. How the needles and knives not only prick at your flesh, but puncture right through your sanity!

I rock back and forth, holding my head between my palms. I can't shake those memories from my mind—the human ones and the ones from Tormentum Tower. I don't dare look up anymore, for I know now what lurks at the end of that tunnel.

Should I be thankful though, for those precious flashes of life that lifted me from the pain while I was suffering through the demons' handy work?

I stop rocking and ball my hair in my fists. I don't know. It hurts to remember. It's *torture* to remember. But, somehow, someway, it eased the pain. And recalling the memories now seems to cool the flaming temperatures in my cell and within myself.

I wet my lips, swallowing the knot in my throat to prepare telling Monica good luck during her torture session. But I hear her voice before my own…

"GET OFF ME!"

I choke on my gasp as I whirl around to see Monica fighting against the demons grabbing hold of her.

"Monica!" I cry, pulling on the bars of my cell.

But it's too late. Thick, blood-stained claws cage her arms as swiveling smoke slithers around her body. The demons—their touch causing Monica to flicker and fade—slowly lift off into the tunnel connecting Monica's tower, then, in Tormentum, they disappear.

"Monica," I whisper, as the echo of her frantic cry dies out.

◉

Monica's been gone for what feels like months. And since I have no one to talk to, I entertain myself with a game I made up—Whack a Flame. I have a bone in my hand, part of a femur I believe, and every time a flame ignites in my cell I whack it. The whispering flames, as they are crushed to death, always go out with an angry *hissss*. This is my way of telling them to shut the hell up. Sometimes I even pretend that the bigger flames are a demon's head. Thoughts of Monica and my own experiences with them come to mind; boiling rage bubbles over then, and I go ape-shit on the fire, thwacking it and stomping it until there's a dent in the ground.

Needless to say, this game helps me manage my rage. Sort of.

Utterly exhausted from so many swings, I drop the bone and rest a while. Staring at the pile of bloodied skeletal remains in the corner, I pant through my teeth, hands curling to fists.

Rage, I have come to realize, finds souls when they are alone in Hell very, very easily, as if they have a big, arrow-shaped, neon sign pointing directly at them. I'm not entirely sure if such anger finds me simply because I am alone; I think it's also how I remembered things today during my time in Tormentum Tower. The memories were like morphine while being tortured, but now that I am aware and not as miserable, the memories are more like the knives that skinned and carved.

Those memories, those *wretched* experiences—they got me here. They drove me to suicide. And the more I think about them, the more

Pertinendi

I yearn to run away from them. I ran from life when they were near, and now all I want to do is run from Hell. Because they haunt me still, lingering like a demon's face before shut eyes.

A body-impairing *thud* reverberates off the walls of Monica's cell. Ash blows out like a sigh from the teeth-like bars, searing my wide eyes that stare in wonder. When the fluttering dust becomes less obscure, I can see the dark outline of the torture victim. The petite shadow twitches inside the cell, body coiled against the rocks, as crimson eyes bleed memories.

I open my mouth to say something comforting to her, but soon realize there are no words to make such torment go away.

No.

There is nothing that will soothe the pain endured in Hell.

Nothing at all.

◉

"Jovie Blue, Jovie Blue, your family found you, your family found you...dead. Now they feel dead, now they feel dead. Jovie Blue, Jovie Blue..."

Warm breath drifts from my lips to hush the whispering flame. This silent evening in Hell is receding to let in the night. Resting my head upon a boulder in my cell, I think of the sun. How it set every night. How the rays of neon pink and ribbons of sherbet orange poised across a brilliant horizon with open arms to welcome the moon and stars, such a loving gesture.

A drilling pang in my stomach hunches me over suddenly. A hard-hitting ripple, from my gut to my throat, elevates a vile substance up into my mouth. It splatters over there in the corner once my lips fly open.

I wipe my scarlet lips, vowing not to remember anything precious from Earth again. Hell reprimands such thoughts…in violent ways.

Blood. I had upchucked blood.

With a sleepy sigh, I lay down on my back, head near the bars so I can eye the cell across from my own. After a minute, I call softly, "Monica?"

"What?" Crudeness intoxicates her voice, as usual.

Her sour tone, as typical as it is, still shoves second thoughts into my head. *Should I even ask her? I don't know. Maybe some other time would be better.* But, thoughts aside and a deep inhale of torrid air, I ask anyway. "D'you think it's possible to—" I shrug. "—I don't know, escape Hell?" I bite down on my necklace charms as butterflies or roaches crawl around in my gut. I detect movement in her cell—the discrete sound of legs scraping on the rocks and the vibration of the bars as hands slap against them.

"What are you getting at little girl?"

I sit up and look to Monica, but her gouged eyes pin me back down. "I-I've been thinking, and I can't stay here anymore. I want out. I *need* out."

"Stupid bitch," Monica spits, "there is no '*escaping*' Hell. And if there is, it has *never* been done before. Even if you were to escape, oh the Devil will come after you and drag you right back. And after that —" She laughs bitterly. "—you'd be better off not existing at all compared to what the Devil will do to your soul for the rest of eternity. This—*this* right here—our own little cell, this is *Heaven* compared to what could be. So if I were you, I'd show a little more gratitude for what I have. We are on the top level of Hell and I don't plan on going down any lower." She paces in her cell, muttering under her breath in Spanish and occasionally in English. "This is like a five star *resort* compared to lower levels. Stupid, ignorant, *selfish*, little girl..."

"Hey, wait," I plead, "what about levels? I don't understand."

Monica whirls around, her blood-matted hair swinging in the air, and laughs snidely at my question. "Oh, you thought this was as bad as Hell gets, eh? Oh no. Oh no, no, *no*. The souls on this level are *nothing* to the ones on the lower levels. Now at that level, that is where your soul... It is not a soul anymore. You are...*truly* a monster. Worse than myself. Worse than a demon. And at the very bottom, oh, I-I can't even imagine what lies there."

"How d'you get sent to the bottom?" I wonder aloud.

"Well, trying to escape would get you a ticket straight to the Inferno, no doubt. But if you're uncooperative you sink to lower levels, and perhaps if your soul goes darker than it already is."

I drink in this information much like I'd drink a glass of ice-cold

Pertinendi

water if I had one.

Okay, so it's an understatement when saying escaping Hell is just a risk. But what do I have to lose? This cell? Take it. I never wanted it. This state of suffering? Screw it. For either way, if I stay in this cell or sink to lower levels trying to escape, I'm in pain. At least attempting to liberate myself from it will bring me some peace as I rot in Hell forever.

"Forget the consequences of escaping," Monica goes on suddenly. "I want to hear your plans of carrying out this action. How the *hell* do you plan on doing it?"

I grin wickedly as I lean into the bars, whispering the plan of action—the plan I have devised over and over again in my head ever since that demon touched my face. How its touch had watered my skin into something that could go right through impermeable things...

"You're an idiot," Monica growls once I'm done telling her everything. "It'll never work."

"Okay, okay. So there're some loose ends in the plan. I'll tie them as I go."

"Escape your cell you may, but Hell is a labyrinth. You will never find your way out."

"Well, at least I'll be out of here," I mutter with whatever dignity is still inside me. "Say what you want. But I'm going. And—" I outreach my hand for Monica's cell, palm upturned. "—I want you to come with me."

The two red bulbs in her cell go out, but glow again as Monica blinks at my hand, dumbfounded.

"Be brave," I encourage, stretching farther through the bars to reach her.

Uncertainty makes the soul across from me take a step away from my hand. She shakes her head back and forth slowly. "Be brave? You think what you're going to do is *brave*?" She leans her face into the bars and seethes, "You're a coward."

"What?" I whisper, my hand dropping from the weight of hurt saturating the air.

"Tortured with memories only *once* and you refuse to face them *again* and *again* and *again*. Forever! At least I know I deserve to be punished."

"You don't deserve this punishment, Monica. Don't think that. I don't care what you did to get here but I want you to leave with me. Leave it all behind."

"Run away is more like," she chides with a piercing stare. "You want to know why the demons never put the chains back on me? It's because the Devil knows I won't leave."

"But you can," I urge, "with me. Tomorrow. We can find our way out."

Monica shakes her head. "Jovie, you don't understand me. I *want* to stay."

My jaw drops, eyebrows scrunch together in utter shock. "Why in the world would you wanna stay here? *Here*, Monica? *Hell*?"

"Because I am here for a reason. To be punished for something horrible I did in life, and I accept that. It is time you accept those things for yourself. You aren't a good soul, Jovie. You are the *worst* sort. And regardless of what you believe is fair punishment, those rules don't apply here. Justice, fairness—those are good things. But look around you. There is no good. Those things don't exist here!"

"That's why we need to get out!" I hiss right back.

Monica heaves an aggravated sigh. She turns her back to me, then, to the darkness in her prison, says, "There is no convincing you. But I will say it one last time. I'm not leaving."

My gaze drops to the fiery brimstone. "Well, sleep on your decision. Cuz I'll come for you anyway. Tomorrow morning. I'm scared, and I don't wanna do this alone, but I will if I have to."

As those final words set in the air, I retrieve the femur bone and smack it against the one, annoyingly illuminant flame in my cell.

All is dark.

◉

Buhboom. Buhboom. Buhboom…

A lullaby, serene and rhythmic, drums in my ears, lulling me in and out of sleepiness. I tightly close my eyes, then open them to clear out the foggy haze in my vision.

Buhboom. Buhboom. Buhboom…

I curl my back to sit up, but I can't move.

Buhboom, buhboom, buhboom…

Glimmering torture tools sparkle like stars in the light shining in my face. But the glimmer goes out when smoke rolls in to make the stars fall upon my skin.

Boomboomboom…

"Jovie," the smoke murmurs in my ear, the voice inhuman and demonical, as if the creature has feasted upon fire every day since its Hell-birth. The demon's nebulous head thrashes, like a hallucination. "We know your plans," it whispers. "We know you want to escape. You will not succeed. You will not succeed." Its voice grows distorted the more I stare at its face, its babbling turning into that incoherent speech the demons usually speak to each other in.

You will not succeed. You will not succeed. Its voice echoes in my head, as the two demons in my tower begin skinning me alive. Wincing and trying with all my will not to scream so their focus on my pain won't falter, I cautiously, with a terrible churn in my stomach and a quivering hand, barely touch the nearest demon's cloak. Gradually, from tip to knuckle, my pointer finger turns into a see-through gray, then eventually my entire arm is translucent. With a discreet lift, my arm goes right through the confining strap, as if the material is made of jelly. I smile, relieved that it works. The demon catches my moment of joy though, and smashes its knife-like claws against my cheek.

Now both my cheeks have demon prints on them.

Once I recoup from the blow, I grit my teeth and officially initiate Operation: Get the Hell Outta Here. With my free arm, I reach for the drill on the silver tray, and, simultaneously, blink, noticing one of the demon's sunken eyes widen at my sudden movement. I clutch a fistful of its cloak; instantly my body is smoke-like. With a gasp, I slip from the belts and straps. In a spiral I fall back down to my cell. I take one demon down with me, drilling and drilling into its head, deeper, deeper, until we smack the rocks in my cage.

My fingers loosen on the demon's cloak as I regain consciousness. Somewhere between the dizziness and pain, I stand back up empty-handed. From the corner the demon lurches at me, claws raised high. I duck them, then shove the demon's face into the wall, stabbing it repeatedly with the point of the drill. After the final stab, I back away, panting, the drill dropping to my feet. The demon idles in the air for a moment, lightning bolts circuiting through its stormy haze. And then, silently, it drops to the ground. Nothing but a blob of cloak is left.

I snatch the cloak. Weightless sensations prickle my flesh as my body morphs into a supernatural blur again. Hesitantly, I run through the bars of my cell, stopping at Monica's prison.

I hear a sharp intake of breath from the darkness inside there and a baffled, "I don't believe it."

"Hurry, we have to go now." High screeching sounds carry in the air from every direction. The floors of Hell begin to quake. "Demons are coming! Let's go!" I reach into her cell with my mirage-like hand and, when my gaze flicks up, I see Monica staring down at it. I shake my hand. "Well take it! Come on!"

She opens her bloody lips to speak but no words exit. She's shaking her head, reaching but then backing away. Indecision scrutinizes her face. She's so afraid. I feel her fear; it's the same fear as my own. "I'm sorry," she finally says, cowering to the back of her cell. "I-I c—" She stops abruptly, gleaming eyes boring into something that's not me. "Behind you," she whispers.

I swing around, donning the cloak at the same time. I'm face-to-face with the second demon from my tower. I blink, and behind my lids it winks at me.

It's over, I realize with a downpour of hopelessness. *I'm done for*, I fret. *I'm dead...again.*

"Down, Jovie!" barks Monica. Without even giving thoughts to why, I do it. Just as my knees hit the ground, something whizzes over my head. I glance up to see a flaming stone jammed into the demon's eye socket—a direct hit!

"Thanks," I breathe.

Monica snorts, "What did I say about manners in Hell, Jovie? Now, run!"

I obey. As I leave Monica behind, hands chopping at the air, wheezy breaths frantic, I hear a soft voice call, "*Buena suerte.* Good luck."

Cell after cell after cell comes then passes right by. Slimy hands stick out of the bars. Some reach to grab and take a bite out of me.

Others, however, beg my soul to free them. But I ignore their heartbreaking pleas and leave them all behind, for a thundering swarm of demons is right on my tail.

There seems to be no end to the hallway of cells. But just as I think this, I come upon an intersection. I skid to a stop, turning round and round, taking in each passageway. The one ahead is dark; red weeds pulsate inside it every time my heart thumps. I turn to the tunnel at my right—it's icy, and I feel an arctic draft wafting from its mouth. To my left is a much smaller shaft than the rest. Its walls blush a peculiar violet color. I step to the left, curious, and, when I hear the snarling demons, take another step, then another, faster and faster.

Inside the stomach of this cavern, it's almost like there's a black light casting over the cave-like features, bringing out a pretty yet unnatural purple glow. Although enchanting, this cave whispers deluding sounds… Nauseating gurgles fill the space I run through, along with guttural coughs and choking moans. It makes my Hell feel cold and empty. It scares me. So I run faster. I run away.

Sprinting and leaping over unpredictable obstacles I am, all the while desperately trying to pinpoint an opening of some sort leading out of this place. But, to my severe inconvenience, there are no exit signs in the deep burrows of Hell. And in this particular burrow, there are no prison cells or creatures to find either. Because of this fact, I am not sure whether to be relieved or even more afraid.

A shrill yelp leaps from my mouth. Something beneath my feet, smooth and rolling, makes me lose my balance and slip. On a bed of scattered pills I fall. I hastily push myself back up to my feet, shrinking away from the spinning pills and their inviting escape. "No," I whimper, my voice faint with emotion. "No."

Yes, a voice pushes itself into my head, picking and pulling at my senses. At first this voice sounds like it belongs to a woman, but then a layer of chalky deepness, like static, conflicts with the softness of the voice. Twisting together, the tones concoct an insidious, sanity-extracting voice inside my head…

You failed at life, Jovie. Look at the mess you've made.

An involuntary shift averts my gaze to the pills; my eyes sting with the last haunting memory of me alive.

You failed. And now you are going to fail again.

My back hits the wall. I grab my head, banging the maddening words out. The cool, purring voice is somehow incredibly familiar, yet I cannot pinpoint its identity.

You will not escape your Hell! You will not escape me!

The pills flee like cockroaches at my feet as I scamper away, venturing further into the tunnel. I leave the voice behind as well—it is the Devil in my head!

It feels like I've been running for an eternity by the time I can finally make out an end to this deranged tunnel. The circular egress flashes a boiling orange grin…like fire.

I've lost a lot of time and, consequently, the demons have caught up to me. Their intimidating howls brush my back and tangle through the dark locks of my hair.

Maybe once I reach the end of this cave I'll be free, I hope.

But I'm not.

With a surprised gasp, I outspread my arms, grasping hold of the narrow sides of the tunnel to keep from falling. My toes curl over the melting edge and, when I uplift my gaze at what surrounds me, I gawk. My soul is awe-stricken at the epitome of trepidation and the desolate infinity it pumps into the ever-branching veins of Damnation.

I stand in the midst of what I believe is the very heart of Hell. Seed-shaped it is, almost like a beehive, but with a sky-high ceiling adorned in a morbid assemblage of limp human bodies. The belly of this dome stretches around in a definite but almost infinite circle. Blemishing the face of Hell are billions and billions of tunnels. From where I stand, they look like tiny pores oozing smoke and screams.

I feel indescribably small looking out at this wickedly-wrought evil, the end to its mighty and belittling horror immeasurable. Gas fumes are suffocating here due to what lies at the very bottom of this abyss, beyond all of the smog and immense distance from where I stand…

The Inferno.

Gargantuan flames slurp and slither against the lowest levels of Hell, relishing in the bittersweet tang of tormented souls.

"That's what Monica was talking about," I whisper, white-faced at the terror. The lowest level is the Inferno. Burning forever and ever.

Though the snaking blaze of the Inferno coils deep down below in the very pit of Hell, the venomous heat soars all the way to where I am. The hair at my shoulders lifts from the blast; eyes tear from the violent gusts, but...

Something...

Something, as I peer up to the tiptop of Hell... The blur of its structure catches my watery eyes.

I squeeze my eyelids shut, then open them to a crisp view of a series of odd earthen platforms hovering in thin air. Steps they are, spiraling like a broken staircase leading up to what I hope with my entire soul is the way out—for a precious light, distant and tiny like a star, glints in the center of the blood-red, corpse-decorated sky. In my eyes it shines *refuge*.

"Well," I say to myself, as I crouch down, ready to leap for the first hovering chunk of dirt, "at least this is the top level." I spring from the edge of the tunnel, the demon's cloak granting me lightness. I land perfectly in place, the squishy dirt caking on my feet; but the platform gives under my weight. "Aahh!" I lunge forward, having to dig my nails into the rock to stay on. After a moment, the rock rises back up, tilting wherever most of my weight is, and steadies.

Whatever optimism I had before is gone with the crumbs of dirt spiraling down and down and down...into the fire.

I glance up at the twinkling light above. Its halo now seems nothing more than a tease, toying with my mind as I struggle to reach it. I look out at the thousands of floating platforms ahead, my muscles tensing with hesitance when the penetrating screech of demons echoes throughout the dome. I twist around to see the tunnel from which I came puking out a dust cloud of demons.

"Oh no," I wheeze. Urgency clenches my fists, draws back my arms, then flings them forward. I'm airborne, skipping two dirt clumps with my expanding range. I cradle the rock once I land, clinging to it and keeping my head down low. The demons scour the thick, acidic air, sniffing me out. Some pummel into other pores of the never-ending walls, searching the nearest tunnels that I may have hid inside. But a few demons stay behind...

I blink...

Their empty eyes wag back and forth, up and down, brushing over my crouching body. Shrieking that high-pitched, rage-driven snarl, they soar through other parts of Hell's sky, not giving up… Never giving up…

I exhale slowly, trying to summon courage back to my guarded movements. I look left, right, and up and down again. *All clear.*

Hellfire's scorching wind kisses my cheek as I fly for the next platform, perhaps to kiss me goodbye, for in the corner of my eye a dark blob outspreads its claws, like a blooming black rose…

"No!" I scream. The demon slams into me, knocking me off course. I miss my landing.

I'm falling!

Falling so fast!

The air stings as I cut flips to dodge the other demons that have me spot. But it's as if all of Hell melts away, the sounds, the smells, the creatures, when I find myself staring face-to-face with the Inferno. The fire smirks, the face of the Devil opening its flame-lathered lips to consume me.

As I fall to my annihilation, my lids sealing shut, a soothing voice in my head, my own voice, hushes my fears with these words… *At least we tried.*

The unspeakable pain entangling my soul relinquishes a primitive howl from my lips. I'm nearing the unforgiving, incandescent mouth of a dark eternity. My fingertips liquefy at the temperature as I claw at the nothingness around. That is, until one of the smoke monsters miscalculates and swoops down beneath me. Just as I enter the flames, a demon and my soul collide. I hang onto its cloak for dear existence as we descend deeper into the Inferno.

The Inferno…

Being embraced by its fire is more like diving into shockingly cold water—the coldest water I've ever been submerged in. I cannot breathe. Only smoke foams from my mouth, escaping to the surface. The demon and I float in slow motion through the flames it seems, as our previous anticipations of the Inferno implode.

My body does not incinerate here. It does not feel hot or burn. It feels cold. Not the excruciating cold, just the uncomfortable sort of frigidness that's enough to turn a pair of chapped lips blue. It's scary quiet too. Dead quiet. It is how I would imagine being locked inside a dead body would feel.

Cold.
Still.
Empty.
Forever.

Despair masks the other souls floating around aimlessly. Their once colorful spirits now sucked dry and bone-white; their hands forever reaching to grasp something that just isn't there.

I feel dead.
Lost.

As if my soul—the only thing left of me—is gone. There is nothing worth existing for.

I am hopeless.

At least in my cell I could communicate with other souls… I could feel… I could remember bits and shattered pieces of the memories of me human, of me alive. And in Tormentum Tower I could at least *hate*. I could blame the demons for my pain. I could channel that rage into hope that I'd somehow, someway, break free.

But here all I have to blame is myself.

And all that hate I have… My soul just simmers in it.

Inside the Inferno there is *nothing*, all I feel is *nothing*, all I am is *nothing*…

I do feel something, though, that draws me out of my blank state. Arms, emaciated and blackened, thrash at my side. Between my fingertips something rubs, the feel slimy like snake skin.

The demon.

I'm still hanging onto its cloak!

The monster in my grasp writhes against the flames, growling, fighting against the souls swimming around in its way. I'm practically skiing atop the fire with the demon dragging me around without its knowledge. Zigzagging we go, swatting our way up through the coldness, straight past the despair…

I feel it, as we ascend, the vise of eternal fire cuffed along my limbs stretching and breaking and…

The Inferno gurgles and gags, then spits out a demon and a soul.

Soaring. We're free.

I suck in a greedy gulp of volcanic air while the demon let's out a jaw-clenching bellow. I cringe, my sweaty grip weakening at the sound. I succumb to panic and thrust the demon into a headlock, my arm clenching tight around its neck so I won't slip again. Panting, I look down at the Inferno. The flames stir round and round hypnotically, coaxing me back into its billowing depths.

I look away, blinking the sight from my vision. Inside my lids I see demonic eyes staring at me, angry and aware of my presence. I open my eyes. "Uh oh."

Bloodied daggers jab at me from every direction; I fight away the demon's claws. The hooded monster takes turbulent ninety degree turns to rid itself of my weight. Other demons try to snatch me, but the demon I'm surfing ducks them unwillingly every time. Punching it in the head, I come to discover, is a *great* way to target its reflexes.

We fly higher and higher, passing the tunnel I'd come from. We crash through the dirt chunks I had tried to climb. Through smoke and fire we rise.

Hell itself the demon and I pass by, leaving it in a crimson blur.

The twinkling light that once taunted me with its distance now grows in size the higher we spiral upward.

"Almost there," I whisper, then dig my knuckles into the demon's squishy head. It flinches in return, but doesn't slow like I want it to. It goes completely haywire! It jerks from side to side, then shoots straight up into the light. The last thing I see before all is white are the blank stares of the corpses in the ceiling…following…my every move.

I can't see.

The light is blinding.

Much too bright.

Somewhere inside the whiteness all around, I lose the demon and crash.

My head cracks against a hard floor…

White light swirls into…

Blackness.

"Oooouch," I groan, unable to move. With a strain, I open my lids, squinting at the bright whiteness. I lay on my side, sprawled on an ultra-white-tiled floor, with my arms bent awkwardly and head limp on the ground.

"*Tsssssss! Tssssss! Tsssss!*" echoes in my bones. It's the demon's pained cries, but nowhere do I see where it lays. I can't see anything really. This white light is thick, almost impossible to see through. Still, the longer I lay paralyzed, breathing heavily against the air, the more the whiteness seems to fade away. Floating like a cloud, it parts, unveiling what is hidden…

A mirror. Large and rectangular. The looking-glass is nothing like a normal mirror though, for flecks of silver swirl around inside, emitting a magical essence. And inside this mirror another one lies. Then inside that mirror lies another, only framed smaller, then another, and another and so on—all of them shrinking in size as they go on and on into forever. A dizzying illusion reflecting me, reflecting me, reflecting me… Reflecting my damaged soul.

My lips part at the sight, all the souls in the mirrors mimicking.

I want to look away from the hideous sight of myself but I can't. I can only lie here, staring, staring, staring…at the ugliness of my soul…

My lids are swollen, tired. Eyes bloodshot and red. Crusted with dried blood are my cheeks, and, beneath the blood, demon scratches blister. My hair, fried and mussed, is scattered all over the floor near my head. I'm wearing a demon's ripped and singed black cloak, the look of it more like broken raven wings. It just barely covers my faded skin that sickens me, because rotting in those dirty pores is the ghastly green shade of a monster; and running underneath is a black serpent—my veins—that lets slither lifelessness through my body.

"Jovie," the dead girl in the mirror whispers. "You can't leave me."

Chilled with fear, I flinch upright, but my reflections stay lying down. They remain staring at me, whispering…

"Jovie, you will never escape me. Us. We will always be here waiting for you, Jovie. When you leave Hell, you leave us. And without us you will never be."

The mirror-girl's eyes are magnetic, reeling me with their alluring intensities into the mirror-world she's trapped inside. But I shake her crawling gaze and stagger to my feet, backing away. I stumble away, the white air lifting completely to reveal only more mirrors lining the walls. All of them reflecting…*me*.

"Oh God," I sob, hands covering my lips. I take another step back, and, this time, instead of the hard floor, I feel something soft and moist squish under my foot. I turn; lift my foot to find a dead worm on the ground. "Gross." Disgusted, I wipe my foot to shed the worm guts. It's no wonder worms would be in my Hell. I *hate* worms.

Following the dead worm are more lively ones squirming near a large black lump on the floor. I pad over to the blob only to jump away when it twitches. It's the demon! But…it doesn't attack… It's—it's whimpering…and dying. Cautiously, I peer closer to its wound. There's a crack in its skull leaking worms.

"No wonder you're all so stupid. You got worms for a brain." I slowly spin away from the dying demon, my eyes taking in the sudden change of surroundings. The mirrors have all gone. The white fog has cleared out. I'm simply in a room with white floors and white walls.

But the light…

I see where it pours from now. I jog to it, head upturned. A narrow, semicircle-shaped window above is where the purest light resides. For the first time in a long, long time, delight curls and vines through my spirit, pulling back the ends of my lips into a smile. This joy gives me the strength I need to bend my knees and jump as high as I can. The demon cloak I'm still wearing gives me just enough buoyancy to reach the opening and grasp hold of its edges. Gently, I press my fingertips to the glass. It responds with a smooth swing, opening up with an easy squeak on its unseen hinges.

Before I go up, I glance back at where I came from…

Hell.

Its ominous shadow lingers still, meshing with the white light, somehow bowing to its luminosity. Looking to the worm trail and following it with my gaze, I see that the demon has disappeared.

Pertinendi

Wherever it went, I don't know. But before it can get me, I pull myself up through the hole in the ceiling with a breathless, "Urrmph."

Out of Hell my soul crawls.

Into a new and curious world I enter, sweet yet alien white light embracing my arrival.

PART 2

PERTINENDI

I stand tall over the window at my feet. Though my bones ache from the strenuous climb, I bend down and, with haste, seal the windowpane. My fingers squeak against the glass as I run my fingers down it, blinking in wonder at the light inside Hell as it dims under my shadow. Then slowly, as I rise to my feet, goes out.

I exhale a long, overdue sigh of relief. "Okaaay," I say, examining my new settings. "Where am I?" I spread out my arms; touch the burnt walls encasing my body. The feel is gritty and rocky, the smell like a campfire. Near my feet are two neatly-placed logs, and in front of them is a square opening letting in light. I look up and see a tunnel of darkness, the stone shaft going up and up and… "*Aaatchoo!*" My sneeze echoes, *Aaatchoo! Aaatchoo! Aaatchoo!* Once quiet, a rustling sound from above draws my attention up into the shadows where a black rainstorm of demons descends to attack me! "AAHH!" I scream, ducking and covering my head with my arms. The black smoke showers me, puffing into the air, making it hard to breathe.

Nothing happens.

"Wait," I whisper, standing up straight. "Ha!" It's just soot. "I'm in a fireplace." I pat the stone chimney twice with a chuckle, then step over the logs, my feet instantly sinking into lavishly soft, cream-colored carpet. My lips part at the room I'm in. It's hauntingly familiar and unnaturally bright, with its semicircle windows letting in the white light from outside. Spotlights shimmer on the carpet, illuminating a path straight to the backdoor of this house.

My house.

"I'm in my old living room," I murmur. It takes me a moment to realize this because everything is bare. The faded beach blue walls are stripped of every picture frame. The carpet is without furniture. No TV. Not one of my mom's teapots and vases are to be seen. Nothing. Just bare walls. Bare floors. Bare everything.

Unsettled by the sight of my home so empty, I run up to my room, soot peppering the carpet wherever I step. Upstairs, before I start down the hallway, I realize that all the doors are shut. White and naked they are, but I recall them never being that way before when I was alive. Slowly, I reach for the golden doorknob to my room. My dark reflection on the shiny knob reminds me of a prowling night monster trying to break into a girl's room at night, quietly and creepily. I twist the knob but it stiffens. I jiggle it.

"Locked?" I kick the door. It doesn't even shake. Intrigued, I move on to where my big sister's room used to be. It's locked, too. "Weird," I say aloud to the vacant house.

I find my way back down the stairs, hands sliding down the mahogany railing just like they used to. I step lightly across the floor, making my way to the kitchen. But all that's left of it is a countertop and an empty pantry.

Sadness hits me then, the emptiness of the house carving a deep hollow in my chest. "MOM?" I call, voice wavering. "DAD?" I jog to the backdoor, looking around for my family. "Olive?" I pucker my lips and whistle. "Pumpkin? Here girl!" Hope erases itself from my soul. "Is anybody here?" I say more softly with defeat. I sigh. I guess it's a good thing they aren't here. If they were, that'd mean they're dead as well.

Standing in front of the backdoor, I find myself squinting at the unearthly light piercing through the curtains and glass windows. I shield my eyes with my hand, reaching with the other to open the backdoor out of this strange afterlife.

Outside I assume I will see the same greenish-yellow grass that used to grow in my backyard when I was alive; I believe I will feast my eyes upon the familiar fence and dinky tree my dad had planted years ago. But none of those things exists here. What lies hidden and dead behind my house now is an eerie garden of tombstones shrouded by wispy gray fog that sparkles mysteriously in the odd light rays piercing through it.

I shut the creaky door behind me, creeping, with a wary stride, down the back porch steps.

Tombstone heads peak just above the mist, each of them engraved with familiar names of people I knew in my life to be dead. "Great Uncle Berry. Dale. Aunt Ciara. Grandma Blue." I glide my fingers along their smooth marble stones, tiptoeing, like a ghost, through this silent death yard.

I stop at the last grave. My knees buckle under when I read the name carved in the rock. I lift a trembling hand to the stone, tracing the bold letter J with my fingertip. "Jovie Blue," I whisper, as the letters blur into a watery swirl.

It was always hard to cry in Hell, but here—wherever *here* is—I find it to be the easiest thing to do.

Breaking down.

I sob into my palms, holding tears that contain no memories. Just clearness. *Good*, I think with a glare, *I don't wanna remember anymore. I know I killed myself, but I don't wanna know why. It hurts too much. I wanna go home. I just wanna go home. God and I'd kill for some water right now.*

Once my emotional falter is over for the time being, I wipe my nose with my sleeve and dab my eyes dry with burnt shirt ends. My swollen gaze flicks up and, to my flinching dismay, my house is gone. Completely vanished!

I press my hands to the ground, an effort to push myself up to my feet, expecting to feel springy grass beneath my palms; however, I actually feel a nip of icy wetness. My attention jerks to the ground. It seems as though while I was crying there was a downpour of rain, for there's a pond of crystal clear water resting at my fingertips.

My throat scorches at the sight. In reaction, my hands plunge into the precious substance, cupping it and clumsily guiding it to my lips. Impatient, I get down on all fours and sip at the water.

"Aaahhh," I sigh once the fire is extinguished in my throat.

Shivering cold streams drip down my lips, as a pleasant wind greets my soul, tousling the dark locks of my hair, whispering into my ear…

"Remember me?" the breeze whispers, luring my gaze down to the water. A familiar stranger's face glows in the pond with a moon-like sort of shimmer, pallid and brilliant, yet mysterious in every pore.

It's me.

Human.

Alive.

Jovie Blue. The tired-looking one, with bluish crescents under her eyes and a bland smile.

This pathetic version of me sickens my dark soul with faint memories of the Jovie I used to be. I bare my teeth in revulsion, then slap the reflection, water ripples drowning the mirage of a loser. When the water steadies, it reflects a demonic monster in the place of the human Jovie…

The monster girl is revolting, as if Hell chewed her up and spit her back out. She knows this is true, the ugliness staining her soul, for it gleams in the black depths of her eyes.

The monster girl is me.

This is my soul.

Rage, sudden and raw, dunks my entire head into the water, the hands of self-loathing scrubbing away the flaws on my face: the dirt, the soot, the blood, the sweat, the Hell. I tease through my butchered hair, yanking out the tangles, ripping them free. And when I'm done, I keep my head submerged in the numbing-cold water in an attempt to drown the monster.

"Don't bother killing yourself again, it won't work," says a voice that pops from somewhere in the swarming silver bubbles.

The threshold of water splashes as I fling my head back out into the air, gasping, though I know my breathing is quite unnecessary—it's just something I'm so used to.

Face soaked, hair raining; I call out, "Hello?" *Clickclickclick clickclick* my teeth chatter, as I wait for a reply. I swipe the water dewed on my lashes and look ahead of me, the thick, ghostly vapor somehow branching down the middle to my wordless command. Clear as the water before me, an island of dry grass appears through the fog, its only occupant a strikingly handsome angel statue.

"Hello?" I say again. "Is anybody there?" Narrowing my eyes, I see a very subtle movement from behind the statue. *Is it hiding from me?* I wonder, pushing myself to my feet. I catch the nearly undetectable twitch of the angel's wing again. *Something must be behind it.* "Hey!" I holler, sloshing through the knee-high water. "Come on out from behind there." I say this with the friendliest voice I can muster at the moment. "It's okay." I stumble to the wings of the magnificent rock, peering with wide, inquisitive eyes behind it. "Hello?"

No one's there.

I stand back, whispering, "I could've *sworn* I saw something back here." I bring my necklace charms between my teeth to chew out of puzzlement.

After a minute of clearing my confound thoughts, I begin circling the angel and studying the piece of art with fascination and envy. The angel, poised in the emerald blades of grass, is kneeling, with a gray and withered hand pressed to its chest and the other hand gracefully outreaching for something, as if it's giving a high five to the air. Meek the statue is at first, but as I trace my fingers along the wrinkled gown cascading to its bare feet and reach up to cup the delicate round cheeks and brush my thumb under the sagging yet steady eyes, the angel's profoundness is there, beautiful, in every crack and crumble.

It's hard to tell whether the angel is a male or female. It's as if the answer is hidden beneath the stone's wavy locks, twining through the strands, all the way down to a pair of immaculately chiseled shoulders. Or perhaps the rock's identity lies somewhere beyond its finely-shaped nose, smooth and faultless. But it's a secret, I can tell; and only the angel knows it, because its thin stone-gray lips curl upward just so.

The angel could be both genders for all I can tell.

The wings on this angel are the most stunning of all its features. Sinuously curved, the elegant wings arch high, revealing the bold, darkened grooves outlining the details of the feathers—they are so realistic to my every fantasy of a guardian angel.

I come to a stop in front of the stone creature and lift my cold hand. I press it against the stone's outreaching one.

"How do you do?" says the same voice I heard from under the

water.

I look at the angel's face confused, then to our hands. I flinch away, shrinking back a few steps.

"Jovie, is it?" The voice... It-it comes from the statue; the lips, though, remain unmoving.

Dumbfounded at the talking statue, I tilt my head skeptically and say, "Jovie Blue. But how d'you know my name?"

"Oh," the angel laughs, "I read your necklace charms while you were observing me. I think you will come to find that I, too, am quite the observer."

"Huh," I say, with a skeptical pucker in my lips. I make a wide circle around the angel again. My eyebrows pull together for the second time when there is no one behind the rock. *Is this some sort of joke?* Taken aback at the thought that this statue really might be talking to me, I say, with a small voice, "Um, how can you talk if you're a...uh...statue?"

"Why, anything is possible here!" So much rejoice is in the angel's voice, and for some reason, in my soul, I treasure the sound. The voice, to my ears, is deep and strong, like my father's, but at the same time soft like my mother's, and...somehow...youthful and fun like my sister's.

"Anything?"

"You were thirsty, correct? Then came the water," the angel points out. "And I believe you wanted to go home, yes? But that house is not really your home, so it disappeared. And—" The voice from the statue takes on a more sympathetic note. "—if you do not like the way you look right now, you can change that if you wish. You only have to desire it and you will receive it."

Keeping a cautious eye on the statue, I walk to the water and lean over. The corpse-like monster still stares up at me from the reflecting glaze. I inhale a deep breath, closing my eyes as I run my fingers through my reflection in the water. I feel the water rippling at my touch, the monster blurring under the waves, as I imagine how I would love to look.

Beautiful.

I feel the delicate tug in my chest pulled by emotional longing. The burning ache to look flawless still dances beneath my skin, letting spin the images of models and actresses and singers and dancers—all seemingly such perfect people.

Reopened are my eyes.

I breathe a quick sigh of surprise at my new reflection. The difference is astounding!

I...I'm pretty!

I press my fingers to my porcelain white skin. It no longer has that seasick green tint, and it's not discolored by pimples and freckles and scars as it used to be when I was human. My eyes now stare up at me with animated, earthy green circles that have glittery violet flecks infused in them. My hair, expelling the floral scent of lavender, flows in lustrous wavy locks just below my shoulder blades. My stomach is flatter, chest just a bit larger, and my smile...not bland at all.

I look more alive than ever.

"Pretty amazing, huh?" the statue smiles.

"Yeah," I reconcile, and, with a giddy laugh, pull at the ends of my burnt clothes as they morph into a stunning off-white dress laced in intricate patterns raveling down to my knees.

The laughter in my face is soon shadowed by caution. I step closer to the angel, tilting my head slightly, and ask, "So, why exactly are you here?" Friendliness softens my voice despite my attempt to be guarded, for I feel as if I know this angel from somewhere, like reuniting with some precious imaginary friend I dreamed of long ago.

"I have been waiting for you, Jovie," replies the angel, "for quite some time, because I am here to guide you to Heaven."

"Heaven?" I breathe. "There's a Heaven?"

Slightly, the statue's boulder lips curl up into a crooked but splendid smile. "Of course there is. Take a look yourself." The angel inhales a deep breath, then releases it into the air in the form of a warm sigh.

Like a magician swiftly whipping off his red cloth to reveal the magic, the fog lifts, evanescing into the air. The odd light shining brighter now, a spectacular display dawns on me as I drift towards it, climbing a small hill I didn't see before in the ground clouds. At the top of the hill, I see it clearly—Heaven. It's there, far, far away in the distance, wedged between two rolling purple mountains, posing as the source of the otherworldly light shining throughout this world. The pale white light, rounded like the sun, is nestled between the mountaintops, frozen in a permanent sunset before my ogling gaze, as if it's waiting for something. Dusk, with all of its pinks and violets and dreamy blues, paints the clouds swirling and curling elegantly at the snowy mountain peaks.

"Beautiful, isn't it?" the statue muses beside me.

"No," I say truthfully. "Not at all. It's *more* than that."

"Riveting? Spellbinding?"

I laugh at the angel's effort to pinpoint the most fitting adjective. "So much more than those words."

"You are...very particular with your words, Jovie Blue."

Reminiscence pulls my lips back into a shy smile. "I write poetry...or...*did*. When I was alive."

"Were you any good?"

"Nah," I say, waving my hand dismissively. "It was more for fun, I guess. And...it was just a way to let out how I was feeling on the inside, you know? I *loved* translating my emotions into words, stringing them together into something that flowed and made sense." I shake my head, smile twisting with sadness. "Because I could hardly ever make sense of how I felt back then. It was so hard."

The angel looks at me, gray face dropping ever so slightly with concern. "Are you okay, Jovie?" And then a stone hand presses gently to my shoulder, comforting but cold, like the touch of a sidewalk.

"Not really. But I think I will be once I get there." I point out at Heaven, then glance at the statue. "D'you think they'll let me in?"

"Who?"

"I dunno. St. Peter? Jesus?" I swallowed. "God?"

"Well, now, now, dear girl, that all depends on if you let *yourself* in."

"Ha!" I laugh loudly at this. "Why wouldn't I let myself into Heaven? That's crazy!"

"Do not be fooled, Jovie Blue. It is much harder than it seems. I have seen many souls find it very difficult to allow themselves into Heaven because they feel..." The sculpted rock chooses the following words carefully, "...*unworthy* of such paradise."

I freeze in place, the word *unworthy, unworthy, unworthy* echoing in my head as I look down to my feet that have trudged the fires of

Hell. "I-I don't think I deserve where I've been." I look to the angel's stone yet soft, concerned eyes. "I was in Hell, but I escaped. I can't really say whether or not I feel good enough to be welcome in a place so…so…*perfect*. But *here*—where I am now with you—I feel like it's the place to be. With Hell behind me and Heaven in front, I'm good. I'm okay. And I think I deserve that. To feel okay." I say this as if I'm trying to convince myself of it.

"Just okay? Not happy or at peace?"

I lift my shoulders then let them slump down. "I'm a Suicide. Being okay is being happy." When the statue doesn't reply, I fidget awkwardly, regretting revealing too much about my soul to a talking rock. I fill the silence with, "So, if that's Heaven and back and below is Hell, then what's this place? Where're we now?"

"We're in Pertinendi."

"Perta-wuh?"

"Pertinendi," the angel repeats. "This is where you will discover where you belong, wherever that may be."

What if some of us don't belong anywhere? I want to say but don't.

"All paths in Pertinendi," Angel goes on, "lead to what was and never will be again. Pertinendi is a patch of space every soul personalizes. It is a wasteland of your memories and structures of pain that have caused you grief in life. Since you are a Suicide, Pertinendi will not be a walk in the park. Here you must face what you do not want to remember—the reasons why you killed yourself. You have to understand *why*. If you face those things and prevail, well, you are that much closer to Heaven."

"What if I don't face them?"

"Then you will forever wander the dead-end path of Nowhere. And going Nowhere in this afterlife, Jovie, might as well be called Hell."

I swallow the hard knot of fear in my throat.

"I understand you have been through Hell, but, whatever it is you are running from, it will only catch up to you here."

"I'm r-running from the Devil," I confess. "I escaped and ran away. And-and they may come after me, the demons and Devil."

"They *will* come after you," the graveyard décor corrects.

I suck in a gust of air, panic constricting my soul. "Then you should go, Angel! I don't wanna put you in danger." A violent shudder snakes up my spine. "They'll hurt you. The demons will get us and the Devil will kill us! You're safer away from me. I don't wanna hurt anyone. Not anyone else. Never meant to hurt anyone…" I whimper into my hands.

"Shhh." A ribbon of peace twirls around my fear and anchors into it. Calming. Soothing. "Do not fret," says the angel. "I am here with you. I am here to help you face what torments your soul still and to help you find peace. Because we all deserve that, Jovie—to be at peace with ourselves."

I inhale a deep breath; hold it in for a moment, then release it into the strange atmosphere of Pertinendi. "Okay," I whisper. "Okay."

The cringing sound of rocks scraping against rocks grates the air as the once immobile statue suddenly rises, standing tall beside me. Concrete wings ruffle in an odd, almost invisible fashion behind the sturdy angel.

"Shall we get going then?" the angel asks, gesturing to the despairingly long path ahead of us leading to the ethereal mountains of Heaven…

Lying between us and Heaven is a long way down a sloping grassy hill, then into the wooden arms of an unfriendly-looking forest. A stormy black sea blinks at me from its circular fit in the middle of the forest. Then beyond that, well, it's too small and distant for me to even make out.

"You wouldn't, by any chance, be able to just fly me to Heaven, would you?" I ask the angel.

"Why, I suppose I could, but I find that taking a stroll can be quite healthy for a soul. So I think it is in your best interest to walk."

"If you say so," I shrug.

Angel starts down the hill while I idle for a moment, second thoughts dimming my mind.

Uncertainty weighs on my footsteps.

I feel a strange emotion manifesting inside my chest.

There's this deep yearning and regretful sorrow crying out in my soul. *Monica*, the cry screams. She's still in Hell. *Maybe I should go back for her. But how? But why? She didn't want to leave.*

"Are you coming?" the statue calls.

"Y-yeah, gimme a sec." Slowly, brows pulling together with guilt, I look back and notice that my house has reappeared...and also the way back to Hell. "Strange," I murmur, narrowing my eyes at the windowpane to my room. Two atrocious green eyes glow in that dark locked room, the owner a curious silhouette. One gaunt blackened hand presses against the glass, scratching down to etch the words:

YOUR SOUL IS MINE FOREVER

My face pales. A horrible burning knot sizzles in my chest and in my bones. "It's the Devil!" I shriek, my certainty of the fact rotten and awful.

The glass window bulges as a hurricane of smoke blenders inside my room, growing, pressing. Glass shards disintegrate when the window explodes from the pressure.

Screeches pierce through the air like lightning bolts, the dark cloud the demons. Scattering, they fly and twist through the wind, their cloaks whipping fiercely behind them. And while they pour from my window, where I used to, as a human, stare out at the world, the Devil smirks, stance awkward, eyes *furious*.

"RUN!" I bellow, heels digging into the mud as I spin around. *Sorry, Monica, I can't go back for you now.*

Down the hill Angel and I sprint, the demons circling like vultures high above our heads.

I glance beside me, amazed at how the stone manages to keep up with my adrenaline-fueled speed. So blurry the angel's strides are. I see one sculpted gray leg in front of the other then it blurs. Another masculine stride, then blur. Stride. Blur. Stride. Blur. Beautifully graceful stone arms pumping then blur. Angel, blur.

The crooked green limbs of the forest jut out of the tree line as we approach it. The thick cover of the leaves will shield us from the demons if we just...make...it...there...

A demon dives down, claws outspread to grab me, but the angel shoves me into the forest where I fall into a shrub. I think I may have been knocked out, for everything becomes very dark. My eyes are open, though, peering through shivering leaves and up through the canopy of tall, tall trees. I see the demons hunting the skies. But in the thick clouds they evaporate with a howl of disappointment.

One minute of still silence passes before the Angel enters the glum brim of forest, stone wings outspread like a concrete shield from the demons' claws.

Two minutes pass…

Then five minutes…until…

"It's safe to come out now," the angel reports.

"The-the Devil's gone, too?" I whisper from my leafy camouflage.

The statue nods, its wings folding carefully back into place.

"Close one, huh?" I breathe, staggering to my feet and wiping the dirt from my clothes. I look to the sculpture, its gray eyes searching the obscure sky.

"They'll be back," Angel states, voice matter of fact.

I gulp. "Then we should get going. The closer we are to Heaven, the safer I'll feel."

◉

Pertinendi's forest is beautiful in its dimness and mysterious in its gloom. The canopy above only allows a select amount of Heaven-light through. But when there is light, it glints in a fascinating glittery way off the bracken at my feet, magic singing in the whispers of the wind rustling through the branches.

We wander for hours or perhaps days towards the unreachable purple mountains of Heaven. Angel and I talk very little, but an occasional question is asked here and there.

"Does this forest look familiar to you?" the angel inquires.

Just as the question suspends in the air, a blue heron bird thrashes in the tree branches above our heads, locus screech, hummingbirds buzz, and a doe runs through my peripheral vision. I look up at the hanging moss in the trees; look down at the rotting logs and swampy green waters. "I lived by a forest like this when I was little. In Louisiana. It's where I'm from." Honeysuckles tickle and kiss my cheek as I inhale their sweet nectarine scent, the childhood within my soul blooming with memories.

"You don't have much of a Cajun complexion," Angel teases.

I try not to smile as I come to my own defense, "I'm aware of the fact that I'm pale as a ghost. But at least I don't have an Oompa-Loompa tan like some girls I knew." I walk ahead in a bit of a huff. Then my luck takes over... My toe catches on an indention in the dirt and I trip forward, arms wagging. Finally balanced, my glare at the ground suddenly melts and I say, "Hey, look." I point down at the spot I tripped over. "Tire tracks." I squat down, studying the thick tread marks, my memory booting up like a slow computer.

"This is your Pertinendi," Angel reminds me, "You put these tracks here for a reason."

"I-I think they're from my dad's old three-wheeler. Yeah! They have to be because, when I was little, my best friend and I would ride through these woods. Wow." I stand up; scratch my forehead. "That was a long time ago. I don't really know why these tracks would be here."

"Sometimes events," Angel says, "traumatizing events, get imprinted on the unconscious without ones knowledge or intent."

Screams quiver through the floral underbrush, scaring me and the birds in the tree limbs above. They bolt from their perches, flying away in a chaotic cluster.

My body responds to the random scream like it did the first time I had heard it...when I was alive and only nine years old. Deeply rooted this memory is in my soul, where it branches into my feet that know exactly where to go. I abandon the tire tracks and Angel, taking off to the left, getting lost in the consuming forest.

Screams buzz through the branches like wasps, electrocuting my panic senses.

"HELP!" I hear a child scream gutturally. My lips puke out the word as well, quietly, *Help.*

I fight off the branches in my way, finally coming out to a clearing in the woods. Harsh, dreamy light halos the field where I see a panic-stricken little girl crying hysterically by a flipped three-wheeler.

Help! She can't breathe, I mouth the words as they are shouted from the little girl. I run for her. Her terror is my terror. Because she is me—the crying girl with thick, tangled, black hair weaving down her back; the oval face with a mousy nose and dark eyebrows framing grassy green eyes. She is me; her short knobby legs tremble as mine do now.

"Nana," the little Jovie cries to the three-wheeler. "NANA!" I near the fallen machine, finding a wheezing child crushed underneath it, her face purple, the handlebar pressing against her chest. *She can't breathe! She can't breathe!*

Lift it! I think and then the younger me does. "I'ma get you out, Nana," she blubbers, as she hurries to the handlebar and, with an adamant "UUUURRRRMPPHH," pushes up on the handle. It only budges. She tries again, bending her knees more and digging her feet into the mud for support. This time the bar lifts higher, and Nana rolls out from underneath it, wailing and gasping.

The younger me lets the handle fall back down with a grunt. She then scampers to where her best friend lay and holds her, tenderly saying, "Oh Nana, are you okay? Are you okay? Please don't die. Please." She plucks the straws of grass out of her friend's short blonde hair.

"I w-want muh Momma," Nana sniffles, pained tears streaming down her muddy face, then falling upon her bruising chest.

"Okay, come on." My younger self helps Nana to her feet. She wraps her best friend's arm around her shoulder, letting Nana lean on her as they walk back home.

Before the past disappears, I, the ghost of the memory, hear Nana —my bestest friend in the whole wide world—say to me, "Jovie, you're muh angel. Muh guardian angel."

A strange, chilling gust of wind blows the memory away, sweeping the fallen three-wheeler and two children off into the forest where they, like sidewalk chalk on a rainy day, dissolve…and disappear forever.

"Nana misses you," a voice says from behind me.

I blanch at the unexpected sound and turn to the statue frozen in place on a fallen log. "That was hard to watch." I manage the words around the lump in my throat.

"You saved a life, you should be proud of that good deed."

I shake my head slowly, brows curving down to an angry arch. "I watched my best friend nearly die. She was turning purple. That was the scariest day of my life." I look down at my toes that Nana used to paint for me because I'd always get the nail polish everywhere except on my nails. "Oh, Nana. I miss her." I look up at Angel and explain how Nana was my best friend and how her real name wasn't Nana but actually Nina; but when we were neighbors a long, long time ago she had written her name in the wet concrete of her newly-built house and my dog had stepped on her name, turning the *I* into a paw shape. Reading it, I thought it said Nana. She never corrected me on it, (she was always painfully shy and quiet) so the name stuck.

"But you know what's funny?" I ask Angel. "After that day she was convinced that *I* was her 'guardian angel', heaven-sent to be her best friend. But really—" I wipe the water from my eyes. "—really all that time while we were growing up she was mine. Nineteen years. I made it to nineteen because she was always there for me. I would've killed myself long before if I never had her."

"But you still did…kill yourself."

"There's only so much a person can do to help someone. There's a point when you gotta help yourself. I failed at that—obviously."

To end the conversation, I turn my back to Angel and walk on. I don't want to talk about what I did; I don't want to talk about my suicide. So I walk fast. Each of my footsteps break the twigs bellow in the ferns. The snapping sounds make me wince; they makes my stomach hurt. I stop suddenly when I hear the giggling of children echoing from all around in the forest. I swallow hard, glance back at Angel who seems unbothered, then face forward, surprised to see a golden light shining upon the fallen leaves before me.

"What is that?" I ask Angel, too afraid to walk any closer to see for myself. But the more I look at it, the more it seems like an opening of some sort, a tear in this dimension leaking the powerful bright light from within it.

"Mommy?" a little girl's voice calls. "Mommy? Where are you?"

My stomach hurts; it hurts so badly now! I fall to my knees, watching with wide eyes as two small shadows step from the sliver of yellow light casting before me. The figures, if I am making them out correctly, seem to me like a small boy and girl.

"Have you seen our mommy?" the obscure shadow of the boy asks.

I shake my head, whispering, "I'm sorry. I-I don't know your mom. I'm so sorry."

The faceless girl takes her brother's hand. The two figures hang their heads as they step back through the golden light…and disappear from this world. The brilliant light soon fades, letting the somber shades of the forest return to my pale face.

Angel is by my side a moment later to help me back up to my feet. "Who were they?" I ask, but Angel only reminds me that this is my Pertinendi and they were here because of me. But I don't know. I don't know those children.

Even though I am at a loss, Angel still insists we continue on to Heaven. But…I don't think I can. "I don't feel so good, Angel," I admit. "I feel sick to my stomach. Can we maybe sit for a little bit? Maybe take a short break? Please?"

"Certainly. I think we have ventured deep enough into the woods to throw your demons off our trail for a while. I saw a spot back that way where we can lay low."

"Okay, good." I follow the gray angel through the maze of trees, over their twisting roots, swiping away the fragrant, floral limbs in my way until the soothing sound of rushing water fills my ears. Abruptly, the angel stops, causing me to lightly bump into the stone. Intricate wings part before me, revealing to my soul a beautifully lush patch of paradise…

A creek, its clarity eternal, fashions itself a winding path through the forest, lined with willow trees that drink its quietly running waters. Huge, algae-coated rocks dwell by the water, glistening as they bathe in Heaven-light.

"This is beautiful," I whisper, brushing my fingers through the willow vines. "I remember this being my *favorite* kind of tree as a human." I hop onto the largest rock getting floundered by the water. Once settled on my belly, I rest my chin on my arm and drop my gaze to the water.

I see my reflection.

I remember…

I remember falling in love with this creek where it carves its mark in the Earth at a small park in Missouri…

My heart suddenly buries itself deep within my chest, cowering behind its numb-shield.

Yes.

I remember now.

We moved to Missouri, away from our hometown in Louisiana, when my mom got a job offer she couldn't refuse.

I was just starting seventh grade that year.

I remember that...

It was hard.

Angel settles in the shade of a mossy willow, resuming its natural pose: kneeling, hand to chest, the other reaching for the unknown.

"Mind if I call you Angel?" I wonder aloud to the stone, even though I know I've already called the statue Angel a few times before. "Or d'you have another name?"

"Angel is fine," the statue says, enchanting voice calm, resting.

"I'm sorry I didn't ask before. I just...I wasn't sure if you had a name or not. I'm still kinda getting used to the fact that I'm talking to a rock."

"I understand," Angel smiles, such a warm expression that even my icy soul melts a little.

Listening to the cool dribbles of water makes me thirsty again. So I desire a cup—a cup that has one of those crazy loopy straws attached to it and an umbrella. It's there, appearing in my hand; the cup is flamingo-pink, the straw lime green, umbrella cherry red—just as I imagined it in my head. And as for its content... I take a sip of the chunky chocolate malt. "Mmmmm." I suck a good portion of it down, its supernatural goodness sending shivers through my soul.

I set my drink on the ground, and, as I'm leaning over the water, catch a glimpse of the dress I'm wearing. I catch a memory too; a quick flash of the dress on my body when I was alive, but in an old family photo. Mom had made us all dress up for the family picture, the annoyance of the itchy formal attire present in all of my family's face except Mom's.

The memory saddens me, barely nudging at the emotion I feel towards my family—how much I miss them. I close my eyes, wishing to forget it, and, when I open them, I am wearing a new pair of clothes: ripped, faded blue jeans, the black Nirvana t-shirt I used to always wear, and, because I could never go anywhere without them,

Pertinendi

my beloved black Converse shoes.

This is much better.

Pleased with my new outfit, I turn over onto my back and let the shades of my lids draw over my eyes. Heaven-light is bright where I lay, shining brilliantly even through my closed eyes.

"Angel," I say after a few minutes, "why's it so easy to remember here? In Pertinendi? In Hell it was so *hard* remembering the good things, the happy times. Only bad memories came to me."

"Well," Angel begins, "Hell and Pertinendi are two *entirely* different realms of the afterlife. When you are in Hell, you become a part of it. You are this negative energy, so all that comes to you is negative. But now you're here, where there is negative and positive energy, and I think you are simply experiencing both for now."

"Oh," I murmur, blinking open my eyes. "Thanks." I turn my head to where the stone resides, behind the draping vines of the willow. "I…" I hesitate, having to take a breath. "I'm glad you're here," I confess, "with me. In Pertinendi. It's kinda…nice…not to be alone."

The willow vines swoosh and loop through Angel's concrete fingers. "My soul wishes to be nowhere but here."

Another gust of wind flows throughout Pertinendi, blowing the willow vines shadowing Angel's face out of the way. "If you don't mind me asking," I say over the rustling breeze, "where is it you belong?"

"Pardon?"

"Well, you said before Pertinendi is where you find out where you belong. So…I was just wondering, where do you?"

"Heaven is my Home," the stone replies simply. "It is a place very, very precious to me. So precious that I venture from it so I can guide Lost Souls to it. Nothing brings me more peace than to share my Home with other souls. You see, I *never* want a spirit to feel inferior to Heaven or unworthy, especially the ones who deserve to be at peace." The statue's blank eyes—seeming to hold the universe—pierce right into my existence. Reading it. Making me feel naked and awkward.

"That-that's," I stammer, "really nice of you to care so much." Finally, I feel the angel's eyes flit away from me; I can breathe again.

I turn my face back to the sky, closing my eyes at its ghostly radiance. It's not even a moment later when it seems as though nighttime has spread its dark velvety quilt over the sky. Confusion furrows my brows, as I open my eyes to a colossal puff of ebony clouds, the shape like a demon claw reaching down from the sky. A single raindrop falls, dabbing along my cheek and streaming down my skin like a tear. "I didn't desire it to rain." I sit up, looking to Angel for an explanation.

"Those are not simply rain clouds gathering above your head, those are *mourning clouds*."

"Morning clouds?" I repeat, lifting my olive gaze to the disheartened sky. "I thought it'd be at least noon by now."

"Not morning, as in time, I mean mourning, as in grief. Those are mourning clouds. They form and precipitate when someone on earth is mourning; and, since this is your own Pertinendi, someone is mourning over you."

Another drop taps my shoulder, spreads along my shirt, seeping, staining. "It's a tear," I point out. It even tastes like one. Warm, salty. Sad.

Chasing the single teardrop is a monsoon of tears descending from the mourning clouds. It soaks my spirit in sadness, in loss; drowning me in the hurt of the heartsick.

Liquid pain churns the creek, rapidly flooding it. Alarmed, I get down from the rock, slipping on algae but thankfully catching myself. "Angel?" I call through the loud patter, squinting to see through the sheet of tears. "Angel?!"

I listen closely for a reply, but it's not what I want to hear…

Lamenting whispers.

In the rain.

Drip, drop, drip, drop, into my ears…

"Why'd you do it? I don't understand."

"I miss you so much. And I love you. Could you not see that?"

"Is it my fault you did it? I never meant to hurt you like that."

"Why'd you make me outlive you, sweetie? I'm the parent. It's not supposed to be like this."

"I don't have a real friend now that you're gone."

"I still can't believe you're really gone."

"I wish you would have come to me for help, Jovie, so I could have saved your life. I owed you that. You saved my life, and I only wish now that I could have taken your pain away. Give and take. I don't know what to do anymore without my best friend."

I recognize the last whisperer's voice; I can even picture Nana's face as she speaks the words, sniffling and red-nosed, with a nasally voice congested by allergies.

Like the tears, the whispers surround me. I try to shake them from my head but the harder the tears fall, the louder the whispers get. I clap my hands over my ears, running from the world I left behind.

It all becomes too heavy to burden.

Whispers and tears swell within my soul.

I drop to my knees, creek water splashing all around, and burst with a guttural scream. The sound shakes my Pertinendi. Trees rustle, their branches bend; the ground shudders, the sky winces, and animals retreat, their eyes wide with the fear of such raw indignation of a confused soul.

The scream echoes throughout my unconscious human chambers; and I bay at the sound, "Just shut up!" I curl into a ball. "Please," I weep. "Just stop."

All is muted.

The faucet of tears in the sky twists off.

I lay in the creek, half of my body submerged and the other half above the water. The aftereffect of the downpour rouses a mysterious steam from the deluged ground. It rises into the air in curvy gray strips that slither through space.

Iridescent willow trees surround me, their dewy vines still as death. Only one tree's vines fumble against a force that is not the wind.

Crunch.

Crunch.

Crunch.

Footsteps.

Behind the willow vines.

"Angel?" I push myself to my feet. "Are you there?" I splash through the creek, jogging to the willow where the sound comes from. I outreach my hand, saying, "Hey," as I draw the curtain of vines.

I find a ghost instead of a concrete angel.

An alabaster-skinned boy with freckled flesh, curly orange hair like a clown's and a gray-blue stare that pins me where I stand. He's wearing nothing but loose-fitting jeans and a perplexed expression that mirrors my own. We stare at one another, our eyes mystified by each other's presence.

Suddenly, through the air, a gunshot thunders. I jump at the rumble, the leaves slipping through my sweaty fingertips. The vines collect between my face and the boy's, raveling down like prison bars.

A threshold between two afterlives.

I look through the spaces between the vines, watching as the boy runs back into the forest. He holds his head as he stumbles, retreating silently, desperately, back into his own afterlife.

A moment lapses when I hesitate. Then, finally, I call after him, "H-hey, wait a second!" I take a step through the vines. Something stops me. A coarse, rock-hard hand carefully snags my shoulder.

"Don't," says Angel. "He will lead you off path. We need to go this direction." The statue points to Heaven.

I nod okay, and, with a twinge of regret, back out of the willow vines that had separated the boy and me.

"You know him," Angel points out, as we set off towards Heaven.

"Yeah," I say, "he looked really familiar."

"His afterlife and your own overlap. So you must have seen him before when you were alive."

My footsteps come to halt by a tree stump blocking my way. I idle there for a moment, staring at the wood, its odd shape grabbing my attention. It looks like a chair, old and terribly carved. As I stare at it, the bark begins molting away into a smooth surface; the fern below transforms into a metal branch. Flawlessly sanded, with a crevasse for a pencil and a compartment for books, the altered stump is a desk.

But the memory within the desk creases my forehead.

"Dale." The name whispers to me from some human breath still in my soul. "The boy... His name's Dale. He was in my poetry class junior year of high school. Sat right in front of me. And...and, well, he committed suicide that year. I never knew him really, never said much to him or even smiled at him. But I remember how seeing his empty desk for the rest of the year made me sad and sorry that I didn't." My puckered gaze meets Angel's, confusion arching my features. "I don't understand. That was years ago. He should be in Heaven by now, not here, not in Pertinendi."

"He's a Lost Soul," Angel says, sympathy sagging the corners of its stone lips.

"Then why don't you go after him and help him?"

"I've tried, but he refuses to remember. And because of that, he will be trapped inside Pertinendi for the rest of eternity. Until he lets in the memories that haunt him and continues moving on to face the next ones, only then will he be free. You see, he remembered you, a tiny detail in his life. You are so like him—only remembering little things, safe things. Never the *important*. The things that got you here. He refuses to face why he killed himself and neither will you."

POP! a second gun fires.

I swiftly turn to the desk, but only a bullet sits in its place now. A memory burning hot inside the shell widens my eyes as I bend to pick it up, feeling the fresh warmth of it in my palm, the texture crusted with blood.

"Dale missed two weeks of school," I explain to Angel. "No one really noticed until the third week. Some people said he moved, some said he was sick. But once the teachers found out the truth, that's when the students started spreading gossip and distorting the little details the teachers would tell us. One of the worst rumors about his death was that he shot himself in the head. Looking at his empty desk during poetry class always haunted me after hearing that rumor. It scared me. Or maybe it was some sort of foreboding to my own empty desk that probably sits cold right now in school."

The statue wipes a strand of hair out of my sweaty face, tucking it back in place behind my ear. Then the stone gently caresses my shoulder, patting it softly, soothingly.

"Can we help him, Angel?" I glance up at the sculpture, eyes glazed over in longing to take Dale's hand and walk with him to Heaven so he won't be so alone.

"The only soul who can help Dale is *Dale*. The moment he accepts his human life as he lived it is when he can know peace. But you have to know yourself, Jovie, memories and all, before you can truly know anything else. Dale is my concern, not yours, although I do appreciate your good intentions. But I must show you something now. Will you please come and sit with me for a minute?"

"Okay?"

The rock cups the side of my face, a shockingly cold touch that bolts through my spirit and launches me through a whir of motion. I gasp as vines slap my face; limbs and trees are dodged without me controlling the movements. Nauseating blurs of green go round and round until all is at a sudden standstill.

Angel lets go of my face, the lingering electric vibe still twitching my soul.

"What in the world did you just *do* to me?!" I peer down at my dangling feet where curly moss frames the incredible heights Angel has brought us to. Perched on the highest branch on a thick-limbed tree, Angel and I sit side by side.

"Oh, that?" Angel smirks, "That's how *I* fly. Teleporting. Fun, huh?"

"Fun," I pant, "would be flying." I flick one of Angel's wings, which, regrettably, kind of hurt. "Teleporting, not so much."

Angel laughs lightly at my insult, then notes, "But look at the perspective it has given us. Don't you like it?"

"Yeah." I peer down through the spaces between the quivering leaves and multicolored flowers, so wonderfully alien and unearthly, where Heaven can be seen. "It's beautiful," I say, though beautiful does not even come close to giving the landscape of Heaven justice— it is so much *more* than that.

"Well—" Angel's inflection has a notch of earnestness now. "— remembering will give you a new perspective as well."

I look to Angel, shrinking under the stone's all-seeing stare. "Angel, I-I can't remember."

"You're dead, not an amnesiac. All of your memories are still there. You only have to let them in. Do you want to be lost like Dale forever? Do you want to exist in denial and wander towards what you think is Heaven but is actually Hell? And here is another question for you, probably the most imperative: Do you want to be at peace, Jovie dear?"

My gaze naturally wanders to the white Heaven-light shining in brilliant prisms throughout my Pertinendi. Oh how my soul starves for Heaven, how it just wants to gravitate towards it and fall from the purple mountaintops into ultimate peace. Letting all its goodness erase my pain, letting all my sorrows be no more. "Yes," I whisper finally. "I want peace."

"Then," Angel says, voice of simplicity, "remember what took your peace away, so we can restore it."

I tear my gaze away from Heaven, and, as I gradually do so, feel this barrier peel off my soul, as if I'm sloughing off a burdensome winter coat. A deep intake of breath helps me to reach into myself and find the surrender I need to let in what I know will hurt, know will kill me again, but will hopefully get me there: Heaven. I release the fear within; it soars into the angel's gray eyes that seem to take my fear and turn it to hope.

"I want to remember," I whisper, as I upturn my face to the lightning flashing in the mourning clouds above.

Flash. Flash. Flash.

I close my eyes, the light against the darkness of my lids lulling me back into a painful past.

Flash. Flash.

Pertinendi is gone.

Flash.

I live again on earth, but in the memories that made me leave it…

Morgan McLendon

PART 3

MISSOURI LOVES COMPANY

Flash. Flash. Flash.
    The sun, glistening between the few still-standing pine trees, kept flashing in my eyes as we drove down the highway, a trailer of furniture lagging behind. Louisiana, my home, was dissolving into a muddy green blur as I squinted out the window of my dad's truck.
    I had moved only twice before. The first time was to a different town when I was six; the second was just to a different house in the same town. I'd never moved states before. My whole life began in Louisiana. The sticky mud had my footprints, the magnolias and honeysuckles had my fingerprints. And the muggy air was all I'd ever breathed in and out. Louisiana was where I grew up, where I had all twelve of my birthdays.
    All the people I ever loved lived there in the south. My grandpa —I could imagine him right now in his garden, replanting and cleaning up the yard. My friends—they were all back at school by now, making up for lost time. And Nana, my best friend—she was probably sitting at school, too, but by an empty desk that used to be mine. I was leaving them all behind now. They existed not out my window, but somewhere in the rearview mirror, too far for my teary eyes to see.
    Mom and Dad jabbered in the front seats about their new jobs with their fingers tenderly intertwined atop the console. Not really. I wished this though—for them to jabber about life and hold hands.

Instead they were silently listening to talk radio, Dad's hands on the steering wheel and Mom's holding a Joyce Meyer book.

Olive, my big sister, sat in the backseat with me, lightly snoring with her head in my lap. It was hard not to notice the bumps of her spine through her t-shirt—a sight I would never get used to. Olive was recovering from anorexia, her brittle but thickening brown hair a sure sign of that. Recovery. I patted her head.

Unlike me, my sister didn't mind moving. In fact, she wanted to. In our hometown was where she shrank dramatically in size; a once broad and invincible athlete slowly deteriorating to a fragile little skeleton. Her friends noticed, everyone noticed. And she knew that they knew. Although she never said, I could tell she just wanted to start over. That was why last night, surrounded by boxes and snug in a sleeping bag, I prayed to God to help my sister find happiness in Missouri since she'd lost it in Louisiana. *I don't care if I'm unhappy, just please,* please, *make Olive happy. Help her heal.* I had prayed that prayer so hard I thought my heart might burst. And I hoped, more than anything, that it would be answered.

I also hoped that she would gain weight. Olive was smaller than me, which upset me a lot of the time since she was two years older. I had to remind myself everyday that she was sick and I was healthy. But still, I felt fat compared to her.

I stopped patting her head, and, with a pinch of envy in my heart, averted my gaze back to the passing trees. I stared out the window for most of the drive, the aftermath of the recent hurricanes a live horror filmstrip constantly flowing through the windowpane. Blue tarps patched up the roofs of almost every still-standing home. As for the buildings not standing, well, their remains were scattered throughout the towns. I saw a slushy machine in someone's yard, a tree penetrating right through another's house, a line of people forming outside National Guard trucks to await food and supplies. Trees that had yet to be hauled away lay rotting with their roots ripped completely out of the Earth.

Mother Nature is a strong woman, I came to realize, along with the fact that the face of destruction was not something a sensitive soul should look in the eye.

But I had to. Especially the day we drove back home after

evacuating from the hurricane. What was left of our home was a foundation, a caved in garage, and our things scattered around the neighborhood. I found my pink unicorn toy in the pond behind our house. *Poor, Pixie,* I had thought to myself; she looked so hurt, as did a lot of other things. And her face was wet…like Mom's.

But the day we lost our house was the day my parents held hands and we all hugged each other. Our house was torn apart, but we were still together. And that was all that really mattered. At least, that was what Dad had said.

Relief finally found me when the mess of the hurricane was no longer visible outside my window. I rested my head against the warm glass, watching as the flat terrain began snaking up and down, twisting through north Arkansas.

I thought a lot to pass the time, trying to imagine how things would be in Missouri. The thought of being popular at my new school tugged the corners of my lips into a slight smile. Out of sheer boredom, I indulged myself with the fantasy of students and teachers taking an interest in me, asking me all kinds of questions. Girls would be jealous because I was the pretty new girl. Guys would get nervous around me, but still ask for my number. I'd make a lot of friends and make them all laugh. I'd be outgoing and fun.

Okay, I indulged *way* too much. But still, I allowed myself the unrealistic optimism for the rest of the drive and for most the time spent moving into our new house.

The morning of my first day at a new school was the day my confidence twisted into anxious knots deep within the pit of my stomach.

"Nervous?" Dad asked me, as he stirred creamer into his coffee thermos.

"A little." *Aaaand understatement of the day goes to…me.* Who was I kidding? I was so on the edge with my nerves that I woke up an hour before my alarm. I had time to straighten my hair *and* paint my toenails this morning.

"You'll be fine," Dad tried, sliding a plate of toast across the kitchen bar to where I sat.

I took a bite of my breakfast, then, with my mouth full, asked, "How come Olive doesn't have to go to school today?"

"Her paperwork hasn't transferred to the high school yet. But yours is all set at the junior high."

"Lucky me."

After breakfast I studied myself in the bathroom mirror for a while, turning to look at my butt, then to the side, then forward again. Considering how nervous I was, I looked alright. Of course, I did have to raid my sister's closet for a decent outfit. I decided with her green Abercrombie polo and my new jeans. As for my hair, I let my black locks down to curtain (or more like hide) my paling face.

"Ready, babe?" Mom poked her head into the bathroom, a sympathetic smile on her burgundy lips. She knew how nervous I really was.

"Uhmmm." I glanced at the reflection in the mirror one last time, pleased with what I saw. "Yeah, I'm coming." I grabbed my schoolbag from my room, then stumbled down the stairs to meet Mom at the front door.

"Ya nervous?" she grinned, as we donned our jackets and stepped out into a gray morning.

"Very," I answered solemnly. And for a moment, I was blinded by the headlights of my mom's car when she unlocked it. *Beepbeep!* the car chirped, the headlights shining, *flash, flash* in my wide eyes.

◉

"One. Two. Three."

I gave a weak, embarrassed smile.

Flash.

"Welcome to Cavern Hills Junior High, Miss Blue. Wait here just a sec, your student ID will print off in my office."

I nodded to the counselor lady named Beatrice or Brenda, (she moved around too fast for me to read her nametag clearly) then shoved my sweaty hands back into my jacket pockets. I exhaled my stored breath of anxiety once the counselor swept back into her office. Alone in the hallway, I turned in a slow circle to imbibe my surroundings…

Cavern Hills Junior High, located somewhere in southwest Missouri, looked to me like any other normal junior high school.

Only, this one was smeared with the colors red, black, and white. Everywhere. Red glossed the lockers armoring the narrow hallways; black darkened the paw prints sponged on every other brick, and white was the color of the beard on the school's mascot—a tiger.

How original, I thought, pressing my sarcasm button on early today. I wished, pining at the glowing double doors leading out of the school, my mom was still with me. I wanted to go home already. And by home I meant Louisiana.

"It's done!" Beatrice or Brenda peered out of her office, waving at me to come on in.

I bit down on my quivering lip, proceeding to her office with heavy footsteps.

The homey scent of pumpkin spice met me at the threshold. I noticed the source of the aroma flickering on her desk. Fake pumpkins sat next to the candle, as did other autumn decorations and Halloween goodies.

"Candy corn?" she offered.

"Thanks," I smiled, then picked out one and let it melt on my tongue. My mouth was drier than the autumn leaves drifting in the wind outside. I'd kill for a glass of water right about now.

"So," Brenda or Beatrice began, as I sank down into the chair in front of her desk, "your mom told me you guys just moved here from Louisiana."

"Yeah," I sighed, popping my knuckles in my pockets. "We lost the house we were renting to the recent hurricane. But about the same time it hit my mom got a sweet job offer here. So all the signs were kinda pointing us in this direction, I guess."

"Ooh, I'm so sorry. Hurricane Katrina?"

"We were more affected my Hurricane Rita. No one really remembers that one," I laughed. "But it hit a few weeks after Katrina."

"Aww, well I'm so sorry for your reason for moving here, but am happy to have you here in Cavern Hills."

I mimicked her cheery Stepford wife smile and thanked her.

The counselor swiveled in her chair to face her computer. I could read her nametag now. Bonnie, it read, in black and red letters.

"Alright, here's your student identification card. It'll make going through the lunch line a whole lot faster. Trust me."

I nodded along, taking the card from her. One glance down at the picture on the card made me look back up with a grimace. As sick and nervous as I felt, I looked it just the same, if not more.

"So what classes did you take at your school in Louisiana? I'll try to put you in similar ones here."

I picked at my brain for a moment, trying to remember. I hadn't been to school in over two weeks because we had to evacuate from the hurricane for so long. Once I was done telling her the gist of my classes, I glanced at the calendar on the wall, the year 2005 a blur next to the month October.

Diiinnng, diiinnng, diiinnng, a bell chimed, a very alien sound to me. I was used to a screeching bell.

"They're going to second hour," Bonnie informed me. "I'll probably be done with you by the time third hour begins."

Did she say this to comfort me? It didn't. I wasn't ready to be thrown into a new school, new classmates, new teachers, new classrooms, new everything. I just wasn't. *Not yet*, the sweat on my palms oozed. *Not now*, my bitten nails pleaded. *Not ever*, my racing heart screamed.

All of my insecurities were amplified when classrooms began spewing seventh and eighth graders. I felt my face getting hot as I leaned out the counselor's office, observing what I would soon become a part of. Some boys were cute, some kind of scary-looking. And a lot of the girls seemed strange to me. They were... I couldn't find the word... Fashionable? They wore skirts over their jeans, scarves around their necks, hats, flip-flops. This I wasn't used to.

"The style here's kinda different," I told the counselor. "We had to wear uniforms at my old school."

"Huh, and did you like it?"

I looked again at all the diversity in the hallway. "A little." I told Bonnie about how I had to go shopping for new clothes once we found out uniforms weren't required at this school, and, of course, that half of my clothes were still laying somewhere on the tattered ground of Louisiana. Before moving here, all I owned were my school uniform outfits, LSU t-shirts, basketball shorts, and a few old softball team shirts here and there. No scarves. No skirts. No fashion really.

"We *even* had *PE* uniforms." I dug in my bag for a second, then came up with a pair of navy blue shorts and shirt. Jovie M. Blue was written in a white strip across the front.

"Ooo, sexy," Bonnie winked.

I laughed at her comment and put them back in my bag.

"I put gym class as your first hour class. That okay?"

"Yes, ma'am, that's fine."

Once my schedule was completed and in the system, Bonnie gave me a tour of the school. She went through it quickly, and I retained about jack squat. Then by the time she said I could go ahead to my third hour class, I couldn't remember where it was. The math building wasn't even connected to the main building. Two gyms. So many hallways. Ugh.

"Can I have a map, please?"

"Oh sure!"

Thankfully, I didn't need the map to find my third hour French class. Bonnie walked me to it, bless her. At the door she introduced me to the teacher, a younger woman named Mrs. Flores.

That same sickening lonesome feeling I felt when my mom had to leave returned when Bonnie left. I felt hot again. Nervous. All the excitement in starting over at a brand new school was nonexistent now; washed away by the sweat seeping from my palms.

Mrs. Flores turned out to be an overwhelmingly friendly teacher. She welcomed my awkward and reddening self into the classroom, seated me in the back, and asked all kinds of questions about my French class in Louisiana.

"Well then, you're ahead of our class. What we're on should be review for you."

"Okay," I breathed, trying at another weak smile.

And it was review, so I didn't pay much attention. Rather, I nibbled away anxiously at the necklace charms that spelled my name as I tried desperately to memorize the school map before the bell dinged again.

When everyone edged on the front of their seats to gather their things, I realized class was almost over. For the first time, I looked up from my papers and noticed all the *stares*. Stares hit me like horizontally-pouring acid rain. They burned. They itched. I hated it.

"Hey, new chick, what's your name?"

I looked to the gothic girl who'd asked me the question. "Jovie," I answered. "What's, uh, what's yours?"

"Francesca. What class you got next?"

"Uhhmmm." I shuffled through my papers, hands shaking, and found my schedule. "American history with Mrs. Wright."

"Oh fun. I'll walk you there."

"Thanks. A lot. I have no idea where it's at," I laughed.

"Don't mention it. Mrs. Flores asked me to."

"Oh."

Before the bell sounded, I talked to Francesca and the other people sitting around my desk. They were friendly enough to tell me their names, but I forgot seconds later what they were.

"So where'd you move here from?" the girl sitting across from me asked.

"Louisiana." I noticed a group of guys in the corner of the room looking at me. I looked back at the girl, embarrassed.

"Why'd you move here?" another person asked.

"Uh, well, a hurricane hit my hometown, and about the same time it hit my mom got a job offer here. She's a floor nurse and she didn't wanna work the floor her whole life so she wanted a managing job—"

The bell dinged.

Everyone I was talking with got up, leaving me with my mouth hanging open in mid-story.

"Come on," Francesca ordered.

The walk with her to my next class was a long one. I was so terrible at making small talk. Francesca, on the other hand, had no problem with it. She talked the entire way there, elaborating on how she'd moved to Missouri from New York a few years ago; and how she knew what it was like to be the new kid and that it sucked big time.

"It's scary," I added quietly, as we walked along the path outside leading to the second building.

Francesca went on and on and on about other things. Walking next to her, I felt oddly out of place. She wore baggy black pants with chains clinking about on the pockets. Her bulky black boots stomped on the pavement. And a black shirt, black lipstick, dyed reddish black hair accessorized her upper half. It was quite a contrast to my jeans and polo. For the rest of the way to class, I had to pretend Francesca was Nana for the sake of me not bursting into tears.

It turned out that my history class was taught by a witch and my following math class was taught by an angel. The history teacher was a witch because she peered down at me with her hot pink, horn-rimmed glasses, slick, pulled-back hair and mole, warning me that if I was late to her class again she'd give me detention. She never let me explain that Francesca had to stop halfway to go to her class, forcing me to fend for myself, so I got lost.

Luckily, the angel that taught my pre-algebra class made me feel better. She let me sit by who she thought were the nicest girls in the class, asked me how I was doing my first day, and complimented me for be so polite when I said yes ma'am, no ma'am. Apparently, no one said that very often here. In Louisiana it was pretty much the law.

One of those nice girls from my math class walked me to the cafeteria when lunchtime came around. Her name was Kayla; a bit of a tomboy she was, with short, sun-kissed brown hair and cheekbones that were always blotchy red. Outside she tried to get me to run with her to the lunch building, but I was too embarrassed to do so—everyone else was walking. I felt bad when her energetic smile kind of faded and her fast pace slowed to match mine. She called me lazy in a joking way. I giggled, but really didn't find it very funny.

Bonnie was definitely right about my student ID getting me through the lunch line quicker. The only thing bad about going through it so fast was that I lost track of Kayla. After paying for my food, I walked out of the line and into a cafeteria full of faces I didn't recognize. None of the staring people had Kayla's face or Francesca's. My eyes darted from table to table; my grip on the tray got slippery with sweat. For the first time in my life, I felt truly and utterly mortified and alone.

Finally, I reminded myself that I couldn't stand there forever, so I started for the empty table in the back. I was halfway there when someone poked my arm.

"Hey, I sit over here," Kayla said, smiling.

"Oh!" I was so deflated with relief that I plopped down at her table and couldn't bring myself eat. I could only drink my chocolate milk, which spewed on my shirt—actually my sister's shirt—when I opened it. I hurried to scrub the stain out before anyone noticed.

"Oh. My. God. I *hate* that movie." The girl saying this set her tray down hard as she slid onto the bench next to me. She looked at me, blinked. "Hi."

"Uh, hello." I half smiled.

"Well *I* think it's funny," a friend of the girl said smugly, taking the seat in front of me next to Kayla.

"What're you guys arguing about *now*?" Kayla groaned. She then introduced me to her friends. "Amber—" She pointed to the girl next to me. "—and Claire—" She elbowed the girl sitting next to her. "—meet Jovie."

They nodded at me with a smile, but kept on with their argument.

Amber said, "We're debating whether or not *Napoleon Dynamite* is a good movie."

"Oh! That movie's funny!" Kayla said heartily.

"It's stupid," Amber countered flatly.

"It's fupid!" I blurted out, then cracked up laughing at my own joke. I held my stomach, giggling for the longest time until I looked up to find that Amber, Claire, and Kayla were all just staring at me. I stopped laughing immediately, reached to chug my milk and awkwardly look away from them as if I did *not* just laugh at my own lame joke. When I glanced back at them, Amber and Claire were glaring at Kayla, their faces seeming to say, "Why did you bring this freak to our table?" Kayla shrugged off their fuming eyes and kept on eating her French fries.

I sighed, vowing not to talk or tell another pathetic joke of mine for the rest of the day.

Of course, I did have to break that promise to myself later, at least the first part. I had to talk because some classmates were actually interested in me. All it took was one person in the class to ask me why I moved here and then a swarm of curious people would come, eager to listen to my story and ask me more questions.

Many students at this school were very friendly; so friendly that some even invited me to their churches. I thought this was the strangest gesture ever but still sweet.

Kelsey, a girl in my last class of the day, was the seventh person to invite me to her church.

"Have you and your family found a church to go to yet?" she asked, her eyes hopeful.

"Uh, no. Not yet." I failed to mention that my family and I didn't attend church on a regular basis…or ever. At least, not since I was little.

"Then you guys should come to my church!" She wrote down the name of it for me. "Hope to see you this Sunday, Jovie." She smiled at me, then turned back around in her desk. I put the neatly folded paper with the church name in my backpack pocket, knowing it would stay there, gray due to the broken pencil lead in there, and crumble because I would never take it out or think about it ever again. I was too busy laughing at the guy who said I had a southern accent to wonder if that was a bad thing or not.

I rode the bus home, my head leaning against the warm glass, a slight smile on my face. The sun was out now, heating the green, ripped seats on the bus and glinting harshly off the sign that read, "Cavern Hills Junior High". But to me that sign sparkled; it was a welcome sign.

As the bus rattled down the road, I replayed the memories of today in my head. I was very pleased with how things went, the people I met, and how I acted (for the most part).

I closed my eyes, thinking, *Maybe things will be okay here.*

◉

"But things weren't okay, Angel," I explain, as Pertinendi's forest settles back around me. The statue and I are still suspended high in the twisting branches of oak trees.

"Why were things not okay anymore?" Angel asks softly.

I stand up from the branch, balance myself, then desire stairs back down to the ground. I open my eyes to hundreds of branches intertwining, twisting, cracking, and bending to form a descending wooden stairway. *It's a stairway away from heaven*, I note, yet the song *Stairway to Heaven* hums eerily through the trees, sings in a whisper within my ears.

I take a deep breath. "Things weren't okay anymore at school after the first two days cuz after that people just…stopped talking to me. Stopped being friendly. Me being the new kid kinda faded, I guess. But it's not like I wanted attention or anything, you know? I just… I just wanted someone to talk to."

"A friend," Angel concludes.

"Yeah," I whisper, starting down the stairway. The moment I take a step down the stairs, the lovely song playing throughout the forest gets fuzzy and distorted, as if it's playing backwards. The bizarre sound scares me; I want it to stop chiming in my ears so badly but it doesn't stop. Not until I jump down from the last stair and take a step towards Heaven. That's when the song plays normally again. "Weird," I mutter to myself, but what's weird to me is not just the song. There's something strange about the ground here. I notice it through the spaces between the undergrowth. I bend to swipe the leaves and twigs away, exposing a grimy tiled floor beneath the soil. My breath escapes me, as a new memory hurls me back into the past…

◉

My face collapsed in my palms. I peaked through the spaces between my fingers, looking down at the dirty tile floor paving the girls' restroom. I sighed, wondering how much longer I'd have to hide in this stall before the morning bell would ding and I could go on to first hour class.

I usually got to school exactly when the morning bell rang so I wouldn't have to stand alone in the cafeteria where everyone else chatted with their friends. But today Dad had to drop me off early because of his work. So, instead of standing alone amongst the boisterous students I didn't know, I locked myself in a bathroom stall and waited.

And I hated it.

Every second of what I was doing.

Hiding.

I never had to do this at my old school. I always had friends to talk to and knew just where to find them. We had our spots outside, in the cafeteria, by our lockers, so many familiar places that I could always count on finding their faces near. Here in Missouri, though, there were no convenient familiarities, no comforting smiles. There was just me. In this gross bathroom stall. Alone.

I stood up from the toilet lid, grabbed my bag, the nerves wringing my stomach warning me that the bell would ding soon. With a breath of anxiety held in my lungs, I unlocked the stall and walked to the sinks. There was a girl dressed in all black washing her hands next to me. She wasn't Francesca, though they dressed the same way. As I dried my hands, I could hear the song blaring from the girl's MP3 player.

Led Zeppelin, I guessed. The song sounded so familiar but I couldn't, for the life of me, recall the name of it…

Just as I was anticipating, the morning bell's three dings sounded overhead. My stomach did a nauseating flip. Gym was my first class. And I loathed it entirely.

Inside the crowded girls' locker room, I quickly changed into my gym clothes and, with the band around my wrist, tied my hair into a low ponytail. After slipping into some tennis shoes, I left the locker room to find my assigned spot on the gym floor. Kayla waved at me from her spot across the gym. I waved back, smiling. She was one of the few people that still talked to me.

Just when I sat down, the gym coach blew his whistle two times, then yelled, "We're playin' indoor softball today! This half of the gym versus this side!"

Crap. Kayla won't be on my team.

"This side bats first! McVey! Here! Put the bases where they need to go. Get to it!"

My side of the gym got to bat first. While most of the guys and some of the sportier girls ran to be first in the batting line, I made sure to walk as slow as possible so that I was in the very back. I got behind a larger girl, freakishly tall for our grade, who seemed to be making it a point to walk just as slow as I was.

It wasn't normal—this hate I held towards gym class. I used to love sports, especially softball. I'd been playing the game since I was eight years old. I was an athlete, with a fairly agile body. I was even on the basketball and volleyball team at my old junior high school. But…something…something inside of me…was changing…

I wasn't sure what it was—this…crippling timidity, like a growth, constantly forming a reclusive shell over my skin. It made me so shy, to the point of feeling physical pain when I had to sit in the front row seat in class or give a speech. And what was even more painful now was that I had to bat with the possibility of humiliating myself in front of a whole gym class.

My team ran on and off of the "field", which was really just the gym. The coach was the one pitching, carefully tossing a wiffle ball at the batter's strike zone each time. It was our fourth time to bat, and not me or the big girl I always stood behind had batted yet. The coach noticed. And he got *mad*.

"Who all hasn't batted yet?" he hollered, pointing at the end of the line. I averted my gaze to the floor, turning my head slightly away. My cheeks burned with heat.

People in front of us murmured, saying they all had all batted.

"Sage! Have you batted?"

The girl I'd been standing behind shook her head.

"Well then get up there and bat," the coach barked. I flinched at his inflection, feeling so sorry for Sage, especially when she struck out.

"Anyone else who hasn't batted needs to get a turn. No one else can bat another time until everyone has batted."

A girl behind me grumbled at the coach's orders, and, with a sigh of defeat, went ahead to the front of the line to bat. While she was doing a few practice swings, I caught a boy staring at me. I recognized him as one of the really competitive guys on our team who batted, like, ten times already. I thought, by some miracle, he was checking me out, thinking I looked cute in my baggy gym clothes and messy pony tail.

As usual, I was wrong…

"Hey," he called to me, "you should get in the front of the line to bat, so people who *want* to play can bat again." It wasn't a suggestion; his tone made it a command.

I shook my head, forcing a smile. "I'm good here." I played with my hair, averting my gaze, but he wouldn't leave me alone.

"Go bat," he pressed, clearly annoyed as he came towards me. I felt his hands on my shoulders, pushing me to the front of the line. "Go!" I obeyed but stopped short. I didn't want to go any further.

"Go!" he yelled again, shoving harder.

"I can't!" I turned on him, brows pulling together in fury. "She's swinging." I pointed at the batter. "I'd rather *not* get hit with a bat today, thank you very much."

"Oh my *God*," was all he said, as he turned to his friends who rolled their eyes at me.

My eyes burned with tears, skin searing with humiliation and anger. When I was up to bat, I let that anger course through my veins, let it soak into my muscles that squeezed the bat really, really tight, like a stranglehold. When the wiffle ball came towards me, I pictured that asshole's face. My teeth grinded together as I swung as hard as I could, with all my fury loaded into that one stride.

Thwack!

The ball soared across the gym. I lost sight of it as I ran to first base, adrenaline and excitement steering my body without any stumbles. I made it safely, and, when I looked up at the first basemen, he told me dully, "You're out."

"What?" I panted, genuinely surprised. I twisted around to see the people in the back of the gym. One of the guys was holding the wiffle ball high above his head, a bright, proud grin on his face.

He caught it.

My shoulders slumped. That was three outs. I trudged to the back wall of the gym to lean against it, my sweaty body feeling cold and numb. The coach did look back at me, I noticed, with an appraising eyebrow raise. "Good hit," it seemed to say. But I got out anyway. Got embarrassed and bossed around. Nothing was good. I looked away from everyone, focusing on the empty bleachers, praying, *God, just let this day be over.*

But just as one day ended, another began. I'd wake up, scowl at my alarm clock, feeling the serenity of my dreams get shoved aside by the awfulness of reality.

Later at school, I'd find myself once again face to face with the grimy bathroom floor, Dad dropping me off early with the same excuse. Work.

Then the dreaded hour of gym class would come around. Sometimes I'd stand by Kayla, but she liked to twirl about like a figure skater and horse around like one of the guys. So on those days

I'd stand by Sage, who I tried to talk to sometimes. We were both quiet people, so there was never much to talk about. I really didn't mind the silence as long as I had someone to fill the emptiness beside me. As long as I didn't appear to be alone. That was enough.

During class teachers would ask questions I knew the answers to.

Photosynthesis.

3.14.

Edgar Allan Poe.

I never said these answers aloud though. I never raised my hand. Something always held me back. It took me a while to figure out why this was so.

It was fear, I guessed. Fear that I would be wrong and that people would make fun of me because of it. I was afraid of embarrassing myself with silly answers and stupid questions. So I never talked in class. Only when the teachers called on me did I speak, which wasn't very often since I always kept my gaze down, hair a closed curtain. No one would ever disturb me. I was invisible. I was silent. I was nobody.

Jovie Blue? Who's that girl?

Weird new kid.

That chick that never talks.

That stranger in the classroom everyone's eyes skim over.

That was me.

The overlooked girl.

How did I become her?

Loneliness.

Only one teacher had the courtesy to ask me repeatedly how I was doing, the angel—my pre-algebra teacher. Everyday I'd arrive early to her class, delighting in her kindness when she'd greet me with, "Hi, Jovie. How're you?"

My answer was always a slight shrug, "I'm all right."

She e-mailed my dad after she thought three weeks of me feeling just "okay" was too much. I should be saying "great" or at least "good" by now. But really, all right was a few emotions better than how I was truly feeling.

I knew about her e-mail because Dad told me about it the night he read it…

"So how's school going?" he asked from his recliner. We were in the living room, the bright TV screen the only light casting pale reflections on our faces.

I was slumped on the love seat, curled against the back cushions. I shrugged in response, realizing how much of an effort it was to shrug. I felt so heavy. "Fine."

"Well, your math teacher sent me an e-mail the other day saying that when she asks you how you're doing, you always just say 'okay'. She's a little concerned about you and—"

"I have an A in her class," I interrupted, "she shouldn't be worried." My tone was flat, cold, but deep down I was sort of touched that she cared enough to point out my sadness to my parents.

"You miss your friends back home?" Dad asked after a few minutes of silence. I felt his eyes on my back, like a swarm of spiders they were on my spine, a tingling torture. The moment he mentioned the word *friends* I had to press my lips together hard and squeeze my eyes shut.

Don't cry. Don't cry. Don't cry, I begged myself.

"I just miss Nana," I admitted, my voice muffled by the pillow I had pressed against my face.

"Why don't you give her a call then," Dad suggested.

He didn't know how it wasn't that simple. How I didn't want to call her, bore her with my uneventful life and complaints about school. I couldn't do that to her. I only called her when something interesting happened to me, which was never. So I hadn't spoken to her in a while.

"Okay, I'll go call her," I agreed with my dad, slowly standing to escape up the stairs to my room. I never did call Nana. I just sat on my bed, looking down at the goodbye letter she gave me before I left for Missouri. Written in her boxy handwriting was "Good luck in Misery". Her misspelling made me smile, but it soon faded when I suddenly felt the real misery growing inside me. It was sad. It was cold. I didn't know till now that it even had a name. And I didn't know till now that, to me, Missouri and misery were the same thing.

I felt tears coming; ready to soak the goodbye letter in a warm, salty shower. Three loud raps on my door made me jump and quickly erase the moister from my eyes. I set the letter on my nightstand, then corrected my lifeless posture into a shoulders back, cross-legged, lively sort of pose.

"What?" I finally grumbled, aggravated that someone had interrupted my sulking.

"Hey." It was Olive who peered through the crack in the door. She entered my room, a possessed skeleton haunting me, so light that not even the carpet captured her footprints.

"What d'you want?" She was holding something in her scrawny alien hands. She looked down at the object, then handed it to me.

"Will you look through the pictures and tell me which ones you like best? I'm working on a layout for the yearbook and I can't decide which ones to use."

Internally I *grrrrrred* a few times, but my conscience made me say, "Fine." I turned on the camera and began clicking through the images. Olive stretched out on my bed, yawning. I should have kept my eyes on the pictures, but I let them stray where they shouldn't. Olive's ribcage jutted out when she breathed in. And her blue veins were thick as worms inside her colorless skin. Her sunken cheekbones were highlighted by the crescent moon glowing outside my semicircle window, and her closed eyes had a natural shade of beige to them. She looked like a model.

It wasn't fair.

"I like these four the best," I said, leaning on my elbow beside her to point out which pictures I was talking about.

"Good. Those were the ones I liked." She turned to me, her autumn brown hair shuffling into her hazel eyes. "So. Got any plans for Halloween?"

I laughed at this, snorting a little. "Nope. Why? D'you?"

Her gaze flitted away as she smiled to herself at some internal joy. "I got invited to a party."

"Whose?"

"You wouldn't know him. He goes to the high school. It's a costume party. What d'you think I should dress up as?"

I had to make a strong effort not to role my eyes. Olive was incapable of making decisions for herself. She always wanted a second opinion that she'd take and make her first before her own—as if to transfer the blame if things went wrong. I sighed, wanting to tell her she should go as a skeleton, but that would hurt her feelings. Again, my conscience took over, and I advised her to go as a goddess or fairy or an angel. Something pretty. It would be easy for her to pull that off. She was a very beautiful girl.

It wasn't fair.

She shrugged at my ideas, admitting she was thinking about going as a sexy vampire. I considered it.

"Yeah! Go as that!"

She giggled and brushed her hair from her eyes with the ball of her wrist. Her laugher abated when we heard the blender scream its mechanical snarl from the kitchen. Mom was making Olive a protein shake—something to help her gain weight. Olive's lips pressed together, her breath exhaling loudly though her pointy nose. Her sour face made it clear to me that those shakes weren't very good, maybe even a bit repulsive. She got up without a word, taking the camera with her. And then the skeleton locked herself in her tomb—the bathroom.

Well, at least she's making friends, I thought to myself, as I turned off my bedside lamp. I was happy she got onto the yearbook staff already, happy she got invited places by boys, happy she was getting involved in clubs, making straight A's and loads of friends, even getting teachers' attention with her sharp intelligence. I was so happy for Olive. She seemed more elated than she ever was in Louisiana, more herself.

She'd gotten her new start at life.

And I was happy that my prayer for my big sister was being answered.

But…now I was sad.

My conscience took over again, deciding for me that sadness was better felt by me than Olive. She deserved happiness after the hell her eating disorder put her body and emotions through.

But don't I deserve happiness too?

I curled in a ball, dozing off underneath the warm blanket of blackness and covers before I could think of an answer.

◉

"You did deserve happiness, as you do now." Angel swoops down from the jagged branches, landing, with butterfly poise, on the tiled ground beside me.

"Maybe," I shrug, though inside I still feel like I don't.

"You do," the statue says sincerely, giving my hand a reassuring squeeze. "And I am proud of you for letting in the memories, Jovie. This is a *good* start. You are doing so well." Angel tugs at my hand gently, coaxing me to continue our walk to Heaven.

"Angel?" I say, as I climb over a fallen tree.

"Yes?"

"Can you see them too? The memories, I mean."

"Of course," Angel says as if it's the most obvious thing in the universe.

"Then can you tell me what was wrong with me?" I plead. "I don't understand why I felt those things during junior high. Being so scared to be called on during class, never wanting to raise my hand, turning into a complete wimp in gym class. I was just so nervous all the time, a *freak*, and I don't understand why." I catch up to Angel's pace, the statue brandishing a concrete wing that curls soothingly around my shoulder.

"Jovie, my dear," the angel says, "you felt that way because your friends, the ones you grew up with, were no longer there by your side. You were vulnerable, out in the open, on your own. Friends have a way of masking insecurities, giving you the illusion of confidence. But when you were alone all of your insecurities made themselves known, attacking you all at once. You never knew just how shy you were until you had to face the world alone."

I stare at the dewy ground, my mouth sagging at the painful reality that Angel is right. "Sometimes," I begin, then clear the strain in my throat. "Sometimes I used to think that if I wasn't so shy all of the time, then maybe I would've—" The lump swells in my throat again. "—turned out differently. Made more friends, you know? Maybe I wouldn't have gotten so sad…"

"Shhh," Angel hushes. "Do not dwell on the What Could Have

Been's. They are bad for the soul." Angel's wing around my shoulder slides off, unveiling my sick spirit. "Come. Let's keep walking."

And so we walk, venturing deeper into the darkening woods of my Pertinendi, obscure Heaven-light our only compass. For a while, I think the thickening canopy of branches above is to blame for the growing dimness all around. But as crickets begin scoring the evening and bats screech as they fly wildly out of their slumbers, I realize dusk is upon us.

Fireflies in the distant brush flicker on and off. But as Angel and I get closer, their lights grow into what looks like actual candle flames…

"D'you see that?" I ask Angel. I run ahead, kneeling down in what appears to be a pumpkin patch. I chuckle to myself, feeling stupid for mistaking fireflies for lit candles inside… "Jack-o'-lanterns?" I look to Angel, then back down at the pumpkin faces. "Why would there be jack-o'-lanterns *here*? In the middle of a forest?" Angel says something in reply, but I don't hear it. One of the pumpkin faces, carved into a malevolent grin, its candlelight flickering on and flickering off, hypnotizes me into a memory…

◎

Sitting in French class, I didn't feel the need to pay attention since I knew most of the material being taught. I found myself, for the majority of the class period, staring at the creepy jack-o'-lantern on my teacher's desk. Obviously, Halloween was near. Actually, I was pretty sure it was today. Well, regardless of what day it was, I wouldn't be trick-or-treating since I had no one to go with. Plus, I was twelve. *Is that too old?*

The bell dinged before I could think of an answer. I bent to grab my books, and, when I stood up, caught Francesca looking at me.

"Hey, new kid, got any plans for Halloween tonight?" She pulled her skull-decorated bag over her shoulder and waited for me while I walked around the desks separating us.

"Jovie," I reminded her. "And, uhhmm." I thought for a moment. "No, I don't think so." We walked out of the classroom, talking as we made our way through the hallway of lockers and obnoxious students.

"Then you should come trick-or-treating with me tonight. I'm going with a group of friends."

My eyebrows arched high at this. "Really? Are you sure?" I didn't want to intrude on her group and all.

"Sure, why not? You don't have any other plans, do you?" We were outside now, making our way towards the math building.

I shook my head in response, smiling. "I'll ask my mom tonight if I can go. I'm sure it'll be fine."

"Awesome. Here." She ripped a page from her notebook and scrawled her number down. "Just gimme a call if you can come." I took the paper from her, still grinning.

"Thanks," I said sincerely, because it was awful kind of her to invite me; it meant a lot to me. "I'll call you as soon as I find out I can go. And I'm pretty sure I'll be able to."

"Okay, well hopefully I'll see you later then." She gave me a subtle half smile, then we parted ways as we walked to our next classes.

For the rest of the day, I was ecstatic and nervous and happy and nervous and eager to tell my parents I got invited somewhere and still nervous. I wasn't sure why I was so nervous though. It was only trick-or-treating…but…with people I hardly knew. *But they could be your future friends*, I kept telling myself, *maybe even best friends*. I smiled really big at this thought as I road the bus home.

The wind blowing from the open window tousled my dark hair violently, conjuring my thoughts to wonder what dark creature I should be for Halloween. I needed…*wanted*…to look good tonight for the new people I would meet. I knew I couldn't pull off a sexy vampire or an angel—I wasn't that pretty. But maybe something cool, something Francesca and her friends may think was cool too… *Hmmm…*

Once off the bus and inside the empty house, I hurried over to the phone; Pumpkin, my golden retriever, attacking me with kisses all the while. I dialed my mom's cell number.

"Hello?"

"Hey, Mom, it's Jovie. I just wanted to ask if I could go trick-or-treating tonight with someone from school."

"What?! Well of course you can! That's wonderful, honey. I'm glad you're making friends." I smiled, pleased to hear such excitement in her voice. "So, d'you want me to stop and pick you up a costume from the store or something?"

"Oh no, I think I'll just put something together from my closet. Thanks, though."

"Okay, sweetie. You be careful tonight. I'll be home later. You can tell me all about it tomorrow morning, okay?"

"Alright, Mom, love you."

"Love you too. Bye."

Click. I hung up the phone, then swung my bag around to dig for Francesca's number. Inside the small pocket of my bag I found the piece of paper with the name of some church a girl had invited me to. I threw it away. "Ah ha! There you are." I pulled out the piece of paper with Francesca's number, and, when I unfolded it to reveal the digits, felt my stomach do a nervous flop. I took a deep breath, then dialed the number.

"Sup?" a voice said on the other end. I knew it was Francesca's. It was hard not to recognize her loud voice that always sounded sarcastic no matter what she was saying.

"Hey, Francesca, it's Jovie."

"Who?"

I pressed my lips together, embarrassed. "Uhh, the…new kid."

"Oh! Duh! Hey, so can you come tonight?"

"Yep," I smiled. "So what time are you and your friends going?"

"Probably around six. My friends are old enough to drive, so we'll pick you tonight. Where d'you live?"

I told her my address and tried explaining directions to my house. "Uhhh," I stuttered once I was done giving the crappiest directions ever. "How about I give you my number just in case you need more directions?" I told her the digits.

"Awesome. See ya, Jovie."

"Okay, bye." I hung up and leaned on the kitchen counter for a moment. *Her friends are older?* I cringed, butterflies swarming around in my gut. *How much older?* I fretted. *Well, old enough to drive. Crap! Now I really gotta come up with a cool costume!*

By the time Olive got home from her after school club meetings, about four-thirty in the afternoon, I was still rummaging through my closet looking for something to wear.

"What're you doing?" Olive asked, poking her head into my room.

"Tryin' to put a costume together. I'm going trick-or-treating tonight."

"By yourself?" She seemed amused by this, as she stepped into my room and leaned against the doorway.

"No," I scowled. "I'm going with someone from school and her friends."

"Well, don't go as a vampire," she ordered. "Cuz that's what I'm going as."

"Fine by me." I stood in my closet for a moment, feeling defeated as I looked around at my pathetic outfits. I peered out of my closet. "Hey, Olive? What should I go as?" I waited a moment for an answer.

No reply.

Must be downstairs, I thought with a sigh. I plopped down on my bed, facing the nearest outfit strung out over my pillow. I grabbed the small black tank top. It said "Rock On" in sparkly red sequins—a pajama shirt Grandma Blue gave me for my birthday a long time ago. I got up from my bed to put it on over my long-sleeved black shirt. I glanced down at myself. It looked decent. I got into some jeans, then went over to my dresser mirror. This outfit looked okay. I could go as some kind of grungy rocker girl. Yeah! I'd go as that!

Finally at peace with an outfit, I found myself in the bathroom digging through Olive's makeup. With imprecise hands, I put on dark blue eye shadow, thick lines of eyeliner, and many swipes of mascara that hung on my eyelashes in clumps rather than smooth lines. Once I was done, I took a step back, studying myself in the mirror. Something was missing. I went back into my closet, smiling down at the coolest pair of shoes I owned.

"What's a rocker girl without her Converse?" I said to myself, slipping on my favorite shoes. *There. I'm ready.*

My shoes tapped the ground nervously as I sat in the living room waiting on Francesca and her friends to pick me up. I checked the clock. It was almost six.

Olive went by the living room in her vampire getup. If it was even possible, the black pantyhose she had on made her legs look even thinner, as did the tight crimson blouse and black high heels. And then to complete the ensemble, she had big white fangs jammed between her teeth. I couldn't help but giggle. "It's a good think Mom and Dad aren't here. I don't think they'd approve of that outfit."

Olive beamed a haughty smile. "Thanks," she slurred, then spit out her fangs. "When're your friends coming?"

"Like any minute now."

"Well, until they do, hand out candy to trick-or-treaters. My ride will be here any second and I still gotta put some makeup on." She started up the stairs, her heels stomping on the soft carpet along the way.

"Fine," I muttered, getting up to fetch the gigantic pumpkin container we stored Halloween candy in. I set it by the front door, then, just when I was walking away, heard the doorbell ring. My heart did a nervous summersault in my chest. I hurried back to the door, opened it up, expecting to see Francesca and her friends. Instead, I found a fairy princess and mini superman.

"Trick-or-treat!" the kids sang in unison.

I smiled at them and their parents, complementing them on their outfits and giving them each a handful of candy.

"Thank you!" they yelled, scampering off to the next house.

I shut the door, and, right when I sat back down on the couch, the doorbell rang again. I hurried to the door, only to open it and find a really cute guy standing with his hands in his pockets and a nervous look about him.

"Uhh," he said, anxiously patting his hair down. "Is Olive home?"

"Yeah, just a sec." I walked to the staircase and yelled up at her, "OLIVE! SOMEONE'S AT THE DOOR FOR YOU!" I heard her curse, trip, and drop something. She came stomping down the stairs again. Her face was beautifully painted with makeup this time—much more carefully than I had done mine.

"Bye, Jovie," she said over her shoulder, as she shut the door behind her and the cute boy. I watched them through the window as they walked to the boy's beat-up car. He didn't open the door for my sister; his eyes just roamed all over her body, checking her out. I hoped she'd be safe at the party she was going to; I really, really hoped this.

I was home alone again, my only company the dog. The house was silent, and time seemed to go by awfully slow as I waited until it was six-thirty. By that time, I tried calling Francesca to see if she was lost. But it was her mom that answered the phone, telling me that they had already left. So I waited another half hour, then another, my good spirits dwindling as the doorbell kept ringing and ringing, but never was it Francesca at the door. Just trick-or-treaters.

When it was almost eight, I turned off the porch light and sunk into the soft cushions of the couch with the candy container in my lap. I ate my saddening feelings away with chocolate, distracting myself by watching the crappy horror movies showing on TV until I realized Mom and Dad would be home soon. I didn't want to be up by then and have to explain that I'd gotten stood up.

I was getting up to take off my costume when I heard honking sounding off from the driveway. I ran to the door, looked out the window. I could see Francesca waving from the car and a few unfamiliar faces in the driver and passenger's seat. I smiled at them, every disappointed and upset feeling I had towards them vanishing immediately. I motioned for them to hold on just one second. I set the huge basket of candy outside for the trick-or-treaters, then raced to the car, panting and smiling like an idiot.

"Hey, Francesca," I said breathlessly, as I slid into the backseat.

"Jovie," she said, "this is Sheila." She gestured to the spiky-haired blonde in the driver's seat. This girl wore a lot of bright blue eye makeup, and two silver piercings glistened just below on her nose and lip. "This is Danielle and Dominique." Francesca pointed to the girl in the passenger's seat and then, with her thumb, to the girl sitting beside her. Both were brunettes. One had long, flat brown hair and the other's was cut short into a spiked mohawk. Both were dressed like hippies. Aside from the hair, though, they looked very much alike.

"We're twins," Dominique informed me as she lit up a cigarette.

"Oh," I breathed, "that's really cool. It's nice to meet y'all."

Francesca giggled, and I didn't know why.

"She's not from here," she briefed her friends, grinning. She turned back to me. "It's funny how you say 'y'all'."

My eyes widened. I didn't know that was a weird thing to say.

"What do y'all say instead?"

"Uh, *you guys* or *you all*," Sheila stated. She kind of talked down to me, as if she thought I was stupid or something.

I didn't say anything back; rather, I watched a group of kids, disguised as various monsters, run up to the pumpkin full of candy at my porch and dump the rest of it into their bags.

My mouth fell open.

"Thaaaat…probably wasn't the brightest idea," Francesca told me.

My face was set in a dumbfounded expression as Sheila backed out of the driveway and turned onto the main road.

"S-so," I stuttered, reaching into my pockets to pull out some plastic bags. "I brought us some bags to put our candy in."

No one said anything.

"For when we trick-or-treat," I went on.

When everyone was still silent, I looked to Francesca, eyes pleading for a response.

"Uhhh," she faltered, "we aren't actually going trick-or-treating."

"We're too old for that shit," Sheila spat, "but we *are* old enough to go partaaay!" She danced in her seat, swerving the car into oncoming traffic.

"And remind me again," Danielle said to Sheila, "why we're bringing not one but *two* junior high kids with us to this party?"

Sheila sighed. "Well, as you all know I got fired from my job."

"Oh, I'm so sorry," I chimed from the backseat.

"I failed a drug test," she muttered dully, looking at me through the rearview.

I shied away from her ice-cold stare, turning to look out the window where Halloween night began to spread its dark wing over the hills of southwest Missouri.

"Anyway, so I'm broke. And I still owe Francesca fifty bucks. *So*, bringing her to the party is me *repaying* her. *Right*, Francesca?" Sheila craned her neck to look Francesca in the face for confirmation of the deal.

"Yep," Francesca chirped cheerfully, her nose scrunched with smugness.

Sheila cleared her throat, then went on to explain, "And the

Pertinendi

reason why Junior High Kid Number Two is joining us—"

Is that me?

"—is because Francesca doesn't wanna be the youngest person at the party."

My lips pulled down from the weight of that last statement. I glanced at Francesca, noticing the redness brightening her pale cheeks. *So that's why you invited me?* I wanted to say to her. *To use me?*

Francesca looked at me, eyes apologetic.

I shrugged, trying not to make a big deal out of it. I wasn't one to get angry very easily, but I was bothered.

"So what're you dressed up as anyway?" Francesca finally asked me, in an attempt, I figured, to change the subject.

"A grungy rock and roll fan girl." I pointed at the phrase on the shirt.

"Ah, that's cool. I'm a goth."

"But you always dress like that," Dominique pointed out after taking a long draw on her second cigarette.

"Same goes for you, ya hippie!" Francesca jokingly jabbed Dominique in the side.

"Yep, we're hippies," Danielle defended her sister.

"And I'm just me," Sheila said, as if it was the best costume out of all of ours.

"Well that's no fun," Francesca muttered. Sheila and Francesca went on and on arguing about what constitutes a good Halloween costume, then about rules for Francesca and me to follow while we were at the party. I didn't pay attention to these rules. I stared out the window, taking note of the businesses and bridge we went over. I'd never been to this part of town.

It wasn't a long drive to the party. But it was long enough for butterflies to multiply in my gut. There they swelled and heated my stomach, filling it with anxiety and second thoughts about not asking Francesca and her friends to just bring me back home. I didn't want to be a hassle for these girls. They weren't the most welcoming bunch, but they were a bunch, they had each other, and maybe, just maybe, I could be a part of that tonight. I hadn't felt belonging in a really, really long time. And that was all I wanted from today, to feel that safe certainty that I was where I should be. But where I was had the opposite effect. Especially when we pulled up in the front yard of a totally trashed, three-story house filled with people I didn't know.

"Awesome. They got good tunes." Sheila's voice held nothing but relief.

"Who-whose party is this?" I stammered, having to raise my voice over the blaring music coming from inside the house.

"Jay Robinson's," Dominique answered, flicking her cigarette into the ground as we got out of the car. "He's pretty popular at the high school."

I nodded, acting like I knew who she was talking about.

"D'you know Scottie Robinson?" Francesca asked me, as she adjusted her black and green stockings.

"No, I've never heard of him."

"Oh, well he's in our grade. That's Jay's little brother. Just thought you might know him. He's in a few of my classes."

I looked up at the house, studying its beautiful garden covered in toilet paper and the manicured lawn fully littered, dotted with red cups thrown about. "They got a really nice house," I admitted.

Sheila snickered under her breath. "It won't look nice tomorrow. Lord I hope his parents won't be home anytime soon. Or anytime this week for that matter. It's gonna be a real bitch cleaning up all this shit." She kicked a plastic cup on the ground, then swiveled around to Francesca and me, pointing a painted-black claw at us with a serious look in her eyes. "Alright, you two, listen up. You best follow those rules I mentioned earlier. First: Do *not* talk to me or any of us while you're at this party until *we* come to *you* about leaving. Second: Do not embarrass us or yourselves; just simply *be* at the party but not seen or heard, got it?"

We both nodded vigorously, our eyes as wide as the full moon out tonight.

"Good," Sheila smirked, turning to the sound of some guy hollering her name.

"Yo, Sheila! Get your ass over here!" The guy waved her and her friends over, his other hand holding a beer.

I swallowed hard. I shouldn't be here.

Francesca's friends ditched us, all going over to the guy then disappearing into the smoky haze of people.

"How'd you become friends with those girls? They're so much older," I said, my voice low. I hoped Francesca wouldn't take offense to my question.

"My sister's older. Older than them, actually. But they're all best friends, so they're kinda like sisters to me."

"Oh." I nodded, understanding it now.

"So. Shall we?" Francesca looked to the house, her black lips set in a mischievous half smile.

"Uhmm," I hesitated, glancing back at the car. I felt like I should sit there until everyone was ready to go home.

"Oh, come on!" Francesca grabbed my hand, dragging me along until the music's deafening base vibrated my legs as we stepped inside the house.

The party was infested with monsters and fairytale beings, all reeking of the odor my Great Uncle Berry used to always smell like—and he was an alcoholic.

"This is awesome!" Francesca yelled back at me, as I followed her closely through the maze of bodies we were weaving in between. I felt so terrible for having to push people out of the way in order to catch up with Francesca, but I was frantic. I didn't want to lose sight of her—not here, not at this party. I didn't want to be alone.

Everyone's voice was a droning hum buzzing in the thick slush of music. The crowd was like torrent waters and I was drowning in it. I felt trapped, squished between all these people. Everyone was so much taller. And the people who noticed me gave me weird looks, whispering to their friends, laughing. I felt like everyone was watching me.

I don't wanna be here.
I don't wanna be here.
I wanna go home.

"Jovie! Over here!" Francesca's voice sounded close by, but I couldn't see her.

I pushed through the people dancing in front of me, stumbling into what looked like a lounge. Francesca was on the couch chatting it up with some guys. With a sigh of relief, I perched myself on the armrest beside her, my heart still beating as violently as the drums in the song playing.

"Who's your friend?" one of the guys next to Francesca wondered. He looked old. *Really* old. Like, much, much, *much* too old for Francesca and me. He had facial hair for goodness sake! And a tattoo! The guy had a creepy smile pulling back his thick lips, and I didn't like the way he looked at me.

"Jovie," I told him, forcing a smile.

"Here," he said, handing me a cup filled to the brim with blood-red punch, "you look like you could use a drink."

"Thanks." I took the cup, peering down inside to see my reflection atop the rippling red surface. My face had a look that seemed to scream, *I want my mom.* She wouldn't want me to be here, Dad neither. My throat got really dry at the thought of my parents, how they didn't know where I really was. I felt like I had betrayed them, but Francesca lied to me first. Did that still make this whole situation my fault? I bit down on my lip, uncertain of an answer. I should have asked to be brought back home the moment I found out we weren't trick-or-treating. *I should have... I should have...*

"Bottoms up, bitches," the guy told us, then downed an entire cup of punch. "Ahhh," he sighed, sliding closer to Francesca. "Drink up." His black eyes fixed on her.

She smiled her smug grin, then chugged her drink just like he did.

His eyes then fell upon me. They were like Sheila's but harsher and colder. He waited for me expectantly.

I took a deep breath, brought the cup up to my lips, barely tilting it back to taste the sour punch. Whatever it was, it was not the punch my mom made during the summertime. It tasted more like sweet cough syrup that burned my throat on the way down to my stomach. I tried not to grimace as I swallowed and swallowed and swallowed the punch down. When there was just a few drops left, I stopped, looked at the guy for approval.

"I'll get us more." He got up, and, when Francesca looked away, winked at me.

"That's good punch," Francesca noted, wiping her mouth.

"D'you know that guy?" I asked her, leaning in closer to her ear so she could hear me. I leaned away, waiting for an answer.

"Of course! That's Stephen. My sister's ex. He's a total douche, but completely harmless." She went on introducing me to the other guys standing around the room. None were paying any attention, just cutting up with each other, all holding a beer.

I felt so out of place.

This wasn't where I belonged.

"Oh my gosh," Francesca gushed suddenly. "It's Cassy!" She turned to me, eyes wild with excitement. "I'm gonna go over there and talk to my friend."

"Okay," I said, my voice small. *Now she's gonna leave me here alone?* I'd much rather be trick-or-treating by myself than sitting here. I looked down at my hands, succumbing to my nervous nail biting habit. When my nails were gnawed to the skin, I brought my necklace charms to my lips, nibbling on the blocks that spelled my name.

Anxiousness swept my throat dry of any moisture... I was so thirsty...

"Round two," Stephan said, holding out another cup for me.

I took it, gladly.

"Where'd Franny go?"

"Francesca? She's talking to her friend," I told him, my voice muffled by the cup. I finished off my second round of punch, and, still, my throat remained sticky and dry.

Stephen laughed at me, taking a seat very close by. "More for you then." He flashed an unsettling smile as he handed me the punch meant for Francesca.

I drank it like I did the others, my throat still not wanting to cool down. I drank almost six cups until my stomach started feeling woozy.

"Want another?" Stephan whispered into my ear.

I shook my head, blinking hard. I didn't like how I tried to answer him verbally, but couldn't get anything out. I felt dizzy, and all the dancing monsters in the room kept spinning and spinning with the slurring music pounding against my eardrums. Sweat dotted my forehead, streaming down in little beads that felt like insects creeping all over my skin. Or maybe it was just Stephen's eyes crawling about on my every pore.

There was another whisper... And a hand touched my leg, the whisper uttering from Stephan's lips saying that I smelled like candy and he liked it.

I looked at him, confused. I tried telling him that I shouldn't smell like candy, because my perfume was lavender-scented. Then my eyes fell down to his hand. It shouldn't be there. I pushed it away. He misread my gesture though, taking it as an offer to grab my hand. I shook my head, closing my eyes. *No*, I told him, but didn't hear myself say it. I got up, swaying a bit from the spinning room, and told him, or at least I thought I told him, that I needed to use the restroom.

Leaving my empty red cup on the table, I started for the next room in the hopes of finding a bathroom. But the group of guys cutting up from earlier stopped me before I left the lounge. Above the music, I heard Stephen yell, "SLOSH AND TOSS!"

The guys laughed; one of them grabbed me by the shoulders.

"Looks like we got a taker for Slosh and Toss, guys," one of them grinned wickedly.

I looked at all their faces, taking them in with wide, horrified eyes. Two were dressed as zombie football players, the other a grim reaper, and the fourth one was a werewolf. *What?* I asked them. *What's Slosh and Toss?*

The werewolf that had me by the shoulders pushed me into one of the zombies, then I was pushed into the grim reaper, and then to the werewolf. They kept shoving me back and forth to one another. I screamed for them to stop but all I got out were sickly sounds. I could feel that awful punch and all the candy I ate earlier sloshing around in my gut. And then, finally, my mouth began filling with saliva, but it wasn't a good thing. I was going to puke.

"Dude, she's gonna barf! I'm out!" the grim reaper yelled, pushing me away until I stumbled into the werewolf again.

"Pussy!" the two zombies yelled.

More pushes.

"Please," I managed, hunching over and holding onto my stomach. "I'm gonna be sick."

"I'm out!" a zombie said, holding his hands up in surrender and backing away quickly.

I gagged.

"Me too," the other zombie admitted, shoving me into the next room.

"I win!" the werewolf barked, punching the air with his hairy fists.

I was free. Holding my mouth, I hurried to find a bathroom. I gagged again as I stumbled on, this time spit coming up. Luckily, I kept it in my mouth, feeling, as I swallowed it back down, my face paling at the grossness of it all.

I couldn't get through the mass of people. They weren't moving out of the way!

I looked to the side. Stairs. I could go up or down. Upstairs I could see, through teary vision, a cluster of people dancing. Downstairs was just pitch-dark nothingness.

I fled down the stairs to the basement of this stranger's house. In the darkness, the sounds of the party from upstairs were muffled, a drunken slur of reality that didn't make much sense to me anymore.

I felt along the wall, tripping over thrown about things, until I found a light switch. I flipped it upward, illuminating the dark room with a dim yellow light. The basement was merely a large slab of concrete and scattered boards—which was what I kept tripping over. It looked like it was being remodeled or something.

My stomach did a nasty twist, growling at me to hurry the hell up. I obliged, quickening my pace on my search for a toilet.

Concrete, sprinkled with sawdust and splattered with white paint, eventually turned to carpet as I made my way down a hallway. This part of the basement looked more finished than the room by the staircase. I turned into the first room, and, when I flipped the light on, nearly sank to the floor in relief. A bathroom. I shut myself in, stumbling to the toilet where I turned the lid up and bent over the ultra-white, porcelain ring.

Everything I had chugged so quickly came back up that much faster. It looked like blood was spewing from my lips, but it tasted like that sour punch mixed with stomach acid. My eyes watered from the burn in my throat.

I coughed and coughed the remains of my stomach out, then wiped my lips dry with my wrist. I flushed the toilet, watching, through blurry vision, the blood-red mistake I made swirl about below me then disappear.

If only, I thought, drunkenly staring at the toilet, *all mistakes could disappear that easily.*

I made my way over to the sink, propping myself up on my elbows as I washed my hands and rinsed my mouth out. I caught sight of my reflection. Black mascara trails blazed their way down the white hills of my cheeks, ending at my red-stained lips. I averted my gaze down, noticing that my hands were trembling. I stood up straight, turned to leave…

Someone was blocking the way out.

I gasped, flinching away.

It was Stephan at the doorway, just now shutting the door behind him.

"What're you doing?" I asked him, quickly wiping away my smudged eye makeup. My voice sounded strange to me, as if I was far away from myself but close by at the same time, kind of like the party happening just above us.

I took a step forward to get by him, but staggered. My legs were so shaky. Why were they so shaky?!

"That doesn't matter," he said coolly, grabbing hold of my shoulders. "What I wanna know is why you're down here all alone instead of upstairs enjoying the party."

I tried to peel myself away from him. He wouldn't have that. His grip tightened painfully around my arms.

"I-I don't feel so good," I slurred, glancing at the toilet. "Please." Fear weighed me down; made my knees feel like they were about to buckle under me. I barley had any control over my body and my words. "I just wanna go home," I finally confessed, a sob making its way into my voice.

"Well," he murmured softly, brushing a lock of hair out of my face, "I can bring you home…if you do something for me first."

I met his murky eyes, a cruel intention burning deep within them. And in their dark glisten, I saw myself, wide-eyed and fearful, reflecting back as a victim.

My body went cold. Mouth dry again. My heart burst with adrenaline, beating against my chest vehemently.

"Leave me alone," I hissed through my teeth, grabbing his wrists and pushing them off me. They remained, squeezing my skin even harder. He pushed me against the sink counter, pressing himself against me so that I couldn't move.

I fought against him, trying to scream, but his hand smashed over my lips. I could only utter, "MMMM!"

He was heavy, breathing hard and sweating as he unzipped his pants, trying to push me down towards a part of him I wanted nothing to do with.

In a frantic blur, I pounded my fists against him, wailing stifled cries that couldn't be heard by anyone, not even over the vibrations of the music.

My body grew weary the more I fought him. Exhaustion spread throughout my muscles, weakening my will to keep scratching, punching, and biting. I was about to give up and go limp but the doorknob jiggled, making me snap out of my defeated daze.

"Who's in there?" a voice yelled from outside the door.

HELP! I tried to scream.

The door flew open, smacking against the wall where it left a dent.

Stephen let me go so he could fumble with his jeans.

I looked to the person at the door. He was shorter, like me, and he seemed incredibly pissed off.

"What the hell's going on?" he demanded, eyes narrowing at me.

I couldn't speak. I just sat there on the counter, tears streaming down my face as I looked to Stephen, down at his open zipper, then to the boy at the door.

I think the boy understood.

"Why don't you mind your own goddamned business?" Stephen grunted, his eyes forming piercing slits.

"Why don't *you* get the hell outta my house before I call the cops?"

"Fuckin' liar. You don't live here," Stephan spat.

"Wanna bet?" the boy asked, laughing without any humor. "Or I know, how about I go get my brother, Jay, and maybe he can convince you."

Stephen's crescent eyes twitched into wide circles. "Fuck you," he seethed, throwing the boy into the wall as he left the bathroom.

"Don't let the door hit you on the way out!" the boy called after him, rubbing his shoulder from the blow.

I slowly slid off the sink counter, somehow able to breathe the words, "Thank you," to the boy.

"Hey, are you okay?" He stepped closer to me, caution guarding his movements as he gently wrapped his arm around my waist, inviting me to lean against him. "Did he do anything to you?"

I shook my head.

He nodded, clearly relieved. The boy led me into another room down the hallway.

I looked around, alarmed by the darkness now.

"Don't worry. It's just my room." He flipped on the light, revealing a large, expansively furnished room filled with scattered stacks of CDs and shelves of video games. Posters decorated the walls, their pictures illustrating rap artists I'd never heard of before. "Here," he said, guiding me down to the armchair.

I sat down, watching him dubiously as he grabbed a pillow from his bed, threw it onto the ground, and sat on it in front of me.

"So what's your name," he asked, voice soft, as if I were a shy animal he was afraid of scaring away.

"Jovie," I whispered, my voice and body still shaking. "Jovie Blue."

His lips parted, eyes beholding some sort of revelation. "Wait. You go to the junior high, right?"

I nodded.

"Jovie," he whispered, looking off into space, "why does that name sound so familiar?"

"It shouldn't," I disagreed, "I just moved here not too long ago."

He snapped his fingers, smiling brightly. "That's why! You're the new student. I've heard about you." Confusion suddenly contorted his features. "What're you doing at my brother's Halloween party? I'm pretty sure only people from the high school were invited."

I hesitated, turning my gaze to the window where a sallow moon floated amongst the wisps of clouds. "It's a long story," I finally answered. I stood up, using the armrest to balance myself. "I should go." I made it to the doorway, but stopped. I turned to the boy. He was still sitting on the floor, watching me closely with soft blue eyes. They reminded me, for a moment, of the fields of bluebonnets that grew alongside the highway in my hometown. I was there, in my mind, safe and warm, in the field of his eyes. "What's your name?" I asked, timidly looking away from his eyes when they locked with mine.

"Scottie Robinson."

"Thank you, Scottie," I said, trying to give him a sincere smile, "for everything."

He nodded once, opening his mouth and lifting his hand as if he wanted to say something.

I left before he did. I just wanted to go home.

Panting and lightheaded, I made it up the stairs, the music's volume increasing with each step I put behind me. Shadows danced along the wall that I slid against in order to make it to the door. I stopped short when I came upon the corner of the room, and it wasn't because someone had bumped into me or wanted to play another round of Slosh and Toss. There, sitting in a white table chair, was the cute boy that had knocked on my front door today. And there, sitting in his lap, was a frail vampire, dressed in crimson and black, with perfect brown waves swiveling down her back.

"Olive?" I gaped.

She couldn't hear me, but even if she were to hear I didn't believe she would have answered. She was much more preoccupied locking lips with the guy holding her in his lap.

So this *is the party you were invited to,* I realized, my mouth still hanging open.

A group of rowdy guys broke out into a fight. Olive turned around to see what the ruckus was about. Before she saw me, I dove into the crowd, disappearing from her view. She couldn't see me here. She'd tell Mom and Dad.

It took me a while, but I finally managed to push my way through the crowd, popping through a door leading outside to the front yard. Sheila's car was still there, but that didn't matter. There was no way I'd be able to find Francesca and all her friends. To be honest with myself, I didn't even want to find them or talk to them ever again. I'd rather walk home alone than be with them—so that was exactly what I did.

I set out along the sidewalk, the eerie moon and yellow smirks of jack-o-lanterns lighting the conclusion of Halloween night for me. I crossed my arms over my chest, shivering underneath my costume.

Each of my sharp breaths was a cloud of fog before my lips. The temperature had taken a nosedive since the last time I'd been outside.

Leaves rustled about at my shoes, the sound like trudging feet behind me. But there weren't very many trick-or-treaters running around high on a sugar-frenzy anymore; actually, there weren't *any* trick-or-treaters outside now. I was alone.

I quickened my pace, not slowing until the booming party music was just a distant rumble, like a long past storm.

I came upon the small bridge we had driven over—a sign I was going the right direction. I stopped halfway across it, resting against the railing. The water lapping below was black as the night, black as the smudged makeup on my face, black as Stephan's eyes…

I ran the rest of the way off the bridge. I ran across the town, following the signs of businesses I had taken note of on the drive to the party. I ran until the lights of businesses were nothing but an artificial glow on the horizon behind me and the landscape before me was just rolling hills of the rural part of town—which was where I lived.

I ran, I ran, I ran…

But how far did I have to run until the party was far enough behind me?

I didn't know, I didn't know.

I had to stop running.

I was too tired.

And the air cut my throat with its icy temperature; stung my eyes with its howling wind. I puffed exasperated breaths; tears formed a new trail of black mascara down my cheeks.

The sidewalk ended. I had to hoof it on the side of the road now until I made it to my neighborhood. It couldn't be too much further.

Mist filled the air I walked through, turning to liquid gold when the headlights of cars shined through it.

Beautiful, I thought in a teary daze. I was freezing, but somehow the mist felt good on my skin, cleansing it, erasing the touch of awful people. I upturned my palms to the sky, cupping the water. Every fiber of my being wanted to be like the mist; wanted to disperse into a million dots that glided along the wind, untouchable, gentle, free.

Honk! Honk! A car screeched to a stop beside me.

Someone shouted my name. I stood still, squinting through the haze at the shadows in the car. The person in the passenger's seat rolled down the window.

"Jovie? Jovie! What in the world are you doing out here? Oh my God!"

It was Olive.

My lips trembled with relief, and tears or mist or rain poured from my eyes now. "Olive," I cried, when she came to my side, collecting me in a hug. "I wanna go home."

"Come on," she said, helping me into the backseat of the cute guy's car. "You can tell me what happened when we get home." She buckled a seatbelt across my torso, then slid in next to me, never letting go of my shaking hand. "Take us home," she ordered the guy, and he did, no questions asked.

Olive wiped the stringy hair from my eyes, erased the cloud of smudged makeup from my face with her sleeve. For a moment, I smiled. It was barely noticeable, but it was probably the most effortless smile I'd ever smiled. For in that very moment, I had my big sister back. The distant creature an eating disorder had turned her into was gone. The tender, loving, kind, and protective Olive I admired so dearly was in the palm of my hand, was laying her head against mine. Feeling the love I felt from my sister right then—a love I never thought I'd feel again—was worth all the humiliation I'd gone through tonight.

The last tear I cried for the night slid down my cheek, then died on the edge of my smile.

◉

My lips, curving ever so slightly upward, slowly bend down as the memory disappears from me, taking my smile with it. Pertinendi settles in around me, but I'm not where I was before when I first saw the memory. The pumpkin patch is nowhere near. I'm sitting amongst large rocks with a campfire crackling before me and a bizarre night sky blanketing my unconscious wasteland.

"We are almost out of the forest," Angel says, watching me carefully from across the fire.

"Good," I say, standing up to rub my butt—I would desire the rock to feel like a cushion later. "How'd we get here?" I wonder, looking around our campsite.

"I brought us here. We needed to find a safe spot to rest a while. I think the rocks will shield us from any eyes that may be watching."

I laugh to myself. "Well, *you're* certainly camouflaged enough to fit right in."

"I guess you are right," the statue chuckles. After a moment, Angel says, "So tell me, if you would like to, what happened after Halloween night."

I press my lips together, feeling heat rising up my neck and burning my cheeks with scarlet embarrassment. "I'm sorry you saw all of that," I apologize, "it's not something I ever wanted anyone to know."

The angel seems puzzled by this. "Jovie, my dear, do not be embarrassed for what happened to you. There is nothing to be ashamed of."

My gaze flits away from the heartbreakingly sympathetic eyes of the angel. I sit back down in front of the fire, taking in a deep breath. "I never told Olive what really happened. I told her about Francesca and her friends—Olive actually knew Sheila and Dominique; they had a class together. Anyway, I told her those things, about how I was lied to and used as more of an accessory at the party than an actual person. I told her about what I drank. She actually thought that was pretty funny. Apparently, it was spiked punch—I didn't know at the time what I was really drinking."

"You were twelve," Angel says, voice softer than the breeze caressing my cheek.

"Yeah," I whisper, staring at the sparks in the fire floating up into the night sky. "It was a sisterly secret that party. And the next morning when Mom asked about how trick-or-treating went, Olive and I just exchanged looks, then I told Mom it was a lot of fun. Olive added that she really enjoyed the costume party she went to. And that was that. Our little lie was bought, believed, trusted."

"So you never told your parents about what happened with Stephan?"

"Of course not. I never even told Nana."

"Why not?" This seems to hurt the statue; agony is so distinct in its angelic voice.

"I was embarrassed, Angel...*humiliated*. I never wanted anyone to know, not even you. What I wanted more than anything after that night was for Stephan and Scottie to just forget that it ever even happened." I laugh with no humor. "What am I saying? Stephan probably *did* forget—he was pretty drunk. But Scottie..." I shake my head, erasing the thought. "Anyway, I couldn't tell Olive because she'd tell my parents if she knew something like that had happened. And..." I trail off.

"And what?"

"I... I...didn't wanna get anyone into trouble. Myself, Scottie, or...Stephan. I just... I didn't wanna be responsible for ruining someone's life."

"He ruined yours," Angel declares firmly.

I shrug, "I just had nightmares about him after that night."

"Things like that," Angel says, refusing to sweep this under the rug, "are not forgotten over time. If they are not talked about, they get buried deep within your unconscious, which is why you had nightmares and is why that memory lies within this very realm of yourself. It has not left you; it has haunted you. I only wish you would have told someone when you were alive."

I nod along, agreeing with every word the angel says. "I wish I would have told someone, too," I whisper more to myself.

Angel, for a swift second, fades away, reappearing right beside me a moment later. A stone finger presses against my lips, silencing my regrets. "You told me," the angel smiles, silently thanking me with concrete eyes. "Now, I think the best thing for you next is to get some rest." The angel reaches for the rocky ground below, curling its stone fingers into the dirt then whipping the ground up as if it is a thick quilt. The statue gestures to it, smiling gently.

I lay amongst the dirt as Angel instructs, expecting this pallet to be the most uncomfortable thing in the world. I'm surprised when I sink a little into the ground, as if it's a water bed. I'm even more surprised when the blanket, appearing to look just like the rocky gravel, is the softest and warmest fabric I've ever snuggled against. "Thanks," I breathe, curling into the covers of Pertinendi.

"Goodnight, Jovie dear," the angel murmurs, then flickers, like a flame, back to its spot across the fire to resume its natural position.

"Goodnight, Angel," I whisper, closing my eyes to the sound of a forest full of orchestrating bugs playing along to the hums of the wind and rushing water.

◉

In my dead dreams, it is still Halloween. In my dead dreams, I am twelve again, wearing the costume I wore at the party. In my dead dreams, I am amongst the rock formations in my Pertinendi, tied to a petrified tree. In my dead dreams, the Devil tortures me...

"Please," I beg, as the Devil drags its razor claws down my neck, leaving deep rivers of blood on my skin. "Let me go."

The Devil's head flicks up, meeting my pained expression.

I blanch at the Devil's face, though it is not real. The Devil wears a Halloween costume as well; masked by a distorted face, with a drooping frown and bloodied horns. A cloak veils the Devil's body, dragging along the rocky ground as it circles me, staring.

A revolting twist in my stomach sends me shrieking in pain. The Devil's presence is unnerving, rotting every speck of my soul! "Go away!" I scream, squirming against the ropes that bound my wrists behind the tree. "Leave me alone!"

The Devil circles faster and faster, slicing away at my skin each time it passes in front of me. Then the evil being slows to a skip, singing, *"Ring around the Jovie! Pockets full of Jovie! Drooling, drooling, we both fell down!"* Its voice is demonic and mocking. The Devil stops abruptly in front of me, drawing a blade from its cloak.

I shake my head, wide-eyed and sweaty. "NO!"

The Devil lifts the blade into the sky with both hands.

For a moment, I swear the drooping mask the Devil wears twitches into a wicked smirk. Then the Devil whispers harshly, "I am coming for you."

The blade stabs through the air, coming down in a blur to pierce straight into my heart.

I scream...

◉

"NO!" *I gasp, jolting upright from my bed in the rocks. I pant,* looking around with frantic eyes.

Angel is still asleep by the fire; stone wings a shawl draped around its body.

I touch my chest, pressing against my heartbeat. I'm still here. I exist still.

The Devil has not come.

I'm safe.

It was just a bad dream.

Releasing a breath of relief into the sky, I lay my head back down on the soft rocks. Restless, I turn over onto my side, closing my eyes in an attempt to go back to sleep.

"I have bad dreams, too," a voice murmurs near my face.

My lids fly open, as does my mouth when I see a pale ghost lying beside me, gray-blue eyes somewhat shadowed by disheveled, bright orange hair.

"Dale?" I whisper, reaching to barely touch his arm. He appears to me so elusive, skin so pale, like my own. I think he may disappear at any moment, like a mirage…or a dream.

He recoils at my touch, folding his hands under his cheek, eyes steady with mine. "Do you remember dying, Jovie?" he asks me, voice husky and intimate.

"Yes," I whisper back, folding my hands under my cheek like he did. "Some of it. I mainly just remember this…dissolving feeling… like, I had turned to mist…or like I was flour being sifted through the pores of my own skin. Then I was weightless. And whatever was going on, it felt like…like, riding in a car. Everything around me, the world, the stars, planets… It was all going by so fast, but *me*, my body or soul, just kinda drifted along with it, not feeling the speed of everything. I was simply looking out the window at it all. Then suddenly everything stopped. Went black. And I woke up in Hell." I swallow hard at the memory, shaking my thoughts free from it. "Dale," I say, changing the subject urgently, "you gotta remember what happened to you. I don't think you've been to Hell yet, but you're gonna wind up there if you don't let in your memories and understand what happened to you. You have to remember... You *have* to... So you can get to Heaven."

Dale nods slowly. "I know," he says, then admits with an averted gaze, "It's just...hard... It...hurts."

"I understand," I sympathize, knowing full and well where he's coming from. "But you still have to."

Dale locks eyes with me again, his cool stare making me go quiet and thoughtless. "You know," he murmurs, "I can remember. I know I'd make it through all of that, but there's one thing I can't do. I can't..." He squeezes his eyes shut, inhaling a quick breath, his body stiff with hesitance.

Something hisses ferociously from inside the shadows of the forest.

I ignore it, eyes intent on Dale's. "What?" I persist. "Can't do what?"

"Forgive myself."

PART 4

THE DESCENT

A yelp escapes my lips as I sit up straight again, sweat dripping down my neck like blood. I look down at where Dale was laying, but only a pool of blood is left in his place. I pale at the sight, glance back at Angel to see if the statue has awakened from the noise.

Angel sleeps still, face serene.

I look back to the blood. It's gone! My lips close, heavy breathing silences. I gulp the confused questions I have for Dale back down and get up to walk off the bad dreams. I wander until I find the edge of the rock formations our campsite sits atop. I perch myself on the edge of the cliff, looking out at my Pertinendi's night sky in awe.

Nighttime in Pertinendi is the strangest of times. The sky lights up in colors I've never seen before. Ribbons of auroras ripple through the darkness. Galaxies so close wind like ceiling fans in the sky. Moons gleam from far away; and foreign planets whirl, their atmosphere's constantly moving, moving, moving, changing and changing…

I reach out at one of the galaxies swirling about, the feel gritty like sand. It is the Milky Way in the palm of my hand. I pull back, lick my fingers. It even tastes like sweet milk, like I always thought it would when I was a child.

I study the sky for a long while, taking in its complex beauty, its unearthly splendor. I study it alone until I hear footsteps clanking against the ground. The sound gets louder and louder the more the shadow behind me grows larger.

It's just Angel, I realize with a sigh of relief. The statue settles next to me on the cliff. "It's beautiful," I say, nodding to the night sky.

"Of course it is," Angel says, "it is your soul, Jovie."

I look to the angel, perplexed by what it just said. "You mean, all this—" I gesture to the galore of perfection, of mystery. "—is me?"

The angel statue flashes a brilliant half smile, face distinctly pleased with seeing me so flattered. "Did I not explain earlier? Pertinendi is *you*. Your memories, and within such memories therein lies your soul."

"Wow," I breathe, "that's incredible."

Angel agrees with a chuckle, and, a moment later, wonders aloud what keeps me up so late.

"Bad dreams," I tell the rock.

"Ah." Angel seems to understand. "Would you like to talk about them?"

Dale's face blurs in my mind, then the Devil skips into my thoughts, eclipsing the ghost. Pools of blood wash them all away... I shake my head no at the angel, pressing my lips together to hide the quiver.

A neon aurora, playful and alive, twirls in electric blue shades at my fingertips. It twitches in circles, splashing against my knuckles. "I did have this dream a long time ago that I'll tell you about," I say, staring at the beautiful light entity. "I had this dream the night before we moved to Missouri. I dreamed of a whirlpool and that I drowned in it. I thought it symbolized a new beginning, cuz that's what I heard death usually means in a dream." I swipe the aurora away from my hand, annoyed at it. "I never thought it was literal, foreboding my own ending." My hands ball to fists at the thought.

"You seem to blame moving from your home the reason for your suicide. Is that the only reason?"

"Of course not," I croak. "Things built up over time. It's not something one event caused; it's something multiple ones caused, all intertwining into this mass inside myself that was like a poison in me, slowly making me sick through the years." I stare down in a daze at the darkness just beyond the cliff's edge, the nothingness below a horror of its own. "It was a long, slow, downward spiral. Moving was the push to the edge of myself, making me see a part of me that perhaps was always there but never made itself known till then."

I slide onto my knees, something in the darkness below catching my attention. I lean over the edge of the cliff, reaching into the darkness at whatever lay at the cliff's bottom. Whatever it is, it has me in a trance. I feel its heavy presence. It's black, dense; it scares me, and yet I mindlessly reach for it, losing my balance off the cliff.

There's no time for Angel to catch me. I fall off the edge into the darkness, my descent a long way down that I do not feel until I close my eyes…and remember…

◉

I collapsed onto my bed after another day of school. I turned to my alarm clock, its glowing red numbers telling me it was only three in the afternoon. But why was I so tired? Maybe it was from having to run the mile in gym today. Or maybe my brain just hurt from internally seething at Francesca during the entire third period of French class.

"So, uh, where'd you disappear to yesterday?" she had asked me.

Solemnly, I told her I just walked home from the party. And that was that. She made a little surprised noise, then turned her attention to the board. There was no apology, no concern.

I had my gaze fixed on my composition book the entire period, the black and white static design on its cover reminding me of last night, of Stephan's eyes, of the chaotic cluster of people, the blaring music that left a ringing in my ears…

The high ringing sound still echoed in my head, even as I lay in bed, staring up at the spinning fan in my room. No one was home. As usual. Mom and Dad were at work. And Olive was still at the high school, either at a club meeting or doing something with yearbook staff. I let Pumpkin outside when I got off the bus; so she was probably pooping in the neighbor's yard or something.

Movies lie, I thought, glowering up at the light fixture. I never met a cute guy who wanted my number; there wasn't even a cute guy living next door like in the movies. Here in reality, there were just grumpy old people living next door who gave death-stares to anyone letting a dog poop in their yard. In reality, or, at least in my life, there wasn't a classmate or teacher that took a special interest in me, believing I was worth a second glance. No. There was just me: going to school, going to class, listening, taking notes, doing what I was told...with no one noticing. It was all just a routine. Nothing special. I was just Jovie. Jovie Blue. And she wasn't the star of a movie. She was just another girl, and that was all she'd ever be.

Yep, movies lie. Big time.

I was still doing homework at the kitchen bar when Mom got home. She rummaged through the cabinets, collecting ingredients for whatever she was making for supper.

"So how was school?" she asked, distracted as she set the ingredients on the counter where my books were sprawled.

I shrugged, taking out one of my MP3 player earbuds so I could hear her clearly. "I miss everyone back home."

This statement made my mom look up at me, seemingly fatigued by my comment. "It's been *one* month, Jovie. *One month*. You gotta give people and places a chance."

"It's hard," I muttered, internally ranting on and on and on about how shy I was, how it was hard to talk to people, hard to even raise my hand in class. Hard to smile.

She gave me a dull stare, then rubbed the puffy gray clouds beneath her eyes. "Hard?" she said, her voice rising with defense. "You think *you're* life is hard? You're so blessed, Jovie. You have parents that are trying to make a better life for you. I took this job so I could give you and your sister more. So we won't have to struggle to get by as a family. I've been working since I was sixteen. I paid for my own car and eventually paid my way through nursing school. My momma and daddy never helped me with anything. So don't sit there and tell me you're life is hard. Especially when there are people in this world who would give *anything* to be sitting where you are right now, living your life. All you see is negative, Jovie. You need to be more positive—"

Blah, blah, blah...

I put my earbud back in, drowning out her speech. *Leave it to Mom to make me feel a thousand times worse by pointing out how ungrateful I am—which is far from true.* I thanked the Lord wholeheartedly every night for all my blessings, especially for my parents.

The thing about my mom was that she just didn't notice in me the weak person she never was, the weak person she never let herself become. My mom's blood coursed through my veins, but that didn't make me her. Her strength, determination, beauty, and intelligence all went to Olive. I wasn't sure if I could ever have that drive my mother had, that confidence in the future…

Chicken broth splashed onto my math homework. I grumbled, and, with a reclusive hunch of my shoulders, slid off the bar, taking my school crap with me up the stairs to my room.

I found remnants of the delicious supper Mom had cooked a few hours later in the toilet, its consistency now vomit. Small bits that didn't flush stared up at me from the clear water, my reflection a dark shadow above them. I flushed the toilet, trying to let the frustration I held towards my sister go down with her purged food.

I undressed for my shower, studying myself in the mirror as the water heated up. My bones didn't stick out like Olive's. A layer of thick skin…or fat…spread out across my body, softening my features, making me look human and less a skeleton. *But skeletons, beautiful ones like my sister, are in magazines, are in movies.*

Maybe I should go on a diet, I considered, then nodded at the unsatisfying reflection in the mirror. *Yeah*, I decided, *I'll cut back.*

After Mom and Dad went off to sleep, I crept into Olive's room, shutting the door quietly behind me. She lay across her bed, her chin resting in her scrawny hands, as her hazel eyes roamed across the pages of her thick biology textbook.

"Olive."

She ignored me.

"Olive," I tried again, plopping onto the bed beside her.

Her eyes flitted to me, then back down to her studies. "What?" She was clearly annoyed already.

I looked down at the floor, drawing a circle with my big toe into the shag carpet. "You need to stop throwing up. You're still doing it, I know you are."

"I'm *not*. So shut up." She rolled over onto her side, curling up with her homework so the book blocked her face.

"Olive," I tried patiently, reaching to touch her jutting shoulder blade. "I wish you'd tell me what's wrong."

She slammed her book shut. "Get the fuck outta my room, Jovie!"

I stared at her, dumbfounded.

"NOW!"

I flinched, then I hurried out of her room. A whoosh of air blew my hair into my face when she slammed the door behind me as a parting gift.

I looked back at her locked door, my teeth chattering uncontrollably for some reason. Olive was the anorexic zombie again, cruel and moody and hateful. I wished I knew what turned her into this creature…

What magazine, what movie, what person, what thought slithered into your mind one day, I wondered, *making it so that, when you gaze into the mirror, you see someone fat, even when you're nothing but skin and bones?*

I shuddered at the thought, locking myself in my room to curl up with feelings heavier than the textbook my sister was reading.

And just when I'd close my eyes, my alarm would go off early the next morning, alerting me that another day had to be lived. The high-pitched scream of my alarm would then morph into the shrieking whistle my gym coach blew; he'd yell at the class to run faster, play harder. Then the whistle would be a ding, then another ding, and another, and another as each class period went by and by. The ding would then distort into a growl—the roaring of the bus I rode home— and the draining ruckus of students would bloat in my head as I stared out the window, wobbling along with the bus's shudders and jerks. Then all the noise, noise, noise would suddenly cease. Silence I came home to everyday. Silence I sat in while home alone, doing homework, petting Pumpkin, biting my necklace, thinking, staring, considering calling Nana. Silence. It was my home. Silence…was me.

The weeks dragged on like this for a long time.

It seemed that while riding the bus one day the scenery would magically transform from fallen leaves to a frosty earth the next day. Thanksgiving passed by with no warning and my birthday sneaked up in December just the same. Too fast and without me knowing until my mom told me happy birthday that morning before work.

I blew out the candles to my thirteenth birthday cake alone, the breath of my friends no longer behind me to help put out the flames.

Mom had offered to help me throw a birthday party, but that idea went out the window after I told her I had no one to invite. Out of guilt, she drove me to the city to have a "girls' day" for my birthday. She took me to this old people makeup store to get a makeover. Olive was forced to tag along, and, after the fifty year old lady had backed away from painting my face, grinning proudly, Olive snickered behind her hands.

"What?" I demanded, looking around for a mirror.

A bell chimed when another customer opened the door to the quaint makeup store. The lady who did my makeup excused herself, then quickly shuffled to the front of the store to help the new customer.

When the lady was out of earshot, Olive's snorting laughter burst through. "You look like you're ready to go work the corners!"

"Huh?" I gave her a furious glare, only pretending to know what she meant by this.

"Behave," Mom ordered sternly, but her lips twitched upward.

"How bad is it?" I pleaded. Mom, surrendering to my panic, handed over the mirror. I gawked at the clown I saw staring back at me—the one with orange foundation caked onto her face, horrendous, bile yellow eye shadow, bright, cherry red lipstick, and two circular pink stamps on her cheeks. "Oh my God," was all I could muster through my painted lips.

"So," the old lady gushed when she waddled over to us again, "whutcha think?"

I opened my mouth, ready to repeat whatever my sister had said.

Mom intercepted me, sensing what I was about to say. "We'll take some of this," she said quickly. "And...*that*...and..." She pointed down at certain products in the glass cases, none of them the colors the lady used for my face.

After that little escapade, mom drove us back home, and, as we flew down the highway, I busied myself with digging through the makeup she bought me for my birthday present.

"Those colors will make your features pop more naturally," she informed me with an expert's confidence.

I thanked her for everything, then turned around to tell my sister to shut up—she was *still* laughing at my face. Turning around probably wasn't the best idea though, because her seeing my face up close just made her giggle even harder.

At least she's laughing, I thought, giving up on maintaining my dignity.

So...needless to point out, my birthday wasn't the best, but at least I had a funny story to tell Nana when she called to wish me a happy birthday. I really loved talking to her when we finally called each other. I felt better after our conversations, but...one thing bothered me...

In my hometown, I thought there were a lot of people, *friends*, who cared about me. But I was slowly realizing that, in truth, I only had one good friend that entire time. Nana. She was the one person who kept in touch with me over the months; the only one who would return phone calls and ask me how I was doing—how I was *really* doing.

"Hey, thanks for calling," I told Nana before hanging up. "It...it really means a lot that you did."

"No problem, girl," she chirped. "Talk to you later."

Click.

I fell asleep at seven in the evening on my birthday, feeling heavy again as I curled against my pillows, snuggling into their soft contours.

Aside from sleeping, watching TV, and eating a little here and there, I didn't do very much at all over Christmas break. Well, I did go outside a few times to stare up at the cotton-like clouds swirling above. The strange gray puffs in the sky dumped these fluttering specks, like weightless white rain gliding through the air.

"It's snowing," I breathed, sticking out my tongue at the beautiful frozen wonderland in the sky. In all my twelve years living in Louisiana, not once did it ever snow. In the south, snow was something eaten on a paper cone during the summertime, never something that created a smooth, powdery glaze over a driveway or the neighborhood or the entire *town* for that matter.

Olive and I, dressed in our heaviest winter clothes, decided to make our first snowman—a task that the movies again lied about. It was *way* harder than they made it seem.

"I'm going inside," Olive stuttered, her entire frame shaking from the cold. Her poor body just didn't have the insulation to keep her warm enough to tolerate this weather, even when she was wrapped up quite snuggly with layers and layers of coats.

I thought this was probably for the best—her going inside. Her skin had turned as white as the snow, her lips as blue as the scarf around her neck. "Okay," I sniffled, patting down the loose snow piling up around the snowman's butt.

In the end, our snowman wasn't as cute and cuddly as a proper snowman should probably appear. Ours looked…demonically possessed, which probably had to do with the fact that it had rotten strawberries for eyes and a banana smile.

I laughed to myself at the finished snowman, feeling too tired to get up or holler for my parents and Olive to come check it out. Instead, I plopped onto my back, staring up into the blindingly white afternoon sky. I waved my arms up and down, kicked my legs from side to side, forming a snow angel. In the angel imprint, I felt numb; numb in the icy residue of winter. What surprised me was that I kind of…liked this feeling, this numbness. It stung for a while, but as the minutes passed by and my shivers became a comfort, the numbness was my friend. My only friend in Missouri. No longer did I feel heavy; rather, I felt weightless, like the snow, flying high with the flurries in the chilly breeze.

It wasn't long, or long enough, until the whiteness blurring all around me became fixed and rectangular. I found myself staring at a whiteboard, feeling numb still, but no longer in the snow. I was back at school—Christmas break was over—and a new semester had begun. I truly couldn't believe that half the school year was already over and that we still had another entire semester to get through.

I sighed heavily in class, wishing I was home… Home in Louisiana, sitting with Nana on the dock overlooking the pond behind her house. I wanted to be there *so* badly, especially during gym class when we began our health unit. Rather than meeting in the gym, we gathered in a classroom every morning to talk about adolescence and all the health issues encompassing these years. We discussed friendship—and that was the first time since kindergarten that I cried during class. No one noticed, but the tears really started filling my eyes when these two girls raised their hands, sharing about how they became best friends.

Loneliness, it pressed down on my shoulders, swelled my chest with this dense emptiness that I couldn't shake. Crammed into this stuffy room with all these people, why did I feel like I was the only one? The only one feeling this way? As if the whole world was crashing in on itself…crashing in on me…

I blocked out the two chatty girls, peering down at the pages in my health book. There was a triangle illustrating the three dimensions of a healthy person: social, mental, and physical well-being. The caption read that each portion of the triangle should be balanced, but staring at it, replaying these past few months, the triangle shrunk in places, growing distorted and ugly, especially in the mental portion… and social.

The bell dinged, forcing me to blink away my reverie. I wiped the emotion from my face, walked the hallways to my next class, clutching my books close to my chest, as if the books and binders were the only barriers holding me together.

Through the spaces between the students, I saw *him*. I saw Scottie Robinson. My lips parted in shock—I *never* saw him around school since Halloween. Not once. Which was exactly how I liked it. I panicked, and, before he got too close to see me, ducked into the bathroom. Besides, I was eager to check the mirror to make sure I hadn't messed up the new makeup on my face from getting all misty-eyed earlier.

I felt better behind the shield of a gross bathroom stall. I caught my breath, waiting for my racing heart to calm itself. I kept thinking and thinking about Halloween night. It took me a while to shake the phantom of Stephan's bitter touch…

I left the stall, stopping in front of the sink. The mirror told me I looked okay; but what it didn't reveal to me in its grimy window was how I didn't *feel* okay.

I took a deep breath before exiting the bathroom. The hallways were empty now, and the only sound was the *tap, tap, tapping* of my Converse shoes along the red hallway…

◉

Tap, tap, tap, tap, tap, went the rain outside, pattering against the roof of our house in a light drizzle. I lay in bed with the lights off, the ceiling a gray shadow, as if the storm was in my room.

Rattled by a cold chill, I pushed my feet underneath the covers. It was still cold out; winter had yet to let up, persistently blowing icy drafts through my closed window. I could go sit by the fire in the living room with my family, but I was tired. I was ready for bed, even though it was only a little after seven in the evening.

I rolled over onto my stomach, which was empty. I had hardly eaten anything for supper. And it wasn't because I was actually going through with that diet; I honestly just wasn't hungry. My stomach was full, but with emptiness. *Is that even possible?* I wondered. *But why, since I'm so empty, do I feel so heavy?* I tossed and turned over an answer, but I couldn't figure one out. I didn't know what was wrong.

It wasn't stress; I had nothing to be stressed out about. My grades were fine, *really* fine, better than they've ever been since all I did was homework once I got home from school. I talked to Nana more often. I was getting used to my routine of going to school, coming home, and doing the same thing all over again the next day and the day after that and so on.

I kept thinking about everything…
Thinking…
Thinking…
Thinking…

And it wasn't until after Mom and Dad came to my room, kissed me goodnight, and shut my door again, that tears flooded to my eyes. I curled into the fetal position, sobs heaving my chest as I blubbered underneath my sheets. But why? Things were okay, weren't they? I had a good life, just what Mom always pointed out… But why…*why* did I feel like I wasn't okay? And where did this weight come from? This weight atop my shoulders, on my chest, even pulling down the edges of my lips?

What's wrong with me?

No one else wondered that question I always asked myself. A version of that question was directed more at Olive, especially as the months got colder and she got skinnier. Mom and Dad argued a lot about what to do with her. Mom wanted to send her to an eating disorder clinic, but Dad wouldn't have that—it was too expensive.

I was scared for Olive. I didn't want my parents to send her away. Which was why I always flushed the toilet when I found puke remnants, and why I never told Mom and Dad about the evidence I frequently found that Olive was throwing up again. I think Mom and Dad figured it out regardless, mainly due to Olive's thighs disappearing into disturbingly thin sticks.

While sitting in my room one night, I overheard a conversation between my fed-up mom and too-thin sister. Olive had just gotten out of the shower, and, before she left the bathroom, Mom led her back in front of the mirror to have a serious talk with her.

"What is it with you and this distorted view of yourself?" Mom's voice was muffled; she had shut the bathroom door.

"It's—helping," I heard Olive say innocently.

"What is it supposed to help?" Mom demanded.

Olive didn't say anything.

"Olive," Mom said, in a clear attempt to remain calm, "talk to someone. Just for one month."

"Talk to *who*?"

"A therapist. Look, I know you didn't like the last one, but this time it'll be someone different. Just give it a try."

"*Why?*"

"Why not?" Mom countered, a frustrated strain potent in her tone.

"They don't listen! They don't understand!" Olive was crying now, but it sounded like it was more from defeat. Her secret that never was a secret for long was out in the open again. Naked she was, wearing nothing but the flesh over her bones that screamed the horrors of anorexia.

"Why don't you wanna talk to someone?"

Pertinendi

"I don't care what they have to say!" Olive wailed.

"Why?!" Mom was pissed now. "So you can make yourself throw up? So you can lose more weight?"

"You have no reason to be mad at me! I haven't done *anything*!"

"Yes I do."

"No. You *don't!*"

Even from my room, I could hear Olive breaking down with sobs, and the softness of my mother's voice when she asked if Olive needed a hug.

"*No*," my sister refused obstinately.

A few minutes later, when the bathroom door opened and my sister's bedroom door slammed shut, Mom appeared at my room. There was a weary way about her movements that made me sad. "D'you need a hug?" she asked from my doorway.

I simply nodded.

She came over to where I sat on my bed, wrapped her arms around me in a sweet embrace. I breathed in her strong perfume, the hairspray in her dark hair, the perspiration on her neck, cherishing this hug so dearly.

"It'll be okay," she whispered, but I didn't think she said it for me. It was for her—a resolution to herself.

"I love you."

Hugging me even tighter, she said she loved me too. And in that moment, I believed her. Maybe things wouldn't be perfect—as if they ever were—but things would be okay…and…that was enough. Mom was rarely wrong about things anyway.

◉

Olive did see a therapist. I went with her sometimes for support, sitting in the drab waiting room with Mom. While Mom thumbed through magazines or read her Joyce Meyer books, I usually stared out the window. The frosted landscape was beginning to gradually slough off the heavy ice of winter. The sun simply melted the burden from the trees, the grass, the dead flowers…

Since it was getting warmer, I'd stand outside waiting for the bus to pick me up in the morning. Gazing up at the sun, I wondered why it didn't melt the weight on my shoulders…

This weight, this emptiness, this loneliness, this—*whatever*—it was getting harder and harder to carry. It made me cry a lot. Every night to be exact. I'd get tired abnormally early, pass by the living room to tell my parents goodnight; and they would watch me trudge up the stairs to my room. They thought I was sleeping. And I wished all the time that I was. But, truthfully, I was crying. By the time I would doze off, my nose snotty and eyes a moistened mess, my pillow would be drenched with salty water.

I never had much to say to my family. And if I did say anything it was a shrug or quiet mumble.

I only ate bites of my food.

I was so sleepy *all the time*.

I felt heavy despite losing weight.

When my weight loss became apparent to my mom, she made me a doctor's appointment. I wondered if she did this out of fear that I may have figured out Olive's dangerous little trick to lose weight.

I didn't think anything of my appointment (I didn't think much of anything, really). Mom told me it was a checkup, nothing to get nervous about. But I did get nervous. While sitting in the waiting room, I nibbled on the five charms of my necklace and picked at the dead skin on the sides of my nails.

Mom bopped me on the back of the head, causing me to spit out my necklace. "You're gonna crack a tooth," she whispered harshly.

I settled with just picking at my nails until a nurse called a name that, for some reason, made me cringe. "Jovie Blue?"

Mom and I got up, followed the nurse. She checked my weight, and, as I suspected, I lost quite a few pounds—this brought a subtle smile to my lips.

After seating me atop the crackling paper on the patient's chair and doing other medical things nurses do, the nurse smiled, saying, "The doctor will be right with you."

She lied. It was another twenty minutes before a knock sounded from the closed door and a doctor slipped into the room. The doctor was a pretty woman, with curvy, cinnamon-red hair and glasses that made her look even smarter than she probably already was. My mom and the doctor seemed to know each other pretty well already—most likely from all the appointments she had to make for Olive lately.

"So what seems to be the problem?" the doctor asked me as she peered over her black-rimmed glasses.

I opened my mouth to say I didn't know, but Mom answered for me. She explained quite thoroughly to the doctor about my strange habits lately: going to bed early, not eating, looking sad all the time, etc. When Mom was done with her little speech, the doctor turned to me, asking, with a very concerned wrinkle on her forehead, "Do you cry a lot, Jovie?"

This question stunned me. All I could do was nod in reply.

The doctor's magenta lips pursed to the side as she pushed her glasses up farther on her nose. "Is school not treating you well?"

There was knot that suddenly formed in my throat; I couldn't speak, so I just shrugged in response.

The doctor nodded, seeming to understand something. "Well, Jovie, I think you may be a little depressed. I know you guys just recently moved here, but sometimes it's harder for some people to adjust to new schools and new people."

I nodded along, agreeing with her. But my attention soon snapped to my mother, who accidently sniffled too loudly from the corner. My eyebrows rose high on my forehead, heart sunk. Mom was crying. Now *I* really wanted to cry…

"I'm sorry." Mom's lips quivered as she hastily took the tissue box when the doctor offered it to her. She carefully wiped the bottom of her eyes, looking up to the ceiling—a technique, I knew now, that helped keep makeup from smudging. "I'm sorry," my mom repeated to the doctor, who, quietly, said it was okay.

I was silent. Numb. I didn't want to be here. I didn't want my mom to be crying over the fact that I was "depressed" or whatever. I just wanted to be in my bed, hidden beneath the covers, safe, unknown to everyone, so I couldn't hurt anyone else, especially my mom. This was unbearable!

To give my mom hope and I guessed to fix me, the doctor prescribed me some kind of antidepressant pill; she also strongly encouraged that I see a therapist. Mom nodded emphatically, dabbing her flushed cheeks one last time. She then set the box of tissues back on the table of magazines…

Only a couple days passed by before I found myself sitting in a cozy little room, a box of tissues sitting atop the magazine table beside me. The magazine topics mostly had to do with psychology, some of their pages advertising the latest antidepressant on the market. The room décor was intentionally relaxing, some kind of feng shui stuff or something. There were seashells placed around the room, a pottery plate filled with sand and a hand-sized wooden rake laying about in it. A messy bookshelf sat behind the large, velvet chair where the therapist sat, her tiny brown eyes studying me intently.

There was something eccentric about this woman—she dressed in a long, flowing skirt and a very light, silken blouse that matched the color of her pouty lips. Choppy, unkempt hair curled at her shoulders, was shedding all over her blouse. The oddness like a halo around this individual was not a bad thing; I liked it immediately. She wasn't normal either. Her name was Monica.

"You and your sister don't look very much alike," she noted after the introductions.

I shook my head, giving her a shy smile. "Nah, we aren't very much alike at all."

"I can tell. So, tell me about yourself, Jovie. Your mom told me you guys recently moved to the area and you're having some trouble adjusting?" She looked up from her notebook for confirmation.

I nodded, swallowing hard and clawing at my hands folded in my lap. "Yeah. I just haven't made many friends. And I really miss my friends back home in Louisiana. Especially my best friend." I shrugged. "I guess I just really miss having someone to talk to."

She nodded along to this, scribbling casually into the notebook on her lap. "You know, Jovie, I'm not from the area either. I moved here many years ago from Puerto Rico. I remember quite clearly what it was like being in an unfamiliar place and being surrounded by people I didn't know. But let me tell you something—" She leaned in closer, a comforting smile on her lips. "—it gets better."

I smiled back, relieved by this news. "Good," I said, my voice small.

She told me the story about how her life turned around after a while. Then her next questions related to my sister, my parents, and my best friend—I told her *all* about Nana and me. It was so nice talking to someone face-to-face. I'd forgotten what it was like conversing with a person; and I was finding that externalizing this world of thoughts inside my head was making me, for the briefest instance, feel lighter.

At the end of our hour session, Monica mentioned that writing down my thoughts may help sort out the things that I was feeling. I thanked her for listening to me, and, as she walked me back to the waiting room, she recommended that I keep a diary.

Mom looked up from one of those psychology magazines and smiled when she saw that I was back. I returned a smile, and this time it wasn't quite as forced.

On the way back home, I told Mom about some of the things Monica and I had talked about. The diary came up, and, without any hesitation, Mom swerved into the corner bookstore.

With the money I'd gotten for Christmas, I bought myself a diary. It was a beautiful little notebook with floral prints and butterflies fluttering on the cover. *Such a gorgeous mask*, I realized, *to conceal my darkest thoughts.*

◉

It was my least favorite part of the school day.

Lunch.

I stood in the bustling line of students, waiting to collect a tray and slide it down an assembly line of tired-looking women with hairnets. They would slop unappetizing food on my plate; give me a dull stare while waiting for me to move over for the next person.

Good thing I was never hungry, because today was chili day. I could smell the goo all the way from my last class. After grabbing a milk carton, I came out of the food line and into the cafeteria, a droning hum of chatting students sitting at tables awaiting me. I looked to where I usually sat in silence, listening to Kayla and her friends babble about random topics. I took a step in their direction, but my foot slipped on something… There was a squeak from my shoe, then I saw my shoe high in the air; and before I knew it I was breathless, laying flat on my back. Something chunky and wet was all over me, seeping through my clothes. My head throbbing, I looked up, and, with a sickened grimace, realized I spilt chili all over myself and had slipped on chili already splattered on the floor.

Laughter roared from all around. Laughing faces were everywhere my eyes flitted. My heart beat fast, filling my face with pink humiliation. I just sat there for a few moments, still registering what just happened, pretending that I wasn't really there and that I didn't actually just fall in front of the entire cafeteria. I squeezed my eyes shut, the darkness behind my lids erasing the world around me...

◉

The sound of roaring water makes me come to. My body aches from the fall, and the darkness I had fallen into from the cliff still surrounds me in Pertinendi.

Something tickles my cheek.

I blink open my groggy eyes, the blinding rays of Heaven-light vanquishing the nighttime behind my lids. A frigid morning greets my sand-crusted face as I lay on what appears to be a shore.

Something tickles my cheek again. I scratch at the source, scaring away a butterfly that had landed on my cheek. It flitters away; but there's something peculiar about its wings. They are paper-white with inky black pen scrawls all over the blue lines going across its wings. *Someone wrote all over the butterfly*, I realize, aghast at the cruelty.

I stand up; dust myself clean of the black sand speckling my clothes. I am on a shore. And before me is the brine of the torrent black waters that expands a great distance throughout the center of my Pertinendi. On the shore, popping up through the onyx pebbles and pepper-black sand, is the strangest assortment of flowers. I've never seen anything like them. They bloom from the sand, their pedals white, and, like the butterfly, have words scribbled on their delicate pedals. I bend to pick one, bringing it up closer to my face so that I can read what's written. It unfolds into a wrinkly piece of notebook paper, dating back to March 2006.

Dear Diary,

Hi, my names Jovie. Im 13 now. I live in Missouri, and its been almost half a year that we've been here. My doctor says Im depressed. And my phyciatrist told me I should start keeping a journal to help with it so I'll try to write down stuff and my feelings as much as I can.

Well, Ive been really sad alot. But I feel all right, right now. I had a test today in science over some of the bones in our body. It went a lot better than I expected. Monica (my phyciatrist) said that everything is better than we think its going to be, because when you worry, all kinds of negative thoughts go in your head. Monica is pretty cool. I like talking to her but I'm scared that when I won't be able to talk to her anymore, I still won't have any friends. I'm scared I'll always feel this way. Well, thats all Im thinkin about right now. TTYL!

I pick another flower, its pedals blooming to reveal my young heart's words.

Dear Diary,

I busted my butt today in the cafeteria. It was definitely the most embarrassing moment of my life! I don't think anyone will forget it. And what's worse is that Scottie saw me run to the bathroom. I stopped for a moment when we saw each other, and probably turned as red as a strawberry! Gosh Diary, it was terrible! WHY AM I SO CLUMSY?????!!!!!!

I pick another.

> Dear Diary,
>
> I've been extra sad lately. I dont know why. Maybe its school. Maybe its the routine I do everyday. I feel so heavy still. Good news though: My prescription for my antidepressant should be ready to be picked up soon. I hope it helps me.

I stop, not wanting to read any more on that one. It's too familiar, too much like the memories I lived again. I crumble the sad little diary entry, then pick another flower. It says similar things. I hover over other flowers, each pedal showing similar words, speaking of emotions I felt in the memories. Some flowers even have sad little poems etched on their pedals.

They make me sick to my soul.

I throw the flowers down into the frothy waves, anger crashing through my soul. I watch the delicate flowers—the *stupid* diary entries—blacken in the oily waters and dissolve into nothing in the rolling waves.

I sigh when they are gone for good, my arms that were folded tightly over my chest now falling to my sides in relief. Such heavy thoughts I held back then, such heavy thoughts I carry still…

A shadow soars overhead. The brief darkness is followed by a loud *clank*.

I turn to the sound, seeing the angel statue standing tall beside me.

"They grow from your sadness," the angel informs me, nodding at the remaining flowers blooming from the black sand.

"What d'you mean?"

"Those feelings you wrote about, they were a product of your sadness. That is why they grow here, on the shore of this black sea."

I roll my eyes, not understanding why these stupid flowers grow *here*. *By the ugly black sea.* It doesn't make sense, and is it even possible?

"So where've you been?" I accuse, attempting to change the subject.

Pertinendi

"While you were sleeping—"

"More like knocked out," I quip, rubbing my head dramatically.

"Er," Angel stammers, "right. While you were knocked out, I was searching for a bridge over these waters. No bridge that way." Angel gestures to the left. "But I'll explore over that way for a moment just to be sure."

"Why don't you just fly us over the sea?" I suggest, raising my eyebrows encouragingly.

Angel gives me a patient half smile. "Jovie, the sea is here for a reason. I cannot cheat you out of the memories that may be in or above the waters. Now, if there is no bridge, we find a different way. Just stay here. I will only be a moment." Angel squats down, then shoots off into the sky, its concrete figure glistening in the Heaven-beams.

When the angel disappears into the clouds, I settle my sights on the black horizon. I stare out over the lapping waters, breathing in the inspiration radiating from the purple mountains standing as a protective guard before Heaven. I can see their tilted snow-covered peaks, the puffs of clouds weaving around the base. The grace is so clear to me, set between the mountains, illuminating my Pertinendi with the light I need to find my way home—home to Heaven.

Clunk... Clunk... Clunk...

My gaze drops back down to the water. There's a wooden boat washing up on the shore, two paddles clunking about against the edges. I start towards them, planning to drag them onto the sandbank. But as soon as the black water laps at my toes, I stop. The water doesn't feel right. It is ice cold, dense, and it leaves me with the lingering sense of the emotions I felt so intensely in my memories. I take a step back, afraid to go any further. The water scares me and I'm not sure why.

The butterfly that had landed on my cheek earlier flutters near my face again, then lands on my left shoulder. I press my finger in front of it, allowing it to crawl onto my nail. Up close now, I can see what the words on its wings say. It's a diary entry of course, but of an excerpt from a poem I wrote long ago—a metaphor of my depression. I swallow hard as I read on, the last lines of the poem reading…

The oily black sea
Was all along the
Inescapable
Depression in me.

The butterfly flutters from my finger to hover over the waves. It then simply stops flapping its wings and falls into the water. Unfolding to notebook paper, it turns black; and the waves take it in, forcing it to crash into the boat. I can still see the messy bold letters of the title of the poem, "Shipwrecked on a Black Sea". My lips part at a realization, as the last of the paper dissolves under the edge of the wooden paddle.

In Pertinendi, the sea is my depression, I finally comprehend, now understanding why Angel mentioned that the flowers—my diary entries—grow on this shore. It is because those thoughts, most of them at least, grew from my depression.

Scowling at the water, it is a long moment before I notice that my hands have balled to fists. I try flexing my fingers, and, when I open my right hand, there is something in my palm. It's tiny and blue and oval-shaped.

It's a pill.

An antidepressant.

I back away, putting more distance between me and the sea.

"I got better," I tell the roaring waves defiantly. "The pills helped me get rid of you."

I set the pill on my tongue. With one last glance at the black sea, I swallow, and, accidently, gulp down a memory as well…

◉

I popped the little blue pill that promised to make me happy again into my mouth.

"Now, it can take a few days," Mom explained, "even weeks, for it to have any effect. Just give it a chance and some time, and you'll

Pertinendi

feel better, okay?"

I nodded, trying to swallow down the lump that had formed in my throat after the pill. Mom left the kitchen. I stayed behind, having to take a few minutes to regain composure.

When I thought really hard about it—this thing called depression—I got even sadder because of the fact that I was having to take medicine to make it go away. *Am I that weak?* I questioned myself. But I guessed what made me even sadder about this diagnoses was my mother's reaction to it. She was trying so exhaustingly hard to give me a good life—her *and* Dad—and still, here I was, sad. She deserved a lot better than that, than me.

This is your depression talking, I reminded myself—just like Monica taught me to do when negative thoughts bombarded my mind. I took a deep breath, trying to access control of the Jovie I used to be. I released my breath, summoning the slightest bit of confidence in that I was going to be okay. I didn't believe it. *Depression talking*, I reminded myself again.

I wasn't sure if it was talking to Monica that helped me so or if the medicine had worked or if it was because summer and its sweltering heat had simply melted the weight on my shoulders, but something was working, *really* working. Over the months, there was a gradual sloughing of the weight on my shoulders, a breaking of the chains depression constantly ensnared my heart with. The real me was resurfacing from the dark depths I had fallen into. I could wake up in the morning, welcome the sun on my face, sit up, and feel *light*, feel *alive*. I could be okay again with that truly being enough.

Of course, just like everything, things weren't perfect. The pills and talking to a therapist hadn't solved all the problems bothering me. During the summer months, I woke up to an empty house most days—Mom and Dad at work, Olive at softball practice. (Yeah, she made the softball team—*figures*). Antidepressants didn't make me any less lonely; they just made me not care that I was. And Monica couldn't tell me how to make friends. But that was okay, because I wasn't sure I'd follow through with any advice she'd give me on that matter. I was too shy to talk to strangers, especially strangers my age.

The pills and a therapist didn't assemble my life the way I wanted it to be: Olive healthy, my parents happily married, holding hands, talking, laughing together, never arguing about bills or petty things; the world finally at peace and every person and animal, at the very least, feeling okay about things.

No.

The pills especially didn't solve any of those problems. Talking to Monica helped a little just to get it out of my system. And antidepressants *did* blow away the cloud of depression within my soul. It numbed the internal agony, put a stopper on my tears, and let this *okay* feeling course through my body and take over my emotions. I was just okay. I felt okay. And that was good enough for me.

The summer before eighth grade went by in a numbing blur, and, even though I was nervous to my very core about going back to school in August, I believed I was ready thanks to the newfound confidence I discovered within me that depression had been stifling all along.

And just as Monica had prophesized on my first visit with her, things *did* get better. Eighth grade was the year I found it in me to talk to people, by letting myself, for the most part, shine through. There wasn't so much restraint in the way I lived my life; I was free from the weights that made me drag my feet, wallow in negativity.

I made friends in gym class that year. Sarah and Sierra were their names, both very lanky girls. They were the two least sporty girls in the entire gym class. Sierra had these thick glasses that bobbed up and down when she ran, and Sarah tripped a lot when she was just walking. It turned out to be that both of these girls had been in my seventh grade gym class; I'd just never talked to them before. But I did this year, because they were the only two people in the entire gym class it seemed safe enough to hide behind during dodge ball. They didn't get pissy like the over-the-top, competitive athletes did when I'd just stand there awkwardly, not wanting to participate—mainly just so I wouldn't embarrass myself.

Sierra was the first to strike up a conversation with me. I had been standing in the farthest corner of the gym, avoiding the balls zooming back and forth across the centerline of the gym.

"That's a good band," Sierra had told me, pointing down at my band t-shirt, as her and Sarah joined me in the corner.

I beamed. "Thanks. They're amazing."

"Hey," Sarah said softly, "you were in Coach Toupee's gym class last year, weren't you?"

"You mean Coach Toup's?"

Sierra sniggered. "Yeah, *that* one. Him *and* the dead squirrel on his head."

I thought back to the coach, remembering that there did seem to be some sort of wig on his head. I smiled at the picture in my mind, finally understanding their inside joke.

As the two girls and I chatted, dodging balls here and there, I came to figure out that Sierra was very brazen in her humor, almost harsh, but it still made me laugh. Sarah was a lot softer than Sierra, more polite and shy. I liked her immediately—she was a lot like me.

We had almost made it through the entire game without being hit, but from the corner of my eye I saw a large guy from across the gym hurl a ball right in our direction. I flinched away, closing my eyes instinctively. Sierra wasn't so quick—she got nailed in the gut. She bent upright after being hunched over for a moment, groaning.

"Alright," she growled, eyes fierce and fixated on the guy who hit her, "tubbylumpkins over there's gonna *die*."

I clamped my lips together to keep from laughing as she jogged to the other side of the court to take her place by the other casualties of dodge ball. My humor didn't last long; it vanished when a ball smacked me directly in the face.

"Are you okay?" Sarah asked me, laughter bright in her eyes.

"Uh," I stammered, turning pink and holding my burning nose. "Yeah, I think so." I gave her a weak smile, then said with a nasally voice, "Good luck." She was definitely going to need it being out in the open now.

I walked slowly across the gym, careful to dodge the number of balls that came spiraling my way. I joined Sierra behind the basketball goal on our opponent's side of the court, as if we were tossed aside chess pieces that had been taken. I didn't mind sitting on the sidelines though, because I got to see Scottie Robinson. Yeah, he was in my gym class this year. As much as seeing him around school bothered me to no end last year, this year I felt different. Like, the memory of Halloween had faded just enough for me, and hopefully entirely for him, so that I didn't have to worry what he may think.

And to be honest with myself, he didn't seem to think anything of me. I didn't exist to him. And, thanks to not being depressed anymore, I didn't care. I simply enjoyed the view of him giving his buddies high fives when they'd get someone from my team out. His eyes were still that homey blue, hair a rich, dark, almond color that was cut short in straight, spiked locks. His olive skin was covered by a concert t-shirt, black like my own... He was a joyous sight to reel in... I especially enjoyed looking at his butt...

A hand waved in my face.

"Earth to Jovie," Sierra said, knocking on my forehead.

I blinked out of my stare, focusing my sights away from Scottie and onto Sierra

"Yeah?" I blinked, still somewhat in a daze.

"Gym's over. Time to change."

"Oh," I breathed, surprised that the time had flown by so quickly. I followed her into the dressing room, and, just before I disappeared behind the door, looked back at the group of guys putting away the balls. Scottie was one of them. He bent down to retrieve one, and, when he stood back up, caught me looking at him.

Yikes! I disappeared quickly then, averting my gaze down at the ground in shame.

The lingering redness in my cheeks finally faded by the time it was fifth period—my earth science class. We were learning about space, and, even though Francesca was in my class, sitting just a few seats away, I remained calm and uncaring. Watching the videos of galaxies, planets, and the billions of stars was soothing to me, like, a lullaby to my soul. Fascinating. It reminded me that there was *more*. More to life than where I sat. And that somehow freed me from the petty crimes of certain people.

During that time in eight grade year, I found it in me to forgive Francesca for what she did the year before. Plus, I kind of had to be civil because we got paired together to do a project over galaxies, particularly the one we lived in—the Milky Way. We talked as if Halloween never happened. And I was okay with that.

Sarah and I became good friends over the year. I sat with her and Sierra at lunch every day, listening and laughing at Sierra making fun of people and Sarah quietly laughing along. It was so nice...to be able to laugh again...and mean it. So nice to have friends I could talk to that would, in return, talk back to me, inviting me in on their inside jokes, their gossip about certain people, their plans for the holidays, their *life*.

I really enjoyed having these friends, but once high school came around, all the friends I made in junior high became acquaintances. Freshman year of high school, I didn't have a single class with Sarah or Sierra...not even Francesca...or...Scottie.

I watched from afar as Sierra joined the debate team and Sarah became friends with the three Ashleys in our grade—a very popular trio. I noticed, while at my locker one day, when the group of Ashleys and Sarah walked by, how Sarah's voice had gotten higher, laced with an airhead accent. Her freckly white skin got tan, her average brown hair dyed blonde, her face caked with makeup and eyes dolled up with thick lines of eyeliner; then she made the cheerleading squad and began dating *boys*.

Sarah was just one of many things that changed in high school.

Kayla, who I sat with at lunch in seventh grade, I found out, was a lesbian. Francesca stopped wearing her black goth getup and began dressing like the twins, Dominique and Danielle, had dressed that one Halloween night—like a hippie. Scottie had a girlfriend, some pretty cheerleader named Cheyenne. And the bell at the high school didn't *ding* like the junior high bell did. It made this awful buzzing sound that lasted three seconds too long.

The only change I seemed to make was getting braces glued to my teeth—exactly at the time when they stopped being cool. I looked like an idiot.

At lunch I sat by people I had nothing in common with. They would talk about video games and manga comics, while I sat silence, politely listening; but most of the time I was actually staring at Olive who sat across the cafeteria, surrounded by the coolest seniors and juniors, laughing it up with them and fitting right in with that large crowd. I sighed, pushing away the chili on my plate. I refused to eat it after it humiliated me in junior high.

Freshman year was the year I pretty much accepted that I was, in fact, a loser, an invisible nobody at school. Just like in junior high, I remained the weird quiet kid in class, the one the teachers were lucky to get a peep out of. Even Olive didn't acknowledge my presence at school—with her being a cool junior and all, it would social suicide being seen with me.

I grew even more envious of my sister, who had obviously made a beautiful name for herself here at school—it was practically her home, academics being the ultimate distraction from her issues. She was still on the softball team, their first baseman; she had perfect grades, a perfectly thin body that was getting healthier as her treatment with the therapist continued on. She was even asked by a senior to prom, and, wearing a lovely cream and gold gown, probably danced the night away eloquently.

The only standard I met that Olive had set for me was that I made straight A's, too. At least, that was until sophomore year came around. Then my grades went to shit—thanks to geometry, biology, and chemistry. Olive had lied to me, saying that they were all totally easy classes.

Yeah. *Not.*

I was disappointed when my grades weren't perfect like Olive's anymore. But that disappointment didn't just stop there; it expanded into feeling disappointed that no matter how much I exercised and dieted, I still wasn't as thinly perfect as Olive, wasn't as beautiful, wasn't as popular and embraced by the school. This disappointment gradually morphed into deep, stewing anger. I was so incredibly *pissed off*, seemingly at the world, but, deep down, I was just mad at myself, for falling short of Olive's standards, for being the loser child of my successful parents. But mostly, for being this drifter in school, this…piece in the large puzzle of life that didn't belong…*anywhere*.

I couldn't tell all of these things to Monica. I stopped seeing her after my successful eighth grade year and responding so well to antidepressants. And it was because of the antidepressants that I didn't feel depressed or heavy again.

That was all the pills gave me, a mirage that I was okay. It put a mask over the things that I felt so deeply before, but couldn't access the sensitivity in me to feel again. I was numb. Simply numb. I thought I was happy these past few years, but I was slowly realizing that happiness was only in the sitcoms or movies I'd watch at night with Mom. Happiness was in the books I'd escape into, the stories and poems I'd write. Happiness, I was slowly beginning to accept, wasn't real at all. Happiness, for me, came in the form of a pill. It was artificial. This "okayness" that I was always feeling wasn't real at all; it was the pill.

But I was better.
I wasn't depressed anymore.
And I felt okay.
So I didn't think I needed the pills anymore.

That was why before my junior year of high school began, I set the bottle of blue pills in the farthest corner of the medicine cabinet, vowing that I wouldn't take them anymore.

I'm better, I told myself, the okay emotion I felt so intensely reminding me that this was true.

And on my last diary entry, the words read…

Dear Diary,

I'm done. I'm done with them. The antidepressants. I want to feel again. Everything. Even the sadness. I think I can handle it now. My depression is gone, and I think I'm strong, even confident enough now, that it won't come back. I can be okay without the pills. I <u>want</u> to be okay without them. It makes me sad just having to take them, knowing that all that I am is because of those pills. I want to be <u>me</u> again, even if that me isn't totally happy. I'm better. And I'll stay better this time.

◉

This diary entry washes up on the shore of the black sea, the bubbling foam sloshing it against my sandy toes. I read again the words I wrote, look up at the black sea that is my depression here in Pertinendi.

"I was wrong," I tell the black waters. "You came back, but a thousand times worse and a thousand times heavier." I wipe the tear slipping down my cheek. "Why couldn't you just leave me alone?" I march up to the water, anger fueling my strides, whipping my hair around wildly. "WHY?" I demand. But in reply the waves just lap at my feet, silently being the omniscient friend it always was to me—cold, unapologetic, heartless, but present. Yes. Depression was always there for me, even when no one else was...

"Jovie!" a voice calls my name from somewhere up above.

I quickly wipe the moisture from my face, then squint at the sky. Obscured by Heaven-light and mourning clouds, I spot, in the distance, a concrete angel flying erratically towards the shore. I smile at the statue, waving politely. My smile soon fades to a frown, skin pales even more when the angel gets closer and I am able to see the panic in its stone features. It's not a moment later when I see the reason for the angel's horror...

Chasing Angel, wearing raggedy cloaks and clawing ferociously at the air, baring their fangs to the sky, are *demons*.

"Run, Jovie! Now!" Angel cries.

Stiff with terror, I turn to sprint down the shore. I skid to a stop when I realize that at the end of this shore is just more forest. And in the forest the trees are parting, making way for the giant, slithering flames breaking them down mercilessly. I know in my soul what is riding that fire-serpent to corner me at this shore. The glowering eyes of the Devil watch the panic seep into my bones, watch me run up to the cliff and unsuccessfully try to climb back up.

I am coming for you! I am coming for you! I am coming for you!

The Devil's words sear my mind. I lose my grip on the cliff and fall back down to the sand.

I'm done for.

I can kiss sweet existence goodbye.

"Hurry, Jovie!" the Angel prompts me frantically.

I stand, look to the black water. The wooden boat is still there, idling in the waves.

It's the only way.

I make a break for it, splashing against the icy black water at my knees. I grab the nose of the boat; thrust it forward against the waves. I charge at the malicious depths of this sea, fearing to my very core at what may lurk in these strange tides. I freak myself out with paranoia and pull myself into the boat, too afraid to swim in this water. I row against the waves as hard as I can, all the while looking to the sky for Angel, who is nearing the shore with a herd of demons on its trail.

Panting with fear, I slap at the water with the paddles, fierce in my movements, but exhausted in every breath the further I paddle from the shore.

Just as the black sand dissolves into the horizon behind me, Angel finally arrives, swooping down to my rescue. The statue reaches for me, but my fingers slip against the stone's… Angel misses! The demons following give up, settling with circling my boat, calculating when to pounce.

One demon dives down at me, letting out a guttural howl as it outspreads its claws, ready to gouge my eyes. Before it gets too close, I swing a paddle. The demon releases an agitated hiss when the paddle makes contact with its skull. More demons dive down. I stand up this time, having trouble balancing my weight in the rickety boat.

I swing as hard as I can at every demon. Their movements are a blur as they cut me when they swoosh by; cut me again when they dive down at me. Screaming, I close my eyes and blindly swing at their unnerving skeletal bodies.

The demons bring with them the presence of Hell. This presence is set ablaze when the Devil makes it to the shore. The fire-serpent's flaming belly coils from far away in the black sand, ready to strike out at this measly boat at the Devil's command.

The Devil hisses in my mind again. I am forced to push against my ears to keep the sound out, to keep the *Hell* out.

"ANGEL!" I cry for help, reaching for the sky. But a demon slashes my wrist, silencing my plea.

Another demon sinks its claws into my stomach, then, trying to retreat, gets its claw caught in my shirt. I try shoving the demon off of me. I heave against its chaotic thrashing, only to be pushed right back, then forward…

The boat rocks violently.

I lose my balance.

The demon and I fall backward, plunging into the black sea…

Morgan McLendon

PART 5

IF I WERE THE MOON, THIS WOULD BE MY DARK SIDE

I am immersed in blackness; whatever Heaven-light there was above the water is no more here in the black sea. The demon snarling beside me disintegrates to nothing in the water. I kick to the surface for air, for Angel, but no matter how hard I kick I am not strong enough against the weight of this water…this depression…of my soul…

I sink.
I sink.
I sink.
Until slimy black sand at the bottom of the sea meets my back.
There is no need to breathe; I am already dead, especially down here.
I stare up at the blackness all around, bubbles oozing from my lips as I cry out, but only silence is uttered.
Something shiny and silver glimmers near my face. I think it's a fish so I wave it away. It doesn't scare though. It merely glides down to the sand, making a soft clinking sound when it reaches the bottom. I turn my head to look at it. It's a tiny strip of silver, something sharp, like a razor.
There's not just one of these things, but hundreds.
I lay in a bed of them, their metallic shimmer highlighting my emotionless face.

Gazing up at the unreachable surface of this sea, I feel a side of my lips curl up just so. I feel…nothing…and I like it…

And somehow…I ease into a memory as I sink lower into the depths of this sea…

This…depression…in me…

◉

I gasped for air, water spilling across my pores as I resurfaced from beneath the soapy water in the bathtub. I rubbed the stinging soap from my eyes, then slumped against the edge of the tub, my chin barely resting in the water. I sighed heavily, staring bleakly at the chipped nail polish on my toes.

The voices coming from all the way downstairs in the kitchen were muffled bits of reality…

"You never help out around here!" Mom yelled. She and Dad were arguing. As usual. "All you do is work. Eat. Sleep. That's it! You don't clean; you don't buy groceries or cook. You don't do shit!"

"I help pay bills," Dad retorted. "Ever think of that?" And then he went on to point out how no one respects him and blah, blah, blah, blah…

I sighed again, sinking into the water just enough so that my ears were submerged.

My parents fought a lot before, but it seemed that ever since Olive left for college a few weeks ago they'd been at each other's throats more than usual. I tried mediating past situations, but right now I felt too defeated to get up and help, too defeated to even listen in on their argument.

I wasn't far enough beneath the water, though, to not hear the front door slam and my mother's car engine roar to life. I winced, guessing their argument had to be cut short because mom had to go to her stress management class for the evening. She'd been attending these classes for a few months now. It seemed that about the same time she began these classes I had accidently happened upon a bottle of antidepressants at the front of the medicine cabinet. But they were prescribed to Sonya Blue.

Mom was depressed, too.

Dad didn't look happy either when he sat in his green armchair every night after work, dully watching the hunting channel on TV.

And then there was me, lying in lukewarm bathtub water staring at my toes.

Where had happiness gone? I wondered most days.

Did it go away with Olive when she left for college? Was it purged from our lives forever? Or was there something blocking it from my family, from me?

The rumbles sounding from my stomach interrupted my thoughts. I pressed my hand to my belly, silencing the growls. Hunger had finally come back to me, or maybe it was just my nerves already sending butterflies through my stomach.

Tomorrow would be my first day as a junior in high school.

Yes.

It was that time again.

The middle of August had come around much too soon, as always, interrupting my jobless summer days that I spent in my room reading stories and writing poems.

The very thought of donning my clothes early tomorrow morning, fixing my hair, swiping on makeup, and then driving myself to school alone brought nothing but dread to my imbalanced mind.

Would I find someone to sit with at lunch? Would I make friends? Be reunited with old acquaintances from previous years?

Gosh. I was sixteen now, but why did every school year feel like the first?

Like Hell.

I inhaled deeply, then sunk back down into the water. Resting my head against the bottom of the tub, I looked up at the world through the thick, soapy lens of bath water. I liked how everything was blurry, so far away that reality became surreal, something I couldn't even feel anymore.

◉

Blurry was the next day at school. I purposely didn't put my contacts in so I wouldn't have to really see anything or anyone. I wanted all to be a blur, so then maybe school, my life, the world, wouldn't seem quite as real.

I sat in my car until the morning bell buzzed. Its echo in the parking lot made my heart drop down to my aching stomach—its contents swollen with anxious butterflies and fat-free cereal. Reluctantly, I threw my bag over my shoulder then hurried into the building.

The hallways were already flooded with students. Conversations of summer, vacations, and parties filled the hallways, reverberated off the locker walls. I swallowed hard, weaving in between the groups of chatting people. I fumbled around in my bag for my schedule. Once I located it, crumbled between two binders, I refreshed my memory on where the hell my first class was.

Ancient world history was my first class of the day and...

Shit.

I was going the wrong way.

I casually turned around, bumping into the person behind me on accident. "Sorry," I mumbled, keeping my gaze down.

"Fuck you," I heard them say to my back.

I took a deep breath, trying to remember comforting quotes Monica used to tell me. They weren't working. I wasn't comforted. I was scared. I wanted my mom, but now that I was older she didn't want me anymore. Her happiness was in a pill now...

My head was spinning. *Where is classroom one-o'-three?!*

Negative thoughts kept bloating in my head, filling my eyes with a teary glaze...

There!

I found the room. But the late bell had already buzzed. The door was shut. I bit my lip hard, forcing myself to march up to the door and politely knock. I could hear the teacher introducing herself to the class, then stop short at the sound I made at the door. She scuttled over, opened the door for me. She didn't say anything about my tardiness—thank goodness—but told me to take a seat over yonder because the desks were almost all filled.

My cheeks stayed red for most of the class period. I felt hot, even though I was wearing summer clothes. It was a little muggy in the classroom, stuffy with all the crammed bodies in the tiny space. There weren't very many people I recognized in this class, but I guessed that was because all I could see were the back of their heads thanks to this cozy little spot in the corner of the room.

The teacher, if I paid attention, was simply addressing information on the course syllabus. But I wasn't really focusing on that. I stared at the Egyptian posters decorating the walls, particularly the ones on mummification. I found myself daydreaming; and in this daydream I was a mummy—preserved, frozen, faceless. I was trapped inside the wrappings, a shell from the mortal world that was just sand…an unfeeling haze.

The bell buzzed.

And then it buzzed again at the end of my next class, then the next one, and the one after that…

I was slowly realizing that all of my classes this year were insultingly easy. This, I remembered, was a result of me being scared out of my wits at the end of my sophomore year after it being so hard and my grades falling so low. By that time, I didn't think I was smart anymore or even capable of dealing with an academic challenge. So, when the time came to schedule for junior year, I made sure to sign up for the easiest classes—the ones slackers took. Like the intermediate courses instead of honors. My electives weren't filled with science classes or anything my future self would be thankful I took. No, I signed up for sewing, cooking, art, and poetry classes. Things dumb people—like me—could master, or, at the very least, get an A in with little or no effort.

Intro to poetry was probably my favorite class of the day so far. It was a class of only twelve people. Amongst these twelve students was a hostile-looking guy with cold, gray eyes and greasy orange hair. And of all the empty desks in the room, he decided to plop in the one right in front of me.

Great, I thought sarcastically, especially when he reeked of cigarette smoke.

Pertinendi

The teacher, after introducing herself, assigned us all a poem to write so she could figure out how many rules of poetry we already knew. It took me a while to get going on my poem, but when I did, the finished product was titled "Mummified". To my mortification, when everyone was finished, she made us exchange poems with the nearest person for constructive criticism. Biting down hard on my lip, I handed mine over to the grumpy kid in front of me. He did the same, with even more hesitation.

His poem was called "I Don't Know What to Write About", and below was line after line of blankness. I half smiled, finding his lack of effort humorous. I wished I had the nerve to pull something like that. The name Dale Dickerson was scribbled in the top right corner of his paper.

Dale's hands shook when he handed my poem back after skimming it for a moment. Taking the paper from him, I noticed on his hand an ugly scar—a cigarette burn maybe?

"It's good," he murmured sincerely.

I returned his poem, stammering, "Yeah, yours too."

Needless to point out, neither of us were constructive critics.

The bell buzzed to commence my most dreaded part of the day... Lunchtime.

Dale and I were the last to filter out of the classroom. We both tried for the doorway at the same time, stopping short when we realized there wasn't enough room for the two of us.

"Sorry," I pleaded to his harsh stare. "Go ahead."

He stood there rigidly for a moment, then shook his head and gestured for me to go before him.

"Thanks," I mumbled, and, after glancing innocently up at his face, immediately regretted not giving him a warm smile. He looked like he could use more smiles in his day.

I could feel this creepy stranger named Dale follow behind me as I made my way to the cafeteria. But when I glanced over my shoulder, squinting through the curtain of my bangs, I saw he had stopped at the library to hide in there for the lunch period. *Smart guy*, I noted, as the distorted chatter from the cafeteria grew louder, echoing throughout the corridors.

My heart thumped pathetically against the anxiety clogging my chest and flushing my skin. I brought my necklace up to my lips, biting down on the charms of my name as I walked into the cafeteria. My eyes flitted from face to face, desperate to pinpoint someone familiar. All were faceless acquaintances, a blur of people that recognized me too but couldn't remember my name.

With my sack lunch, I sat by some girls I had a few classes with last year. I gave them a warm smile and asked them how their summers were. After telling them about my uneventful summer, the girls talked about other things. I remained quiet, drawing a blank on what else to say.

I truly sucked at socializing.

Evidence of this fact was there across the cafeteria. And over there. And there. Other new students over the years. There they were, sitting beside people who seemed to enjoy their company, laugh with them, and let them belong in their little group. Why was I so incapable of that? Making friends? Belonging?

The only belonging I ever felt was in books, with the made up characters and worlds. *Maybe I should've just sat in the library like Dale...*

After a few more dreadful hours, the final buzz of the day sounded, letting loose the obnoxious blurs around me called my peers. I trudged to my car, dodging the rowdy JROTC students, feeling very thankful I didn't have to ride the bus anymore now that I was old enough to drive my mom's old car.

Most of the students in a raving dash to beat the after school traffic all had to go to work. It seemed like half the high school was employed either at the grocery store or some fast food place. I was amongst the unemployed losers. So I went straight home after school.

I shut the front door to my house gently, the silence of my surroundings heavy. Pumpkin came bounding down the stairs, all excited and carefree. I bent down to pet her. Stroking her silky fur, I longed to be able to talk to my dog, so I could ask what her secret was to happiness—she seemed to embody the emotion so effortlessly.

"How are you always so happy?" I asked her, mussing her hair. I kissed her head, then raced her into the kitchen.

I did my normal routine: feeding Pumpkin, letting her outside, then settling at the kitchen bar to work on homework. While I was in the midst of organizing my new binders, I caught myself looking up at the medicine cabinet frequently. Finally, I scooted my chair out from under the bar, hopping down to make my way over to the cabinet. I opened the door, revealing the many orange and white bottles with all kinds of medicine inside. I reached into the very back corner to fetch my pills. I grabbed the bottle, but didn't open it. I just stared at the blue pills inside that waited patiently to be swallowed.

I closed my eyes, trying to feel something. *Anything.*

I wasn't depressed.

This I was certain of because I felt absolutely nothing.

Nodding once, I set the bottle back inside the cabinet and shut the door on my depression once again.

I'm better, I promised myself.

After letting Pumpkin back inside, I checked the mail. Sifting through the bills and magazines and junk mail, I found a lot of different college brochures. We'd gotten them before, but they were always addressed to Olive. Since she was at the big state school now, they all had my name on the front. *Ew*, was all I could think when I saw them. So I threw them in the trash.

Sick of dealing with school crap, I ran up the stairs to my room and shut the door. I fell onto my bed, staring up in a daze at the winding ceiling fan. *Why do I feel nothing?* I wondered. It seemed to me that I could lay flat on my back in bed all day. Staring at the ceiling. Staring at the puppy dog calendar above the light switch. And not feel a damn thing.

I guessed the scarier question was this: Why don't I care? There might as well be a welcome mat on the outer threshold of my heart where this numbness stood. I didn't mind not feeling. No. I didn't mind it at all.

Because as time went on and on and on, I didn't have to feel any of it. I could walk the hallways at school, emotionless. Then plop down on my bed at the end of the day, not caring about how I *hated* school, *hated* the people, *hated* that everyone was already taking the ACT and I didn't want to take it. I couldn't even feel how much I *hated* that everyone was dating, had a lot of friends, and already knew exactly where they were going for college, what they wanted to major in, what they wanted to be, while I didn't even know what the hell I was doing the next day, much less the rest of my life!

Numbing indifference—it blocked a lot of things I should have felt. Things I should have been dealing with.

The truth was, I'd just lie on my bed and watch as the squares on my calendar kept getting marked off as another day was lived…then another…and another…until my calendar told me it was the middle of October already.

And still…

…

…

I felt nothing.

…

…

I felt so little that I could hardly write anything decent in my poetry class—which killed me, because I adored the class. At least, I loved it up until the day the seat in front of me became vacant, as did some unconscious spot in my life that Dale had unknowingly occupied.

"Dale is no longer with us." The solemn look on my poetry teacher's face told us all that Dale hadn't simply switched schools.

"Suicide," someone whispered. And then the whispers became rumors of all kinds of awful ways he killed himself.

Staring at the empty seat in front of me, I felt very, very cold.

And empty.

When I got home that day after hearing about Dale's suicide, I sat in my room for a long time. Just staring. Trying to make myself feel some sort of remorse. Some sort of sadness for this guy I sat behind in class. This guy I should have smiled at. Should have talked to and befriended.

Still, all I felt was nothing. I couldn't pick at the ends of my heart, bend them down into sadness, heat them up with anger, or even preoccupy them with staring to turn this nothing into boredom. I tried falling inside myself to feel, only to come back up with the discovery that I was saturated with this numbness. This nothingness that remained a cold and empty void inside of me.

And it was *wrong*.

I stood up from where I sat on the edge of my bed, stumbled to my dresser mirror. An emotionless zombie stared back at me.

And it was *wrong*.

I was wrong. All this time. Not to feel. To allow this foreign anesthetic to take over my body and shut down my emotions.

"I can't do this anymore," I whispered down to my trembling hands. A weight pressed down on my shoulders. I felt heavy. Dizzy. Numb.

I met my reflection's dead eyes. *I am empty*, I thought lifelessly. My name was a label for a reflection I didn't know anymore. My skin enveloped a vessel but no soul.

Numb.

That was me.

And I felt the weight of something unbearably heavy pressing down on my shoulders.

My lips parted when I realized what this weight was, this numbness, this zombie...

My depression never left.

Scissors. There they were on my dresser, lying about perhaps because I never put them back in the kitchen after clipping the tags off my new school clothes. I grabbed them, then, with a determined stride, marched into the bathroom. I sat on the toilet lid, studying the dull blades of the scissors.

I had heard stories of people intentionally cutting themselves. I always felt sorry for them, though I never understood why they did it.

Until now.

I let the blade drag across the back of my arm. It left only a white mark on my skin. I tried again, pressing harder this time. Nothing. Grumbling with impatience, I kicked my leg up on the bathtub edge to try cutting the skin there. In the process, I accidently I knocked over my pink razor and shaving cream. They tumbled into the tub, both landing near the drain. I stared at the razor for a moment, contemplating trying them instead of the scissors.

I did.

And when that wasn't enough I tore apart my razor with toenail clippers, picking out each blade placed between the pink plastic. I let one of the blades, wedged between the pad of my thumb and pointer finger, hover just above my wrist. I pressed down a few times, feeling the thin blade sinking in. My skin resisted its sharpness. So instead of pressing harder, I dragged the blade slowly. It stung like a paper cut. But when I lifted the razor and saw the blood, something else was lifted too... From that ever-deepening void inside; from the secret place that not even my soul would let me or anyone touch or peek into. Maybe this was where my depression made its nest and spawned, creating a black cavity within my spirit, growing, burning... constantly.

Rising with the blood, a tempestuous emotion screamed in its silent surfacing. Everything that I couldn't make sense of, I cut out. Everything that was held in, I cut out. Everything I regretted and didn't want to remember, I cut out. Everything I knew I wouldn't be, I cut out.

And then a thick glaze of tears filled my eyes as blood dribbled down my hand. I yanked a tissue from the box to dab my self-inflicted wounds. *Beautiful*, I thought, as I took in the sight of crimson.

It was getting late, and my parents would be home soon. I had to stop what I was doing, but I didn't want to. I simply got up from the toilet, locked the bathroom door, then twisted on the showerhead. I undressed, stepped into the shower with the razor still in my hand.

I saw the water drip down in lovely diluted red streams... And the hazy numbness I was so deeply infested with seemed to externalize and swirl all around me now in the fog from the hot shower. All around me this numb, but I didn't feel it anymore. All I felt was the warm water beating against my skin, stinging my cuts and burning my body.

When I was done washing off in the shower, I stood naked in front of the mirror, the red cuts an ugly contrast against my pale skin. I swiped at the fogged mirror, revealing a teary girl's reflection. *What have I done?* I asked the blurry stranger in the mirror. I shook my head slowly, staring into the faded green of my eyes. "I don't know you anymore," I whispered, then the steam still floating in the air fogged the mirror again, veiling my reflection with more elusive blurs. I flipped my head of sopping hair over, twisted a towel over it, the warm, clean, laundry-scented darkness closing in...

Pertinendi

◉

Darkness is all I see here at the bottom of this black water in Pertinendi. I force myself to summon the strength to get up from the bed of razors I lay in. I am cut all over; my skin stings. Still, I push myself from the seafloor, floating in the water for a moment, then landing on my feet in the sand free of razors. The razors haunt my vision still, as they lay there in the silence of my depression, sharp, cold, lethal. I look up at the blackness all around, my depression…

"I didn't wanna feel you again," I say to my depression. "So I cut. To feel a different kind of pain…that wasn't *you*. To force myself to feel something instead of nothing. To reverse this zombie-effect that would kill you in the process. Depression," I address it, angrier this time, "you stained my world. Turned everything black. Negative. It's all I saw when you clouded my mind…when you took over my soul." My lips quiver at the chilling silence that depression responds with. Tears spill from my eyes, only to swell in this sea that is already filled with black tears.

Sniffling, I peer up to the rippling surface. I want to escape this God-awful place, but the sea's surface is so distant and elusive. I can't swim to the top. Depression is gravity here in the sea, weighing me down in this black, negative perspective of my soul, of my life. So I look ahead to the direction I was trying to reach in the boat—the other side of the sea. Closer to Heaven.

I decide I'll just have to walk. Besides, Angel said it's good for the soul…

Worry creases my forehead when I think about Angel, suddenly remembering that the statue is still up in the sky with the demons, somewhere far away from me. I worry about Angel. *Is the statue okay? Have the demons gotten it? Because of me?* I bite my lip anxiously, then call out for Angel in the darkness several times. There is no response. Not even a whisper.

I'm alone.

And alone I push through the water, stumbling over shells and rocks…and even a…rocking chair? I bump into the darn thing after a while of walking.

"What the—?" I step back from the chair, confused as to why its here. The floral carvings in the wood are a familiar sight; the scathed wooden legs tug at some old fuzzy memory… Suddenly, I have an instant flashback to my mother: She's rocking a baby in the chair—*me*. The memory morphs into my mother sitting in the chair again, but she's reading a book to a thumb-sucking toddler with a head full of black hair—me again. The memories of the swaying, soothing, back and forth, motherly comfort of the rocking chair then dissolves back into what is before me—an empty chair. And it doesn't rock anymore, doesn't soothe. It's frozen.

I wonder, for a moment, why my mother isn't here in my Pertinendi. I want her to be, but then she'd have to be dead, right? Or wrong? It's my world after all. But, as I think more about it, she *is* here with me. She is the rocking chair. A symbol.

I remember reading somewhere—maybe in a book about dreams—that the unconscious part of humans speaks in a language of symbols. Which is why dreams are so bizarre; they are architectures of symbols.

Looking down at the rocking chair, I know for certain that this is my mom. A symbolization of my mother…sitting in the haze I saw her through when I was depressed.

I remember that the rocking chair used to be strong as ever, but it became wobbly, vulnerable, as I grew up. My mom, so sweet, loving, and funny, was swallowed up by work, overwhelmed by utter exhaustion.

The rocking chair rocked…no more.

My mother was tired. Old. For too long she was the support of the family. At first gradually, then suddenly, setting adrift, alone and lost, in her depression.

And I think, as I reach out with a shaky hand to touch the arm of the rocking chair, Mom simply, over the years, got tired of being a mom.

The chair, at my touch, suddenly crumbles into a pile of frail pieces.

Responsibility took my mom from me. And responsibility doesn't have much time to give hugs, kisses, or love. No, it's much too busy being responsible, being tired.

Poor Mom, I think woefully, as I kneel down to the rocking chair pieces. Hopelessly, I try assembling the pieces as they were, but they won't go back, they won't stay, they won't rock, they won't comfort. They are withered to the core. So, defeated, I resolve by setting the pieces around me in a circle. Dense with emotion, I curl in the fetal position in this circle, what was my mother when I was depressed… when she was depressed…

Sobs heave my chest as I wail at my depression caving in on me… "You made me think she didn't love me anymore!" My words echo through the void… "MOM!" I cry… "Mommy…"

Sobs rattle my soul, as I curl even deeper into a defenseless, needy little ball.

◙

Ornament balls decorated the Christmas tree, and, under the fake limbs, carefully-wrapped presents waited to be opened. The blue lights were up, twinkling along the edges of the roof; pies were baking, glasses of eggnog sat on the kitchen counter filled to the brim.

It was Christmas.

But it didn't feel like it. I supposed yet again the Christmas spirit didn't touch me this year. It was just another routine to do. Play Christmas music. Eat a lot of fattening foods. Open presents. Hug my parents. Go to sleep. And then it'd be over.

That was how Christmas felt without the warm, tender, loving feeling of the Christmas spirit hugging me tightly like the thick winter clothes I donned that morning. Such a joyous holiday feeling, I guessed, went away after I found out Santa wasn't real, or maybe this was just how Christmas felt to someone depressed, or worse… someone growing up.

Olive was back from college on winter break. She seemed to be doing very well, though still a bit hesitant when it came to eating a lot of food. She had gained some weight over the months; her bones still stuck out, but they were covered by the sun-kissed skin of someone who seemed alive and not dead anymore. She wore bright pink and lime green shirts with Greek symbols often. She was in a sorority now at the big state college she attended on a full scholarship, studying nursing, like everyone else it seemed. She went clubbing now, had already gone through two boyfriends at her new school—something that was totally out of character for my big sister, at least the one I used to know, the one I'd last seen on Halloween many years ago.

She was changing, or growing, and that was natural. But it made me sad. People who changed, like Olive, Sarah, and everyone else I knew, made me worry about the fact that I *didn't* change. Sure, my hair grew longer, I got better at applying makeup to my face, my braces were off, and I plucked my eyebrows now, but my character was still the same. Deep down, I was still the person I always had been. Depressed now, of course, but still the same. I just wasn't sure if this was a bad thing or not.

Dad was tired. So was Mom. And ripped and crumbled wrapping paper was sprawled across the white living room carpet. The Christmas CD that had been playing was over now, and so was Christmas for this year.

"I'm goin' to bed," Dad announced, slowly getting up from his recliner with a groan. "Goodnight, love you." He kissed Olive and me on the forehead, telling us merry Christmas one last time before he went to lie down. Mom stayed up a little while longer to clean up the wrapping paper and empty boxes. I helped her, growing worried every time she sighed deeply, rubbed her puffy eyes, and seemed to avoid going to bed. I was tired, too, and Olive had already passed out on the couch (she had a little too much rum in her eggnog). So I gave up trying to stay up with my mom. I told her goodnight and merry Christmas and that I loved her.

"G'night," was all she said back.

I paused for a moment at the staircase, watching my mother's busy shadow in the kitchen. Maybe she didn't hear me say that I loved her, so she didn't say it back. *Yeah*, I blamed it on her bad hearing.

But as the December month continued on into January, love was a word rarely spoken in my world, and even rarer to be genuine. It was a feeling clearly not shared between my parents as they went to and from work, talking very little to each other and only about bills. Love was a word never returned after I'd say it to my mother before bed. Love was gone; and I truly had no idea where it went. Maybe it was wherever happiness had gone off to...

Pertinendi

Mom's lack of response when it came to affection really troubled me. I'd stay up late lying in bed, agonizing over what I did wrong as a daughter to make her not love me anymore. One night I couldn't take anymore of my negative thoughts; I was at my limit. So I tried distracting myself by reading. And of all the genres of books I had on my shelf, I grabbed a romance novel—I needed to feel some sort of affection, even if it wasn't real at all.

While I was devouring the book, there was a soft knock on my door. Olive opened the door to a crack, peaking in my room. "Hey," my big sister said casually, walking over to where I sat on my bed. I looked up from the page I was on, watching my sister's breezy façade dissolve into an expression of concern. "Does Mom tell you she loves you?" she asked, eyebrows arched high and innocently on her forehead.

"No," I answered, swallowing down the emotion that had instantly formed a lump in my throat.

"Okay, I thought it was just me. What's wrong with her?"

I flipped my book shut with a sigh. "I think she's just stressed," my sensible side said to my sister. But what I really believed was that our mom was tired of being a mom. Tired of cooking, tired of cleaning, being a wife, being a mother, making appointments, paying bills. Just tired. And I understood this. But understanding her exhaustion didn't make it hurt any less. Mom was falling out of love with the children in Olive and me. And I understood the difficulty in loving the adults we were becoming—one recovering from a terrible eating disorder, and the other crazy, depressed, and full of angst. At least Olive had some redeeming qualities—her academic success, lots of friends, dating, a scholarship. I had none of these things. So what reason did my mother have to continue loving me? Why would any parent be proud?

They wouldn't. And my mother was beginning this process.

Olive seemed relieved by the answer I gave her. The lie. "Okay, I was worried I looked like I lost weight or something." Mom usually got pissed at Olive when she seemed thinner—another thing I totally understood.

"No, you look fine," I reassured her, then changed the subject by asking how college life was. It worked. She babbled on and on about her classes, her roommates, her ex boyfriends, and a number of other subjects. When she got bored with me, she said she needed to get her school stuff together since she was heading back to her dorm in the morning. She then left my room, shutting the door behind her.

Yawning, I got up to turn the lights off and set my book on my nightstand. Curling in bed beneath the covers, I felt a draft of icy coldness wrap around my heart; and it wasn't the frosty January air seeping in through the cracks of my window. Loneliness crept into my room, making me turn over onto my side restlessly. Unable to sleep, I gazed through my semicircle window out at the stars glimmering in the velvety midnight sky. I tried feeling the love the religious people at my school always talked about—the love of Christ, of God, of whomever. I wanted to feel that again. I used to feel it every time I looked at the night sky—that feeling of something more, of infinity, of love.

"God," I whispered to the stars, "please help me. And please help my mom."

There was no deep connection felt, no speck of hope rising in my chest. I might as well be whispering to my pillow, to my blankets, to the darkness in my room. The coldness.

Love.

It was harder to feel now.

Love was a routine, a word, four letters, that, when put together, meant nothing in my life.

Love was frozen in my heart, turning to cold, hard stone, weighing me down like the densest depression it was.

I needed a hug, but I wasn't sure if even the warmest hug could break the depression frozen on my shoulders, weighing on my spirit, on my life. Depression was a part of me for a long time. Depression was my friend. Depression felt real. It always felt real—more real and present than love.

There was no one to curl up with at night, no Mom or Dad or big sister to tuck me in. I was seventeen. Those things couldn't be anymore. But depression understood my selfish, childish needs, and I could curl up with it at night, feeling heavy, tearful, but not alone. Because I had depression there on my back, silent in the darkness, invisibly watching, watching, watching me go numb under its spell. Frozen.

Frozen was my car early the next morning. Olive left to drive back to college. Mom and Dad had already left for work. And only my car sat in the driveway, baring ice sickle fangs in its grill, coated with a layer of winter's ice. I took a deep breath before going out in the cold to turn on my car and let the heater blast. I nearly busted my butt on a sheet of ice in the driveway, but luckily made it back into the house with only a red and runny nose.

"It's cold!" I told Pumpkin, whose face seemed to say "No shit?" when she perked her sleepy head from where it lay near the crackling fireplace.

The Christmas decorations and stockings that had hung on the fireplace mantel were put up for the year. Christmas was officially over when the decorations were gone.

And so was Christmas break.

I had to go back to school today.

I sighed, went into the kitchen to grab something to eat. On the counter were highlighter-pink paper notes. Notes my mom left me to find in the morning that read: *Fold towels* or *Put dishes away* or *Noodles to fix spaghetti in pantry*. This was how I talked to my mom now—a relationship built upon a foundation of tiny notes.

My appetite was gone. I left the kitchen to sit in the living room with Pumpkin while my car finished defrosting. I plopped down in my mother's ancient rocking chair—a rickety old thing that I worried might collapse under my weight.

I closed my eyes, thinking back to a time when my mother and I were close. When I was small and she used to let me lay in her lap as she gently stroked my hair. Back when love was as easy to feel as the wind on my dirt-smeared face while flying high on the swings at the park in my hometown.

Right now, I wished I could talk to my mom, make her proud of me, make myself less a burden for her to have to support. But more than anything, I wished to be someone different for her, a better daughter. Grow into the woman she always wanted me to be.

I reached down to feel the cuts on my legs, hidden beneath my jeans. I reached into the long sleeve of my coat to feel the cuts there on my arm…

My parents didn't deserve a daughter like me, especially when they raised me so right. They deserved a lot better, and I felt like I cheated them out of that, turning out this way. The big fat pile of nothing…that was going to be late for school today if she didn't get going…

"Shit," I muttered, blinking myself out of the past and back into the present. I got up from the rocking chair in a hurry, and, when I reached to open the front door, looked back at the living room. The rocking chair squeaked every time it lurched forward, but, as I shut the door behind me, I saw through the frosted glass that it became still.

School. It was second semester now, which meant I'd have a few new elective classes to find today. My day went about as usual. Ancient world history, English, math, and then my new elective that would replace the semester-long poetry class I'd been in.

Parenting.

Yikes.

Why'd I sign up for this class?

Right. It's supposed to be easy.

Wrong.

And to make matters worse, Francesca was in the class. I hadn't talked to her since eighth grade. Hell, I hardly even saw her around the high school because she was always at the community college already taking stupid college courses. *Why am I the only weird person in this school who isn't brilliant?*

She took the seat next to me, nodding at me like the old acquaintance I was to her. "Heeeey, *you*. Have a good Christmas break?"

I tried at a smile, but I think I scrunched my nose instead. "Jovie," I reminded her…*again*. "It was all right. How was yours?"

"Crappy. I worked all break. My stupid boss is a dictator."

I pressed my lips together, attempting, this time, at an expression of sympathy. "That sucks."

"Tell me about it."

Actually, *she* told *me* about how much it sucked. Bitched an entire ten minutes before the teacher finally came into the classroom to go over the course syllabus. Francesca, besides her now choppy auburn bob, hadn't changed one bit. She even still had that whole hippie vibe going on and the same annoyingly sarcastic attitude.

I tuned her and the teacher out, settling my sights on the posters on the wall beside me. They were all gruesomely disturbing, with their diagrams of how a pregnant woman's body looks on the inside after nine months. They portrayed the baby curled snugly in the fetal position, crushing the mother's internal organs to the side.

Ooouucchhh, was all I could think, as I stared at the helpless little baby, my mouth set in a disgusted cringe.

◉

I lay still, my arms folded at my chest, back curled in the black sand that is gooey at the touch. It is a long time before I find the will to stretch myself out and leave the pieces of the rocking chair behind.

But they're gone.

I shove the sand away, digging and digging, only to find more sand. The rocking chair pieces have disappeared. I want to cry out for my mom again, but I press my lips together and push myself to my feet.

I have to keep going.

But it's hard. Especially down here in the sea, because not even the inspiring view of Heaven can be seen from these gloomy depths. And Angel isn't here to guide me anymore. Lord knows I need a guide since every direction I seem to take is the wrong way—at least, that's how it usually went when I was alive.

And so it seems to be here, even in Pertinendi.

I take another step through the ambiguous waters, only to find soon after that no sand is there, but a deep groove in the seabed. I fall, but slowly thanks to the water and my decent swimming abilities. I finally touch the sand again with my toes; and from somewhere up above—but not Heaven—artificial lights beam down where I stand. The lights glitter before me, illuminating a path of elegant destruction. In the sand are toppled over tables and chairs, broken punch bowls, and a shattered chocolate fountain. Popped balloons blemish the sand's smooth surface, as does the fallen disco ball shards. I look down at myself, puzzled when I see that I am wearing a beautiful, sparkly violet gown—something one might wear to a fancy ball or... *prom*.

As I step forward to study the wreckage more closely, the silver-jeweled heels I'm wearing accidently stomp down on something beneath the sand. I bend to unbury the artifact. My lips part in awe at the piece that I find—it's a mask, something that reminds me of Mardi Gras in Louisiana, and...also reminds me of...someone.

The mask has turquoise and purple sequins, with bright pink glitter outlining the eyes. It's stunning, handmade. I put it up to my face, peering through the eye-slits. I am at a loss of breath, of words, of feeling when I see through this mask. The darkness of the sea all around is suddenly lifted, gradually turning into a tantalizing electric blue color that sends my heart into full-blown flutter mode.

I am weightless in this blue water. I find myself not freezing anymore, but melting inside, soothingly, gently. I love it.

I blink.

Behind my lids that are framed by the mask, there...a memory resides...

◉

My eyes fluttered open—I had them closed so I wouldn't get glue on my eyeballs. Fine art was one of my new elective classes. And in this class today we were making masks. I thought they were because Mardi Gras was coming up soon, but really they were prom decorations. Masquerade was the theme. And my class was the free labor making the ornaments.

I didn't mind making the masks. I really grew a liking to mine actually. I thought it was quite pretty with its intricate patterns of multicolored sequins and glittery pink outlining of the eyes. I was so proud of my mask that I had to try it on.

I pressed my creation up to my face, squinting through the holes. I blinked a few times, looking down at the glitter-speckled floor. Suddenly, a pair of untied, black, high-top Converse shoes stepped onto the tile I was looking down at, framed by the mask. Slowly, I turned my face upward to see who the feet belonged to. My mouth fell open at the sight of this person's eyes. Instantly, I was transported to a lush field of bluebonnets. I was warm, melting under the hot Louisiana sun, the wind rippling the field of electrifying blue I was lying in. I was home. Happy. Weightless.

Free.

But then I blinked, and reality came crashing back into my vision.

"Are you done with these?" the boy with the magnificent blue eyes asked me, holding up a pair of scissors.

Completely dumbfounded, I nodded with the mask still stuck to my face.

Scottie Robinson said, "Thanks," with a polite smile, then turned to sit down in his seat way across the classroom.

When I registered what had just happened, I ripped the mask from my face. My cheeks burned with shame. How awkward could I get? Especially around Scottie! I hadn't had a class with him since middle school and he *still* made me nervous.

Taking a deep breath to calm myself, my eyes unwittingly traveled to the orange glitter container on a classmate's desk. Spellbound, the burnished bits let a memory from long ago sneak into my thoughts...

Halloween.

Bright and orange.

Pumpkins and candy.

Black eyes that belonged to Stephan. I could never forget his name. I shuddered away from the thoughts, swallowing hard to keep them from bothering me.

I couldn't help myself. I glanced up at Scottie, something I never once let myself do in this class so far. To my horror, he was already looking at me. Quickly, he averted his gaze back down to the mask he was making, and I did the same.

Does he remember? I wondered frantically... *Does he know? That it was me he saved at the party years ago?* I hoped not, because I remembered the night well enough for the both of us *and* Stephan. Plus, how embarrassing would it be, to have this gorgeous guy remember me—a nobody—and how he saved this nobody at his brother's party that I wasn't even supposed to be at. I didn't like how he had seen me at my weakest, crying and afraid.

It was like he had something over me, a superior debt that I owed him. I didn't like that. I didn't like that at all.

But I did like *him*. I couldn't resist admitting at least that to myself. My heart fluttered in my chest when I, very shyly and discreetly, looked at him again. His skin was still tan despite it being too cold to go out in the sun. His hair was coffee black, cut short and naturally spiky straight. He was slender, but not quite as lanky as he once was in middle school.

He chuckled at something his friend said beside him, parenthesis dimples lining his cheeks.

Cute.

And he seemed really, really sweet.

Damn it, Jovie! Stop! I yelled internally at myself. *You don't like this guy. He probably has a girlfriend still. Probably doesn't even know who you are or that you exist. You were just the girl who had the scissors to him. That's why he talked to you. HE. DOES. NOT. LIKE. YOU.*

I huffed at my negative thoughts, though I agreed with them wholeheartedly. Still, I couldn't deny myself the pleasant homey place I went to in his eyes. Such a sweet feeling stuck with me, and I longed to be there again. In his eyes. Home.

◉

January was the first month in years that I wasn't home very often. Francesca was to thank for my absence. Being reconnected with her in parenting class and her forgetting all about Halloween night when we were twelve meant she invited me places again. To the movies. Out to eat. Bowling. Shopping. Just her and I. Mostly because *she* wanted to do these things, just not by herself. I was merely an accessory to her, like the hemp bracelet she always wore—something to fill the empty spaces around her. I understood this. Which was probably why I never told her no when she asked me to go places with her. Plus, I supposed it made my parents happy that I went out and did stuff now—I had friends, or so they believed.

Friday came around—*finally*. My parents were probably a little shocked by the fact I wasn't home when they got back from work; I owed this to Francesca again. She'd told me to meet her where she worked—the cell phone store in the mall of all things. And I couldn't even get a job at a fast food joint...

The mall was packed. Rosy red and suave pink colors embellished the inside of almost every store. Heart-shaped objects were displayed behind glass windows and the gourmet chocolate stores were flooded. Was it seriously almost Valentine's Day? Where had January gone? And every other month within the last five years?

Like Francesca told me to, I met her at the booth she worked at. Her shift was over, and she came around the counter to meet me.

"Hey," I greeted her, smiling, though I didn't really want to be at the mall, especially when it was *this* crowded.

"Come on. I wanna go in here." Francesca dragged me into the gothic store called Fang You.

"Uhmm, what're you lookin' for?" I asked her over the screaming music inside. I was attracted to the shelf of band t-shirts, but Francesca whistled, catching my attention—I was so like a stupid puppy...

"Do these look good to you?" Francesca turned to me, totally serious about an answer.

I couldn't contain it. I snorted with laughter, pressing my palm over my mouth. "They're penis-shaped lollypops, Francesca. They look disgusting!"

"Perfect!" Francesca grinned wickedly. She bought the bouquet of them, then made me accompany her to a few other shops.

"What in the world are you gonna do with those?" I asked her, still giggling.

"Give 'em to somebody."

"*Who*?" I begged.

"Well, I'm tempted to send them to Stephan, just to piss the bastard off."

I stopped short, heart freefalling all the way down to my feet. "Is that the guy that—" My throat suddenly scorched with dryness. I swallowed, but it was like swallowing leather. "—that was..." I trailed off, dizzy and unable to finish my sentence. I lost my breath, my hands trembled, voice shook with anxiety.

"You met him before. At the Halloween party, remember?"

How could I forget?

"The stupid piece of shit knocked up my sister," she confessed, walking on casually through the mall.

"I thought you said they weren't together anymore."

"They weren't," she answered blankly. "He raped her."

Now it felt as if my jaw had fallen to the floor, right next to my heart. "*What?!* When?"

"A year ago. She'd been in rehab for a while, but when she finally got her shit together, she came back home. Ended up meeting up with him to catch up and… Yeah. Shit happened. But don't freak out. She aborted. She's fine now. Just back on drugs."

I had my fingertips pressed against my quivering lips, eyebrows set in a genuinely sympathetic arch. "I am *so* sorry Francesca." My heart ached for her. For her sister. For her family. How terrible. "Are *you* okay? That's a really scary thing to see someone go through. Especially a sister."

"I'm all right," she shrugged. "And Stephan's in jail, thank God."

I wanted to tell her. Right then and there that Stephan had tried to rape me too. And maybe he would have gone to jail earlier and would have never gotten the chance to hurt her sister if I would have said something. These words were right on the tip of my tongue, my lips were parted, voice ready to speak up, but only silence came out. I couldn't say it. It was too private of a thing, nestled too far inside. It only came out through cutting. And I didn't think Francesca would understand this. Besides, Francesca would be furious with me, right? Knowing that it was…in some way…my fault that her sister got hurt…because I didn't have the courage to say a damn thing, to turn him in years ago.

I truly and utterly hated myself.

For being the person that I was. A coward.

I drove Francesca home that night, the headlights of passing cars like grounded shooting stars that granted no wishes.

Francesca had changed the subject hours ago, but what she told me earlier remained in my thoughts. At least until the chatterbox in the passenger's seat got onto the subject of boys that were *our* age.

"You don't know him, he goes to a different school," Francesca said, blushing. "But I like the guy. Met him at the rock festival last summer."

"D'you talk to him still?"

"Nah, not really. Just through Facebook every once and a while."

"Oh, okay. Well maybe you should try getting his number or something." I was actually quite surprised that she hadn't. She was so outgoing, made friends practically wherever she went.

She scoffed at my suggestion, dismissing it with a wave of her hand. "Yeah right. So. D'you like anyone at school?"

My grip tightened on the steering wheel. I trusted *no one* when it came to talking about crushes unless it was Nana. "Um, no, not really."

"You're a *terrible* liar," Francesca laughed, prodding me in the arm with a penis-shaped lollypop. "Come on! Tell me who it is. Please? I won't tell. I promise." She even held out her pinky to pinky swear.

I sighed, giving in to her begging. "Fine. Um…" I nervously tucked a lock of hair behind my ear, already feeling red-hot humiliation rising up my neck. "D'you know…? Uh…" I pressed my lips together, peeking over at Francesca to see if she was still interested. Ugh. She was. She looked as bubbly as a puppy about to be given a juicy steak.

"Yeeess," she prompted, leaning towards the console so she could hear me just in case I mumbled the name, which I did.

"Scottie. Robinson? Know him?"

"Aaaawwwww!" she gushed. "That's adorable! You know, I'm friends with him on Facebook. I could talk to him for you if you want—"

"*No*," I interrupted firmly. "Please don't say a word. You promised!"

"Aggh, fine. Fine." She acted like she was zipping her lips, then throwing the key out the window. "Your secret's safe with me."

I relaxed a bit behind the wheel, exhaling the stored up breath I was holding. "Thanks."

Morgan McLendon

◉

The next time I thanked Francesca went more like "Thanks a lot," but with a whole lot of sarcasm. It was Monday; and that morning I had woken up to find a voicemail on my phone from Francesca—she'd called around midnight when I was dead asleep. Rubbing the crust from my eyes groggily, I pressed my phone to my ear to listen…

"Jovie! You need to wake your ass up! I have the best news in the world! Like, I am seriously bursting with excitement for you! *Because*…I talked to Scottie last night! Aaaaand you guys are gonna go out on a date! So you need to call me as soon as you wake up so I can give you his number and you can set up a date with him sometime next week. So. Call me back when you wake up. Okay? Bye!"

I sat bolt upright in my bed, puffy eyes wide with horror. "WHAT THE—!" I ripped open my phone and pounded Francesca's number.

"Ohmygosh! Jovie! Hey! It's about time you called!"

Francesca's chipper morning attitude pissed me off even more. "Thanks a lot!" I growled into the phone, cueing the sarcasm. "I can't believe you told him! What am I gonna do now?! I have a class with him today! Shit!" I grabbed at the nest of frizzy hair on my head, yanking down at the strands that were probably turning white from distress.

"Calm down. *Jeez*. Just tell him hi. That's all you gotta do."

"Gosh, Francesca, why? *Why* did you tell him?" I paused a moment, thinking about the whole situation. "What *did* you tell him?"

"I messaged him on Facebook. Look, I gotta get ready for school right now, but I'll tell you everything later. Just know that he said you seem cool and that he wouldn't mind going on a date with you."

"What if he would've minded?" I demanded, not quite as angrily as I intended after hearing that Scottie thought I seemed cool.

"Uh, I probably never woulda told you that I talked to him."

I laughed at this. "Uggghhhh, I can't believe you."

"You're welcome," she said smugly, then hung up.

I threw my phone into the covers, burying my head deep into the pillows. I didn't even want to start this day…

This day. Today. Today was normal, like any other day. At least, that was what I kept telling myself. Everyone at school seemed like themselves, those colorful blurs I couldn't identify. I managed to avoid these blurs, making it to ancient world history class with not one sighting of Scottie.

Later in parenting class, Francesca told me about her and Scottie's conversation on the Internet. As much as I wanted to sock her in the face for not keeping her promise, I couldn't help but feel somewhat giddy about his positive response.

But I still had to face him in art class next hour. I struggled all through parenting class to come up with some excuse to tell Scottie for what Francesca had told him. How her Facebook message was a joke. How it was just something to embarrass me. But every excuse I made up in my head wasn't convincing, not even to myself. I liked Scottie, ever since I looked into his eyes that Halloween night. And that was the truth. There was no way around it.

I was a frantic mess while sitting in art class, having to resort to the silent treatment when he entered the classroom. It was the only thing I knew how to do—ignore him. It seemed to work well enough all these years.

We were working on our self portraits again today. If the teacher were to wander through the room, studying everyone's portrait, she'd find that most drew their lips curling upward, their eyes wrinkled with a smile. When she'd get to mine, though, she'd observe my penciled lips as they always appeared—an emotionless line.

I kept my head down, eyes fixed on my drawing throughout the entire hour until the last few minutes of class. Everyone had gotten up to stand by the door, ready to make a break for the cafeteria once the lunch bell buzzed. To avoid the crowd—and Scottie—I remained seated, deciding to get a head start on the book my English class was assigned to read this semester. I wasn't even on the second sentence when I felt the heat of someone's presence hovering over me. I swallowed hard, continuing to pretend like I was reading.

"What're you reading?" a deep voice so near wondered aloud.

I slowly lifted my gaze from the book, letting my eyes settle on the simple blue-eyed boy that I couldn't believe was in front of me. "Uhh—" I cleared my throat. "Kill a Bird..." I shook my head, closing my eyes in embarrassment and hastily shaking my head at my stupidity. "I-I mean—" I held up the book idiotically. *"To Kill a Mockingbird."*

"D'you have Miss Cook for English?"

I nodded.

"My class has to read it, too."

"It's not bad for an assigned book," I commented, pinching the pads of my fingers between the pages nervously. I wet my drying lips, barren from the anxiety flushing my skin. Confessions then slipped from my mouth out of nowhere, without my control. Like a reflex, I defended myself from the humiliation Francesca had thrust upon me. "I swear I didn't put her up to it. Francesca, I mean. Whatever she told you. I didn't want her to…" I looked at him, eyes wide and innocent. I hoped he could hear the honesty in my embarrassingly desperate inflection.

He gave me a simple smile and a simple shrug of his broad shoulders. "Hey, it's all right."

I opened my mouth to speak out of obligation, but the bell rang. Scottie was saved by the bell from suffering through my terrible small talk.

He glanced back at his buddy waiting for him by the door. Hesitantly, he slid his hands from his pockets and reached for a broken pencil lying about on the table. "Well if what Francesca told me is true—" He leaned against the table, scribbling a set of digits onto the folded paper I was using as a bookmark. "—here's my cell number." He wedged the paper between the pages I was reading, gently shutting the book when it was snug. He left me with a sweet half smile, then turned to meet up with his friend for lunch.

I sat there in my seat, watching him walk confidently from the room, disappearing into the herd of students. I pushed my book closer to me, opening the pages to the paper he wrote his number on. I touched it, and it was real. I hadn't imagined it.

Scottie Robinson just gave me his number…

◙

And thus was the beginning of my very first relationship. Our first date was that weekend. Dinner at a Mexican restaurant. I had lied to my mom through a text message, telling her I was going to be at school working on an art project. Truthfully, I was too embarrassed to tell her I had a date—we didn't talk about boys. That was way too awkward. And I didn't do well in awkward situations, which was proven to me on this particular date…

Awkward silence sat beside Scottie and me in the booth, saturating the humid air that reeked of refried beans and beef.

"So what d'you like to do for fun?" Scottie asked me. Turns out, we were both awful at small talk. This made me smile internally.

"Uh, well I like to hang out with friends." Such a typical and pathetic answer. By friends I meant Francesca, and when I said I liked it I meant I hated it. "I read a lot. Sometimes I write."

"What d'you write?"

"Poems mostly," I answered, reaching for a salted chip in the chip basket. "I took a poetry class last semester, and I think it's been my favorite class so far in high school."

Scottie told me he was more partial to history classes. He could talk all day about it, knew dates and historical events off the top of his head!

"Well if I ever have history homework, I'm definitely giving you a call," I joked. Then a miracle happened—I made him laugh. I smiled with him, ecstatic to my very soul.

Alive.

I felt it.

Vitality beat in my thumping heart. Pink timidity burned in my cheeks, sweat from my palms. But I was smiling. And it was real.

I felt real. In the present. More in the world rather than my own head—I hadn't felt this way for years.

"S-so what kind of music d'you like?" I asked him after our food came out, steaming hot and smelling delicious.

"Rap." His voice was muffled from the huge bite of stuffed burrito he had just thrown into his mouth.

I nodded once, looking down at the platter of quesadillas before me. Saliva filled my mouth, allowed me to lick my chapped lips, but I wasn't hungry. Butterflies had already filled my stomach, shook my voice and my hands, made me an awkward mess that somehow Scottie tolerated.

After forcing myself to swallow down a bite of my food, I told Scottie I was more into heavy metal and grew up listening to country music. He didn't seem to have a problem with our contrasting musical tastes, but he was considerate enough to change the radio station in his car to a classic rock station when he was driving me back to my house.

Our next date was at a Chinese restaurant, very close by the restaurant I found out he worked at.

"The local sushi bar," he said, "I bus tables there."

I admired that about him—he had a job. I was pretty sure he already figured it out, but I was too ashamed to admit that I didn't have one. I also felt ashamed when he asked me if I was a fan of sushi. I shook my head vigorously, a grimace set on my face. "No way!"

"And *you're* from Louisiana?" he clarified dully, as he speared a shrimp with his fork.

"I know. I'm the worst Cajun ever. I don't like seafood and I'm as pale as a ghost. Sue me."

"I probably could, you know? My dad's a lawyer."

I considered this for a moment, allowing myself, only for a moment, to think back to the completely trashed but gorgeous house I'd visited on Halloween night many years ago. "No wonder your house is so big," I said absently, still lost in the past.

Scottie suddenly stopped eating, set down his fork and met my eyes. "You know where I live?"

"Uhhh." *Shit.* "I-I mean..." *Now you've done it!*

He stopped me with a slow shake of his head. The laidback essence he'd been giving off before became very rigid and serious. He leaned over the table towards me, eyes intent on my face. "I have a question for you," he said, "and it may seem kinda weird, but just bear with me, okay?"

I promised with a slight but cautious nod of my head.

"Halloween," he began, the simple word cutting the air like razors, "about four or five years ago, were you ever at a party across town on Fritz Lane?"

I finished chewing the small chunk of orange chicken then swallowed hard. "I don't really know about the street name and all, but I was at a Halloween party across town before." I looked down at my hands folded on the edge of the table. Only I could detect their trembling, and only I felt Stephan's hands on my shoulders still, his eyes on my chest, on my legs, on my face. Everywhere. "I know what you're gonna ask me," I admitted softly, gaze steady on my greasy fingers. "And to answer you... Yes. I was at that party. And I was the girl in the bathroom. It was me you saved from that...*guy*." I met Scottie's eyes. The dim lighting of the restaurant seemed to gray his irises, turning them somber instead of their intense blue.

I wasn't expecting it; and it took me aback for a moment when Scottie reached across the table, brushing his fingers over my hand. Only then did they stop shaking.

"I've wanted to tell you for years now how sorry I am that that happened to you." Gently, he gave my hand a comforting squeeze.

"Nothing happened to me thanks to you," I reminded him, my hand melting under the heat of his touch.

"Still, the situation alone is traumatizing enough. No one deserves to go through such a thing."

I shrugged off his sympathy. "It's okay. I'm okay. And I owe you a huge thank you because of it."

Scottie shook his head in disagreement. "I didn't bring it up for another thank you. I just wanted to know if you really are okay. It's bothered me for years. And, I feel like I owe *you* an apology, for not calling the cops that night or-or making you stay until someone came and got you. I shouldn't have just let you go." His grip tightened on my hand, fiercely and surprisingly protective.

"I walked home," I confessed to him. And from there I rewound the story, telling him all about that night, from Francesca, to the lie about trick-or-treating, and then Stephan. I told him about what he did, what he encouraged me to drink that I was too naive not to question.

For some reason, it felt okay now to tell Scottie these things. Maybe because he knew the worst of it already. Or...maybe...because it was inside me for far too long. I longed to speak it out and not have to cut it out anymore.

"How come you never talked to me after that night?" Scottie asked, voice low and earnest. "In middle school, I used to see you around all the time."

I was at a loss of words, of an explanation. So I just shrugged and threw the question right back at him. "Why didn't *you* ever talk to *me*?"

"I didn't know what to say," he said honestly.

"Well neither did I. Not to mention I was still completely mortified at the whole thing. That's not something you go around making conversations about."

Scottie understood, and he shut up about that for the night. Well, it did come back up one last time. It was after he drove me back to my house. We were standing beside his car as I thanked him once again for taking me out to eat and paying for everything. I tried paying him back, but he was a gentleman and refused.

"So you *are* okay?" he asked again, his face, though lit only by the near streetlamp and stars, I could tell, was full of concern and sympathy.

"Well, right now, yes. Back then, absolutely not. But," I sighed, "nothing happened. And…I'm alive. So I think I'm luckier than most in that situation."

"Right."

I tilted my head to the side at Scottie's hesitance, confused by the worry deepening the wrinkles on his forehead. "You didn't just take me out so you could ask me if I'm okay, did you? To see if I'm okay after something that happened *years* ago? Cuz that's really sweet and all but—"

"That's not the only reason," he interrupted, taking a step closer to me. "Sure, I've wondered about you every day since then, but there's—" His voice grew softer, dropping down to a whisper as he brought his palm to my cheek. "—something else…" He never finished his sentence. He didn't have to, because I understood, and I felt it, too, after all this time, I still felt it…

The almost-bridge that had been built between us the day he interrupted Stephan's assault was finally being connected right now, as Scottie's lips brushed against mine. Despite the freezing February night, I was warm and whole and melting against Scottie's lips. I felt real. Exhilarated. Alive.

And for the first time in years…I felt…happy.

Scottie leaned his head away, his breath vapors like a cold phantom against my cheeks. "Goodnight, Jovie," he murmured, as a sweet smile formed on his lips and dimpled his cheeks. "I'll see you tomorrow at school."

It was never spoken, the fact that we liked each other. I believed we admitted this through the kiss, in the way we held each other's hand the next day at school and every day after that.

It was never spoken.

That we were officially "boyfriend-girlfriend".

But we were.

And it seemed like overnight the emptiness inside of me was filled with this sweet, wonderful person: Scottie Robinson. I didn't have to hate myself or drown in depression. The very fact that Scottie liked me made it okay for me to like myself. And the way he made me feel—wanted, like I belonged beside him, in his arms, against his lips—made me forget about the void inside of me. My depression became dormant.

He was all I looked forward to at school, over the weekend, during the day when we'd text each other.

After a month of dating, I was introduced to his parents—a moment I was a nervous wreck for, but still managed through with some poise.

The day I met his parents was the first time I'd been to his house since that dreadful Halloween night years ago. It was strange, like stepping back into an altered past, except this was the present, the now…

Scottie's parents were amazingly sweet to me. They all had awesome Jersey accents, something that made me smile since I supposedly had a southern accent—I didn't feel like such an oddball here.

"We moved from New Jersey when the kids were younger," his Mom explained to me from the kitchen. She explained why, then asked me about why my family and I moved here from Louisiana—I guessed Scottie had already told her that much. So I told her a story about a hurricane and my mother's job offer. Her bustling behind the kitchen suddenly halted. She turned to me, giving me a sweet, somehow sympathetic half smile—kind of like the way Scottie smiled at me. "Well, I'm sorry about all the hurricane mess, but I'm glad you're here now. I'm making pizza tonight, by the way," she mentioned, throwing me a subtle wink.

Scottie tugged at my hand, nodding to the staircase beside us. "We'll be downstairs watching movies," he told his mom.

She waved in acknowledgement, giving us the green light to head down the stairs.

The stairs.

I had a flashback to me five years younger, drunkenly stumbling down the steps, my hand clutching my woozy stomach, the other blocking the punch fighting its way up my throat and through my lips.

Reality.

At the bottom of the stairs, I was expecting it to appear how it did years ago: a cemented basement with paint splatters, nails and boards strewn about. But this time around, my bare feet stepped onto squishy beige carpet, a spacious living room welcoming my entrance.

"We remodeled everything," Scottie informed me when he noticed my surprised expression.

"When?"

"That year," he admitted hesitantly. "This part of the basement went through the last of the renovations. That's why it probably looked like shit when you last saw it." He ran a hand through his hair, laughing lightly. "Aaand this is where my brother hid me when he threw that party."

"That's awful."

"That's Jay," he shrugged.

"Where were your parents that night?" I wondered, checking out the wall of DVDs in the corner.

"Oh, they were in Kansas City at my sisters' dance recitals."

Scottie had mentioned his sisters before, and I knew one of them already. She was a grade above us, a dancer on the school's dance team. "Jenny, right?" I guessed, since we were on the subject of his siblings.

"And that's Jessica," he added, pointing at the youngest girl in the family picture nailed to the wall.

I laughed to myself, reciting, "Jay, Jenny, Jessica. All J names. Were your parents not able to come up with one when you came along?"

Scottie smiled, "They did, actually. My first name's Joshua, middle name Scott. Scottie's just been my nickname as far as I can remember."

"Ooh, okay, I see." And I also understood now why Scottie was so accepted by the more popular kids at school—because of his siblings. Not only Jay's obvious legacy, but also Jenny's. She was a very pretty, very amazing senior dancer.

As Scottie led me down the carpeted hallway towards his room, a memory stalked the past corridors of my mind. Slipping by the bathroom, seeing the mark that still blemished the wall behind the door, a cold chill shuddered my spine, something too chillingly deep that not even Scottie's warmth could heat. And then we were in his room. The harsh intensity whispering from the bathroom was no more once Scottie shut the door to his room.

Scottie's room.

I was in it.

For the second time.

And this time it seemed plainer, with only a few band posters on the walls. The only things that had remained constant about it were the scattered stacks of CDs all over the floor. I bent to pick up the CD closest to my foot.

"I *love* this band," I told him, the excitement in my eyes reflecting in his.

"I can burn you a copy if you don't already have it," he offered, taking the CD from me to check out its cover.

I beamed, "That would be *awesome*."

He returned a smile, setting the CD back down carefully atop the rickety stack.

We had planned on watching movies for this date night. Old gangster films that Scottie adored, like, *The Godfather* and *Pulp Fiction*. Instead of putting in one of these movies, though, Scottie got really close to me, leaning in towards my lips. So near, I could feel the heat of his breath, the beat of his heart…

I vocalized my concern that his mom was right upstairs; she might come in.

"She's making pizza. Trust me. She'll be up there for a while."

I relaxed, allowing Scottie's lips to close in on mine. His hands grazed along my back, slowly tracing down my spine, but stopping at my ass. He squeezed there once, then picked me right off my feet—a sudden surprise that took my breath away.

It was only a moment later when my back was cradled by the soft, navy blue sheets on his bed, my hair sprawled all over his pillows. His body hovered over mine, hands near my head, holding his weight. Our kiss deepened. His lips were fervent against mine, opening them slowly, pressing his tongue against mine.

I was amazed at myself in this moment; how I seemed to move against his lips so effortlessly, when, in truth, this was my first make out session ever. My hands somehow knew to travel to his hair, gently tug at the short, spiky strands. My lips knew how to open against his, meeting, with my tongue, the hot wetness behind his lips.

He felt indescribably wonderful...

Kissing Scottie was like kissing happiness...

And happiness was something my heart opened up to, would do anything for, would never let go, would welcome in no matter what.

Scottie was unlocking the barriers around my heart that depression had built.

Trust.

It was somewhere deep down the dormant dark pit in me, but now it was resurfacing, reaching against the impossible depths it'd fallen into, and coming out into the light of Scottie's room as I kissed him, touched him, and let myself truly like this person that made me so unbelievably happy.

Scottie pulled his face away from mine, his eyes hungry when they looked down at me. "Just tell me if I go too far, okay?" His voice was husky and drawn, breaths a rugged whirl of heat against my skin.

"Okay," I breathed, nudging his face back down to mine.

In the back of my mind—the very far back since most of what was racing through my head was Scottie—I wondered just how far he would try to go with me. Touching my butt seemed far enough for now...

Besides, this was only my first make out session...

I was new to all of this...

All of *this* especially:

Scottie's body was all over me, pressing against my skin; his hands roamed across my hips, making their way up to my breasts. It seemed almost like he was testing me, seeing just how far I'd let him wander about my skin until there came a stop sign.

His hands slipped under the back of my blouse, fingers brushing up my spine until they fumbled at the back of my bra.

I suddenly registered what he was trying to do. "Too far," I breathed under his lips. "Too far."

"Sorry," he murmured. He stopped immediately, looking down at me with genuinely sorry blue eyes. He cupped the side of my face, saying again wholeheartedly, "I'm sorry. I'll slow down."

"It's okay," I assured him, then settled back onto his pillows, allowing him to kiss me, but not proceed with what he had intended.

Scottie having more experience with this stuff shouldn't have surprised me. He did, after all, date Cheyenne Whore... *Oops.* I meant Cheyenne Moore. All the gossipy girls I sat near at lunch always had dirt to say about this girl. Like, how she was Queen Skank Bitch of the cheerleaders, and that she slept with half of the football team. I wasn't sure how much of that stuff was true, but the things they said about Scottie and her... Well, before, I liked to tell myself they were just rumors... Now, I was beginning to see that maybe they weren't.

I never asked Scottie about Cheyenne. The jealousy that brewed in me towards her getting to have him first simmered in me enough already. Bringing it up would only stoke the fiery jealously burning in my green eyes. He liked *me* now; he was dating *me* now. Cheyenne didn't matter to him anymore.

But at school I wasn't so sure...

Sometimes when I'd reach for Scottie's hand in the hallway, he'd pretend not to notice, brushing me off. And sometimes when we were holding hands, our fingers intertwining beautifully, he'd suddenly let go, allowing my hand to drop by my side idly. Every time when this would occur, I'd always look up at the blurry faces passing by, and one would always be close enough to be clear in my vision: Cheyenne.

Ouch didn't even begin to describe how much that hurt.

Hurt. I buried it within the deep dark pit inside of me, letting Scottie's presence bandage the void, mask the pain that I would always ignore.

The silent screams my dead depression sometimes uttered would be hushed by Scottie's lips when we'd park in empty parking lots after dinner and a movie...

He'd kiss my pain away, my sadness, my confusion, my worries. All I had to think about was Scottie in those moments of peace, trapped beneath his body that I surrendered to willingly every time.

But surrender couldn't arrest the doubts I had about our relationship. Sometimes Scottie would really hurt me; only, I would never admit to myself just how much.

He would never text me during the day unless I texted him first, wouldn't even call—we'd only text. And most of the time he'd blow me off in order to play video games with his buddies. (Okay, maybe that was karma since I'd blow Francesca off sometimes so I could hang out with him.) But the worst of his bad tendencies was how he forced conversation between us, only seeming to look forward to the physical part of our infatuation.

Part of me questioned if Scottie just simply didn't care about our relationship as much as I did. I could understand why though, he was dating *me* after all.

But I would forgive him for all of those things and more, especially when his lips were against mine, hands in my hair. I loved this feeling of being wanted, of belonging...

I'd ignore all of the bad things in Scottie, his negative qualities, because I didn't want to lose him or his family. I loved going to his house, talking with his mom, dancing around with his little sister; I loved eating dinner with his big family that seemed to welcome me in so effortlessly. I loved this sense of belonging I felt near him, at his house, under his arm, against his body...

I felt whole when I was with him, and I didn't want to lose him and feel empty again.

Empty were the glitter containers in the art room. For months now my art class had been working tirelessly on prom decorations since spring was finally here, letting bloom a bubbly atmosphere.

Massive banners hung from the locker walls, there to advertise prom ticket sales. The gym was no longer in use because it was filled with hanging masquerade masks, black paper-mache columns with beads spiraling down the sides. The scuffed wooden floor was paved over by the black and white checkered paper that I had helped paint. Glitter-filled balloons hung everywhere, and a red curtain—that I even helped sew—framed the entrance to the gym.

I was never one to get all enthusiastic over school events, but the fact that I helped make most of the decorations made prom seem more appealing. I was kind of excited about the event, even though I wasn't going. Well, not unless Scottie asked me to.

"When's prom anyway?" Scottie asked me, clearly annoyed by the whole occasion and the fact that we had to help make the decorations during art class.

"This weekend," I answered, as I cut out the mask outlines Scottie traced for me. "Are you gonna go?" I wondered, trying to be subtle about hinting that I wanted to.

Scottie shrugged. "Jenny's got a big group going and she said I could go with them." He stopped tracing a mask, then looked at me. "D'you wanna go? I know you said before you can't dance, but I just thought I'd ask anyway."

My eyes gleamed. "*Yeah*, we can go. It's about time you asked me," I joked, elbowing him lightly. "That sounds really fun."

He nodded once, lips mirroring the smile on my face. "Cool. I'll probably borrow a tux from Chandler; he can't go this year anyway."

Chandler was Scottie's good friend, the friend that used to sit next to him in this class. But I sat in his chair now, right next to Scottie.

"What happened to Chandler?" I wondered, then noted, "I haven't seen him in class for a while."

"Didn't you hear?" Scottie said, surprised. "He got suspended for painting marijuana pictures on the prom posters."

I snickered to myself at his friend's idiocy. "Does he smoke the stuff?" I asked Scottie, thinking it was safe to ask since the entire class was chatty and the teacher was out of the room.

"Yeah," Scottie laughed, "all the time. He's baked outta his fucking mind most days."

I giggled, and, for some reason, asked, "D'you smoke?" I wasn't being serious; I was still laughing. My laughter ceased, though, when I detected Scottie's hesitance. I stopped what I was working on; set down the scissors, studying Scottie's face more carefully to measure his uncertainty. I asked the question more earnestly this time, "Well, do you?"

"Uhhh." Scottie looked down at his pencil nervously.

"Come on." I bumped his arm playfully. "You can tell me. I won't get mad."

"Then…uh… *Yeah*. I've tried it."

I chuckled lightly at his answer to hide my disappointment. "Did you like it?"

"Well…yeah," he admitted slowly, then asked, "Have you ever smoked?"

It was my turn to avert my gaze. I simply shook my head no and went back to cutting mask outlines. I did notice, through the corner of my eye, Scottie looking away too, seemingly nervous and embarrassed. Or maybe just disappointed.

◉

Disappointment filled me and the prom dress I stepped into, the slick fabric ensnaring my body much too tightly. I reached for the back to zip it up, but the zipper jammed halfway up my back. I let go, sighing. The dress was too small. Or I was too fat to fit in Olive's old prom dress.

"We can get you a new one at the mall," Mom offered, remaining hopeful and positive.

"Okay." I undressed slowly, careful not to turn towards my mom and reveal the ugly scars I made on my leg with a razor.

"I'll go get my keys," Mom said, as she left me alone so I could

Pertinendi

change back into my regular clothes. A few minutes later I could hear her keys jingling from down the stairs; and it wasn't long until that sound became the scraping of hangers dragging across the dress racks at department stores in the mall.

Mom sorted through the dresses promptly and at record pace, all the while throwing ones at me to try on.

I was ready to give up on the whole endeavor after about the fifth dress that looked ridiculous on me. But my hopes were raised when Mom unexpectedly gasped, "Ooo, Jovie. Come here! Look. This is perfect!"

I peered over her shoulder at the long, plum-colored gown that, when the florescent lights hit a certain way, sparkled mesmerizingly.

Mom immediately yanked it from the rack and shoved into my arms.

While trying this dress on in a dressing room, I realized how right Mom was—as always. *It's perfect,* I thought, aghast at my own reflection. The gown breathed fluidly down my body, snuggling against my skin as if it were tailor-made just for me. Its length was perfect, cascading all the way down to my toes. There would be no need for alterations or hems.

I turned to admire the backside of this dress. The straps crisscrossed in the back, adding a sexy flair over my pale skin.

"How's it look?" Mom asked, knocking on the stall door.

"Perfect," I breathed. "It's perfect."

Well, it was perfect until I looked down at the price tag. "Two hundred bucks?!" That was way, way, *way* out of the price range I usually shopped in.

"I'll get it for you," Mom insisted, despite me saying no out of sheer guilt. But she bought it anyway, with a slide of her credit card.

That night unending, torturous guilt haunted me in the form of an expensive dress. I couldn't go to sleep; I kept thinking about how I didn't deserve the dress, didn't deserve Mom's kind gesture, didn't deserve it one bit. Unable to take the internal agony anymore, I crept to the kitchen and slipped two one hundred dollar bills inside Mom's wallet—money I'd gotten for birthdays and Christmases over the years.

I sighed in relief once the debt was repaid. Things were okay now. The irrepressible guilt subsided, and I was able to, with a smile, hang my dress up in my closet, feeling excitement bubble in my gut for the impending day of prom...

◉

Prom fell on the last Saturday of April, which was the day I gently took my dress from its hanger and carefully slipped into its breathtaking fabrics. My hair was done up in a simple bun that my mom had styled for me, along with braids she delicately crafted and wrapped around the bun. Mom even did my makeup; patiently painting my lips with red-violet lipstick, my eyes with sugar plum eye shadow, and swiping my eyes with black mascara and eyeliner. Her finishing touches were dusting my cheeks with faint hues of blush and adding about half a bottle of hairspray to my hairdo.

I was still coughing from all the hairspray I inhaled when the doorbell rang.

It was Scottie.

My stomach did a nervous summersault. I hurried to tell my parents he was here to pick me up. This was the first time they'd be meeting Scottie—I'd been putting off introductions for a while now. I wasn't sure if they'd approve.

"You look beautiful," Scottie whispered in my ear when I opened the door, greeting him with a tight embrace. I stepped back, letting him into my house.

"Hi," was all Dad said, as he very firmly shook Scottie's hand, intimidation purposely smoldering in his eyes.

Scottie was suave and this didn't faze him. "It's nice to meet you finally." He welcomed a handshake from my mom next, then promised he'd take good care of me tonight.

Mom insisted on taking pictures of us. So, with redness in my face that wasn't because of makeup, we awkwardly stood in front of the fireplace to pose.

We posed a few more times later at the park where our prom group of fifteen people met at. The group was mostly a cluster of Jenny and Scottie's friends. The park was beautiful; I'd never been to it before. It brought back memories of Louisiana with all of its gorgeous willow trees and the glittering creek that sparkled more than my dress. Instead of introducing myself to the group like I should have, I drank in the creek's natural beauty. It almost made me want to cry. It was like home. I could lie on the big, craggy boulders with the turtles, soaking the sun into my pale skin, letting the willow fines flow through my fingertips.

"Jovie, smile." Scottie brushed me with his shoulder, tearing my gaze away from the creek.

I smiled, even though I didn't know why. Then I turned to the group, realizing that everyone's parents were taking pictures of us...

Flash.

Flash, flash.

Flash, flash, flash.

Dizzying strobe lights flashed rapidly at prom, lighting the gym in the blink of an eye, then making it go dark the next half second.

Scottie and I were sitting at a table, the glitter and masks we had made in art class decorating the tablecloth.

"Having fun?" he yelled over the music.

I nodded, a genuine smile on my face.

Scottie couldn't really dance either, so here we were at the table talking—more like yelling—at each other over the music. When the occasional slow song would come on, we'd join the web of dirty dancing high school kids, getting caught up in the song wrapped in each other's arms. It was quite romantic, especially surrounded by the wonderland of decorations we made together.

About the time prom was over, one of Scottie's friends stopped by our table, his tux noticeably stained with sweat. He gulped down a large glass of punch. He couldn't talk because his mouth was full, so he nodded to Scottie, holding up two of his fingers in the form of a peace sign.

But peace didn't find Scottie and I until prom was over and we sat in his quietly-rattling car, parked in an empty lot.

"That was really fun," I told him, sipping on the water we had stopped at a gas station to get. "Thanks for taking me. And thank you again for paying for dinner." I gave him a sweet smile, then took a long swig of water—it had gotten really hot in the gym after so long.

"Hey no problem," he said, after taking a sip of his fruity drink.

We set our drinks down in the cup holders, sitting in awkward silence, both waiting on each other to make the first move. Scottie's impatience made him succumb first. He leaned across the console to barely touch his lips to mine.

In the heightened moment of our kiss, I could feel the seatbelt buckle digging into my thigh painfully, but I ignored it; all my senses were under Scottie's heady spell...

I parted my lips against his, tasting his fruity breath, breathing in the thick scent of his cologne. My hands eased through the soft spikes of his hair as he pressed me closer.

Scottie touched the skin that my dress didn't cover, slowly working his fingers up to my shoulder where he tried to brush one of the dress straps off to the side. But the straps crisscrossed in the back —they weren't going anywhere. I was thankful for this, so I wouldn't have to speak up and tell Scottie not to go that far.

Somehow, though, he persisted on...going further and further but finding that there were no more stop signs...

If Scottie were water, I would be drowning beneath him in joyous agony...

His hands had given up on the dress straps, settling with touching my breasts over the silken cloth of the gown. And for some reason unknown, I never told him to stop.

I liked it.

Him touching me.

Even though it was much rougher than I would have preferred...

He didn't stop after my breasts. From my chest his hands slid down my stomach, plunging all the way down to my legs, then back up but under the fabric of the dress. His fingers brushed in between my thighs, just barely touching my panties.

"Wait," I breathed under his lips. I sat up a little in the passenger's seat, looking at Scottie with wide, innocent eyes. I swallowed hard, unable to tell him that I wasn't sure if I was ready for what he was about to do. He was edging on a part of me that was much too private, much too sacred to let him enter without at least talking about it first.

Scottie sighed heavily as he leaned away from me, brooding in his seat, clearly frustrated and withdrawn. He was angry, annoyed, and the internal wound he masked was slipping away too, uncovering the void that wanted to resurface at any given chance. I could feel it coming, the pain that came with his absence, without his touch…

I squeezed my eyes shut for a moment, thinking hard about what he was going to do. I persuaded myself frantically that I wouldn't mind him touching me there. I would be okay with it.

"Wait," I said again, fumbling on the words, "Okay. It's okay. I'm sorry. I-I'm just nervous."

Scottie's hardened face finally softened with a smile. "You're such a virgin." It was a joke, but I was too embarrassed to laugh. To my relief, Scottie came back to me. There was a new excitement in his movements that lured me back down in my seat as he climbed closer. His lips reunited with mine, hand back between my legs, gently sliding my panties to the side.

My heart hammered against the reddening walls of my chest. It was all I could hear until a soft noise escaped my parted lips. I relished in Scottie's touch, my eyes closing as I gave into the sensation, some part of me screaming in horror but delighting in the exhilaration.

◉

Summer finally came, and, along with it, the sweltering heat of two bodies wrapped up in each other. I spent most of those hot days with Scottie, in his room, on his bed, only to leave at about three in the morning—a time that far exceeded my curfew.

On the couch in Scottie's refurnished basement we'd watch movies, then, once the credits went up the screen, leaned into to each other, beginning what we started doing on prom night. One of these nights Scottie guided my hand down to his pants, pressing it there against the stiffening part of him.

I knew what he wanted me to do…

I looked into his eyes, seeing the black pupils and also seeing Stephan's black eyes that had hungrily gazed at me on Halloween night.

I didn't fight Scottie like I did Stephan. If doing things for him meant keeping him close and having him as a distraction, I'd do it.

Desperate.

That was me.

I needed Scottie.

I needed to fit into the beautifully mysterious puzzle he was; I wanted to be the puzzle piece he always needed to be full, to be complete. Or maybe it was the other way around...

But summer simmered in its baking rays a pain that wouldn't fade like the sunburns I had sustained while at the pool with Scottie and his family.

Distancing himself from me, Scottie became cold and indifferent about everything that involved us. Our dates were quiet and awkward. His texts were short. His sense of humor that used to make me laugh so hard became hurtful and dark. And his electrifying blue eyes that once shocked me back to life were now cold and heartless—they killed me.

There was no more respect in the way he talked to me or even in the way he touched me. It seemed to me that our past was too far gone; the way he had saved me from Stephan, then, years later, helped me to open up about that night instead of bury it further into my depression. Rather, the past, *our* past, was buried in lust. In the way Scottie and I would spend more time kissing and touching than talking and holding hands. Realizing all of these mistakes broke my heart, even before Scottie texted me on the fourth of July, asking if I could go get lunch with him.

Of course I would. I was all dressed up for him and at the restaurant within an hour. I opened the door, spotting Scottie at a booth in the corner. He had already ordered himself a drink, but nothing for me. This was unusual; he always ordered me water if he got to the restaurant first.

I sat down, greeting him with a smile and a, "Hey, how's it going?"

"Fine," he said dully, keeping his eyes on the chips and salsa before him. We were at the Mexican restaurant he had taken me to on our first date. We spoke a lot then, but now I didn't like the way he hardly said a word or looked at me. Something was off. And the horrible queasy ache in my stomach that made the burrito in front of me look highly unappetizing confirmed that something was very, very wrong.

"Is everything okay?" I asked Scottie, a pleading crack in my voice.

He shrugged. "Yeah."

No. It wasn't. I could tell.

We ate in silence. Maybe other tables chatted and our waiter came and went, but my world was quiet. All I could hear was my fast-beating and already broken heart; all I could feel was a familiar numbness seeping through the bandage Scottie had formed over my sadness.

"So what d'you wanna do after this?" I asked after the waiter gave us our ticket.

Scottie shrugged again.

"Well…" I picked my brain for things to do. "There's a new zombie movie out we could rent. It looks pretty good."

He didn't say anything, just slid out of the booth. I followed him like a stupid puppy.

"So?" I prompted when we were outside in the parking lot, the sun beams heating my face already with sweat. "What d'you wanna do?"

"I don't feel like doing anything."

"Oh." My shoulders slumped. "Okay. Well, uh, thanks for lunch. And… Have a good day, I guess." I went to my car, searching my purse for my keys.

"Heeey," the voice dragged out the word. I turned to the sound, surprised to see Scottie still standing behind me.

"Yeah?"

He swiped at his hair nervously, then popped his fingers, his eyes dropping to the pavement. "Look, I've never had to do this before, but I-I think we should stop seeing each other."

A transparent gust of rejection hurled at me, punching right through my chest. But I remained calm and unflinching. I kept my gaze steady with Scottie's pointy nose, as I slowly lifted my hand from my pocket to claw my arm. *Avert the pain*, I kept telling myself. *Focus on* this *pain.* I clawed myself harder, though the stinging in my heart burned more.

"Why?" I asked pathetically, my voice tight and small.

Scottie struggled to explain, but nothing made sense. "—I don't want you to change. And..."

I nodded on and on, taking it in like a zombie. Emotionless. Dead. "Did I do something wrong? Is there someone else?" My thoughts immediately went to Cheyenne Whore, and then to Hayley McAllister, a girl Scottie and his friends always swooned over.

"No," Scottie assured me. "It's not that at all." He kept trying to explain, using those senseless, strung-together words that phrased some sort of a sentence I couldn't fathom. He was trying so hard to explain but none of his words made any sense.

I finally looked up, stopping him short. "Okay," I said softly. "Okay." Why torture him? He didn't know what to say.

He outspread his arms slightly, an invitation to a hug. *This is it; the last time you'll ever hug him. Make it last.* But I didn't. I leaned in, only halfheartedly pressing myself to his body. I didn't even wrap my arms around him to keep him near, because there was nothing I could do anymore to make him stay, to make him want me.

I got into my car, shutting the door with all the strength I had left. When I faced the windshield, I couldn't believe it. It happened. We were done. Over.

I started the engine, and, when I pulled out of the parking lot, saw that Scottie was pulling out, too. We turned opposite directions, each going back to our own separate ways.

I held it in.

All that I was feeling.

Because I had to go home. But I didn't want to go home. I didn't want to face my parents while exploding with tears and heartache. I just wanted to go away, evaporate into nothing, feel nothing. But I didn't make the right turn onto the back roads when the time came. I found myself in the driveway.

"You're home early," was the first thing I heard when I opened the front door. It was Dad talking. He sat in his recliner, watching the hunting channel on TV.

"Yeah," I said, my voice straining to blockade the tanks of emotion charging in. "Me and Scottie just went out to lunch."

"Well that was quick," he noted. He then looked up, muted the TV. "Everything okay?"

"He broke up with me." The words tumbled from my lips, flipping through the air and crash-landing on my dad. I ran up the stairs to my room, locked the door, and collapsed on my bed. I cried…

Cried.

Cried.

Cried.

For hours.

Scottie used me. He used me up until he got bored. Interested at first only to clear his guilt, then from there it was just a game to see how far he could get with me. And when he'd taken all the territory of my body he knew I'd let him roam, he dropped me. I got that. But I used him too…

Through the tears in my eyes, I had a moment of clarity. I realized that, all this time, I was never in love with Scottie Robinson; rather, I was in love with the mask he put over my pain. His presence made me forget why I was even sad in the first place. Going out to dinner, to the movies, then parking somewhere to make out—all things that distracted my mind from what was really wrong.

He came back into my life, showed me a degree of kindness, when I couldn't, for the life of me, be nice to myself.

A mask.

That's all Scottie Robinson was to me, disguising my depression with his pretty face.

The mask.

It was gone now.

◉

I throw the mask from my face, watching the memory float back down to the black depths of Pertinendi. Without seeing through the mask, the once blue water is black again. Black as the depression that came flooding back into my life after Scottie had left me. It feels heavier even now, the depression, this sea. And being alone with it seems so much scarier than before…

Because Scottie was a reminder of how happiness could feel. Now, crashing back into its contrast, the feeling is so much worse, so much more intense than it ever was before.

Why did it always have to come back? The depression? Scottie was my most successful antidepressant that allowed me to feel again. Without him, everything went rotten. Without Scottie, I was numb. Heartbroken.

I fall down to the prom wreckage in the sand; the shattered mirrors and masks welcome my collapse into a shattered identity. When I was alive, I had tried *so hard* to be everything Scottie wanted, to do anything he asked. I longed to be his perfect girl, not realizing at the time that to achieve such a wish meant sacrificing being myself.

I turn my face to the mirror shards, seeing in their reflection a mysterious fog looming above. I sit up, only to have my face bombarded by the white wisps of vapor. Scared, I get up from where I lay, hurrying through the obscurity all around. I think I'm going the right direction through the sea, the way to Heaven, but it's hard to tell; all I see is gray and black.

I take another long step through the sand, noticing that the prom heels have dissolved from my feet. My gaze then follows up my body, and I see that I am no longer in my prom dress, but wrapped in a simple white gown.

I stop running, look up to find a peculiar little shack in the fog. It almost looks like a church, but terribly ramshackle and forgotten. I take a step towards the building, the feel of the sand suddenly piercingly cold. It's snow! Even the roof of the monument is snow-covered and frozen.

My shallow breaths join the fog in the air, as I walk up the three wooden stairs leading to the church. The door is opened to a crack; I hear a voice inside. The voice is sad. The voice is scared. The sound is that of someone crying…

I open the door all the way, revealing a spooky underwater altar with five rows of benches and a still-hanging cross on the wall before the aisle. Broken stained glass windows decorate the sidewalls, but no light is down here to make them shine, to make them beautiful. I see a girl sitting in the second bench, her head bowed but buried in her arms. She's the one crying. I take a step to tend to her, but I see someone else at the edge of the aisle.

"Angel!" I breathe, hurrying to wrap the stone in my arms. I pull

Pertinendi

away from our embrace, gasping, "What're you doing down here?"

The angel smiles, warming even this sea. "I came after you," Angel says, "I could not leave you behind now, could I?"

"Well, I would have, if I were you," I wink, grinning brightly. "But what about the demons? I thought they got you."

The angel shakes its graying head but quakes its stone structure too roughly. Bits of the stone crumble to the ground; cracks splinter throughout the statue's cemented skin.

I gasp, trying to catch the falling rubble of Angel. "Are you okay?"

"Yes. Yes, I am fine. Just weak. It is hard for me to be here in your depression. That is why you lost me."

"I'm so sorry," I apologize sincerely. "We can get going. I don't want you to break anymore."

"Now, now," the statue hushes me. "Let us go on together, but more carefully this time. There is still much to remember. Come." Angel presses its withered hand to my back, nudging me forward to the little girl at the bench.

"What's wrong with her?" I whisper to Angel, the sounds of heartbroken sobs filling the void of this sea.

"You tell me."

I swallow hard, turning my gaze to the wooden floor in shame. "I-I'd say she's…embarrassed about something…ashamed." I walk closer to the girl, reaching out for her but too afraid to touch her long, frosted, black hair and ice-blue skin. Her shoulders heave with sobs; tears hit the floor only to be absorbed in the black sea.

"Or maybe she's mourning over something," Angel guesses, watching me closely as I bite down on my lip. "I know about Scottie," Angel tells me. "I know." Understanding flows from the angel's tongue, wrapping around my soul like a warm blanket.

I break down like the girl, my sobs echoing hers. "I…" I take a deep breath, pressing my fingers to my lips to hide their tremors. "I cannot explain the…*shame*…I feel. Or felt." I stare at the colorful stained glass windows, their images illustrating the Virgin Mary. "I mean, Scottie was my first hot and heavy make out session. I'd only pecked a boy on the cheek before. Me and Scottie… We never went all the way with each other. I wouldn't let him. But we did…*things*—

things that I wasn't ready for. And I knew I wasn't ready but I did them anyway because I didn't wanna say no. I couldn't for some reason. I think I was just afraid that my saying no would hurt or upset him. I was so concerned with his feelings that I never once acknowledged my own. But when I finally did after he broke up with me I felt this—I *feel*—this *filthiness* inside of me that I can't clean. And no matter what I do, no matter what I tell myself, I can't shake it. I feel dirty, Angel. Something wasn't the same after Scottie. I just don't know what. Maybe it's shame. I'm just so ashamed..." I press my hands to my face, sobbing, "And I feel humiliated and embarrassed. And-and that's all I can say out loud."

The angel is calm. The angel is patient, so wholesomely understanding. "Jovie, my dear, you do not have to feel ashamed of those things. I understand that it is hard to forgive yourself for doing something you were not ready for, but know: that is simply a part of growing up. You mature. You learn lessons. And that is *nothing* to be ashamed of. And perhaps the 'filthiness' that overwhelms you so is there because you did not mean what your body said when you were intimate with him. You didn't loved him. If you would have truly loved him and he returned it, that dirtiness would not be polluting your heart, your soul. Love makes those things beautiful. But for other reasons, they can make the experience very hurtful, even selfish."

I wipe the tears from my eyes, then sit down next to the crying girl that is frozen. "I think," I admit, "a piece of me still lays in his bed—naked, raw, and exposed. It's a part of me I'll never get back." I look at the girl's empty hands, her arms that hold nothing.

"Innocence," Angel says softly to complete my thought.

It belongs to Scottie now, wrapped in his navy blue sheets, trapped in the feather bristles inside his pillows, cast away in the very pores of his chest, so deep I could never find again. "I gave him too much of me," I confess to the statue, to the girl. "Parts that he didn't deserve or handle with enough care and respect. It wasn't until after he left me that I realized what he took with him. In those months that we were together, I grew up too fast. And I wanted to retrace time, go back to being a kid, innocent and ignorant. Because those things I did with Scottie—they *disgusted* me. Or maybe...I'm just disgusted with myself that I ever did those things with him. That I allowed myself to let him take a very precious part of me."

I look up at the cross hanging on the wall behind the altar. All I can do is bow my head in shame and feel the crying girl's sobs rising in my own chest.

"Come," the statue says. "Let's move on." Angel guides me down the aisle; we leave the crying girl behind—there's no way to restore her, only accepting her for what she'll never be again. Innocent.

Angel steps out into the snow, but I stop at the threshold of the church door. "Wait," I tell Angel, an ambivalent panic in my face. "There's something else about this place, why it's a church and why it's so empty. I think I know." But so does Angel…

"During that time in your life," Angel says, "you were beginning to lose your faith. In men, in the world, in yourself, even a higher power."

I can only nod in agreement, but also in shame. Angel, to my surprise, offers a forgiving hand to me, leading me out of the building and down the icy steps.

We walk around the church, continuing our journey across the gloomy seafloor of this depression. During our walk, Angel asks me about the cuts all over my skin.

I try to make light of them, laughing, "Well, the fish around these parts are razors if you haven't noticed. They don't bite…they cut." I rub my scars dramatically, then look up at Angel to see if my answer is enough. It's not. I sigh loudly. "It's hard to explain."

"Jovie, please try."

I comb my fingers through my hair, letting the long strands gather as a curtain to shield my face. "It's just…cutting. It-It's not something I did to hurt myself on the outside. I was trying to carve out what was causing me so much pain on the inside."

"Your depression?"

"Yes, but it's not just that. Over time there became not one but *numerous* reasons why I cut. First, it was just to feel something other than my depression when it came back. Another reason was that sometimes when I got mad or frustrated with something, the anger would just boil inside me, getting all pent up, and I knew no rational way of dealing with it, no way of stifling it anymore, so I'd cut it out.

Let all that rage ooze out in red streams down my skin. Eventually, I cut because I wasn't angry at the world or anyone in particular. I was just mad at myself."

"Why? What could you have possibly done to convince yourself that you deserve such self-inflicted pain?"

"I'm not perfect," I told Angel, stopping dead in my tracks, feeling the anger rising again in my soul. "I wasn't good enough for *anything*. You can tell me that that's just my depression talking, but back then it was the truth. My mom was the successful manager at a hospital, my dad the radiologist, and my sister the soon-to-be nurse. But me? Who was I? The Nothing. The big fat failure with no future. I couldn't even get a job at a fast food restaurant. I was a mistake, Angel; everything I did was wrong. Cutting was a way of punishing myself. Because when I looked in the mirror, I didn't see who my parents wanted me to be, not even who I wanted to be. In the mirror—was a monster. A zombie. And I *hated* her. I hated me. Cutting was a way of showing that hate, making me feel it, making the *monster* inside of me *hurt*."

"No one is perfect, Jovie," the angel reminds me.

"I know, but I didn't care. I still wanted to be. Because if I was perfect, then maybe, just maybe, everything would feel and be perfect too."

"Perfection, and trying to accomplish it, can make one very, very sick, Jovie," Angel warns. But this I already know…

I suddenly hunch over, gagging violently. Angel comes to my side, holding me upright so I won't fall to my knees in the sand…

But the sand isn't sand anymore…

It is some awful chunky goo that is so putrid that I gag again, only this time something comes up…

A memory…

PART 6

HER NAME WAS BULIMIA

Blood-red chunks of what was spaghetti splattered down in the shower drain, along with the water raining atop my back from the showerhead. I took my finger out from my throat, panting, vision blurring with tears.

I had overeaten. Too much spaghetti meant fat. So, I did what Olive used to do after we'd make her eat—I threw it right back up. But only once. Just enough to make the sickening fullness in my stomach subside. I was too scared to do it again—I didn't want to hurt myself. I just didn't want to get fat. That was all.

I wanted to be skinny. I wanted to make Scottie notice me tomorrow in the classes we had together this year…the last year…

Senior year.

The beginning of the end was tomorrow. Words couldn't describe how nervous I was about the things I was always nervous about every year. Like, if I'd be able to find someone to sit with at lunch and if I'd have anyone to talk to in my classes. I'd have Scottie in anatomy and drawing classes. But, as far as I knew, we weren't on speaking terms. I hadn't heard a word from him since the fourth of July, not even a text.

Screw him, I thought angrily, twisting the shower knob off. I threw back the shower curtain, grabbed the towel, and twisted it around my dripping body. I ripped a brush through my hair, scowling down at the ACT practice booklet I sometimes skimmed through when I was using the bathroom.

And then I had to admit it to myself...

I wasn't only nervous about the usual things this year. I had to start thinking about college, and I had to take the ACT again, since, when I took it over the summer, I had made the pathetic, measly score of only sixteen.

My parents were so proud.

Not.

My goal for the second time around was to score at least a twenty—because I was pretty darn certain I'd never be able to surpass Olive's solid thirty.

After changing into some comfy pajamas, I grabbed the ACT study booklet, then settled down in my bed for the night. I turned on my nightstand lamp, illuminating the multiple choice hell of the ACT. I flipped to the first question. It was about grammar. I read the question twice, the answers more than five times, then sat up, my brows furrowing in confusion. "All the answers sound right!" I hissed. Sighing, I guessed an answer then turned the page to the answer key. "What?! It's B?!" Of course. I was wrong. *Fuck it!* I clenched my teeth, threw the booklet across the room, and flipped my lamplight off. I yanked the covers over my shoulder, burrowing deep into the cozy nest of blankets.

I glared at my pillow, frustrated tears streaming down my cheeks. The world felt like it was crashing in on me. So heavy. I wasn't ready...

I wasn't ready for the ACT...

I wasn't ready for senior year...

I wasn't ready to grow up.

◙

Grown up was everyone at school the next day. With their afterschool jobs, their college applications all filled out, their high ACT scores... their entire fucking futures planned out flawlessly. It pissed me off. *They* pissed me off. *Everyone.* School. The entire institution of it. It was just stupid.

Or maybe I was stupid, and I just didn't fit in with all the smartness going on.

Grown up was how everyone looked. With their dyed hair, their fake-baked skin, dolled-up faces, 'roid-raging biceps, and name brand clothes.

All this growing up made me want to throw up. I especially wanted to upchuck from the nervous ache in my stomach when anatomy class came around. I would soon have to face Scottie...

I was the first one to the class—as usual—so I took a seat in the back. I chewed on my necklace as the classroom filled up, the faces familiar but none belonging to Scottie—the face I'd seen in the dark, so close to my lips...

But as the bell rang there he was at the threshold, looking nervous like me, but keeping it cool. That confident strut he asserted now seemed cocky to me and his pants were hanging off his ass—Dad was right, he needed to pull them up. He took the last seat in the front, eyes never grazing over me in the back. He didn't see me. That was probably for the best. I guessed, "I think we should stop seeing each other" literally meant he never wanted to see me again. I understood that. But we had classes together! How could we stop "seeing" each other? I'd see him all the freaking time! And maybe he'd see me too if he paid attention, but he didn't.

It was truly amazing how *wrong* I was about him. Once perceiving this beautiful soul within, dreaming about him so much that I felt like I knew his heart already, even when I'd only uttered a few words to him.

But, all this time, I was always in the background of his world, thinking of him as this wonderful hero, this mysterious character, tough but gentle, quietly popular, and a suave gentleman. Though after dating him and seeing how much he had changed since the last time I'd talked to him, he wasn't who I thought he'd be, the guy I'd fallen in deep infatuation with over the years. Or maybe he always was this person, but that infatuation, that blind fondness I had for him, made me not see all the ways he disrespected me and treated me like a toy—something he used up until he got bored.

I closed my eyes for a moment during the class, letting school wrap up in the darkness behind my lids. Because I felt him. I felt Scottie still. Then I felt Stephan. I felt them both, on every inch of my skin that they had touched, that Scottie had kissed, licked, and had his way with. Every pore on me perspired the deepest regret and disgust.

I felt so much toward Scottie during class, and all he seemed preoccupied with was fiddling with his pencil!

It was like we never dated at all. Never said a word to each other, never kissed, never touched or hugged. He ignored me. In the hallways, in the classes we had together. We existed now as we did in junior high, both of us simply not knowing what to say to each other anymore.

I sighed in the middle of the math syllabus lecture. Algebra two. I was put in it with all the juniors because my math skills were embarrassingly awful. But to make math even more torturous, my teacher was a prick, and then the cherry on top of it all was that he had a whole lot of pent up sarcasm in his system. Cue the sigh and my head falling into my palm, as I aloofly skimmed through the Latin book we were given in anatomy class.

My anatomy teacher informed us that knowing Latin root words would help us learn the big medical terms we'd be studying later on in the year. I was quite intimidated by the class, especially as I flipped through the Latin dictionary part of the book. I turned through each section; having to stop at the P's when my teacher looked up at the class to make sure we were all paying attention. I looked up at the podium he stood behind, eyes focused. Once the teacher averted his gaze back down to the syllabus he was reading from, I turned my attention back to the Latin text.

The first word my eyes fell upon jumped out at me for some reason and, in doing so, stuck in my mind. I tried pronouncing it in my head—it had a cool sound to it. *Perta... Pertin... Pertinendi? Yeah! Pertinendi.* I especially liked what it meant. It had a few definitions, but the one that stood out to me the most was "of belonging".

Belonging.

I didn't feel such a beautiful emotion sitting here in this desk. I didn't feel it with the girls I sat by at lunch or with my mom and dad when they'd get home from work.

I was like the autumn leaves that flew through the air that fall, always wandering, always floating, trying to find a place to land, but never knowing just where that should be.

Belonging wasn't even in my reflection. My pale skin, dark hair, green eyes—they made up a stranger. Wherever Jovie had gone, I didn't know. She wasn't beneath the fog in the mirror after a shower, wasn't behind the makeup on my skin. She was nowhere. She was…

◙

"Are you depressed again?" Mom asked one day out of the blue.

I shrugged.

"All you do is mope around the house. What happened to Francesca and Sc—" She was about to say his name, but then it seemed to dawn on her memory that he'd broken up with me months ago. And I didn't even want to get into the whole Francesca ordeal. She'd been upset with me all summer since I blew her off to be with Scottie. I deserved what she was doing to me now—blowing me off.

"Francesca's busy," I lied, turning my attention back to my homework on the kitchen countertop.

Mom turned from the macaroni boiling on the stove, her lips pulling to the side in concern. "D'you think your medicine isn't doin' what it's supposed to anymore?"

I shrugged, then, with my voice muffled by my hand over my mouth, said "I stopped taking them, like, a year ago."

"Why would you do that?" Mom gasped, her face a disapproving scowl.

"I thought I was better."

"Clearly you're not."

I shrugged again, and, this time, it was hard to shrug. A weight pressed down on my shoulders—the old familiar friend. My eyes suddenly filled to the brim with tears that I didn't want to shed, especially in front of my mom. I hated the word depression. It was so heavy, like an entity of its own, always waiting, pressing, containing…forever haunting me.

"Jovie, what's the matter? D'you think you're depressed again?"

I could only nod.

"Why didn't you tell me?"

I sniffled loudly, wiping the water from my face. "Cuz I didn't wanna make you cry again."

"What?"

"You cried last time at the doctor when she told me I was depressed. I didn't wanna make you sad."

Mom looked to the ground, then back at the stove to hide her face. "I'm sorry you feel that way. Start taking your medicine, okay?" She only looked back at me to make sure I nodded.

I took my antidepressant that night, thinking that maybe Jovie Blue existed somewhere in the tiny blue pills, waiting to dissolve back into my system once consumed.

So I consumed them.

Day after day.

Gradually feeling lighter, more myself, but I knew deep down the pills weren't expelling the demon always haunting my senior year…

The future.

Seniors in high school had to start thinking about it, planning it, finding themselves in it. But, for some reason, I couldn't. I'd research different colleges, only to break down in tears, even bang my wrists on the computer desk to avert the pain raging inside me, the *fear* that not even the pills could hush. I'd research careers and majors and minors only to figure out that I couldn't see myself pursuing any of them.

A teacher?

I'd lose my mind.

A surgeon?

I'd throw up on the patients.

A therapist?

I'd cry with the patients.

Another career, another excuse as to why I wouldn't be able to do the job. All just labels. They weren't who I was—a poet…or…at least I wanted to be. But what sap would pay be to be one? To write?

No one.

The future, to me, had a dark halo surrounding it. In my mind, the future wasn't bright, happy, or fulfilling. It was nothing. Just blank uncertainty.

Blackness.

Pertinendi

◉

Blackness filled my vision during anatomy class one day later in the semester. We were discussing bones, facial bones to be exact.

Now, I was not one to be incredibly squeamish by any means—I was a horror movie addict after all. But, for some reason, the way the teacher kept touching the skeleton dummy, jamming her finger through the…zygomatic arch? Whatever, the cheekbone. It was revolting!

And I could see Scottie in the corner of my eye now because the teacher assigned us seats after the first day of class. He sat in the row next to me, a few seats behind. He could see me. Always see me.

It made me nervous.

I sat in the front, where I hated to be, all eyes behind me, watching, judging, laughing.

It made me nervous.

The teacher kept touching the skeleton, then scribbling on the white board in her messy scrawl. She talked too fast, reviewed the bones too fast, wrote on the board too fast.

I didn't understand anything that was happening.

And I could still see Scottie, there, far in the corner of my vision.

I was getting dizzy. So I blinked hard a few times, setting down my pencil. I tried concentrating on the board, but I couldn't focus. My heart beat against my chest much too fast, palpitated painfully, then raced even faster.

Pink anxiety highlighted my hot skin, glaring with sweat.

It was so stuffy in this room, so many bodies, so much heat.

I kept tapping my foot on the ground, a steady pulse to focus on instead of the chaos within.

Black static filled my vision suddenly, caving in, then blowing away—a tease. I pinched myself to snap out of it, but it wasn't enough. So I clawed at my arm, scratched my wrists—an attempt to stay in reality, because Jovie was fading. I was so far. Far away in my head. Like a glass wall separated me from reality.

I could no longer focus; it took too much effort, more energy than I had. My mind just wanted to sleep; body shuddered with confusion, with anxiousness.

I couldn't take it much longer. Blackness was descending in my vision again, this time staying and not going away. I needed to go to the nurse.

But I needed to finish taking notes first. This was a hard class; I had to stay and get all the information on the board.

I held my breath, picked up my pencil, and tried to take the notes, focusing until class wound down.

Finally, the teacher finished the lecture, asking the class if they had any questions over the material.

I raised my shaking hand.

The teacher looked at me, nodded for me to go ahead and speak.

"Can I go to the nurse?" The class was so quiet. Why was no one talking? Why did everyone look at me so strangely?

"Of course. I'll write you a pass," the teacher answered, her eyes holding a bit of concern when they studied me more carefully.

I slid out of my chair, holding onto the desk so I wouldn't fall. I could hardy see, barely breathe. I took the pass from her, and, just when I was about to open the door to leave, the teacher asked me if I was okay. I wanted to whip around to her and snap, "No fucking shit?! I'm asking to go to the nurse! Of course I'm not 'okay'!" Instead, though, I said faintly, "No. I feel like I'm about to pass out." I opened the door that used to be green but now looked like static on a TV screen. I turned the corner of the darkening hallway…

The last thing I saw before all was dark was the vomit-colored floor of the school as my face hit the tile…

Then blackness engulfed my world.

It seemed like only a moment later my head was throbbing and classrooms and lockers were passing me by in a nauseating blur. I looked down at myself.

A wheelchair?

Why am I in a wheelchair?

"Jovie?"

I turned around to the voice. An older woman was pushing me along.

"I'm the school nurse, Mrs. Ellis. How's your head? Your teacher said you may have bumped it when you fell."

"Uhh…" I was getting dizzy again.

"I'll give you something for the pain here in just a second." She turned me into the nurse's office, then helped me onto one of the beds. Gathering some painkillers from the medicine cabinet, she asked me if we had been dissecting something in class today.

"No, just taking notes," I answered.

This seemed to puzzle her. "Are you squeamish?"

I shrugged. I honestly didn't know anymore.

"Here you go." She handed me two paper cups, one filled with water, the second containing two pills. I tossed both cups back, first the pills, then the water.

"Thanks," I sighed, lying on my back again and letting the world settle back around me in its usual, less dizzying place.

Nurse Ellis pulled up a chair next to the bed, proceeding to ask me a few questions about my symptoms. When she was done considering my explanation, she said, "Sounds like you may've had an anxiety attack or something. You may wanna see your doctor and get that checked out." She rolled back to her desk, shuffling through the paperwork on her desk. "By the way, you can lay there till you feel better." She gave me a nice smile, then whirled around to her computer.

The bell rang a few minutes later. I waited for the hallways to clear until I headed to the cafeteria for lunch. Before I got up, though, I reached into my bag to fish for my cell phone. I flipped it open, checking for any messages…particularly worried texts from Scottie.

Zero messages.

Figures.

I flipped my phone shut, then stood from the bed slowly. "Thank you for your help," I told the nurse. "I think I feel better now."

"Not quite as woozy?"

"Yeah." I tried to smile. "Thanks again," I said over my shoulder, as I pushed the glass door open.

The cafeteria was its usual boisterous volume flooding into my ears in a thick, hazy drone. I sat down by the group of girls I normally sat by, unable to ever keep up with their conversations. I kept my eyes down on my sandwich and yogurt. But when I looked up at the bodies all around, the blurs, their sounds a distorted hum, it frightened me, made me nervous and shaky again.

And there, at the table in front of mine, a couple was arguing about something. The girl fumed at the guy who didn't seem to give a care. Then it seemed like all of school billowed away in the freezing air-conditioned draft. All I could see was the couple. All I could hear was their bickering…

Hours later, the bickering I'd heard in the cafeteria became the voices of my parents. They argued in the kitchen, whispering harshly about bills, about work, about everything.

I listened to the conversation from the bottom of the staircase, my mind still bloated with the hums of the cafeteria and now the voices of my parents…

Fighting.
Fighting.
Fighting.
Their voices, voices…
Always fighting…
I *hated* it.
I hated the sound of it, harsh and piercing and heartbreaking…
The sound was all I could hear until all fell silent after two doors slammed.

My phone vibrated then, interrupting the unsettling stillness in the house. I flipped open my phone, surprised to see a text from Francesca. She was asking if I wanted to go with her to the local animal shelter tomorrow to help her get more community service hours for some honors club she was in. I considered going for a moment, looking around the sinister house, its quiescent scream morphing into crippling tension.

I texted Francesca back, agreeing to go with her tomorrow. I really needed to get out of the house anyway.

But outside the house another storm brewed. It cracked the sky with lightning bolts, vibrated the floorboards with pounds of thunder. Alarmed by the ruckus, Pumpkin stood up, her ears perked. From her throat a guttural bark ripped through the house, seeming to echo into the next day…

Early the next morning at the animal shelter, barking echoed through the fur-contaminated air and the many cages all around. I shed my jacket once inside, shaking off the light rain from my hair. Francesca stood by the front desk, chatting with the other volunteers that were from a local church. I greeted her with a smile, then waited for instructions like the rest until the founder of the establishment finally came to the front.

"Hi, everyone. The name's Lydia. Thank you all for helping me today." She clapped her dark hands together, smiling down at us. "Well, let's get to it. I want *you*, *you*, and *you* to clean the cages outside. And *you* and *you*—work on cleaning the indoor cages. Pooper-scoopers're in the back. And…" Her chocolate eyes fell upon Francesca and me. "You two replenish the food and water bowls. Got it?"

"Food's this way," Francesca murmured, tugging my shirt in the direction she wanted me to follow her. We broke into the food bags, scooping out mountains of dog food then dumping them into the small silver bowls. "So," Francesca began, attempting to break the awkward silence. "How've you been?"

"Uh, all right, I guess. You?"

"Stressed." She went on to brag about all the prestigious colleges she applied to, rant about how work was busy because the holiday season was near, and complain about the mess of dramas going on in her life.

"Aww, I'm so sorry. I really hope things settle down soon."

"Me too. So did you take the ACT in October?"

I nodded, reluctant to talk about a daunting subject such as the ACT. "I don't know my score yet. I kinda don't wanna know." I made an anxious face, then scooped more dog food into an empty bowl.

"Did you hear about Scottie and Cheyenne?"

"What about them?" The letters, the sound of them strung together forming his name, let seep an awful pain into my gut.

"They both went and got high together after the ACT."

"Scottie smokes?"

"*Duh.* He's hardcore with that shit. You didn't know?"

"He told me he tried it... But-but I didn't know it was a regular thing." I felt even sicker, this time filthiness dusting my soul, like a stain setting in—something I could never, ever clean.

"Well, now you know."

I stood upright, brows narrowing in anger down at Francesca. "Why didn't you tell me that before?" It was all I could do not to yell at her. "You knew he was a pothead and didn't warn me before you set us up? What the hell, Francesca?!"

She laughed at my aggressiveness that was equivalent to that of a kitten. "I thought you knew," she shrugged. "And hey, I was just trying to help you out cuz you liked the guy. Look, I'm sorry you guys broke up. But at least you got to spend a few months with him, even went to *prom*."

I heaved a sigh, picking up a few filled bowls to put in the cages. My cheeks burned with ferocity, heart beat in adamant pounds that set my skin ablaze with sweat beneath my long-sleeved shirt.

I set bowls down in two cages, then came upon a small pin encaging a tiny dog, its coat fuzzy and white. I set down the last bowl in its cage, and, when I stood up, felt someone behind me.

"She won't eat it."

I turned to the voice. It was the owner of the place, Lydia.

"Her owner passed away recently. I think she's heartsick, so she won't eat anything, not even a scrap." She bent down, nudging the bowl of food forward, but the dog turned her face the other way. "See."

"Poor thing," I frowned, sorrow lacing my voice.

"Her name's Willow, by the way." Lydia gave the dog one last sympathetic gaze, then went back to the front desk.

I reached down in the pin to pet her, but let my hand drop after a moment. I saw in the dog's eyes something familiar, something that made me sad...

I saw myself.

My lips parted at the sight, uneasiness wrinkling my forehead. I quickly turned around, rushing back to assist Francesca with the dog food.

Around lunchtime, the volunteers and I took a break. The others sat down together by the front desk, talking about other volunteer projects and church activities. Francesca had left for the break to go cash her paycheck. So I sat in the back with the animals, nibbling on the peanut butter sandwich I had packed.

I swallowed down a small bite of bread, unable to eat much more. I kept thinking about what Francesca had said about Scottie and Cheyenne and drugs, feeling more and more like I was going to hurl. I gave up on eating; wrapped the sandwich back up in the paper bag. I got up to throw it away, but stopped by Willow's pin. I looked down at her scruffy face, her glazy eyes.

Determination, just a faint flare of it, suddenly ignited inside of me, whispering to me in the back of my mind that it was okay to try and help this dog with its sadness, even when I didn't know how to help myself with such a problem.

Holding my breath, I stepped inside the dog's pin and knelt down beside her curled body. I slid the sandwich from the bag, peeling the two slices into smaller pieces. Very gently, I patted Willow's back to coax her attention my way. She perked her ears, turned her face to me just barely. I held out a piece of bread smothered in peanut butter. She gave it a dubious sniff, then, to my giddy surprise, a lick. Eventually, she took the entire piece into her mouth.

"Goooood girl," I cooed, petting her soft coat as she practically inhaled the rest of the sandwich pieces. She licked her lips hungrily, sniffing the paper bag up and down in search for more sandwich crumbs. When she found nothing, she got up from her bed to lap at my fingers. An effortless smile broke out onto my lips when I noticed her tail wagging. Willow looked up at me, her black eyes reflecting a grinning stranger, a beautiful girl I didn't see nearly enough.

The cloudy skies observed this girl from afar when I stepped out into the breezy cold at the end of the volunteer day. I started up my car, pulling out onto the back roads that led me home. In my window, the green hills of Missouri went by, then the gray statues and headstones of a cemetery—the stone angels smiling at me as I drove along.

I rolled down the window to let in the crisp, cool breath of winter sigh against my face, kiss my chapped lips. I breathed deeply, my lips curling into a smile as I took in the sight of beautiful sunrays leaking through the cloud cover like heavenly gold.

Today is a good day, I thought, a rare feeling of peace washing away everything but myself. Today, I was okay. Today, I felt like Jovie Maureen Blue. Me again. And completely me. As if even depression had a vacation day, leaving me at ease for a while. Or maybe it was that I had helped someone. Willow. I gave her a moment's peace. Now, in return, I was given my own…

I tapped my thumbs along to the radio, nodding my head and humming.

I was alive.

And I was okay.

Life seemed worth living.

I could feel myself letting go, letting go of the sickness within… It was gone for now, maybe long enough for me to move on.

If only depression were so kind…

It was as if the mental illness had an elastic noose tied around my neck; because every time I'd feel myself getting better, embracing just a tiny sliver of hope and distance from the darkness within, I'd just snap right back to where I was before.

Only worse.

The impact of falling back into the nightmare of depression and having to relive it from the beginning was Hell. It was when such relapses occurred that I'd question the cycle of my emotions that always led to it—the inevitable domination the illness had over my mind and now my soul. How could I ever make it end?

◉

THE END crept up the television screen at the conclusion of a Christmas movie showing. Rudolph the Red-Nosed Reindeer was flying off into the snowy night, saving the day while triumphant music blared in the background.

I sniffled and wiped my own red nose, then reached for a tissue on the computer desk. Lighting my face in ominous blue shades, the computer screen featured the different colleges I was applying to. I had the applications here on the desk, a pen ready to help me fill them out. The only problem…

I still didn't know which college I wanted to attend.

And I had no clue what to major in.

But I filled them out, writing my new and improved ACT score of twenty-two on the line.

Where do you see yourself in four years? another line demanded. I pressed my lips together, oh so tempted to scribble down: *Being in debt up to my fucking eyeballs thanks to the ridiculously criminal price tag of this college education! That's where I see myself, you assholes!*

I didn't write that down of course.

The truth was…I didn't know what to write that was both the truth and what would give them the answer they wanted. Maybe this would suffice: *In four years, I hope to succeed in a career that brings me both purpose and happiness. In four years, I also see myself applying to graduate school, getting married, having children, and being happy with my life.*

No.

That was a lie.

What I meant was this: *How am I supposed to know? I don't know who I am. I don't know who I'm supposed to be. And you sit there, and you tell me that I have to figure it out NOW. Know NOW. Well guess what?! I don't fucking know right NOW!*

But Mom tells me not to worry; she tells me I have all the time in the world to figure things out. But if that were true, why does everyone at school demand that I have a plan, demand I know what I want to do with my life? Demand that I know who I am and who I want to be? *Why?*

And why was it so hard for me to answer their questions: *What do you want to be when you grow up? Where do you see yourself in such and such years? What career? What major? What minor? What future do you want?*

Plan it NOW, know NOW, act on it NOW.

Because time is running out, and if you don't you'll work in fast food for the rest of your life. You'll never get a job. You'll be a fucking loser!

Loser.

Loser.

Loser.

The college applications screamed up at me... "LOSER!"

And I can't make decisions. Losers always make wrong choices. I'm still a kid, I'm still a kid. I'm just a kid. I can't make decisions... I'm... I'm...

Afraid.

Afraid of deciding, afraid of failing. So afraid that I don't even want to try.

My breathing became disturbingly jagged and broken as more sobs erupted in the back of my throat. I bowed my head, fingers reaching to my hair where they pulled at the strands with utter vexation.

I felt like I was having another anxiety attack, but my medicine was supposed to stifle such feelings...

I was just so angry though...

I didn't know what to do...

I didn't know who I was...

I didn't know how to face the future...

So the anger toppling through the borders of my control finally burst. Like a reflex to the stress of it all, I threw the college papers into the air. Then, sitting in a daze as they fell down all around me, time seemed to pass me by and by and by...

◉

Graduation caps fell down all around. The red-gowned blurs all laughing and smiling because our class of 2011 had finally made it through high school. In the midst of all the commotion, a quiet voice in my head was the clearest, wondering, *Is it really over? Is it really time to grow up? Or did that time pass long ago?*

I swallowed hard, getting up with everyone else to make my way through the mass of people in search for my parents. I spotted them ten minutes later outside in the parking lot.

"Congratulations!" Nana appeared from the group my parents and sister formed. Her arms wrapped around me in a tight hug. It had been so long since I'd last seen Nana, my best friend. It had been much too long.

Pertinendi

"Thanks for coming, girl," I smiled, pulling away from her. Nana's hair wasn't the sunny blonde I remembered as a child. I supposed it no longer got the chance to absorb the sunshine because we never played outdoors anymore. It absorbed fluorescents, thanks to having to study and work. But that didn't mean her sunny personality had dimmed. She was still the towering, lanky gem she always was, remaining, still, an amazingly sweet person. She hadn't changed at all.

Instead of going to project graduation with the rest of my fellow classmates, I hung out with Nana since she'd driven all the way from Louisiana to see me graduate. She spent the night at my house. We stayed up all night catching up, while old Disney movies we put in around the clock played in the background. Candy and junk food were sprawled across the living room floor—something I'd need to clean before my parents woke up in the morning.

"So did you ever figure out where you're goin' to college?" Nana asked, then popped some candy into her mouth.

"Yeah. *Finally*. I only applied to two colleges, and the one that's closest is the one I'm going to. It's, like, maybe two or three hours away. So it's not far. I actually went to the campus before but didn't realize it till I researched the school. My art class in high school could get extra credit if we went to one of the art shows held by the art majors there. Me and that girl, Francesca—I think I've told you about her—well, we went, and I actually really liked the campus." I shrugged. That was my decision in the end. I had no clue if it was the right one though.

"Are you sure you don't wanna go to school with me in Louisiana? We could be roommates," she offered with a bright beam, her soft brown eyes full and hopeful.

"I can't, remember? Out of state tuition."

"Right," she frowned. "That really sucks."

"Yeah," I agreed with my mouth full of the cookies we had baked. "I mean, I would *love* to go back to school with you and all our old friends again. That would be amazing!"

Nana's face suddenly fell, her eyes dropping to the candy wrappers on the carpet. "Everyone changed, Jovie. I think, besides me, you wouldn't recognize anyone. You remember Casey Monroe and Tori Vincent?"

"Mhhmm."

"Well, Casey's not a virgin anymore, and Tori gave Trenton Baker a blow job! It's disgusting!"

"What?! You're kidding!"

"Nope, I'm not."

It was a long moment before I could stop laughing from the flighty shock.

"Those aren't just rumors either," Nana went on. "They tell me those things cuz they're all I really have to hang out with now." She gave me a sad look that I returned wholeheartedly. "I don't mind that stuff, I really don't; it's when they turn the question around to me. I've never had a boyfriend and…"

"They look down on you for that," I guessed, pursing my lips in annoyance at her friends.

"Yeah. More for being a virgin, I guess."

"Well, there's nothing wrong with that. I think it's sweet you wanna wait for marriage." And Nana *would* wait. She was very conservative. I was always convinced she was born in the wrong era. She belonged more in the fifties or even the eighties since the majority of space on her iPod was filled with music from that period. "Just," I said, "don't worry about what they think. Okay? People… change. And sometimes it's not always what we'd want them to turn into but you still have to let them go do their own thing. One of the nice things about us is that we don't. We're still the same nerds we were in the fifth grade."

Nana's eyes seemed to reminisce to the past. Laughter then filled the living room at whatever she was remembering. "Yeah," she giggled. "You're right. We are." Nana finished chewing her gummy candy, her face growing more somber by the minute. She swallowed, saying, as her eyes met mine, "But Jovie, you *have* changed. I've noticed. Every time we talk on the phone you sound so sad and distant. Like you're fading away. So what's wrong?"

I waited till the burning lump in my throat cooled before I spoke. "I just… I mean… High school. I was always a nomad. And…now college. The real world. The *unknown*. I-I feel like I don't belong anywhere in it. I look in the mirror and… And I don't know who I am."

"You're Jovie," Nana tried to console.

"That's just my name," I reminded her. *I'm empty. Something's missing, Nana*, I wanted to tell her, to cry to her.

"You shouldn't talk like that. You'll do great in college. All you gotta do is study and you'll be fine. Your roommates are gonna love you cuz you're a good person. Okay? Don't worry so much."

◉

But I did worry. All summer I worried and worried, fretted and fretted, picturing myself in college, in class, in a dorm…losing my mind.

I worked my first job that summer cleaning apartments. And every day, I'd think about college, finding myself scrubbing harder and harder at the baseboards, the white paint nearly rubbing off.

I had to stop myself, take a deep breath, and summon gratitude for this job that I didn't want to lose. I was lucky enough to get it in the first place.

I really didn't mind the job at all. I…actually…kind of…*liked* cleaning. I could make things once ugly and tarnished pretty again. I could wash away the grime, the scuffs, the imperfections.

I could make things appear perfect.

But, deep within my mind, the black stain of depression lingered; I couldn't clean it, not even with the pill I swallowed every day. The quietly rumbling storm in my head had blown far into the back regions of my mind, where it stayed there, numb. A winter storm, frozen inside. Such a storm didn't scare me as much as the external one did. The world outside my own head. The real world. And never did it fail to frighten me with its looming thunderclaps…

Lighting bolts slashed the squares on my calendar, leading up to August nineteenth—move in day at my dorm. As the marks neared that number, my room became bare, stripped down to the walls and stuffed into the boxes stacked all around my room.

Then, all too soon, before I was ready, I had to leave home. The boxes were all in my car now; my room was, for the most part, empty. My body trembled with nervous emotions and second thoughts about my decision.

It was time for college.

It was time to grow up.

It was time to move on.

The goodbyes broke my heart. Mom cried and even Dad got emotional—something so rare.

As I pulled out of the driveway, I saw a bird flying from a tree. In my head, I pictured myself as the bird being kicked out of its nest...

Only, its wings hadn't grown yet...

And the bird was falling, falling, falling...

Like the tears slipping down my face as I drove...

Falling, falling, falling...

Because wings...I didn't know how to grow.

◉

Bluebirds flew over my head as I walked to class, their wings flapping and flapping until they disappeared into the soft gray skies. I sighed into the beating sunrays, longing to go with them, wherever they were going...just...*somewhere*. As long as it wasn't to a classroom, which was where I had to go.

My first class of the day looked more like an auditorium. I sat in the back—my usual habitat. I was fifteen minutes early, so there were few people sitting in the rows ahead. I didn't recognize anyone, and I was surprised to feel a bit of freedom in that. No one knew the shy outcast I was in high school. Here, I could be anyone I wanted. I could start over. Best of all, I never had to see Scottie again.

What. A. Relief.

Another relief was that the three classes I had today weren't all that bad. I already had homework, chapters to read, math problems to solve, but other than that, I survived.

My roommate was already in our dorm when I got back from the bookstore.

"Hey," I greeted her, as I set my used textbooks on my desk. "How'd your classes go today?"

She yanked the earphones off her head, turning away from her laptop to me. "Sorry. What?"

"How'd classes go today?"

"Oh, they were great. In PT all the professor did was show us how to wrap an ankle. Then class was over."

"Wow, that's awesome!" I was so jealous. "What's PT again?" I bit down on my lip in shame a moment later. She'd already told me when I first met her but I forgot.

"Physical therapy."

"Oh right! Right. I remember now." That was her major.

I sat down in my desk chair to skim over the list of things I needed to get done today. I scratched out purchasing textbooks. The next task was buying a parking permit before my car got ticketed. I opened my mouth to ask my roommate if she'd already gotten a permit, and, if not, if she'd want to go with me. But before the words came out, she stood from her chair, swung her backpack over her shoulder. She stuck a granola bar between her teeth, mumbling over it, "See ya later."

The door gave a cringing groan as it shut, the silence following louder than every noise outside my window.

Sighing, I leaned back in my chair, eyes roaming over the walls that looked different now. My roommate must have hung more of her stuff up. The white walls were now covered in volleyball and athletic posters; the ceiling had Christmas-like lights ornamenting its border. And then there were the letters above her desk, spelling her name...

MACY

Macy Evans. My roommate. Yeah. She was one of those girls who just seemed to have all of her shit together: Like, a flawlessly planned out future in a career that had a great job outlook and pay; she worked at the local hospital in the field she was studying; she helped coach volleyball at her high school. She was sinewy and athletic, went to church every Sunday. And, as if those things didn't make me annoyed at her already...to top it off, she had a face that hardly needed any makeup to look perfect, if none at all. She was perfect. A parent's dream.

And her parents were *my* dream. I met them on move in day. They were so kind to me, offering me lunch and help carrying boxes. I loved how they held hands, worked together, *talked* instead of yelled. They were pleasant, happy. But what muddled me about Macy was that she had no pictures of them, not even a photo of her four brothers. Just sports posters. It was quite a contrast to the collage of pictures I had taped all over the wall beside my bottom bunk. All of them photos of my parents, Olive, Grandma Blue, Nana, and Pumpkin. So I could stare at them at night, try to imagine that they were here with me; try to grasp the faintest feeling of company, of not feeling alone, trapped beneath the top bunk that squeaked like rats in the night.

Macy Evans, I came to realize, simply didn't need pictures of her family. She didn't need pictures from the past, to feel like the future would be okay.

Envious I was of her independence, of her unfaltering confidence.

The stillness of the dorm was interrupted when I heard laughter erupting from my suitemates' room. Carina and Amiya were their names—the girls next door that I'd be sharing a toilet and shower with all semester. I had yet to meet the duo. I only knew their names since they were posted outside their door, just like mine and Macy's names were. But whoever these strangers were, it wasn't hard to gather that the pair was coveted, donning friendships like clothes, so effortlessly, a second nature. Laughter always spurted from their dorm, since day one here, and it seemed like every time I was leaving, guys were letting themselves in next door.

I considered, for a moment, knocking on their door to introduce myself. The idea soon got shot down when I glanced at my planner where all my assignments were scrawled. I needed to get to work... I needed to get to work right now...

I had to study.

There was no time to make friends.

I opened to page one of my psychology textbook, the words spiraling up at me in a dizzying haze of black and white.

◉

Black and white snack cakes called to me from the shelf above my closet. A place where I stored all the junk food Mom sent me away with. I hid it away for one reason and one reason only—so I wouldn't eat it. The potato chips, the cream cookies, the snack cakes, all a mouthwatering delight.

My stomach rumbled; my head pinched with throbbing pangs. I didn't eat much here in college. Most days I ate cereal for breakfast, cereal for lunch, then salad for supper. I was terrified of gaining weight my first year. The "freshman fifteen" myth was like a bright, neon billboard in my head, telling me *no*, don't eat the hot lunch, don't eat the pizza, don't eat the thick subs or the packaged meats and potatoes. *You'll gain weight. You'll get fatter than you already are.*

God but I was so hungry! I couldn't even concentrate on the math problems on my desk. I wanted, no, I *needed* to eat!

I got up from my chair, stood before my closet, my eyes transfixed on the snack cakes. *Just one will be okay*, I promised myself. But then I reached for the package, making the mistake of looking at the nutrition facts. *Yikes.* No, one would not be okay. *Maybe just half then. Yeah, okay. Half*, I agreed. I opened the plastic wrapping, saliva oozing all around my tongue as I brought the cake up to my lips.

Biting, chewing, tasting, swallowing.

It was heaven, this food. Nothing mattered but the pleasure I found in the bubbling taste, the tantalizing sweetness of it that I yearned for so often. *Yum* was all I could think. Until I found myself unable to stop eating, eating, eating it till it was all gone.

I pressed my lips together in shame, looked to the sink…

Well, I thought, *my roommate's at work right now. So…I could just…throw it up.* Like I did in high school sometimes if I overate.

But I didn't throw up. Not yet. I kept eating and eating, ripping open the wrappers and packages; biting, tasting, indulging, until bliss saturated my tongue. And the stress of the exams I had to take tomorrow, the chapters I had yet to read, the papers I still needed to write, all simply melted away with the chocolate on my tongue…

The frenzy, the high, I came down from it when my eyes fell to my stomach. It bulged out—a horrifying sight of fat was all I could see there on my gut, dangling from my arms, jiggling my thighs…

I hurried to the sink, jammed my finger far back into my throat to coax out the mistake, the sweets. Disgustingness came up and up, splattering into the sink. I purged, purged, and purged, tears and snot spilling down from violent, emptying heaves. I couldn't stop; I couldn't stop, not until it was all out of me, every last calorie.

Panting and coughing, I leaned against the counter, my body trembling. In the mirror, there, a nasty monster wheezed. But behind the puke-covered lips and the black mascara trails, there was release. Freedom from the stress. My headache had been purged; the rumbles in my tummy were gone. And…somehow…when I looked down at myself, I was thin again. I didn't have to worry about gaining weight anymore, as long as whatever I did consume left me the way it came.

Bulimia was always a distant acquaintance in high school, but I believed here in college…her and I were going to be best friends.

◙

Friends were in short supply lately, well, as always. It shouldn't have come to my surprise that I was incapable of conversing with others I didn't know very well. But to realize that I still had problems making friends was *really* frustrating. Even my roommate, I could tell, didn't like me very much. I figured it was because I was always in the room studying, so maybe she was annoyed because of the lack of privacy. But even at dinner, I'd sit with Macy and her friends, finding myself clamming up into this shy entity, choking on words, fumbling on sentences. Why was so gosh darn awkward?!

I took my medicine, but it didn't make me a more outgoing person. It only tamed the beast caged inside—the one that was freed when I didn't take the pills. The one that made me into an angry person, ready to lash out at any anyone who pissed me off. I'd get so furious at everyone, the world; then, in shame, curl up and cry over the monster I truly was without the medicine. This happened a lot over weekends when I'd go home. I'd forget my medicine, somehow leaving myself in the pill bottle as well.

I didn't like myself at all. I was still the loser I was in high school, only, I studied a lot more and I was stressed out of my mind and I had a face full of pimples because of it.

My life was mashed between the pages of textbooks. All I did was study, all I did was outline chapters, edit papers, scribble notes, read, read, *read*, until I'd have a migraine. I just didn't want to fail. I couldn't fail. I needed to make A's. I needed to make my parents proud.

I needed to be *perfect*.

Perfect. I was desperate to attain such a state, such a feeling, such an all-conquering trait. Maybe if I were perfect...I could *for once* make *myself* proud. Be proud to simply be *me*. Perfect.

But trying to be perfect was an awfully lonely task. Sitting alone in my dorm because my roommate was never there, alone in the study lounge, alone in front of the mirror applying makeup, alone at the sink with puke-matted lips...always alone. This loneliness stared at me from the white walls in front of my desk, a haze before my face. Some days I yearned to somehow split myself in two, have the mirror-girl step out of the reflecting glass and come to me. Wrap me in her arms, kiss me, stroke my hair, then my face, all the way down to between my legs, whispering into my ear that things would be okay, that I wasn't alone, and that she loved me still. Hold me as I fell asleep at night, curled against her warm body that fit against mine as if we were one.

Love.

I wished I felt that way towards myself. So I could embrace my reflection, embrace *me*, and, eventually, embrace others, the world, instead of the loneliness saturating the void that filled my dorm, that filled my soul.

Maybe the emptiness inside was from not knowing who I was. Because at school everyone seemed to have some sort of way of identifying themselves, as if their majors, their job, their social life, made them somebody. That was Business Major there. His name was Biology Major. Her name was Teacher Assistant. And their names were their students ID numbers.

But who was I without a clue of what I wanted to be? Not a clue of the future? I didn't even have my student ID number memorized. I was Undeclared. Did that make me a nobody? Someone without an identity at all? Someone empty, without a personality...without even a future to behold?

"Jovie, hey! Jovie?"

I blinked out of my stare, focusing in on the blur sitting beside me at dinner. It was Karen speaking to me, one of Macy's volleyball friends. I sat with their group at the circular table in the cafeteria for dinner most nights, and, today, for some reason, this chick was talking to me. "Huh?"

"We're all going to the lake on Saturday, you wanna come?"

"Uhhhm." I pushed a carrot around on my plate, surprised that they were inviting somewhere. Quickly, I thought back to all I'd written in my planner for Saturday... I was pretty much all caught up on reading assignments. And...I didn't really want to go home. There was too much tension in the house—Mom and Dad always angry with each other. Then there was me, sick at heart, needing to get out of my dorm. I swallowed hard, saying, "Yeah," with a slight and rare smile. "Yeah I think I'll come. Thank you."

"Awesome! We'll leave at ten in the morning Saturday. Oh, and bring a swimsuit."

"Okay," I breathed. "Yeah will do."

The table seemed to light up with conversations of the lake and how the weather was supposed to be beautifully warm—perfect swimming weather. Boyfriends were tagging along, bringing their friends.

Great, I thought, *I'll be around a lot of people I don't know while wearing a swimsuit.* This was a recipe for awkwardness.

Laying my head down atop my pillow that night, my eyes remained wide open, fixed on the calendar I had taped on the side of the rickety bookshelf beside the bunk. Tomorrow was Saturday. And the landscape picture on this month of the calendar was of a pristine lake, ocean blue, with puffy white clouds swimming in the sky. I dove into the picture, later in my dreams, floating on my back in the lake... Only, the water was black...and the sky was purple... And, when I couldn't float anymore, I disappeared beneath the water.

Sinking.

Sinking.

Sinking.

I resurfaced the next morning with a loud, frightened gasp, as I threw the sheets I'd sunken down into from over my head.

Still breathing unsteadily, I reached for my phone to check the time…

Figures.

My alarm would go off in five minutes. I turned it off, but stayed motionless in my bed. I didn't feel like getting up. So I listened to the rhythmic snores Macy made from the top bunk and the muffled TV sounds coming from our suitemates' dorm.

A few minutes later, I heard the shower come to life from the bathroom, steam, as it built up, clouding out from the cracks of the bathroom door. One of my suitemates was in the shower, very loudly singing Taylor Swift songs. I closed my eyes, trying to tune out her off-key voice, and focus on the pattering water from the showerhead, the sound like rain…and like the splashing sounds I would later hear at the lake…

Nearly bare bodies, their contours shapely and athletic, splashed around in the lake, their skins all evenly enveloped by sunrays, tan and glistening in the murky water.

The girls I sat with in the cafeteria most days had all shed their sundresses, tied their hair into ponytails, and, with confident gulps of fresh air, jumped into the lake from the rocky cliffs. Their boyfriends eagerly following their foamy splashes shortly after.

I watched the large group of people from the gravely shore, my toes planted firmly in the sand. My hair that I kept down flapped like a black flag in the wind from the boat-made waves. And the white beach skirt I still had on—something to cover up the cutting scars on my upper thighs—rippled violently in the breeze.

I wanted to join in on the fun, I really did, but I didn't want to get my face wet. I was afraid that the makeup I used to cover up the pimples on my face would wash off, revealing the hideous skin of Jovie Blue hiding behind the fake powder and blush. I needed to keep my perfect mask on, even if it meant being alone here on the shore.

This perfect mask was a devious illusion, I discovered, when a couple of guys just arriving at the lake nodded at me with impish grins on their unshaven faces. They thought I was pretty—how stupid of them. I returned an expression that was something between a smile and a grimace. But once they ditched their shirts, I turned away, deciding to keep my eyes to the ground where I would search for shells and rocks.

Wandering down the shore, it seemed I entered a world of rocks and boulders, the muddy water welcoming me as it lapped at my ankles. Stone cliffs looked down at me from above, their profound curvatures modest in a palette of earthen colors. Bracken waved at me from the tops, the vibrant nature giving life to the dead rocks all around.

I found a boulder a few feet out into the water, an algae skirt fitting snugly around its bottom. I hopped onto it, careful not to slip on the wet spots. Sitting down, I hugged my knees to my chest and looked out at the group of people splashing, screaming, laughing with one another in the water, enjoying the weekend, the sun, the water, the world—life. It was a beautiful sight to see, and I'd bet, an even better one to experience.

My toes curled over the edge of the rock as I leaned forward to look down at the water. I saw below not my reflection rippling in the lake, but what seemed to me like a question mark. My heart suddenly beat sporadically in my chest...

Who am I? Who am I? Who am I?

But misty waves, caused by a boat speeding across the horizon, hushed my thoughts with their sounds...

*Sssshhhhh...sssshhhhh...sssshhhhh...*the waves soothed, as they splashed into the boulder repeatedly, the sound so similar to that of a Louisiana downpour, only such rain made the sound of a constant sssssshhhhhhhhh, hushing all worries for a long while.

A smile stretched my lips, as my fingers brushed over the necklace around my neck...

The noise conjured a memory from far inside my mind, maybe even my heart—a place where memories of Grandma Blue were stored.

This memory in particular was the last one I could remember of Grandma Blue alive. She had been in a nursing home, sick with Alzheimer's and lung cancer. I visited her a lot, always enjoying our porch swing talks during a rainstorm. The constant patter made it so that I had to practically yell in her ear, but that was okay; it was kind of funny to me.

Grandma Blue sometimes didn't know who I was—I thought then she was just being silly, but I know now it was because she was sick. But that rainy day, her dark green eyes looked to mine, their wrinkly frames brightening when she smiled. "I got you sumtin, sweet girl," she said, her voice hoarse and low. She reached a shivering hand into the pocket of her gown where she pulled out a black chain adorned with five silver blocks that spelled my name.

I answered her gesture by turning around, lifting my hair from my neck so she could latch the necklace together. When it was on securely, I turned to my grandma, grinning down at my present.

"It's tuh help me remember who yuh are. So I won't forget." She stroked away the damp hair in my eyes with her frail fingertips, brushing them back behind my ears. "And maybe one day," she went on, "when yuh all old, it'll help yuh. So yuh won't forget, too." She winked down at me, laughing deep in the back of her throat.

I thought it was rain on my cheeks, but when I opened my eyes I was still on the boulder, the mist from the waves spraying in my face. I glanced down at the charms around my neck…

JOVIE

The blocks told me who I was…but they didn't tell me who I was supposed to *be*.

I yanked the necklace off angrily, letting the five withered charms collect in the palm of my hand. There, right before me, lied the answer to the constant question going through my mind—*who am I?*

JOVIE

I moved away for college, moved to a new town, been all over Louisiana, Missouri, and many other places, countless attempts to start over, to run away from what was wrong… But, all along, I was the problem…

Because I am the sadness within.

I am the loneliness.

I am the…depression.

It is so far inside, a mass of black tendrils ensnaring my soul, always strangling, always heavy, always, always, always, growing.

I am the disease…
I am what my medicine needs to get rid of…

I glared down at the necklace, at my name, at myself, remembering who I was and who I would never be…

Someone…*more*…than just Jovie.

Someone like those people out in the lake, able to embrace the happiness around them, the company, the *love*. There was a chain around my neck—I thought it was depression—but, looking down at the necklace, I saw now that it was *me*…holding *myself* back.

Anger, tempestuously raw, made my teeth grind together, ball the necklace into my fist, and fling it out into the lake…

Bloop! It landed far out into the water, where it sank, sank, sank…to the very bottom. It could rot there for all I cared.

"HEY! JOVIE!"

I turned around to the shore where someone was yelling my name. Squinting into the sunrays, I saw that it was Macy, dripping wet and holding her boyfriend's hand.

"WE'RE FIRING UP THE GRILL!" she hollered, her free hand cupping the side of her mouth for more volume. "COME EAT!"

"Coming!" I tried to yell back, as I pushed myself to my feet. I jumped back to the shore, having to catch myself on the other slippery boulders nearby. Once I was safe on the sand, I looked back at where I'd thrown my necklace. Absently, I rubbed the bare skin of my neck where the charms always dangled; I felt naked without them.

As I walked on, I felt, for a moment, a bit of remorse for what I did. Grandma Blue gave me that necklace, and I wore it for years ever since that day. I stopped walking, the question, *What have I done?* suddenly making me sick to my stomach.

"Come on, Jovie!" another voice yelled; a softer voice that belonged to Karen. "We're about to have lunch!"

Reluctantly, I turned away from the water, waving at Karen in the distance to let her know I heard her. I started running to make myself leave the necklace behind, but found myself looking back for it, hesitance making me stumble…as I ran, ran, ran, faster and faster… further and away from myself.

Old, graying tennis shoes stomped along on one of the treadmills tucked away in the corner of the college gym. These were my shoes, attached to my feet, as I ran, ran, ran against the fast-paced speed of the treadmill; my only motivation to keep going was the angry music blaring in my ears from my iPod.

I started running every night after I'd call it a day on studying. At first it was just exercise to me, something to help me lose weight and get toned. But then, as I kept raising the speed more and more each day, running became…something else for me…

It was pain.

I couldn't cut anymore; I couldn't binge and purge—there was so little privacy in a dorm. So, exercising was the next best thing, for in the pain, there was release. The rage inside oozed through the pores of my skin in sweat, as my heart drummed *I hate I hate I hate* in my chest.

Most nights I'd run until my knees felt like they'd eroded to sand, till my ankles popped, feet ached, dizziness swelled inside my head, and black dots crowded my vision…

I'd run…until I…*hurt*.

Later, after walking back to my dorm, I'd stand in front of the mirror, smirking at the sweaty monster in the glass, her eyes burdening a tragic glisten. *Help*, they screamed, but then I'd mouth the words *fuck you* to the reflection; lock myself in the bathroom where I'd turn the shower on and scrub so hard at the monster, trying desperately to wash her away.

Violence laced my behavior, haunted my thoughts. The anger swelling inside…it was hard to control…hard to make sense of…

College, being away from home, being alone—it was so…*hard*. And I became so angry with myself for falling short of my own standards that I had raised to perfection. I was angry for getting C's on exams, for failing that last math quiz, for doing that English paper completely wrong, for that reason, angry because of this… There were so many reasons…countless reasons… But there was one that scared me most. One that I put off, was terrified to admit to myself that I was even aware of it…

Aware of a presence inside me—a little girl. This small girl was childish, innocent, and carefree. Yeah. My childhood. It blossomed in the still sunny part of my soul; skipped across my heart frequently, singing and singing, longing and longing, needing…needing…to be free again.

I wanted to be her. A kid.

I didn't like this thing called growing up. No. I didn't like it at all.

But there was another part of me who knew I had to grow up despite the protests of the child—the woman inside. She was wise, steady. She was my future. But I couldn't access her as much as I needed to; I couldn't be her—not yet. Because the child in me was way too strong, wailing against her, crying, throwing fits. *No, no, no, no, no!*

I wasn't sure who the monster was inside: the child I could never be again or the woman I would never become.

Or perhaps…the monster was the fragile girl I saw in the mirror. The teenager. The indecisive sap who didn't know which one to be.

I knew I needed to be the adult, the woman. But what I wanted with all my heart and soul…was to simply be a child again.

Pain was a way of silencing the inner hysteria of all these voices —voices that were all mine but had different thought processes, different goals, different desires. Pain gave me peace; pain shut everyone up inside my head. It shut me up. So all there was to worry about was the physical pain, not the internal wasteland of a life inside this pale skin.

I turned off the treadmill after a fifty minute run, as usual. Still winded and red in the face, I made my way down the stairs and out the double doors of the gym. Blustery night wind cooled my face, chilled the sweat dewed on my skin, as I walked across the black pavement of a parking lot. I could hear the blaring rap beats from the fraternity house party down the street. Even above my own music plugged into my ears, the laughter of the guys cutting up over there across the lot was audible, the clicking of high heels sounding from a group of girls as they made their way to the club was piercing—the noises were unnerving, provoking the invisible entity I knew too well. It suddenly coiled around my neck, weighed down my shoulders, sagged my lips, filling my head with thoughts like…

I don't belong here…

I walked faster, the wind tousling the locks of my hair along with the vines of the willow tree lining the sidewalk. One of the branches reached out to me, brushed beneath my chin, luring my gaze up to the sky where my eyes locked with the beautiful night above…

There, so far away in the heavens, were the stars peering down at me, while I stared back at them. I stopped walking, took out my earbuds so I could welcome in the sudden extraordinary silence muting all the ruckus of the city.

All was quiet.

All went away.

The world.

The people.

College.

Everyone.

Except the stars, except the moon, except the beautifully dark void above that wielded mystery in all its emptiness—something that I was drawn to, for it practically reflected…*me*.

Belonging… I felt it there in that beautiful somewhere, that refuge of velvety black—the nothingness. How I so intensely longed to evaporate to mist, to lightness, and lift off into the dark, become a jewel inside the vast space, burning fiercely from afar—safe, untouchable, silent, but always present, always seemingly perfect in the emptiness all around, and bright…always, always, a light.

My legs began to tremble, maybe from the cold or maybe from exhaustion, but I had to sit down for a moment. I rested on the bench near the willow, its branches swaying beside me as if they were dancing in the wind, cupping the moonlight in every leaf it grew.

I sighed into the wind, finding my sights guided up to the sky again. It was an awfully lonely feeling, seeing how the emptiness above seemed to mirror what was within my soul. I talked to someone inside my head in that moment. And that someone was God…

I prayed a lot most nights anyway. An endeavor to feel less alone perhaps, but whatever the reason, I prayed, I talked to God, unsure if I was even doing it correctly.

My family was never one that attended church every Sunday; and

Jesus was always the static channel on television. But, living in the Bible Belt of the US, everyone said the Father, the Son, and the Holy Ghost were much more. So much more. And I believed it, certainly, of course. I just didn't feel it, though I wanted to with all my heart.

I wanted to feel God, or grace, or the love and forgiveness of Jesus, but I didn't know how. Did I need to rip my heart out? My soul? Send it off into space so I could get better reception? Get a better feel? A reading?

I didn't know, but I still tried...

God, I thought, *why'd you make the world, the universe, so big? Some people, people like me, get lost easily, so lost that they don't even know exactly where it is they belong. I think I love you; I'm just not sure if you love me. I understand why, though. I don't love me either. But just don't forget that I need you, I need help...*

I sighed heavily. This was useless.

I felt nothing but wetness in my eyes and the chill of the cold night closing in.

There was no voice talking back, just the increasing volume of the world returning to me—the sounds of police sirens in the distance, the swoosh of cars passing by on the road, the party music, the laughter of others, the world...the night, time...going, going...on. So unlike the stillness of the stars and me on the bench...going, going... nowhere.

Before I left the bench, I gave the darkness one last glance, noticing how the stars twinkled on, off, on, off...on...and...off.

◘

Christmas glowed in the darkness of the wintery nights. Lights hung from the rooftops of houses, swirled up the streetlamps and trees—all embellished like the stars in the sky. The flickering red dots everywhere reminded me of the pimples all over my face, formed because of the stress finals week brought with it in December.

I couldn't *wait* for the semester to be over; to be home finally with no homework, no studies or papers. Just family, comfort food, and the cinnamon-sweet scent of Christmas mixing in the frosty air.

Most of my finals—including, to my surprise, math—were fairly easy. I blazed through the bubble sheets with my pencil, piecing together what I'd studied all semester with the questions on the test. And when my last final came to pass, I hurried to my car, slid inside with my suitcase in the passenger's seat, and hit the road that led me home.

Home.

Home was empty when I got there.

Mom and Dad were probably still at work; Olive visiting with her boyfriend one last time before the Christmas break distance came between them. So, with Pumpkin lapping at my face, I sat down on the couch, settling in with the remote to simply relax a bit. I turned on the TV, and, after a few minutes of channel surfing, heard my stomach growl obnoxiously loud. My eyes flitted to the kitchen…

Empty bags of chips, ripped open boxes of cookies, opened jars of peanut butter, trails of crumbs, led anyone who was home to me hunched over the sink, throwing it all up. But no one was home, so no one knew…

No one knew that when the house was empty I'd binge; I'd ravage the hidden chocolate bars, the divine snack cakes; consume all the pleasures of the kitchen chilled inside the freezer, stacked high inside the pantry.

Even during the semester when I'd come home for the weekend, I'd always succumb to this disgusting habit.

I was possessed by decadence, so far under bulimia's vile spell that it was impossible to stop…

Once I began eating, there was no stopping until I felt like I would burst. Then I would, by throwing it all up, hating myself every second during the purge.

I wondered if I threw up my soul somewhere along the way, because once all was down the toilet or drain or sink, I was empty. Not just in my stomach, but in my entire body, mind, and heart.

Empty…

Because I'd given myself completely to her—to bulimia.

◉

It took a lot of restraint not to throw up after consuming Mom's remarkable Christmas day supper: the warm juicy turkey breasts, the sweet, gooey candied yams, buttered rolls, cheesy homemade macaroni, the deliciously crunchy green bean casserole, and freshly baked pecan pies and pumpkin rolls—my stomach was unbearably full within ten minutes.

But I held it in, trying to enjoy this special time with my family as we sat together on the floor after supper, the presents with our names on them sitting before us. It was at this time, not at the table, when I noticed again the tension between my parents. It was obvious now, because they exchanged no gifts, only accepted the ones Olive and I had gotten them, giving us a few in return.

Christmas seemed…strange…

Or maybe it wasn't Christmas…but my family that was different.

Dad fell asleep in the recliner for another night in a row. And Mom, without returning another *I love you* to me again, stood before the microwave, absently watching the popcorn bag she put in expand and…

◉

POP! POP! POP! went the fireworks outside on New Year's Eve, welcoming in the year 2012.

Another ending…

But Mom said it was a new beginning for our family.

That night, as fireworks exploded in the sky, Mom sat Olive and me down on the living room couch. Tears suddenly formed a glass window over her eyes, toppling over her painted lashes, then over the pink curves of her cheeks, leaving a trail of makeup behind it. Emotion convulsed her body, trembled her red lips…

"Mom?" Olive gasped, horrified at the sudden breakdown of our mother. "What's wrong? Did someone die?"

Mom quickly shook her head no. "D-divorce," was all she could sputter out.

But the word was all that was needed to quake the very foundation of my world and turn my motivation to live into dirt and rubble.

Olive burst into tears with my mother, hounding her with questions of *Why? What happened? Are you okay? What's going to happen? Where will you go?*

I cried silently to myself, finally realizing that, even after living through a hurricane, still, I never did know what it was like to be in a broken home. Because the boards, the nails, the walls—that was just the house. The lives inside and the love between a family made up the real foundation…of a *home*. The torrential agony the word divorce always brought me as a child was real now. This wasn't a nightmare. It was real. Right before me.

I turned my attention away from Olive and Mom's conversation, my eyes falling upon the Christmas tree in the corner by the dining room table. I watched the lights that twisted around the limbs, like a Christmas noose, growing envious of how they could be on one second…then off the next. And, once unplugged, could live in their darkness forever…

◉

Shadows fill my vision as Angel tries to steady me on the puke-covered seafloor. I cough gutturally, finally retching myself free of the memory inside.

"Jovie," the angel calls to me, "Jovie, are you okay?" The statue gives me a gentle shake, and I am able to open my eyes to Pertinendi again.

"Yeah," I croak, coughing one last time from the rancid vomit below.

Angel, so tenderly, wipes the mess from my lips and tucks the loosened locks of hair back behind my ears. "Let us get you up," the statue says, lifting me back to my feet.

"Thank you," I breathe, having to hold onto one of Angel's stone but cracking wings for support. It is a long couple of minutes before I can settle down, catch my breath. When I am able to stand on my own, Angel holds me still in its stare of a thousand years, gray and hard, but eroding with confusion and pain.

"Now," Angel begins carefully, "can you tell me why you put your body through such torture, such violence, all to look a certain way—an *unrealistic* way?"

I slowly shake my head, keeping my eyes down with shame. "It wasn't just about losing weight, Angel. It's never just about that." My hands curl to fists, white knuckles pop. "It's about *control*. If you don't eat, you don't gain weight. If you eat but purge, it seems to cancel out the calories. It's about certainty." Emotion rises up to my throat like puke... "Because nothing was certain anymore in my world," I cry. "Who knew about tomorrow, if I'd be happy or sad, if I wouldn't kill myself that night, if my parents would love or hate each other the next day, or if we'd be financially secure. Fuck, if even gas prices would be the same. I was so afraid, because growing up meant realizing that everything was out of my control... I-I did the only thing I could control—I self-destructed."

The tearful confession falls from my eye, but it is not absorbed into the black sea. Rather, the tear falls to the ground, splashing on a button-eyed teddy bear half buried in the vomit. The tear slides down the brown furry face, then dies on the blue bow tied around its neck.

I pluck the toy from the sand, whispering to the angel, "I think... all that time I was trying to purge the child inside of me, the devastated little girl that knew her time was up. That knew her time of control—of being the master of her toys and stuffed animals—was over, never to return." I clean the bear's face with the tenderness of a child; shake the puke from its hide. "It was the woman's turn to shine through; the little girl had to play the quiet game now...forever. I had to grow up." My grip suddenly tightens around the bear's neck, forming a stranglehold. "But...I was afraid to be her, to grow up into the woman...because..."

"It's the unknown," Angel finishes for me, precious understanding carved deeply into its stone face.

"Yeah," I murmur, wiping the emotion dripping from my eyes.

The angel wraps a consoling wing around my shoulder, saying softly, "It is okay to be afraid of the future, but not to the point where you kill yourself so you will not have to live it."

I look to Angel, whispering honestly, "I see that now." And with my sighing breath the black water exonerates the gravity of depression.

Pertinendi

We are weightless…
I float up to the very brim of the sea with Angel by my side, holding me steady.
Our heads break the surface, the inky water dappling our faces.
"Look," Angel urges, pointing behind me.
I twist around, wide-eyed and gasping, "It's the end!"

PART 7

MY APOCALYPSE

We made it to the end of the black sea! Over there, just ahead, the shore is only a few yards away. Stretching behind it are emerald ribbons of grassy hills, the sight reminding me of Missouri's landscape. But there, beyond the hills, towering above the horizon is the inspiring purple mountains, their white snow tops and the light wedged between—Heaven. It's there, so, so close…

The Angel and I swim to the shore, collapsing when we make it to solid ground. Sopping wet, I stagger to my feet to assist the withering statue, electric urgency rushing my movements. "Come on, we're almost there," I encourage hopefully, as I pull the stone back up to its feet. To my utter shock, part of the angel's wing breaks off, crumbling to the ground. I inhale sharply, squatting down to quickly gather the pieces and try reassembling them the way they were on Angel.

When I grab at the last rock fragment, my hair is blown back by a searing hot wind that stings my eyes. Stunned, the rocks fall from my hand as I look up to find that it is the breath of Hell on my skin, burning my soul…

A giant flame slithers across the sea, its fluid form much like a snake, as the Devil rides its thrashing heat.

"The Devil's coming!" I scream to Angel, whose knees have given out. The statue falls in the black sand, paralyzed. The statue is…frozen.

Demonic howls fill the air; demons scatter in the sky, circling above us.

I look to Angel, desperate for an answer, for hope, but there is none.

Soon…we will exist…no more.

"Jovie," the angel says to me, "you have done so well. I am proud of you." A concrete hand cups my cheek, brushes the tears rolling down my face. "But you must keep going. You are almost there. Home is so close."

"I'm not leaving you!" I refuse, looking back at the Hell pummeling towards us. I turn back to the statue, face falling in the stone hands… "*I need you,*" I whisper, tears swelling in my eyes again.

The hand I'm holding feels like sand a moment later. I open my eyes, grief crippling my will to even try, to even run away when I see that the Angel has turned to dust. "No," I cry to the remains, shaking uncontrollably at the loss of Angel—sweet, loving Angel…

A devilish sneer makes me snap out of my hysteria.

My hair whips around as I turn to see what is still pursuing me—Hell. It is time to either pay the consequences for breaking out of Hell or keep running from them…

I run.

I can't face it.

I can't, I can't, I can't…

So I run… I run hard…

Hard as I possibly can, until the sand turns to emerald blades of grass; and I'm sprinting down a valley through the hills…

Demons claw at my back, snarl from the sky, trying to delay my break for Heaven. But I run up the hill; I keep running. It's difficult, though, to make my feet move as fast as I need them to. It's like I'm in a dream, a running dream, and my ankles have weights on them—I simply *can't. run. fast. enough.*

At the top of the hill a demon swoops down, claws slashing at my shoulder. The impact knocks me off my feet, sending me tumbling the rest of the way down the hill. I land flat on my back at the bottom, puffing a loud, exasperated groan of pain. In a daze, I pick my head up from the ground, watching as the top of the hill is engulfed by flames as the Devil reaches the top of the fiery mound...

It's over...

I let my head fall back to the grass in defeat, surprised when I feel a plush memory softening the blow...

◉

"Just lie back and relax," the therapist instructed me in a calm but mannered voice.

I did as I was told, lying back on the grassy green couch, letting my head rest upon the emerald pillow with tassels dangling from its corners.

The small window in front of Monica's computer desk shielded us from the harsh January weather. Frozen raindrops kept tapping the glass, as if they wanted inside, as if they wanted to melt in this stuffy heated room and become rain.

Mom suggested I see Monica again after I seemed to have taken the news of the divorce too well. So, again, I did as I was told, making the appointments with the clinic from the dinky desk in my dorm room at college.

And here I was...back in Monica's office.

I remembered quite distinctly the eccentric character this therapist was years ago, so enlightening and fun to talk to. But, when I shook her hand in the waiting room, she didn't share the same recollection as me. She didn't remember, she didn't remember me at all.

"I read what you wrote on your forms," Monica mentioned. "You said you're having trouble with anxiety, correct?"

I nodded from the couch.

"Okay. Well, that's why I'm having you lie down. I want to try some relaxation techniques with you."

I nodded again, "Okay."

She asked me to close my eyes and focus on the spot in the middle of my forehead. I did that until she directed my focus on another part of the body.

But I couldn't relax.

I couldn't focus.

I kept shaking, picking at the dead skin in the corner of my fingernails; frantically thinking about the forms in Monica's lap that I had filled out while in the waiting room…

They weren't the truth…

I'd scribbled lies all over them.

Because one of the questions asked me to describe what was wrong, but I couldn't explain, I couldn't say…

Shame stopped my hand from writing, taped my lips from speaking…

That I'd been cutting myself for years, binging and purging recently—and it was getting worse, out of control, which was the opposite of its very purpose. That I couldn't, no matter how hard, no matter where I went, shake my depression; it was there, always locked inside me, refusing to leave. I couldn't explain that my parent's marriage of twenty-five years had ended, or that I had no direction in college, in life, in the world, and that I was afraid of everything… especially growing up. Especially…the future.

The only thing I felt was sane enough to write was that anxiety attacks had been troubling me for a while.

So that was all Monica could see on the paper. But if only she could see inside me, actually look into my eyes, into my soul; she'd see all of what I wanted to say…and more.

"Very good. Now, are you relaxed?" Monica asked, watching me with her dark, beady eyes.

"Yes," I lied, the crescent smile fading from my lips. "Thank you." I sat upright, adjusting the jacket I had on as I faced Monica in her chair.

"So, how's your family?"

My eyes dropped down to my fidgety hands. "Uhhh, not so good, I guess. My, uh, parents are getting a divorce."

"Oh no," Monica empathized, her brows pulling together with concern. "When did this happen?"

"A few weeks ago."

"You know, having to cope with a divorce is very similar to mourning a death."

I reflected on this statement for a moment, finding that in divorce there was, in fact, an absence about it, even in the very sound of the word. Like, something went missing and died, just by saying it. "Yeah," I finally agreed with her, "I guess it is."

This seemed to give Monica the go ahead to dive into the stages of grief, emphasizing the last stage—acceptance—quite heavily.

She went on and on about this stage, but never really addressed the part I wanted to know most, which was *how?*

How could I learn to accept the space between my parents now? The quiescent love or lack of any love at all? From the beginning they were my parents, like one entity, but now, they were becoming two—the pair I loved most splitting in half—*divorcing*.

I would always love them, of course, but…I wasn't sure how to love the gap between them. I wasn't sure…if I ever could be okay with it.

I understood it, though. Truly, I did—the divorce was longtime coming. But understanding it didn't make it hurt any less.

"It just…" I murmured to Monica, getting choked up during her speech about acceptance. "It breaks my heart." I patted my chest lightly, fighting back the big fat globs of tears blurring my vision. "And I'm nineteen, but I feel like I'm handling this like a little kid. I'm angry and upset. I can't get over it."

Monica yanked a tissue from the box on her desk, then reached to hand it to me.

I dabbed my eyes with it, wiped my nose, trying hard to quickly regain my composure. Monica was being polite, looking down to scribble on her papers while I let out my emotional kink. I took a deep, silent breath, balled the tissue in my hand, and let my eyes wander back to Monica. She was oblivious to my watching, but, in that moment, I realized how old she'd gotten since the last time I'd seen her years ago. She wasn't the bubbly eccentric she was before. She was solemn, graying, and tired. I could tell that the years of listening to people yap about their shitty lives had taken its toll, as impatience willed her quick scribbles on the papers in her lap, tapped her feet, drew her eyes back up to mine and reflected a dull sort of indifference…

That same indifference was present in my doctor's eyes later that week. Instead of papers in her lap though, she had a laptop propped on her knees; her fingers spread across the keyboard, adamantly typing out the symptoms I spoke of.

"I don't think I've really slept since December," I explained, "It's like I can't shut my mind off. I keep thinking and worrying about everything when all I wanna do is sleep."

She nodded, her eyes caught in the computer screen's glow, illuminated by its cold, robotic soul reflecting on her weary face. She kept typing, nodding, clicking, typing, clicking, nodding, typing, typing, typing, typing… The sound became an agitating *tap tap tap* in the sterile room. I imagined standing from where I sat, ripping the computer from her hands, slamming her against the wall by the hazardous used needle box, and screaming in her face to *look* at *me* instead of the stupid computer, *listen* to *me*, try to *understand*…and *help me!*

I blinked away the reverie, remaining quiet atop the crackling white paper on the patient's seat, calmly folding my hands in my lap, awaiting a diagnosis.

Insomnia.

I could only hope that the sleeping pills she prescribed me would free me from this dark world of restlessness. Make me sleep instead of stare at the top bunk all night, fretting about how the bars holding the mattress above looked like bars—prison bars—locking me inside this cell of darkness.

◉

The sulfurous odors that plague the prisons in Hell waft in the fiery winds the Devil casts down the hill. The smell conjures a fear in me, a dreadful terror of the place—Hell. And it is fear that makes me get up from the grass and stumble towards Heaven. I keep running through the valleys, avoiding going to the tops of the hills where the demons lurk so close in the sky.

I run, I run, I run…so hard…until Heaven's glistening gates can be seen in the distance, and, even more so, the snow-dusted purple mountains…

I'm almost there!

I gasp for air, for the stamina to keep pushing through the tension, panting, panting, panting as a memory drizzles down my temple in the form of sweat…

I hurried into my dorm room, panting from the fast-paced walk I exerted all across campus to get to my dorm as quickly as possible. The door slammed shut behind me, letting the dimness of the room close in before I could turn on the lights.

Macy was gone, as usual; probably in class or hanging out in her boyfriend's dorm. Whatever. I needed to check something on my computer. I was in such a hurry that I didn't even shed the thick winter coat I had on or wipe the sweat running down my brow. I couldn't wait...

My teacher finally had our grades up... The grades to our huge research papers—the paper I spent so many hours slaving away for in the library, on the Internet, in front of my damn computer typing; putting all this effort into what I hoped would pay off to be a perfect A...

When I logged onto my student account, clicked on the course grades, I was severely disappointed...

C, the grade read.

I'd gotten a C.

My lips parted as I leaned back in my chair, staring blankly at the screen.

C

The thick winter coat I wore suddenly became burdensomely heavy on my shoulders, so I slid out of it, but didn't find that the weight on my shoulders had lessened any. I got up from my desk, wandered over to the sink. I felt sick. Sick in my head, sick in my stomach...

C, C, C, C, the mocking letter glowered from the computer screen, vibrating my soul with a feeling of unworthiness. *You're not perfect*, it seemed to scream, *you're failing your parents, wasting their money, and failing yourself.*

C, C, C, C...

I drew a quick breath, looked up in the mirror...

See.

I stared at myself for a long time, desperately searching the glass

Pertinendi

for someone worthwhile reflecting back.

I'd once heard that eyes were supposed to be the window to the soul. So, I looked into my own eyes for my soul. But all I could see were the black pupils embedded inside the green, as if they were a window, not to my soul, but to the ever deepening darkness inside—my depression.

If there is a Hell, I thought, *it'd exist right there inside of me.*

Because the void within just kept expanding, tugging; freeing terrible thoughts into my head…scary thoughts, *bad* thoughts.

I wished I could erase these thoughts with a shake of my head, but they wouldn't go away!

I looked to the side of the mirror, seeing what was reflected in the background. It was all of Macy's things—her perfect everything.

I broke down then, bowing my head, succumbing to the cold, awful fact… "I can't do it," I confessed to myself in a whisper. *I'm not perfect.*

And I saw no potential, not a speck of hope in the monster in the mirror—me. I was a disgrace, a disappointment, never to be the perfect daughter my parents deserved or even the perfect soul the crucifix on Macy's wall deserved to see.

I am…nothing.

I am…

I thought back to my last session with Monica before I cancelled all of our future appointments. She'd told me something…something that hurt… It was the truth…

She spoke the words shortly after I had explained to her how I felt about college, how agonized I was over my lack of identity and belonging in the world; how I felt like a had no future, couldn't even think of one…

"You know, Jovie," she said with a hint of impatience, after the mouthful that poured from my lips, "you are the *worst* sort of person."

Wait. Did she say worst person or a negative person? My mind was playing tricks on me.

"You have all of these opportunities," she went on, "You're in college, you have parents who love you and want you to succeed in life. They care about you. But all you seem to see is the negative side of everything. You need to think more positively. Don't say that you have to go to college, be proud to say that you *get* to go to college." She clasped her spidery hands together, saying, "I want to talk to you today about gratitude…"

From then on she talked to me about it, making me feel like a self-indulgent, whiny little bitch for saying all the things that I'd said to her. I hated her for making me feel worse about everything. *She can rot in Hell for all I care! Screw her!*

But…the worst of it all…was that she was right.

I was the worst sort of person. Because, while in this hole of depression, I had all these ropes hanging down, there to help me get out, but I turned my cheek, looked away; I refused to acknowledge their presence.

But why?

I'm scared, I cried internally. *Of expectation, of risk, of responsibility, of the real world. I'm too afraid to see it to the end, because I have no faith that it will be okay, that tomorrow will be a better day.*

I am such a child… And all my fits, anxieties, depression, rage… It's all one ultimate temper tantrum…to self-destruct. Because I'm not getting my way, I no longer have control… And I can't accept any of it…I can't…

"Grow the fuck up," Dad had told me before I left back for college after Christmas break. We'd been discussing careers he'd approve of me going into, but all of them were in the medical field. I'd told him *no, I can't handle that. It's too much pressure. I don't want a job that has that kind of responsibility…*

Then Dad told me to grow up, inserting a curse word in between the sentence. "You sound like a twelve year old."

As the words he told me spun around in my head before the mirror in my dorm, I couldn't help but piece together what he said and how I felt…

All of this happened…my depression…the leap into the downward spiral…when I was twelve.

Would I always be trapped inside of that little girl? Forever reverting to her when I needed to look forward to the adult I needed to try really hard to be?

My breathing became erratic; my heart pounded in my chest like the drums at the gallows. I wished I'd stop thinking, I wished I could go home...

But there was no home. Home was shattered by the turbulent winds of divorce...

I should call Nana, I thought, but then I remembered our last conversation...

I had called her to tell her about the divorce, and, after she said how sorry she was, there was an awkward silence that set in between us; silence turned to static through the phone...

"Are we growing apart?" I asked her, tension wringing my voice tight.

"No," Nana breathed into the phone, "just growing up."

My grip tightened on the counter; I squeezed my eyes shut, not wanting to let the tears fall through...

"I can't do it." The tearful truth burst through. But this time, I wasn't referring to being perfect. *I can't grow up.* I shrugged, eyes wide at the girl in the mirror. *I don't know how*, I told her in my head. *It's too hard.*

So there was only one option left if we couldn't be the child again and if we were never going to be the woman... Only one option. Because we were never going to be the daughter our parents deserved, never going to be the woman the future needed to see...

Because we were nothing, the mirror girl and me. We were the reflection in a puke-filled toilet. Blackness, a stain on society named Jovie Maureen Blue. But we were going to clean that stain today. I was tired of avoiding the mirror where the monster lurked, so tired. I wanted to put an end to her...*once and for all.*

I drew back my fist, and, with a faint grunt, thrust it into my reflection's face as hard as I could. My hand recoiled, bloodied and trembling. I breathed out heavily, letting go of the rightness in my mind and giving in to all the chaotic wrong thoughts spinning and spinning and spinning inside my head.

My hands curled to fists as I walked away from the shattered monster in the mirror, deciding that I was going to make it all stop inside my head; I would put it to an end.

◉

The end of Pertinendi is there, so close; I can almost reach out and touch Heaven's gates...

"PLEASE!" I holler, waving my arms in the air. "LET ME IN!" I plead as I near the gates. "THEY'RE AFTER ME! THEY'RE GONNA KILL ME! PLEASE!"

A demon plunges down from the sky, claws outspread. They tangle in my hair, pulling me back away from the gates...

I let out a restrained cry, as I fight off the memory knotting and pulling my hair...

◉

I ran my fingers through my hair, wheezing with indecision and yanking on the strands of my hair, releasing a quiet cry. I didn't want to do this...I didn't want to do this...

But I had to...

It was the only way...

I reached for something at the top of my shelf; something I tried to keep out of sight so it'd be out of my mind, less tempting... I reached...reached...reached...but was afraid to grab...

◉

I finally break free from the demon. I reach for the gates of Heaven, but come to a sudden halt when I realize what the gate is made of. It's a lustrous orange beam of intricate patterns, expanding before the purple mountain Heaven. I look out at what's beyond the gates and am crushed by disappointment when I see that Heaven's light is farther off in the distance—almost unreachable—because what lies through the mountains is a white frozen wasteland, expanding for hundreds of miles before the setting Heaven-light.

My eyes focus back on the gates. Curious, I reach out to touch it. But...they scare me... I don't like what lies inside the orange beams... It's something poisonous... Something lethal... Something that holds a memory…

The very last memory…of me alive…

The pad of my finger barely brushes against the gate, but it's enough pressure to make the beams convulse violently and…to my horror…open…

◉

I ripped open the tops of the orange pill bottles, every kind I had hidden away at the top of my shelf. My chest was racked by sporadic, uncontrollable sobs as I upturned the bottles, let the ridged edge touch my lips…

The pills came toppling down into my mouth, spreading across my tongue…

◉

The open gates of Heaven—or what I thought was Heaven—come crashing down. The gates, all along, are made of pills… So many of them flood all around as they burst from the bright orange gates.

I slip amongst the chaos, finding myself caught in the massive current of pills crashing into my soul. I scream at the demons whirling around my head, scratching, taunting, teasing; the Devil's fire-serpent coils round and round, snaring my soul, letting loose the hellish memories in my head…

◉

White hot pain whirled around inside my head, replaying images from the past, images of a bleak future, and bad thoughts…so many bad thoughts…of the present…

I'm not good enough… I don't wanna be here… I can't grow up… I don't want to, I don't know how… I can't face it… I can't do anything right… I'm weak, I'm so weak and I know it… I'm not strong enough…

My face was pinched with tortured sorrow when I finished off the last pill bottle—the newest one that would simply make me fall asleep. I couldn't stop crying, though an eerie stillness washed over me, allowing me to get a grip on my actions and scribble something on the nearest piece of paper...

I wrote a letter, something short, something simple. It didn't say much; it was only the truth. It was how I felt right here, right now...

When I was done writing it, I crawled into my bed, tears already dotting my pillow, and curled up with the empty bottles...

I sighed heavily into the quiet room, staring at the calendar taped to the side of my bookshelf. The landscape picture for this month was the most beautiful place I'd ever seen... It was of these fantastical purple mountains, powdered with fresh snow on the tops. The two mountains seemed to lean in towards each other, leaving just enough space for the sunrays behind to shine through in brilliant prisms...

I thought, in a sleepy daze, *If there's a Heaven...it's gotta look just like that...*

The eerie stillness of the room was suddenly interrupted by the blaring TV that turned on in my suitemates' dorm—they always had the volume up so loud. I was just too tired to roll my eyes and be annoyed by it this time. Today, I was actually thankful for it, because Carina or Amiya was watching *The Wizard of Oz*. And Dorothy was singing a lovely song that brought one last tear to my eye...

She sang of somewhere...

Somewhere where?

Somewhere over the rainbow...

But I wanted to be somewhere else...

Somewhere there, in that picture on my calendar... How beautiful it seemed to me, how peaceful...how...*perfect.*

I wanted to go there...

Why oh why can't I? I thought with Dorothy, as shadows of darkness began descending down my vision...

◉

Demonic shadows have me in their claws. I watch helplessly in horror as the Devil jumps down from the head of the fire and comes for me, just like it always said it would...

The Devil stands before me, but my vision is too blurry to see its face… Everything is getting so dark… Especially when the Devil whips its hand across my head, knocking me unconscious…

The feel of scalding wind makes me come to moments later. I quickly gather that I am in the air, trapped in the clutches of the demons as they fly me back to Hell. The Devil leads the way, blazing a trail of fire that the demons plow through with no pain.

I am stuck in a sleepy daze that I can't shake. Pertinendi is passing me by way down below, all the miles Angel and I traveled rewinding in seconds.

Maybe it is the grogginess in my mind, but to me, as I watch the landscape from far up in the mourning cloud skies, my Pertinendi, with all of its mysterious green forests and emerald hills circling around the black sea in the center, looks familiar…like…an eye…my eye… As if my broken soul is still trapped inside the dying Jovie, and Heaven—the last tear—slipping off the corner of my eye, is sliding farther and farther away…

The suffocating winds of Hell engulf my soul in pain—so deep, so fiery, that I can only pass out to escape the agony…

◉

The heater kicked on in my dorm, its deep drone distorting the sounds of the movie playing next door. I was so sleepy and my heartbeat felt weird; I felt weird.

My thoughts were fading, like they did when I was too tired to think… But this time the thoughtlessness frightened me, because I didn't know if I'd wake later or fall into some eternal nightmare.

The hot air blowing in my face lulled me into the darkness behind my half closed lids. I slowly curled my body into the fetal position, the form punctuating the end of my life…with a question mark…

…I want my mom…
…I wanna go home…
…Sorry…so sorry…
…But I'm tired…think…I'll…sleep…now…
…
…
…

"*Wake up... WAKE. UP... WAKE UP!*"

Something slams across my face, sends my head reeling to the side and blood spouting off into the darkness...

I open my eyes, the blur in my vision slow to fade, but, when it does, reveals to me a dimly lit cave. Rocks pave the ground and cavernous walls enclose this dark Hell. And, somehow, they emit a dreary blue color into the darkness, as running water seeps through their cracks...

I expect the air in this place to be tortuously hot, like in my cell. However, here, it's cold. *Freezing* cold.

There's another blow to the other cheek. My face wags from side to side. "Don't," I slur to whoever did that, as drool or blood spills to the ground. It's hard to pick my head up. All is so bleary from where I kneel down in the spot the demons had thrust me before they evaporated into the gloom...

The *drip, drip, drip* sounds of the water trickling down the rocks suddenly turn to a rhythmic *click, click, click* as the shadow from which the noise emits from grows larger and larger in the darkness before me.

It's the Devil... I know it is...

But there is no feeling of dread inside at its presence; there is only...defeat...

I don the bravery of a coward and let my eyes drop to the ground, too ashamed to face what I've been running from all this time...

The final click of the Devil's shoe echoes in the cave. As the echo fades, I feel ice cold fingers near my collarbone. The necklace that spells my name is suddenly yanked from my neck...

"*Hey*," I scold, but the fury changes to wonder when I see the Devil's...shoes. "Nice shoes," I whisper more to myself, gawking in shock at a pair of sleek black heels. I slowly raise my gaze to finally feast my eyes upon the beast that fills the heels and clasps the necklace around its own neck...

But...it can't be... The Devil is...a woman... A familiar stranger dressed in a tattered white blouse and half ripped black skirt—a massacred business attire barely covering her corpse-like skin. Her singed dark hair is short and matted in her monstrous green eyes, sunken into a body that is skeletal, frail…broken.

"That's right, Jovie, I *am* the Devil," she spits, "*your* Devil. You killed me when you killed yourself." Her hands are a blur when they snag my shoulders; lift me up into the air, squeezing tightly, *furiously*. Our eyes look into each others, hers holding a devilish glisten… "I am the woman you were going to be," she explains through gritted, fang-like teeth, "I am your future. And I'm *angry* with you! I *hate* you! I *hate* you for killing me!" She throws me back to the ground.

"Ow!" I scream, skidding along the icy rocks and cracking my head against the wall.

But my Devil has only just begun…

She evaporates to shadowy smoke, then, like a mirage, appears right in front of me. She bends down, slapping me across the face. I squeeze my eyes shut, hold up my hands as a shield as she beats me. Punches keep coming, followed by slaps. She rips out strands of my hair; kicks me all over until I feel like my soul has been pulverized. Finally, she throws me against the opposite wall. I fall down, along with the rocks I knocked into…

I tremble all over at the truth…

The Devil is me.

How can I fight against myself? I can't; there is no way. I'm too scared.

I don't know what to do but cry, "Why are you doing this to me?" I can already feel my face swelling, my bruising skin weeping the crimson tears of a tormented soul.

"Because I want you to know how it feels!" she screams, kicking me in the gut. "You did this to me all the time, Jovie! You always beat me, distorting me into something ugly and dark as I am now!" She gestures to her monstrous figure. "You battered me, mutilated OUR FUTURE with your negativity! And now I want nothing more than to shove you down a blender so you can feel how I felt!"

My skin tingles all over with razor sharp pain… I am pulp, barely hanging onto my beaten limbs…

The Devil—me—finally relents in her rage. She steps back, falls to her knees as emotional sobs break through her demonic rage. She crawls closer to me, her face just an inch away. My shoulders are in her tight clutches, her glowing eyes pleading for an answer… "Why were you so afraid of me?" Desperation cracks her voice…

"I didn't know you," I whisper, trying to lean away from her, but the wall has me pinned.

"No one knows me!" she suddenly bellows, her fury taking over again.

"I didn't trust," I quickly pant, "that you would be good. That there would be happiness in you."

The woman I was going to be stares at me for a moment, then stands to her feet. "I'm the unknown," she begins, pacing back and forth slowly, "I get it. I'm scary," she mocks, fluttering her fingers in the air. "But to throw me away, to kill me, to not take a chance and *live* me—" She strikes the wall behind me, shuttering the very foundation of Hell. "—THAT'S WORSE THAN THE DOUBT YOU FELT! Was erasing me what made you feel better?" she inquires desperately, but I have no answer. She recoils into the shadows of Hell, laughing with no humor. "No. I know. You hated YOU. Where you were at the time. It wasn't the past and it wasn't the future making you sick. It was you," she whispers, as if it's a precious secret. "The present you."

"You're lying!" I retort bitterly. "You don't know anything!"

The Devil slaps me again. "I do know, Jovie. You can't lie to me, because I *am* you!" Her fingers coil around my neck, lifting me up, dragging me against the wall. "I want to know," she says earnestly, "I *need* to know…why you pushed me away. Why you gave up on me? The future? On us?"

"I was sad, I was lost," I manage through her choking stranglehold.

"Then you figure it out! You don't give up!"

Her lack of understanding awakens the temper in me as lethal as hers… I slap her hard across the face. The blow weakens her grasp, allowing me to fall but still land on my feet. "Don't tell me what to do when you have *no* idea how I felt. How I *feel*. You don't know any of my problems."

"And how do you feel, Jovie? I wanna know how you feel after throwing away a future. A life. What were your problems? Come on, let's hear them. I wanna know what made you believe that your life sucked *so badly* that you had to go and off yourself to make it better. Because you had it all, Jovie. Opportunity. Parents that loved you, that were going to help you pay for your—*our* college education. So tell me again, what problems did you have? You spoiled, selfish, *stupid* little brat?"

"I was thankful, so thankful everything I ever had but…"

"BUT WHAT?!"

"I DIDN'T BELONG ANYWHERE!" I scream, pushing away my future self. "I wasn't who they thought I was. I was nothing. I had no potential. I didn't even know what I wanted to be or who I was."

My future self pushes me right back, forcing me against the wall again. "A writer!" she reminds me, "You wanted to write! We were a poet, Jovie."

"It was impossible! Everything I ever wanted to be…could never happen. My dreams… They were just that… *Dreams.* They would have never come true. Because, may I remind you, that *you* sucked! THE FUTURE *SUCKED*! The economy was shit—and probably still is. Grocery prices were scary high and gas prices were insane. A war going on overseas. You had no chance anyway. *We* had no chance in the world. We would have never survived doing what made us happy —writing…poetry. It doesn't work that way. You have to settle for a mediocre job that is all about money so you can survive in the world. Happiness doesn't pay your bills."

The Devil slaps me on one cheek and then the other. "I was worth taking a chance on!" She throws me into the wall, profound indignation fueling her violence. "I was *worth it!* But you didn't believe in me, you tossed me away, you didn't believe that things would work out, that things would be okay, so guess what… Of course I—the future—was scary. Because you thought of me that way. But the thing is… We would have been okay. We would have been *alive.*"

"Yeah, in a world that fucking sucks!"

"In a world that's hard," she compromises, "but is also worth the trials. *Worth it*, Jovie. Because life is precious. You don't throw it away like you did! It would've gotten better," she promises.

"No, it wouldn't have! That's what everyone always told me.

Right from the get-go. 'It gets better'. But guess what?! IT. GOT. WORSE!"

"Exactly, because you didn't believe it would ever get better." She grabs me by the shirt, shaking me gently to highlight her point... "There's this thing called *faith*, called *hope*. And that's what makes the future better. But you lost that—you lost all of it—in me. So, of course, to you, I was dark. I *am* dark. I'm scary. I wasn't worth the chance. Because YOU didn't believe in ME!" She jabs an awry finger to her chest, her breaths rasping through her fangs.

"I couldn't decide," I mutter above the tension.

"Decide what?" she demands, letting me drop back down to my feet.

I sidestep out of the corner she has me backed into, walk away until my face is half shadowed in darkness. "How I wanted to live you —the future—or who I wanted to be. I was clueless, without identity, slowly turning into someone I didn't like, someone I couldn't *stand*. Why feed the monster I was turning into?"

"Depression was the monster," she points out, watching my movements with caution, as if she thinks I may run away again. "The monster wasn't you and it wasn't me. It was the *disease* and all the self-destructive habits it led to."

"Maybe," I agree, turning to face her. "But don't you see? I couldn't get better. It was never going to stop."

"You weren't sad every day. There are good days, even in depression." Her hands ball to fists and her devil eyes stare straight into the green in mine. "You should have lived for *those* days. Because I can tell you right now that you would have not grown up into a monster. Happiness would have found you, maybe not constantly, but in certain moments, like it does for everyone. Happiness was in you, Jovie; it was in our future too—in me. It was in the unconditional love and devotion in our future husband's heart; it was in our future children's eyes, in the love from Mom and Dad and Olive. Even Pumpkin. Look." She comes closer, letting the blue light cast upon the delicate skin beneath her eyes. She points at them. "Laugh lines. It *is* possible to laugh again, even after resurfacing from the deepest depression that we felt. It's possible. And we would have pulled through. But you were a coward, Jovie. You never dealt with what was wrong. You always averted your pain, you turned the other way. You cut. You scratched. You banged your wrists. You threw up. You ran. Anything you could do instead of dealing with what was in front of you." She steps even closer, "Which was *me*. Your future."

I step away in response to her close proximity, but find that my back is already pressed against another wall.

"Your demons, your devils, your fears, YOUR PROBLEMS—you never dealt with any of them. You were immature, lazy, a coward…a child. You didn't wanna grow up!"

"I know, I know!" I cry, squeezing my eyes shut and pressing my palms over my ears. "I was too afraid! I thought I would fail at everything!"

"But you didn't even try! And that's failing, too!"

"I felt like I was still just a kid," I sob, my hands dropping to the sides of my face. "I didn't know how to grow up. I didn't know how, I still don't know how!" I hunch over, tears pouring from my soul at the confession…

If it's at all possible, I detect, in my future's voice, a trace of mercy in her suddenly soft tone. "Your childhood was your foundation," the monster says, "You never had to burry it or rid yourself of it completely. That's not what growing up is. It's about building your life up from the foundation of a childhood, then on the layers of adolescence. Just because you were entering adulthood didn't mean you couldn't miss being a kid, you just had to accept that you weren't one anymore. Responsibility was growing, and now was the time to use what you learned all your life to achieve your childhood dreams, any dream you wanted.

"You had the power then, Jovie," she goes on, "to make whatever you wanted possible. That's the beautiful thing about me—the future—I can be whatever you want me to be. You didn't see that then so I'm pointing it out to you now. If you had hope, just an ounce of it, you wouldn't have killed me. Us. If you would've believed that I would have been okay, you'd—*we'd*—still be alive."

"Why are you telling me all of this?" I ask, as a violent sickness swells within in my soul.

"Because I want you to regret what you did to me!" she yells, snatching my soul and throwing it down to the rocks again. "To us! To *yourself.* I want you to understand what you threw away, what you wasted. Possibility. Hope. A future. All good things, Jovie. *All* good things."

"W-what about all the bad things?" I blubber feebly to the ground.

"That's just life, Jovie. You have to accept life for what it's not and for what you can never be: *Perfect.* Nothing's perfect. Not even me. But when you accept imperfection, Jovie, you welcome a perspective of goodness that allows you to see beauty, even perfection at times, in a scary world. A silver lining, if you will. But you were depressed, I get that. It's hard to think positively in that state. I hear you out. But you should have kept taking your medicine; you should have talked to the ones who loved you, who *still* love you. You should have expressed all of your hurt in poems, in our diary, not with a razor, not with throwing up or self-hatred. Instead of putting all of that effort into hurting yourself, Jovie, you should have been putting that energy into *loving* yourself. Putting down the razor and picking up the pills that could help us get better. Opening yourself up to the light that was darkened by depression. Having hope. Having faith in yourself, in the future. In *me.*

"Things fall apart," she explains on softly, as she lures my gaze up to hers with a lift of my chin.

"Like our mom and dad's marriage," I sniffle, wiping the blood from my nose.

"Yes, like Mom and Dad. But that doesn't mean *you* have to fall apart. And even if you did, Jovie, believe it or not you are strong enough to put yourself back together." Her hand moves from my chin to caress the bloodied skin on my cheek. "Some things are worth fixing. And by God you were and *are* one of them."

To my surprise, she bends to offer me her hand. Hesitantly, I take it. My future self helps me up to my feet, dusts the embedded rocks and blood weighing down my soul. When she's done, she stands before me and says, "All this time, you were trying to belong in the world, in a state, a clique, an occupation, even a certain beauty form, like a model. But really—" She unchains the necklace from her around her neck. "—what you needed to realize was that where you belonged was within yourself." She, very gingerly, puts the necklace that says my name back around my neck. "You can't expect to feel belonging anywhere unless you first feel like you belong in your own skin, in your own mind… In your own heart." A tear sparkles on the edge of my Devil's eyes, dropping to the rocks where it freezes on the floors of my Hell. "You were a beautiful puzzle, Jovie Blue. The missing piece all along was me. The future, what you could never imagine for yourself. I was hidden, and I know I was hard for you to find but you would have found me if you wouldn't have—" She closes her eyes, tormenting anguish pressing her lips together like a levy… "—killed me." The tears of my future rain upon Hell, her sobs quaking my very soul…

Her hands cover her face to hide her emotion, but when the vulnerability subsides, her hands slip down, unveiling the wrath of a future I was too afraid to live…

"I am going to kill you," my future states simply. "If I can't exist, then neither can you." As she offers a few unforgiving throttles to my face, the demons lurking in the darkness of Hell storm all around, howling their high shrieks and brandishing their razor claws.

Justice is present in the hostility attacking me. I feel it in every searing slap, every gushing slice, every unrelenting punch and kick. The violence soothes the affliction within her, within us, because she has every right to hate me, to want to kill me. After all, I killed her.

She wails against me as demons skin my soul. I am pinned to the ground, my face being grinded into the rocks with the Devil's fists. Agony drowns me from the inside out, rising up my throat where metallic crimson sputters from my lips. Gasping for existence, choking on regret, I'm slipping away into the darkness as my Devil reels back her fist, ready to strike me one last time…

I hold up my battered hands, and, above the chaos, finally cry, "I'm sorry!"

My future's hand stops suddenly in the air, along with every demon swirling about. She swallows, eyes narrowing to slits down at me. "What did you say?"

"I said," I pant, "I'm sorry. For giving up on us. I'm sorry I'll never know what it's like…to grow up into you. A woman. I'm sorry we'll never be alive again. I am so, so, *so* sorry." The tears pouring from my soul dilute the crusted blood on my cheeks, creating a blood-red downpour of rain in Hell. "And I'm even sorry we'll never stay up late with Olive watching horror movies and stuffing our faces with cookie dough. I'm sorry we'll never be able to kiss Mom and Dad goodnight again. I'm sorry for taking away our chances at college and of ever being with a guy that we love. I'm especially sorry for that—for never knowing what that's like, to be loved in that way."

My future self silently lifts her shirt, revealing to me the saggy skin over her belly, its puckered wrinkles telling me they are stretch marks.

I bow my head, let fall the lamenting tears as I whisper, "I'm sorry I took away our children, the ones we *would've* had. I'm sorry we'll never grow old, never listen to the rain again or look up at the stars and just believe. I'm sorry…for giving up on you, on us. I'm sorry," I wail, curling in on myself with regret. "I am *so* sorry!" I cough up blood, but continue speaking from my soul, "If I could, I'd do things differently. I'd have faith in you; I'd believe in you with hope…and I would *live* you. I'd *live* you to the *very fullest*. Every second I'd be thankful for the air in my lungs, for the possibilities you hold. You were my future…and I am *so sorry* for killing you when I couldn't handle the present." I shake my head slowly, popping the broken bones in my neck. "I shouldn't have done what I did to you. And I'm sorry."

My future self and the demons stand there idly, frozen in the silence setting in. Unexpectedly, the demonic shadows floating above disperse into a million glistening blue dots. Like mist, they gently drift down towards my future self, showering her in glowing light. The dots flutter to her shoes, then swirl in a mystical spiral back up her figure. The haze polishes her blemished soul, erasing all of the Hell it's been tainted with.

The glittering cloud gradually fades, revealing to me an inspiring future…

She's tall and lean, but a maternal softness outlines her structure. Her hair—shorter than mine—is still beetle-black, wielding the shimmer of moonlight in every strand. Her skin, it's like a magnolia pedal, pale and soft…beautiful. And her eyes—they are the liveliest green I've ever seen, and they seem to encompass all the potential in the world.

Pertinendi

My future self looks down at her restored body, then, for the first time, looks to me with an angelic smile. She reaches down to me, but I think she may hit me again, so I recoil. But she doesn't. Rather, she touches her fingertips to my heart, feeling the rhythm of our souls vibrating as one.

I look into the eyes of my future, seeing the past reflecting back —me.

"I'm sorry," I whisper to her again.

The woman I killed doesn't shudder with irrepressible malice; she doesn't yell or hit.

No.

She wraps her arms around me with the tenderness of a child, and then, with the boldness of a woman, whispers back to me, "I forgive you."

She sighs during our embrace, her breath growing colder as she gradually dissolves to a cloud of shimmery blue dots that, somehow, seep back into my own spirit. They settle there in my heart, where the emptiness always grew, reassembling back inside my soul, and, for the first time, maybe in forever, I feel whole…

I exhale the same cold air, the life inside that is no more. Hell, Pertinendi, Heaven—it's all blown away with the sigh. All turns to white sand beneath my feet. Then I turn to mist, too…rising, rising, rising…out of the body named…Jovie Maureen Blue.

Morgan McLendon

PART 8

NO HAPPY ENDING, JUST AN ENDING

Exonerated from my mistake, I lift from my body as if I am weightless, as if I have no body and am only a soul. The white desert below, as I float higher and higher, slowly gets smaller, appearing more to me like a closed eyelid—my eyelid.

But the world is distorted and blurry; I try to focus my vision but I can't…

Then a door gently closes behind me.

All is dark.

It is a moment before I can collect where I am.

I'm in a hallway of doors—that much I am sure. And each door has names stuck to them. The door behind me reads MACY AND JOVIE. But I can't go back in there; the door is sealed.

So I waft around. And there, glowing brightly enough for me to see in neon red letters above a doorway—EXIT. It's the way out…

I drift toward the exit door out of this dark hallway, passing by all the dorms—I can hear girls laughing, blow dryers howling, life being lived…

But I can't stop; the gravity of this afterlife pulls me toward the exit door.

When I pass the threshold, white light takes hold of me and all is silent…

Then, at the speed of light, for hours or days—I don't know—I race with the light as it guides me to a place unknown...

◉

When the light finally fades, my perspective of the world is clear again. I can see even myself as I used to be—only, I seem to be somewhat transparent, and draped around my body in intricate weaves is the light, like a glistening white gown.

I walk up the stairs of what seems to be a crypt. It leads me out into a vast lawn, glumly ornamented with snow-dusted rows of tombstones. Icy dread creeps into my soul when I realize I'm in a graveyard, but my fears are calmed when a stone hand reaches down for me from atop the stairs...

"Angel?" I whisper in utter disbelief, as I take the beautiful statue's hand and am pulled up onto the snowy landscape. "You're alive?" I touch the angel's immaculate face, the coarse but solid texture so familiar that Angel *must* be real; I can't be dreaming this.

"Of course I am," the angel says softly, returning a brilliant smile in response to my own. "Come." Angel gently tugs at my hand. "There is no more to remember, only more to see."

Angel guides me through a countless number of frozen statues watching over other graves. We weave between hundreds of tombstones until we come upon a funeral procession taking place at the edge of the cemetery.

There, dressed in depressing black outfits, I see my parents standing together by a casket, their eyes red and wet. Olive stands behind them, her hands trembling with a magnolia flower wedged between her cold fingertips.

"Angel, this can't be real, can it?" I ask, my breath invisible in the wind unlike all the other bodies who breathe out into the cold with visible vapors before their lips, before their red noses...

"I am sorry, Jovie, but yes. This is real. This is your funeral."

"But, why's everyone so sad? I didn't think anyone would care if I died." I let go of the Angel's hand, hurrying to the shivering, black-clothed group. I come up behind the preacher man giving a eulogy about my life...or death...and, in my ghostly presence, listen in about...

My suicide.

"—the bereaving family may also wonder where in the life of one so young can choose such a fate. But as it goes, these circumstances often go unnoticed. Darkness can consume even those with the most light. And in that, we all may wonder where in the darkness was the all-telling frown of deep, internal sorrow?"

"It was in my smile," I whisper the answer.

"And what cries were uttered that no one could hear?"

"It was in my silence," I tell him, all of them.

"And where were her hands in the darkness when they didn't reach out for help?"

"They were reaching for pills," I clarify, but no one can hear.

"But most imperatively, where was the love she couldn't feel?"

I open my mouth to speak, but soon realize, with a gust of sickening hurt, that I have no answer for him...or anyone...

"I see it all around," he says, "in everyone's eyes that mourn this tragic loss. Love is here. But where is it for her? I think...we will all be left with this question. But as humans, we can join together in our hopes and prayers that love and peace find this young woman in a better place."

Everyone dressed in black walks by my casket with their heads bowed, eyes hesitantly looking at my body, then dropping to the snow as liquid melancholy drips from their eyes...

Mom cries the hardest, her chest heaving with untamable hysteria. But Dad... Dad doesn't show emotion like Mom. His face is rigid, silently smoldering in the blaze of burning redness in his cheeks —maybe he's irritated from the cold...or maybe he can't breathe...

I spot Nana through the crowd, weeping with Olive, the pair clinging to each other in their thick black coats. I wish to hug them, tell them how sorry I am, that I never meant to hurt them or anyone... but myself.

Nana and Olive follow my parents, but the two stop before my casket. Nana pulls a bag of my favorite candies from her pocket, then sets them down inside my casket. Olive does the same with the magnolia flower in her hand.

The rest of my loved ones follow, each slowly passing my casket and whispering things, mournful things, while crying into the cold winter snow.

I am the last to pay my respects...to myself...

I stand before my body, my soul trembling not from the cold, but with grief, with regret, with longing to go back inside the place I belonged. I lift my hand to barely touch my pallid cheek, then touch but not feel the magnolia that Olive had tucked behind my ear. "I can't go back, can I?" I ask Angel, who stands close by my side.

"You chose to die," the statue reminds me. "This is the consequence of that decision."

I nod remorsefully, looking out at the worst consequence of all—the despair, the loss, the pain...that I brought upon my family and my best friend. "There is no happy ending for a suicide, is there?"

"No," the stone says honestly, "just an ending. But how you end is dependant on a choice you must make."

"What d'you mean?"

"I mean, it is time to decide where you feel you belong. Back in Hell or—"

"I-I don't know where I belong, Angel," I interrupt, "I don't know. I don't feel like I deserve to stay where I've been. I don't wanna go to Hell." The sorrow in my soul rises, clenching my throat with sobs, pouring from my eyes in glistening tears. "I just wanna go *home*," I cry to the angel. Looking up this time, I repeat in a whisper, "I wanna go home."

Angel's stone lips stretch across its face into a smile. "Well, Jovie, my dear, take my hand and I will show you the way home."

Willingly, I let our fingers intertwine, palm to palm, a perfect fit, as if, all along, they were separated puzzle pieces only now being joined together.

I walk with the statue towards the road winding through the valley. Standing in the middle of the two lanes, my feet brushing against the yellow stripe, I watch the cars of my family all driving away in the distance. I believe Angel and I are going to follow them back to my house, but we don't. Instead, Angel guides me across the road, down the glittering, snow-covered hills of Missouri that are beginning to melt in the rays of the sun.

But just as the sun begins to set, another light rises, but from within the statue... "Angel?" I gasp, eyes widening at the light piercing through the stone's features.

"I am more than an angel, Jovie," says not the stone but the light inside it... What remains of the statue, before the light shines through it, are its outspread arms. "I am Love, Jovie," the white light says, "and it is *okay* to feel me again."

Understanding immerses my soul, as humility weakens my knees and allows me to fall into this perfect entity's arms... "Don't ever leave me," I cry to the light, embracing it tightly, fiercely.

"I never did," it replies, "You froze me in your mind, like a statue, and you blocked me out with indifference and negativity. But those barriers are no more. Come," the light tells me, "let us go home."

In the pure light of Love, I am weightless, turning to a tingly blue mist as beams shoot from all around. I slowly flow into the current of light, acceptance allowing Love to take its place back in my soul where I will never let it turn to stone again...

As the pale sun sets on my human life, another sun—grace—rises within my spirit...

I fade into the Love eclipsing my imperfections, as the rising Heaven-light echoes with beautifully familiar voices...

"Hey, sweet girl!" I hear Grandma Blue gush from somewhere in the light... I even hear other voices, voices I never knew on earth but was told of their love...

Somewhere...

That's where the light takes me...

Somewhere...

It's an otherworldly kind of perfect...

And all throughout my soul a rejoicing song sings, *I'm home, I'm home, I'm home,* but what whispers from my lips is...

"I belong."

Pertinendi

...I know I don't belong anywhere. But that's okay, I don't want to be just anywhere. I want to be Somewhere, and hopefully Somewhere I will find what I couldn't when I was just anywhere.

– Jovie Blue

© Black Rose Writing

CPSIA information can be obtained at www.ICGtesting.com
Printed in the USA
BVOW081246240413

318987BV00002B/141/P